# the
# thing
# is

# Kathleen Gerard

RED ADEPT PUBLISHING
Unlocking New Worlds

*The Thing Is*
Copyright © 2016 by Kathleen Gerard All rights reserved.
First Print Edition: January 2016

Print ISBN-13: 978-1-940215-58-7
Print ISBN-10: 1940215587

Red Adept Publishing, LLC
104 Bugenfield Court
Garner, NC 27529
http://RedAdeptPublishing.com/

Cover and Formatting: Streetlight Graphics

"The Thing Is," Ellen Bass, from *Mules of Love*. Copyright © 2002 by Ellen Bass. Reprinted with the permission of The Permissions Company, Inc., on behalf of BOA Editions Ltd., www.boaeditions.org (22-2438531).

For my mother
who taught me what it means to believe
and is the greatest storyteller I know
&
For my sister Patricia
who always cheers the loudest

## The Thing Is

*to love life, to love it even*
*when you have no stomach for it*
*and everything you've held dear*
*crumbles like burnt paper in your hands,*
*your throat filled with the silt of it.*
*When grief sits with you, its tropical heat*
*thickening the air, heavy as water*
*more fit for gills than lungs;*
*when grief weights you like your own flesh*
*only more of it, an obesity of grief,*
*you think,* How can a body withstand this?
*Then you hold life like a face*
*between your palms, a plain face,*
*no charming smile, no violet eyes,*
*and you say, yes, I will take you*
*I will love you, again.*

—*Ellen Bass*

# One

Prozac

THE MINUTE THE BREEDER OPENED the crate, my littermates went nuts. They charged out and made a mad dash, scattering the newspapers covering every square inch of tile floor, including the glowing review I had been reading for *A Chorus Line*, which was being performed at the local community theater.

My two Yorkshire terrier sisters and one brother—tails wagging, yet still wobbly on all fours—made a beeline across the laundry room, heading straight for the sweet-smelling lady with wispy white hair and a cane. She sat on a folding chair in front of the clothes dryer, engrossed in our yipping and yapping.

"Oh, look at the lovelies!" The woman's British accent was as demure as her outfit—a black-and-white skirt suit with a brimmed hat to match. She plucked off her gloves and, bare-handed, leaned down to the pups at her feet. She ruffled their soft black fur and tried to get a look at their tan faces. But the crew was all wound up and accosting the poor lady, whimpering and pouncing all around her thick ankles.

Still in the crate, I sat up taller and took it all in. I held my gaze on the woman and tried to figure out if I knew her. Something about her seemed familiar, especially that British accent.

*Liz, is that you?*

The sight of her single strand of pearls answered my question. Queen Elizabeth never wore singles, always double or triple. And the woman's teeth were much whiter than the Queen's. I would know, as I had once been considered for a position amid the Queen's royal pack of beloved Pembroke Welsh corgis. I didn't make the final cut, but Liz gave me as a wedding present to one of her dressers, an unassuming young woman who took me to work with her during the summers when she accompanied the Queen to Balmoral Castle.

"Well, you're the very first outsider to set eyes on this brood," the breeder said as she gathered up the great volume of her long brown hair into a ponytail and twirled it into a messy bun. She stood in the laundry room doorway, allowing the Queen Elizabeth look-alike to have something of a private audience with the whelps. "And as we promised, Helen, you can have the pick of the litter."

*Aha. It's Helen Hendrix. I should've known. She's just as described.*

My brain tingled, and my heart swelled with love. But my poor littermates—oh, the pitiful creatures! The pack of little clueless canines simply didn't understand that an elegant, sophisticated lady wasn't in search of a puppy with sharp nails that would rip and put runs in her expensive support hose. She didn't want a panting slobberer who got in her face or chewed on the laces of her orthopedic shoes. *Yikes, a very big no-no!*

"How do you tell them apart?" Helen asked the breeder.

"The colored bands on their necks. Cymbalta's in pink. Lipitor's in yellow. And the boys are in the darker shades: Cialis is in red. Prozac's in blue."

"Those names!" Helen laughed with apparent delight. "How did you ever come up with them?"

"You can blame my husband for that. He's a pharmacist and thought it would be clever to name all the pups after popular prescription drugs."

"Sure is clever. But tell me about that one," Helen said, pointing at me. "Prozac, right? Why is he staying in the crate all by himself? Is something wrong with him?"

The breeder sighed. "Oh, I don't think you'd be interested in that one."

*Wanna bet?*

Helen asked, "Why not?"

"From the time he was born, he's been something of a loner. Keeps to himself, away from the pack. I think he's got an independent streak, but my husband's convinced he's a snobbish old soul."

*You're both right!*

"He looks like a proper English gentleman, regal and debonair," Helen said. "Do you think you could lure him out so I could take a look?"

As the breeder walked across the room to fetch me, I sprang from the crate, bounded toward her, and leaped into her hands. Then she carried me to Helen and set me upon the fine woolen fibers of Helen's skirt and her fleshy, cushioned lap that felt as cozy as a warm blanket. With my littermates all squirmy and whiny below, I snuggled into the indentation between Helen's thighs and rolled onto my back, offering her my belly, my moist nose, and a doleful gaze.

"What a handsome little love," she said, her eyes sparkling.

I stared up into her wise, compassionate face. Her skin was pink and powdery. She caressed and smoothed my coat with tender care. A whiff of her floral-scented perfume tinged with talcum proved as intoxicating as the feel of her fingers.

*Oh, I could learn to live like this!*

Helen picked me up and cuddled me close to her heart, anointing my head with a kiss that imprinted my fur with a seal of her lipstick. "Sold," she said. "I'll take him."

# Two

*PAST PERFORMANCE IS NO GUARANTEE OF FUTURE RESULTS*

## Meredith

**A**LWAYS KEEP A CAMERA CLOSE *by at weddings, baptisms, and bar mitzvahs.* That was the cardinal rule of survival I'd devised when trying to navigate my life as a shining example of unexpected spinsterhood. The world, I'd learned, traveled in pairs—like Noah's Ark—or with families. But people, perfumed and ready to party, could never resist mugging for a photo. Latching on to a camera could create a sense of security and purpose, something to hide behind. In my case, I had a tendency to cut off people's heads in pictures. But that didn't matter. Aiming a camera—a point-and-shoot or even just my smartphone—and pressing the shutter was a simple enough task that could occupy my time while couples were out on the dance floor.

The thing was that, after a while, there were only so many pictures to take and so many trips to make to the ladies' room. At some point during social events, I always found myself alone at my table, surrounded by empty chairs, dirty plates, crumbs, and soiled napkins as I slugged back another sip of wine and wished—wished so hard that it hurt—that they'd hurry up and bring out the cake to signal that the party would soon be over.

That was the very dilemma I was facing at the bar mitzvah that day. The firstborn son of my old college roommate, Sarah, was celebrating his coming of age, while I was sitting alone at my empty table. I forced an admiring smile as dolled-up couples and pimply-faced teenagers crowded the dance floor, shaking and shimmying to a live rendition of "That's the Way I Like It."

At first, I didn't even realize that Sarah's youngest, five-year-old Jed Jr.—JJ—had climbed onto the chair next to mine. But when I felt a tug on my sleeve and heard him ask, "How come you don't have a husband?" his presence was announced, loud and clear.

"How come you don't have a wife?" I countered.

"'Cause I'm too little," he said. "What's your excuse?"

I laughed. JJ certainly had no inhibitions. And he was a real cutie. His fair skin, disheveled angelic-blond hair, and saucer-like blue eyes guaranteed he'd break hearts someday.

"Well, not everyone is married."

"Mommy says your husband died."

*Thanks, Sarah!* "He was my fiancé. Not my husband."

"What's a fiancé?"

I had to stop and think. Even though I wrote books for a living, award-winning romantic sagas with convoluted plots and subplots, my trying to define the word *fiancé* for a precocious child was like reconciling the meaning of the universe into a single sound bite. "Well, before people get married, they get engaged, like when a man gives a ring to his future bride. Did you ever hear of that?"

"Of course. Everybody's heard of *that*, dummy."

*So much for little Prince Charming!* "Well, before the wedding, that's what a bride or groom is called. After the engagement ring is given, you would say, 'He's my fiancé,' or in your case, you would probably say, '*She is my fiancée.*'"

"How did your fiancé die?"

*What's taking so long with that damn cake?* "Well, the thing is…"

I froze and stared at a tiny drop of red wine that had spilled on the starched white tablecloth, suddenly transported back three years to the night of my thirtieth birthday…

*Kyle and I were having a beautiful, candlelit dinner on the patio at Andrea's, my favorite Italian restaurant. We watched a mango-colored July sun slip down into the evening sky.*

*Kyle held up his glass. "Happy birthday, Meredith. I'm looking forward to spending all of your birthdays with you."*

*That was the same thing he'd said when we'd first celebrated together on my twenty-third birthday...*

*Our bellies full of pasta, crab-filled calamari, veal parmigiana, espresso, and tiramisu, we walked arm in arm back to the lot where we'd parked the pickup. Kyle kept whistling the birthday song...*

*A St. Florian medal and a replica of Kyle's fireman badge dangled from a chain looped over the rearview mirror. I leaned toward Kyle, and the light from the dashboard illuminated the warm pools of his brown eyes as I pressed my lips tenderly to his...*

*And then a jolt—the urgent sound of a fist rapping upon the driver's side window. "Yo, get a room! We're waitin' for this spot. You leavin' or what, dawg?"*

*My heart pounded in my chest.*

*The menacing, crazed face of an eighteen or nineteen-year-old kid filled the square window frame. He was wearing a ski cap, and lots of gold chains surrounded his neck.*

*Kyle reached to open the door.*

*"Don't," I said, my fingers firming around the sleeve of his polo shirt and his rock-solid arm. "You only promised me dinner, not fireworks. C'mon. Let's go."*

*"No," Kyle snapped. "This is exactly what's wrong with the world."*

*Even with both my hands clamped to his arm, Kyle swung open the door and forced the kid to take a step away.*

*"You stay here," he ordered. "I'll be right back."*

*"Kyle, please," I pleaded, but he broke free from my grasp and hopped out of the car.*

*I inhaled a deep breath. I knew how Kyle was—strong and domineering in a calm yet take-charge, assertive way. My gentle giant. That contradiction made him a good, caring fireman and an even better person. But he could also be principled to a fault.*

*Kyle and the kid came face-to-face behind the bed of the truck. The young punk kept moving closer, invading Kyle's personal space until the two were nose-to-nose, recycling the same air. From the indecipherable flurry of their words, I sensed a flash of white-hot fury.*

*I hurried out of the car as fast as I could, my pulse racing.*

*Neither was backing down, and I could see the flex of Kyle's jawbone as he said, "It's called common courtesy and respect. Try showing a little next time."*

"Kyle, let's go." My voice was shrill and urgent. I prayed that my words would defuse the standoff.

The kid backed off, and so did Kyle. I breathed a sigh, thinking my prayer had been answered.

In the cone of light spilling down from a nearby lamppost, Kyle glanced at me over the bed of the pickup. The fire in his eyes gave way to a twinkle. He winked.

And then, a voice from behind us yelled, "Scumbag! Here's your respect..."

When I turned, the kid was winding up like a baseball pitcher. Something darker than the night was hurtling through the air. Kyle's head jerked back. It smashed against the side-view mirror of the pickup before he collapsed and disappeared from my sight. I screamed and hurried around the truck. Through the shadows, I found Kyle facedown on the ground. I tried to lift him, but he was too heavy, so I rolled him over. I clutched at him, resting his head upon my lap.

"Somebody call an ambulance," I cried, my words shredding through my vocal cords as I smoothed Kyle's closely cropped hair.

"It's gonna be okay. It's gonna be okay." I brought my face close to his and kissed him. My trembling hands felt warm, wet. I looked at my palms. Blood was all over my fingers, even my engagement ring. A large chunk of broken asphalt lay next to us. "C'mon, stay awake." My voice was thin and wavering as I shook him. Kyle's ashen face was slack, cold to the touch. His eyes were slits. My panicked, terror-filled heart clenched like a fist—

"So what is it? What's *the thing*, Meredith?" JJ's voice ripped me from the memory of that night.

"Meredith?"

A pang of grief as sharp as any I'd suffered in the early days of mourning gripped me. I squeezed my eyes closed, my mind burning as the details unspooled all over again. I ached for Kyle. That sense of loss was so acute it felt like panic.

"Meredith?"

I looked at JJ. My mouth felt dry. My gut, tight.

"The thing?" I asked.

"Yeah. You said, *the thing is*, and then you stopped."

My mind felt like a shaken-up snow globe. It had taken years for the dust to settle—for the truth of Kyle's last moments to stop creeping into my brain at all hours, often when I least expected—yet with one simple question, a little boy had stirred up all that horror again.

I cleared my throat and choked out, "What was the question?"

"Ummm..." JJ scratched his head as if trying to remember. "I think I forgot."

"You forgot?"

JJ grinned, coy. "Oh, Meredith, you're funny—"

"Not as funny as you."

I tickled his side. He quickly folded over upon himself, erupting into giggles. Relief filled me when he scooted from his chair, took off, and ran around my table. Envying his short attention span and carefree antics, I picked up my wineglass and gulped the last drop. My head throbbed to the thumping bassline track of the music. A bottomless longing for Kyle swallowed me whole.

*If only we had stayed home that night, and he had let me cook for us... If only it hadn't been my birthday... If only it had been later... or earlier... if we'd picked a different restaurant... parked somewhere else... hadn't shared that last kiss... If only...*

JJ uttered my name in rounds. "Mer-a-dith... Mer-a-dith..."

His gleeful voice cascaded in waves, receding from me then circling back again each time he neared.

"Mer-a-death... Mer-a-death..."

His singsong was overpowered by the music, but I could make out his reciting the syllables of my name slower and slower until it sounded as though he was chanting, "Merry-Death... Merry-Death."

# Three

*WHEN LIFE CHANGES, IT CHANGES FAST*

Meredith

"**M**EREDITH, ARE YOU THERE? ... C'mon, pick up..."
A gravelly voice blared through the tinny answering machine speaker, and I groaned, stirring beneath the bedcovers. A bag of potato chips rustled atop the comforter, and an empty cereal box toppled to the floor, crashing into a mound of half-used tissues that went airborne.

"Okay, be that way! I just hope you haven't already spent your advance, because if you keep up this silent treatment, the publisher is going to force you to give the money back. Don't say you haven't been warned."

*Click!*

I squinted against the early morning light then pulled the covers over my head, curled into a tight fetal loop, and succumbed again to tears and sniffles.

After the trauma of the bar mitzvah, I came home and wrapped myself in one of Kyle's old flannel shirts, burrowing beneath the soft sheets and heavy blankets of my bed. A windy, rainy nor'easter pummeled my little corner of northern New Jersey and cast the world outside the windows of my townhouse into lingering shades of gray more dismal than my despair.

Day after day, morning lapsed into afternoon then evening. I listened to doors slamming, car horns honking, and the bathroom faucet dripping hollow, ominous plunks. The kitchen sink piled up with dirty dishes. Mail spilled through the front door slot, and I let it all rise like a swelling ocean tide upon the foyer floor. I didn't brush my teeth or shower. My legs even went unshaven.

Kyle had been gone for almost three years, and all the life I thought I'd been living without him suddenly seemed like such a sham. A pointless waste of time.

I had heard it said that love never ends. But maybe it would've been better if it did—if love simply evaporated so people like me wouldn't wade into deep reflecting pools that had the power to pull a soul down into a vortex of grief and sadness as dogged as quicksand.

Even work, my one great escape and salvation, couldn't rescue me. I was already past deadline in getting pages to my editor, but I couldn't concentrate on finishing the sixth book in my Ghost Ranch series. I figured that if I didn't care about some loner, a handsome 1950s rancher with a V-shaped physique and bulging biceps—who was falling for a woman artist, also a loner and trying to reinvent her life on a canvas—then a reader wouldn't care about the characters either. Even the persistent emails, texts, and telephone messages from my agent pestering me to turn in my manuscript couldn't light a fire under me.

And neither could my sister, Monica. She had been calling more than usual, harassing me daily.

"I know how you are when you're on a deadline, but call me. I need to speak with you." It killed me that Monica never seemed to have enough time or breath to give closure to her calls. Why couldn't she offer a simple hello or goodbye?

The only other contact I had with the outside world came from the flickering television. Held captive by sleep and hours of brainless sitcoms, I became an expert at manipulating buttons on the remote control without looking.

I was inching past week two of my hibernation when the doorbell rang. The sound made me lurch up in bed, as if I'd had a defibrillator shock.

I fumbled for the remote, muted the TV, then froze in the silence.

*Am I hearing things?*

When the doorbell chimed a second time, I flung back the covers and tiptoed to the front door. My heart pounded as my bare, cold feet slipped upon piles of mail and glossy catalogs scattered all over the floor. I cautiously pressed my eye against the peephole and found a distorted-looking image of my one and only sister—a tall, normally well-tended woman, a locally respected workaholic CPA. Something about her looked severe. Her dark sunglasses accentuated her pale face, furrowed brow, and tight lips. Light gray roots poked through the center part of her long brown hair. Was she going to ask me to color it for her again? I called it being too cheap to go to a salon. She called it knowing the value of a dollar.

When Monica leaned in toward the peephole and pressed the doorbell a third time, I noticed the breast pocket of her blazer was stuffed, overflowing with crumpled tissues.

*Uh-oh. Does she have a head cold?*

When I heard a whimpering sound and spied a dark little dog in her arms, I quickly put to rest all my pseudo-hairdresser and rhinovirus theories.

*I don't like the look of this!*

Monica pounded on the door. The fierceness of the vibration shot right through the painted steel, straight into my eyeball.

"C'mon, Meredith. I know you're in there. Open up," she commanded.

When her head jerked forward from a loud sneeze, traces of what I gathered to be her infamous dog allergy sprayed upon the lens of the peephole and fogged it up.

I jerked my eye away.

*Yuck!*

I turned on my heels to make a beeline straight back to bed. But when my sister bellowed, "Meredith, open this door right now—or I'm calling the police," I stopped in my tracks.

*The police?* I already feared that I was billed as the crazy, reclusive writer who lived at 22 Rosebush Lane. And my sister certainly wouldn't improve my reputation by carrying on, making a scene on my front porch. I quickly undid the lock and dead bolt.

I opened the door and held it ajar, trying to obscure myself behind it. Monica peeled off her sunglasses. She bore through me with a bloodshot, blue-eyed gaze. "I've been leaving you messages for days. I've been worried sick, picturing Mom when we found her after the heart attack—"

"Oh, stop being so dramatic."

"*Me*, dramatic? You're the one not answering your phone. Would it have killed you to pick up or call me back? Even shoot me a text?"

She was so upset that the blackish-brown dog let out a shocked yelp that seemed to defuse her anger. She picked up a large, rather unwieldy-looking shopping bag that had been resting against what appeared to be a playpen. When I refused to open the door to accommodate her, she swept a judgmental gaze over what she could see of me—my bed head, Kyle's old flannel shirt, and my hairy legs.

I said, "Nice to see you, too, sis."

"Here." She pushed herself inside, thrusting the scruffy little black and brown creature right at me. I was afraid the ball of fur was going to drop onto the ceramic tile floor of the foyer, so I had no choice but to take him. He weighed less than a sack of potatoes.

Shopping bag in one hand, playpen in the other, Monica barreled past me, trailing a fragrant blossom-scented perfume. As she trod over the mail-strewn floor, her pumps slid on a catalog from Harry and David. The glossy cover ripped, and she almost wiped out atop the colorful image of their Deluxe Easter Gift Basket promotion.

"Geez, Mer, it's bad enough you won't pick up your phone. But what have you got against the mail?" Monica set the playpen in the middle of the living room. Then, with bag still in hand, she hightailed it back to the foyer, where she gathered up armfuls of letters, catalogs, magazines, and flyers.

I stood there holding the germ-laden animal in my arms, keeping them outstretched as far as possible. What if the thing had rabies—or fleas or ticks or something?

"What's going on? What's this all about?" I chased my sister as she paraded through the living room and straight into the kitchen. Pieces of wayward mail fluttered to the floor.

"The dog's name is Prozac."

I could feel my face shrivel up. "Prozac, like the antidepressant medication?"

"Yes. It's a long story." My sister slapped the mail onto the kitchen table. She heaved the shopping bag up onto a kitchen chair. Then she reached for a napkin and launched another annihilating sneeze that seemed capable of blowing the tiles right up from the floor.

"*Gesundheit*," I said.

My sister offered a nod of thanks. She blew her fuchsia-colored nose while picking up envelopes and catalogs on her way to the living room.

"He belongs to one of my best clients, Helen Hendrix. I really like her.

She's such a nice lady." Monica fumbled through the drapes in search of a means to open them. "I think you might've met at the banquet when I was installed as president of the State Society of Accountants."

"Yes, the British lady." I conjured an image of a meticulous-looking elderly woman with billowy white hair and pearls. She carried a cane and spoke with a proper and distinguished accent.

"Well, I feel so bad. She took a spill—broke a bone in her foot." My sister finally ripped the pulley cord, and the drapes parted with a loud *swoosh.* "She might need to go to a rehab center."

"Gee, that's too bad." A glare of dreary daylight spilled inside and forced me to squint.

"The thing is, I sort of made a promise that if anything ever happened, I'd help Helen out with Prozac here." Monica sneezed again.

"Didn't you tell her you're allergic to dogs?"

"I honestly never thought it would come to this—"

"But Helen must be ninety years old."

"She's only eighty-seven."

"Only?"

"Look, I don't want to let this lady down. I need your help."

"*Me? My* help?" I pointed a stiff finger at my chest, jostling the dog. Suddenly, I got the gist of things, and I didn't like where we were heading.

"Yes, we're sisters. We're supposed to help each other out."

"Oh? And is this a law or something?"

"I'm up to my eyeballs in tax season. It's March—"

"I'm sorry about your client. I am. And I know how you get with April fifteenth looming. But don't expect *me* to take this dog—"

Monica cut me off with a sneeze. She charged back to the kitchen, flung open a napkin, and blew her nose loudly. The sound heralded like a foghorn that drowned out my pleas of protest. I tried to hand the dog back, but she sneezed again, sighing to emphasize her misery.

"But Prozac doesn't even need to be walked," she said. "He's a house dog—answers Mother Nature's call right on these Wee-Wee pad things." My sister reached inside the big shopping bag and pulled out a handful of some medicinal and absorbent-looking square white pads bordered in Caribbean blue. She held one up as a bullfighter might fling out a cape.

"You throw one down like a rug in your bathroom, and that's it. Business taken care of. Prozac knows exactly what to do."

With short, firm shakes of my head, I said, "No way."

"It's only for a few days."

"Absolutely not. And you know me. The only animals I *care for* are those that are grilled or fried, sitting before me on a dinner plate."

"But I made a promise."

"Take her to a kennel."

"He—Prozac is a *he*. A male dog."

I raised the dog over my head and peered under his carriage. There was his little twig but no berries. He was obviously neutered.

"Mer, I don't feel right about leaving him with anyone else. Helen's my best client, and Prozac here means the world to her. And she's referred a ton of business my way."

That was the difference between my sister and me. She was the numbers gal, always seeing things and breaking them down, calculating the world and people in it via tax brackets, dollars, and cents. I was the word gal, always trying to give meaning and form to abstract feelings and concepts. Our conversation was making things clearer than ever—Monica and I might've shared a bloodline and similar sensibilities, but we certainly didn't speak the same language.

"You know, I'm really surprised at you," I said as the dog wiggled in my grasp. "Why would you even consider this proposition, especially after what happened with H&R Block?"

H&R Block was Monica's pet parakeet. Only a twelve-year-old numbers whiz—a kid who used to keep ledger books on how much she spent on chewing gum and hair barrettes—would have named a pet after a retail tax service mogul. I always hated that bird and how he shed his feathers and spilled birdseed onto the hardwood floor on only my side of our shared bedroom.

One day, while Monica was at her youth Mensa meeting—she'd always been *that* smart—I prayed for something, anything, to liberate my tortured nine-year-old soul.

When fate didn't intervene, I took matters into my own hands. I did a bad thing. A very bad thing. Something I still felt guilty about. I opened the window in our bedroom, unlatched the door to the birdcage, and swung it open.

Later that same night, as my sister blotted her eyes and nose with tissue and sobbed while pecking away at her calculator—its long, narrow tape spewing figures of all she'd invested in caring for that stupid bird over his lifetime—H&R Block tapped on the glass of our bedroom window as if he were some sort of homing pigeon skilled in Morse Code. The familiar sound of numbers crunching must've lured him back. After his return, my sister invested in a lock for the cage, and only she knew the combination. The living, feathered hell went on for another seven years, long after she left me behind and went away to college.

"H&R Block is all the more reason you owe me," Monica countered, snapping me out of my reverie. "And it's not forever—just until this lady gets back on her feet..."

The dog was growing heavier to hold. I was tempted to set him down. But I feared that once his paws made contact with the floor, he'd claim my townhouse as his own territory. Then I'd really be stuck with him.

"And who knows, Mer. Maybe this is like Mom used to say—it's providential."

"Providential this lady broke her foot?"

"No. Providential that this dog should remain in your charge. He might be just the thing to keep you company—"

"Puh-lease!" I cut her off. "Save your psychology for the IRS or whoever it is you deal with!"

"When are you going to admit it? You've been holing up like a thirty-five-year-old Miss Havisham, living in solitary confinement, ever since Kyle died—"

"I go out sometimes. And I'm only thirty-three," I corrected.

"All I'm saying is that Prozac might be the best thing for you. The two of you can keep each other company. Unconditional love and all that. Besides, since ancient times, bona fide hermits have always kept dogs as companions."

The dog sneezed, and I pushed him in my sister's direction. She put up her hands and took a step back.

"I am *not* a hermit. And I am *not* keeping this dog—"

"You don't have to *keep* him."

"Look. This is more than I can handle right now," I shouted, my voice trembling. The dog must've sensed my upset because his body quivered and his heartbeat took off like a rocket beneath my fingertips.

"There's nothing to handle. All he needs is a place to stay. Dog food and water. And if you go out, plop him inside the playpen."

"Playpen?"

*Oh, why did I ever get out of bed? I should've let her call the police!*

"Yeah, it's a cinch." Monica scrambled around me to the portable enclosure in the living room. She flipped out the sides to open it. Tiny yellow ducks and pink and blue sheep dotted the padded liner encased in fine netting. "Helen says he feels safe and secure in there. And it's easier to dump him inside than having to finagle a dog crate."

I put up a hand. "Stop right now. This is *not* going to happen—"

"But it's not much more care than you're giving to yourself right now." To reinforce her point, Monica swung her sights to the dishes piled up in my sink, the empty soup cans and frozen entree wrappers filling my garbage pail, and the haphazard deluge of mail she'd dumped on my kitchen table. "Besides, I've been telling you for years you should be on Prozac or some other antidepressant to snap you out of your grief. If you won't take medication, then maybe this dog—caring for someone, something else—can help you get on with your life."

"But the townhouse association—I don't think they allow pets. I never see dogs around here—"

"I already checked. There's nothing in the bylaws about pets. And don't worry. If there's any problem, I'll pay the fine."

It was just like my sister to know all the angles and come prepared for cross-examination. Her meticulous attention to detail made my life easier. I could always count on her to take care of the legalese and figures that came with my being a midlist novelist who mentally glazed over whenever it came to addressing the noncreative details of life—things like paying the mortgage and filing my taxes on time.

When the dog licked my hand, a sick, queasy chill shivered through me. Monica said, "Look, he likes you already."

As if to affirm my sister's comment and seal the deal, that furry little germ magnet finally broke free of my grasp and leaped to the floor. His nails clicked against the tile until he circled and sat down next to me really close, his fur tickling my bare feet. His pointy, triangular ears sailed back as he craned his neck to look up at me. His bashful gaze and his tentative, moist brown eyes met mine. I had to admit he was sort of cute, in that fluffy, stuffed teddy bear kind of way.

When my sister sneezed again, I couldn't decide which was worse—Monica's germs or Prozac's.

"What is he, anyway? What kind of dog?" I asked.

"A Yorkshire terrier."

"How old is he?"

"Two or three, I think. Does it matter?"

I nodded. "If we're gonna be roommates, I'd like to know more about him."

Monica beamed, convinced she'd won the battle. "I'll check with Helen, find out some more details, and shoot you an email or a text later." Before my sister left, she studied me up and down as if seeing me for the first time since she had paraded in that morning. "I hope you're going to tend to *those* soon," she said, pointing at my hairy, unshaven legs.

I pulled at the hem of Kyle's old flannel shirt, trying to stretch it to my knees.

"A shower and shampoo can work wonders, too. I mean, God forbid something happens to you or Prozac. The paramedics are likely to rescue the dog and ditch you like roadkill."

"Very funny," I said.

"You watch. Someday you might thank me for this, Meredith."

"Get out," I said, "before I change my mind."

# Four

*I'M GONNA WASH THAT MAN RIGHT OUTTA MY HAIR*

Meredith

AFTER MY SISTER CLOSED THE front door behind her, the townhouse felt cold and eerily quiet. Prozac pressed his grungy warmth against my bare, stubbly calf. I looked down and stared at the copper-colored crown of his head.

When he looked up at me with sheepish, compassionate brown eyes, I sighed and said, "Well, it's you and me now, mister. And first things first. We must rid you of Monica's germs."

I reached down and picked up the furry, four-legged creature. He retained a spicy, stale odor, something like what wet Doritos might've smelled like. With outstretched arms, I carried him down the hall to the bathroom where I rested him atop the vanity, opened the medicine chest, and pulled out an economy-sized container of hand sanitizer. I scanned the ingredient panel. *Isopropyl alcohol? Is that safe for pets?* Not being sure, I put the bottle back, reached for toilet paper instead, and rolled some off around my hand. I pumped out a smidgen of fragrant antibacterial soap from the sink dispenser onto the paper wad then drenched it with warm water. The natural part in Prozac's silky black-brown coat was wiped and dampened as I tried to disinfect every square inch of him from the crown of his head to his paws—in between each little pad—and beneath his chin and undercarriage. Along the way, the wet, soapy paper disintegrated into soggy little pieces, making the poor dog look as though he were plagued by a bad case of dandruff.

I dropped what remained of the toilet paper into the bowl and flushed.

Then, I used my fingers like the tines of a comb, smoothed and fluffed Prozac's matted, clammy hair, and picked out some of the paper flakes until his coat revived, retaining a lingering scent of clean soap.

"There. Good to go." I pushed some loose strands of copper-colored hair away from his eyes. Then I took his damp face in my hands and stroked him under his chin. Staring into his wide eyes, I wondered what he was thinking—if anything at all. Did he realize that Helen, his beloved mistress-master, was injured? And what did he make of being whisked away by Monica and dumped on me?

He wormed his head from my grasp as if perturbed by my mental analysis, and I set him on the floor. He scampered away, dashing into the hall. After I doused the counter and my hands with alcohol, I went after him. With his snout, Prozac pushed open my bedroom door and threw himself onto the plush area rug at the foot of my bed. He shimmied on his back—upside-down, paws skyward—rolling and wiggling side to side. He was shameless in his effort to dry himself and be rid of that soapy scent.

"Prozac!" I shouted. There was no doubt that the dog—probably along with my next-door neighbors—heard me, but my scolding didn't stop him. I made a beeline for the linen closet, yanked out the oldest towel I could find, and hurried back to my bedroom. I flung out the towel and tried to maneuver Prozac onto it, but he wasn't interested. He wanted at those bristly carpet fibers in a big way. I finally gave up, standing in the doorway to my room, puzzled by the weird gyrations of the uncomfortable, alien-looking creature that had invaded my personal space.

---

I did as Monica had instructed and took out one of those Wee-Wee pads from the diaper-looking pack, smoothed out the rigid seams, and placed it between the toilet and vanity. Then I picked up Prozac, who'd shadowed me around the townhouse since his arrival. He was nearly dry, although his hair—thanks to the carpet-cleaning episode—retained a ton of static cling, with some of the strands standing on end. He looked like a canine troll.

I placed him atop the pad and said, "Okay, this is our bathroom. I get the bowl, and you use *this* area when Mother Nature calls. *Capisco?* Got it?"

The dog studied me as if he could understand what I was saying. I stroked his head, smoothing down some of those wayward electromagnetic hairs, and told him, "I'm going to take a shower and shave these legs of mine. You run along and be a good boy, okay?"

The dog didn't move.

"Go on. You're free. Go. Scat!"

When he still didn't budge, I tried to read between the lines of his doggy gaze. "Oh, I get it. You need some privacy. All right, then I'll get my clothes and leave you here to do your business."

I set off for the bedroom, where I gathered clean underwear, jeans, and a turtleneck. By the time I returned, Prozac was gone, and the Wee-Wee pad was clean. I tiptoed back into the hallway and found Prozac sitting erect, looking reflective and philosophical, a majestic statue atop the back cushions of the living room sofa. Murky daylight streamed from the front picture window into the room and cast him in a cool glow. From his high perch, he had a clear view of the world outside—and he seemed more interested in that than in me.

"Good boy," I said. As I turned for the bathroom, I added, "Maybe this won't be so horrible after all."

I set my clothes on the hamper and topped them with a clean, folded Turkish towel. Then I slipped out of Kyle's old flannel shirt and dropped it into the laundry chute. Before I stepped into the tub, I decided to leave the bathroom door open a crack. After all, what if the little guy had to go to the bathroom while I was showering?

But I soon regretted that decision as the open door created a draft, something of a wind tunnel. The vinyl shower curtain kept billowing into the tub, sticking to my wet, soapy body. With the handheld showerhead, I doused the vinyl, trying to weight the curtain so it would adhere to the white painted steel of the tub. But the curtain kept ballooning back toward me, which made shaving my legs and armpits, and even shampooing my hair, a challenge.

At one point, Prozac's nose suddenly popped around the shower curtain.

Surprised by the sight of him, his beige front paws resting on the side of the tub, I asked, "What are you doing?"

Prozac whimpered and stood there panting.

"I'll be done in a minute," I said as I yanked the curtain closed, forcing him from my sight.

When I was finally through and flipped off the water, a bright flash of lightning pierced through the bathroom mini-blinds. A peal of thunder growled. I squeezed the water from my hair. A few drops of hard rain pelted the roof, and another thunderous quake clapped as if ushering in the next round of storms taking hold overhead. Thank goodness I'd gotten my shower over and out of the way.

As I ripped open the curtain and stepped out of the tub, something caught my eye—a splotch of beige and brown rising up from inside the toilet bowl. I did a double take, reaching for my towel and drying my eyes to get a better look. Two triangular shapes, like dueling dorsal fins from baby sharks, rose from inside the seat.

The pointy ears and wet face of a bedraggled-looking Prozac emerged.

I gasped.

The dog was shivering. A pitiable look was etched on his face, and his big brown eyes telegraphed, *Help! Get me out of here!*

I was stunned, standing there wet and paralyzed.

There was a flash of lightning, then another low rumble of thunder started to break until it snapped with a roaring *ka-boom!*

The slippery, cold tile floor quaked beneath my tacky feet from the explosion. I flinched, my gaze still riveted to Prozac. He quivered inside the bowl—a drowned rat with sad eyes.

*Oh, God, please tell me I don't have to reach into a dirty toilet!*

Bile filled my throat as I flung down the towel and draped it onto the floor. Then, naked, I approached the bowl. Feeling my face shrivel up with queasy repulsion, I narrowed my eyes and turned my head away as I reached into the toilet.

"Yuck!"

Prozac jumped into my hands as if my fingers were magnets and he were made of iron.

Keeping my arms out straight, I lifted Prozac from the bowl and placed his four paws atop my good Turkish towel.

Rain hammered the roof. I wrapped the chenille around Prozac, but the still-dripping-wet dog wormed away from the folds and took off, racing out of the room.

"No," I shouted, watching the dark ball of wet fur scurry away.

I looked at the empty hook on the back of the bathroom door, realizing that I'd forgotten to hang my robe. I shifted my sights to the towel on the floor but couldn't bring myself to wrap it around me, not after using it on a dog drenched in toilet water. Instead, I ripped the hand towel off the rack, but it was much too small to cover me. I positioned it over myself as best I could as I hurried out of the bathroom. Like a crazy lady at a nudist colony, I sprinted down the hall, tracking the dark, hairy shadow moving briskly across the polished oak floor of the living room.

"Prozac, stop!" I bellowed. But he bolted away. The dripping tangles of his hair released water droplets as he made a beeline over my imported oriental rug and skittered under the bottom flap of the upholstered sofa. He was gone, vanished from sight.

I heaved ragged, wheezing breaths and stopped dead in front of the picture window, shifting that hand towel between my private parts. With the heavy brocade drapes rippling from the velocity of the chase, I heard a whistle, an approving sound, like a heckling man who's spotted a beautiful woman on a city street. Realizing that the noise was coming from outside, I turned and saw my paunchy, middle-aged mailman, Carlos, rooted in place on the other side of the raindrop-splattered glass. There he was in his blue uniform and white waterproof postal helmet with a large brim. A toothy smile filled his face. He held a stack of mail in one hand and gave a big thumbs-up with the other, offering another whistle.

Appalled and mortified, I dropped to the floor. I didn't move a muscle. All I could hear was distant rainwater coursing through the gutters outside and the rasp of my own heart thrashing. I hoped that either A) it was all some sort of twisted bad dream, or B) the mailman had gone on his merry way and had tripped, fallen—nothing severe—and suffered a sudden bout of short-term amnesia.

A few moments later, with my body motionless on the floor, the bottom flap of the sofa moved. In slow deliberation, a moist little black nose emerged. Out stepped Prozac, who gave his cold, wet body a good hard shake that launched sprinkles of toilet water right into my face. Then he lurched onto the couch and settled his scruffy-looking body like King of the Mountain atop his perch, as if nothing out of the ordinary had happened. I, on the other hand, was down on all fours with my exposed derriere pointing up like a flag at full mast. I crawled over to the drapes and yanked the cord to pull them closed.

*How will I ever go out in public again?*

I slammed the toilet lid and toweled off. Then I channeled my wet head through my turtleneck and squeezed into a clean pair of jeans. Knowing what a gossip Carlos was—whenever I had to sign for a package, he would go on and on, spouting all the news and dirt from the neighborhood—the writer in me imagined him blabbing away about what he'd witnessed.

*Did you hear the latest about the reclusive author in Unit 22? She was standing there, buck naked, right in front of her picture window. You've should've seen it... I've got no idea what she was doing. Maybe role-playing for her next romance novel or something... Or maybe she was coming on to me!*

God only knew how Carlos would misconstrue and distort what he'd just seen. That was the problem with keeping to yourself and trying to be private—people could draw all kinds of wild conclusions.

But there wasn't a thing I could do about any of that other than hope for the best and get on with life.

The skies were brighter and finally settled into calm. I wrangled up Prozac and headed to the kitchen sink. When I saw the dirty dishes and empty soup cans, I made an about-face and carted him off to the bathroom, plunking him inside the tub while I got down on my knees. With the shower curtain partially closed, I regulated the tap then aimed the remote showerhead at Prozac, who became a moving target. He trailed back and forth in the concave steel, desperate to escape the blasts of warm water. When he realized he was trapped, he let me lather him up with lavender-infused shampoo. With delicate fingers, I pressed the tension from his scrawny body. As soap bubbles rose up between us, he was softening—trusting me. He dropped his hindquarters and finally sat down, succumbing to a groaning yawn. As I rinsed away the bubbles, his tired eyes blinked heavily as though he might nod off. The warm water ran clearer, and I let it cascade over him longer than needed. I hated to disrupt the peace of the moment.

That all changed, however, once we moved on to the blow-dryer phase.

I was tempted to dry him off atop the bathroom vanity, but conjuring images of his taking a high-flying leap onto the ceramic tile floor—or flirting with the potential for electrocution from the wet sink nearby—I decided instead to set off for my office. I snaked my way around columns of books rising from the floor and placed the dog atop the credenza behind my desk. It was crammed below the corner windows and covered with papers and books. I piled things up and moved the stacks, arranging them like a blockade to confine him. Keeping one firm hand on the dog, I plugged in the hair dryer and pointed it like a gun at Prozac.

As soon as I pressed the on switch, Prozac transformed from Toto into Cujo. Strongly objecting to my styling efforts, he bared his fangs and bit at the blasts of air as they hit him. He was wiggly and unwieldy, but I managed to keep him cornered and channel the air his way, minus a few misdirected blasts that sent some pages from my novel-in-progress airborne. I let them fly, wafting around the room like a large spray of confetti, as I raked my fingers through the short strands of Prozac's thin, fast-drying hair. When the dampness was replaced with a warm, super-fluffed coat, I set him down on the floor, which was by then carpeted with so many papers that when Prozac bolted from the room, a path of pages fluttered up in his wake.

# Five

*IT'S ENOUGH TO MAKE YOU WANT TO GO POOP!*

## Meredith

IT WAS TURNING OUT TO be one hell of a morning, and it wasn't over yet. Prozac once again nestled atop the sofa. The copper hair atop his head looked as shiny as a brand-new penny. I did a load of laundry, picked up the catalogs, letters, and the newspaper Carlos had dropped through my mail slot, then put on a pot of water to make myself a cup of instant coffee. While I waited for the kettle to boil, I clicked on my laptop and checked my emails.

There were a ton of messages, mostly bogus advertisements and spam, but I stopped scanning subject lines when I came upon "Prozac." The sender's name was listed as one word: HammondCederholm.

I stared at that name and subject line, leery of opening the email. I certainly didn't know anyone named Hammond Cederholm, but I did, unwillingly, know a dog named Prozac. Inhaling a deep breath, I clicked on the message and began reading.

> Dear Ms. Mancuso:
>
> Hello. I am writing on behalf of Aunt Helen (Hendrix) who is in the hospital, convalescing from foot surgery.
>
> First of all, she thanks you sincerely for agreeing to take care of her canine companion, Prozac. He's a very special little dog!
>
> We both suspect that your sister has already passed along instructions regarding Prozac's daily necessities, but

Aunt Helen would also like you to have a copy of Prozac's weekly itinerary (see the Excel spreadsheet attached).

Prozac is a CTD—a Certified Therapy Dog—and Aunt Helen makes it her priority to ensure that he keeps to his schedule and visits "his people" regularly. She understands you are very busy, but if you could and are willing, she would appreciate your at least keeping Prozac's standing appointment with the good folks over at Evergreen Gardens. It is an independent living facility for seniors in Oak Park, not far from your own hometown. Prozac is committed to visiting at least two hours, once a week, on Wednesdays, and Aunt Helen feels these folks, her good friends, would be sorely deprived by Prozac's absence.

Of course, if you'd like, and your schedule permits, you can also consider filling in for Aunt Helen at any of the other stops on Prozac's weekly itinerary. Aunt Helen claims that Prozac is most in his element during hospice calls and whenever they visit the dementia wing over at the Veterans' Home.

As an aside, I, myself, had wished to take Prozac. But between the added responsibility of caring for Aunt Helen, long hours spent commuting and working at my job in NYC (plus, I live alone), I'm unable to give Prozac the care Aunt Helen feels he needs and deserves. Monica has assured us that you are an animal lover and you work from home, which is a perfect arrangement.

Aunt Helen and I are extremely grateful for your support during this difficult time. Feel free to contact me at any time with questions and concerns.

Best,

Hammond "Ham" Cederholm

(on behalf of Helen Hendrix)

I couldn't believe what I was reading! *Me, an animal lover?* Monica had out-and-out lied? It was bad enough to have the damn dog thrust upon me against my own will and better judgment. Now I would have to be further inconvenienced by taking time out of my life to traipse him around the county, too?

*And who said anything about surgery? I thought Helen only broke her foot?*

I was even more enraged after I downloaded the document attached to the patronizing, guilt-trip-laden email—a thoroughly detailed spreadsheet that itemized Prozac's calendar of daily events, broken down hourly. I was astounded as I read through the entries. In addition to visits to hospice centers, nursing and veterans' homes and hospitals, there were stops at halfway houses, schools, Read-to-a-Dog programs at a host of local libraries, even a weekly cameo appearance at the Stitch-and-Bitch group that met at the local craft store on Monday evenings. How could a five-pound ball of fur have a more active social life than I did? And how in the world did an elderly lady, the eighty-seven-year-old likes of Helen Hendrix, even keep up with him? Some middle-aged heads of state didn't have such vigorous commitments!

Those were exactly some of the points I spouted when I picked up the phone and blasted Monica, telling her that I had a limit.

"And calling *me* an 'animal lover'? That is total deceit, lower than low," I said, pacing the floor between the kitchen and living room.

"Oh, stop," Monica said. "I just stretched the truth a little, based on your liking a good steak—"

"Yeah, like you stretched the truth about Helen's broken foot?" I was so furious that my spittle was spraying around the kitchen. I heard it singe on the hot stainless steel teakettle. "Why didn't you tell me she had *surgery?*"

"Because that was an unexpected complication—"

"Oh, really? I'll give you an unexpected complication. Try me fishing this damn dog out of the toilet bowl."

Monica burst out laughing. "Were you trying to dispose of him or was he in search of an escape route?"

"It's not funny. It sickened me. He jumped in there while I was in the shower."

Monica couldn't contain her amusement. "I hope you had flushed first?"

"Of course I flushed." I felt a queasy shiver prickle up my spine. "Look, I've got much better things to do with my time than babysitting and grooming someone else's spoiled little pocket dog."

"Like what? Like sitting on your duff another year, licking your wounds, and watching marathon episodes of *Law and Order*? Like cultivating your agoraphobic tendencies—"

"That's enough."

"No, maybe it's not enough. Maybe it's about time someone gave you a swift kick in the—"

"I'm hanging up."

"Wait. I know you're upset, Meredith. But this is the most lively I've seen you in years."

"Lively? This is called me being ticked off. Big-time!"

"Whatever it is, it's refreshing to see that you've still got some spunk left in you. I was beginning to think you died right along with Kyle."

"I wish I had."

"Well, you didn't. You're still here. And it's about time you started living again."

"I'm living. My heart's beating. I'm still breathing."

"Honestly, I don't know what to do for you or how to help you anymore."

"I didn't ask for your help. And I sure as hell didn't ask for this stupid dog."

"Oh, right, I forgot. God forbid! Meredith—proud, stubborn Meredith, a pillar of self-reliance—would never ask for or want anybody's help. No, that's *so* beneath her." I could envision my sister sitting in her high-back leather office chair, phone crooked between her head and shoulder while she tossed up her hands in exasperation. "Nothing you're doing to help yourself is working. So maybe it's the best thing that you do someone else a good turn."

"Oh yeah? Like helping my disingenuous, manipulative sister be the savior for some rich old lady with a busted foot and a spoiled dog?" I took a much-needed breath. "Stop with the reverse psychology. Get over here and take back this animal. Now."

"Can't. My next appointment is walking in—"

"Get your bony ass over here right now! This dog is *your* responsibility, not mine—"

*Click!*

Blind with rage, I felt my chin unhinge. When the piercing sound of the dial tone filled my eardrum, I poked a finger onto the off button of the cordless phone and slammed the receiver down onto the kitchen table.

I screamed, my angst welling forth in a painful roar of "Dammit!" With my heart thrashing inside my chest and my hands balled into fists, I turned toward the kitchen sink, feeling my left shoe squash into something soft. I looked at the floor and saw only the cold, hard ceramic tile. But when I picked up my foot, a fetid stench rose. Brown glop stained the floor and the sole of one shoe.

"That's it!" I marched toward the living room to reprimand Prozac, but as tracks of squalid brown sullied the tile, I stopped abruptly.

The room was silent. There was no sign of Prozac perched atop the sofa or chairs.

"Bad boy," I shouted, hoping my scolding would reach him—wherever he was. I slipped off my shoe and held it far away from me as I traipsed toward the laundry room washbasin. En route, I mumbled, "And they call this bag of bones a Certified Therapy Dog—a dog to provide affection and comfort? Ha! If I keep him another second, *I'm* the one who's going to need the therapy!"

# Six

Meredith

WITH A TOOTHPICK, I PRIED the squashed doggie turd from the rubber crevices of my left shoe and thoroughly rinsed and disinfected the sole beneath the spigot of the washtub. Once I slipped my foot back inside the damp, soft leather, I marched straight into the living room, collapsed that playpen, and reached for my car keys on the library table. Enough was enough. It was time to pack up that dog and return him and all his paraphernalia to Monica.

But my clear resolve was impeded by the fact that Prozac was nowhere to be found. His hide-and-seek routine was growing old, even after only ninety minutes in my charge.

My first line of defense was to check for Prozac under the sofa. But he was MIA. I tramped down the hall, flung open the partially opened bathroom door, and looked at the toilet. When I found the lid closed, I breathed a sigh of relief—it was the only thing I'd done right all morning. From there, I bounded for the bedroom, and lo and behold, Prozac's stubby tail and his rear paws pointed out from under the bed skirt. I was reminded of the story of the ostrich that stuck his head in the sand, thinking he was obscured. I shook my head, and my smirk verged on a smile.

*Damn dog!*

Knowing if I moved too quickly, my four-legged canine nemesis might shrink deeper beneath the bed, I tiptoed closer, hoping the floorboards wouldn't creak. When he was within arm's reach, I swooped down like a determined hawk in pursuit of prey.

"Gotcha!" I exclaimed, clasping my hands like a vise grip around Prozac's middle and sliding him out from under the bed.

Keeping his squirmy body glued to my side like a shaggy clutch purse filled with a million dollars, I returned to the kitchen and rummaged through that shopping bag in search of a collar and leash. I pulled out several cans of dog food; bones and treats; some tiny little shirts, bow ties, and bandannas; even a doggy toothbrush and chicken-flavored toothpaste. When I dumped the remaining contents of the bag onto the kitchen floor, out rolled an impressive array of plush and rubber squeaky toys, balls, colorful ropes, and a canvas doggie Frisbee. At the very bottom of the bag was a tangled harness-and-leash combo.

I suited him up and said, "All right. Let's go, mister," giving him a tug met only with resistance. In protest, Prozac had plopped his derriere onto the ground. Stubborn, he made it clear he wasn't going anywhere. But being almost thirty times the weight of the four-legged monster had benefits. I simply reached down and scooped him up. With dog in one arm and playpen, purse, and shopping bag in the other, off I went.

---

Prozac sat in the front passenger seat of my Toyota and stared straight ahead at the dashboard until he finally lay down, pressing his head upon his front paws set atop the soft velour upholstery. He refused to look at me.

Monica's office wasn't far, only three towns away, and each small community had similar landmarks—one chain supermarket, a few strip malls and gas stations, the public library, and post office. By the time we drove past the sign that read Welcome to Oak Park, I could already feel the weight of my responsibility for the dog beginning to lift.

But before we arrived downtown at Monica's office, we were stopped by a flashing red signal at the railroad tracks. Red-and-white-striped gates lowered. The ground began to quake, and the distant thrum and wail of a whistle blew, indicating an oncoming train. Once I spotted a slew of rail cars with CSX and Norfolk Southern logos, I shifted the Toyota into park. Clearly, the train was carrying freight and not commuters. Staring through the windshield and listening to the shuddering and clanking of gears upon the rails, I was lulled by the panorama of cars, some of them sporting wild and colorful graffiti as they spooled past. Prozac leaped upon the door to look out the window. He, too, became hypnotized, soon releasing a great big yawn and settling back onto the passenger seat. He lowered his head, pressing it upon his paws while shifting his soulful eyes toward me.

I looked at his furry face and tried to put myself in his shoes—or paws. It couldn't have been easy for him with his master taking a fall, vanishing from his world, and leaving him something of an orphan. He was then schlepped to my sister, a classic workaholic Type-A personality, who was probably freaking out over having to deliver on a promise she never thought she'd actually have to keep. And then, he was dumped on my doorstep—placed in my charge, against his will and mine.

Prozac looked so small, so sad and lonely, nestled there on the big bucket seat. He looked up and, with eyes bright and pleading, tilted his head as though petitioning me to reconsider my decision to take him back to Monica.

"Don't look at me like that," I said, banishing any glimmer of a second thought. "I'm sure, in your own environment, you're probably a pretty decent dog. But this would never work. I'm not in a good place in my life right now, and you wouldn't be happy with me. I'm not a dog person. And after you pooped in my kitchen, you don't strike me as being an admirer of mine, either. So let's call a spade a spade." I reached over and patted his head, realizing that Prozac and I had things in common—namely that we were alone and on our own. We'd both been abandoned, unwillingly and by forces beyond our control, by the people we loved—and who loved us—the most.

But such sentiments were short-lived. When the railroad lights ceased flashing and the candy-cane-striped gates lifted, I left all those feelings behind. The tires lumbered over the bumpy tracks, and I accelerated, focusing on the road ahead.

---

A few turns put us on the main drag of Oak Park and in mounting downtown traffic. Prozac rallied, propping himself on his hind legs, anxious to look out the window. As we passed through the shopping district and wound onto more residential side streets, Prozac's breath lightly steamed the glass, and his stubby little tail wagged furiously. My gaze roamed, curious to know what had caught his attention. A lofty, rectangular stone turret rose above an immense, gothic-looking structure. Mature foliage surrounded a limestone dome, and tall recessed windows—possibly stained glass—loomed beneath a myriad of steep pitches and gables. The place looked as though it might've been an Ivy League prep school or some kind of church, complete with tall, well-tended evergreens and shrubs. A sprawling, snow-covered front lawn sprouted traces of greenery, and shoots from daffodils and tulips bordered a long horseshoe drive. Prozac scratched on the glass of the passenger-side window as though trying to claw his way out. But as we drove on, his enthusiasm waned. We soon came upon center hall colonial houses, doctor's offices, and an obviously affluent large brick residence that had apparently been added onto and converted into a daycare center with more flags than the United Nations.

When I spied the embossed sign that read Dean's Electric, I flipped on the turn signal and hung a right into the parking lot of an updated two-family Victorian house that had been modified for commercial use. Tucked behind the building was the sign for my sister's office—Monica Mancuso, CPA: Tax and Estate Accounting.

"Modest but with curb appeal" was how a realtor might've described the place. The front half of the house served as an electrician's shop. Workers were rarely on-site, but a fleet of vans remained parked on the side drive after business hours. The other half of the house, the rear portion, served as Monica's tax office. To the untrained eye, the house was all office. Most folks didn't know that Monica not only worked there as a sole practitioner, but she also lived in the same place, behind a locked door—down the hall, past the bathroom.

Monica's "living quarters" were part bedroom, part recreation room and den, part library, and part gym. She also shared the space with her longtime beau, Larry, whenever he was home on leave—which was only a few times a year. Larry was a senior-level military bomb squad engineer whom Monica had been "dating" since the Gulf War, when Larry first began taking consecutive tours of duty in the Middle East. He was also an acrimoniously divorced father of two grown boys of left-wing, anti-war persuasion— "just like their mother," Larry would say. The boys wanted little to do with Larry, as he had been vocally opposed to their joining the Occupy Wall Street movement full-time after they'd graduated college. Many years later, the rift remained.

Larry, like Monica, was a workaholic, so they were a perfect match. They spent the bulk of their respective waking hours putting out fires and averting catastrophes with terrorists—whether said terrorists were on the battlefield or with the IRS. They supported each other and seemed content despite the lack of a legal commitment. The arrangement worked for them as they inhabited living spaces, together and apart, with trappings as sparse as barracks.

Monica lived in that one room of her office, a rather large master bedroom crammed with a queen-sized bed, a dresser, no TV, piles of books—Monica escaped with westerns and romances, including my novels—and an exercise bike, an enormous fitness ball, and hand weights. She had a tendency to hoard things, but the size of that room served to keep her Feng Shui inclinations in check. Only my sister could make the practices of hoarding and Feng Shui compatible.

For years, it struck me as odd that a high-powered career woman with the letters CPA after her name lived and worked so frugally in all of three rooms—one large, main office room, a kitchenette, and the storage room-slash-bedroom. But to know my sister was to know that she was always crying poverty. She was always inundated with too much work and facing some sort of pressing deadline, and if said poverty and overload weren't part of the equation of her life, she was usually miserable. Monica was married, for better or worse, to her job, and she lived to work. She thrived on it and was so committed to helping and doing right by her clients—for instance, fulfilling the promise she'd made to Helen Hendrix about Prozac—that she sometimes dreamed of them, along with numbers and laws, amid the REM cycles of sleep. That was what I most admired about my sister—she lived her life the way that felt right for her despite the expected conventions. She was always true to herself and marched to her own drumbeat regardless of how the world judged and operated. If only I had possessed a shred of her conviction and confidence.

But all of that was about to change as I pulled my Toyota into the parking space alongside Monica's Saturn.

As I cut the engine, I said, "Okay, time to go, little man," to which Prozac responded by leaping into the floor well of the car and burrowing beneath the seat.

I groaned as I reached down and, foraging for fur, swiped my hand against carpeting and metal brackets beneath the upholstered seat. My fingers met with a few cellophane wrappers. I heard heavy panting behind me. I craned my neck to the backseat and found Prozac, his long tongue lolling from his mouth as he looked me in the eye.

I refused to be ruffled again by that furry five-pound bully, so I hopped out of the car and ripped open the back door, determined to overpower my opponent once and for all. But when my fingertips were just inches from him, Prozac lurched up onto the rear platform of the car, the narrow, wedge-like crevice above the back seat at the rear window. His determination to evade capture was making me grow more and more peeved. As I lowered myself onto the seat in an effort to put an end to the madness, Prozac leaped down in an unexpected arc from platform to footwell, completely bypassing the seat. I grabbed for his leash, but my reflexes were too slow. Prozac bounded out the opened car door, straight into the parking lot.

I gasped.

Before I could maneuver up and out of the car, I screamed for him. But my pleas were futile. He took off, obviously gaining momentum and motivation. His red leash looked like a long, bright, skinny tail flapping in defiance as he raced behind the buildings bordering Monica's office.

Like the crazy, completely irrational lady I was fast becoming, I ran after him and kept hollering his name. I sent up loud, pleading petitions of "Prozac! Prozac!" as if I were an antidepressant junkie in the midst of a nervous breakdown, desperately in search of my next prescriptive fix. I was frantic to get that dog back. I didn't like him, and I sure as heck didn't want to keep him, but the thought of that dog charging toward the busy, traffic-laden main street district of downtown… Horror of horrors!

Prozac bounded behind buildings and houses. I decided the best way to pursue him was via a route parallel to the one he was traveling. I figured if I came at him from a street side, I might be able to redirect his path and corral him toward the quiet back roads.

My strategy seemed to work, and soon I was gaining on him, as he had far more obstacles to cross in his path than I did in mine. His short legs and paws skittered around cars and concrete parking stanchions, garbage pails and fences; he leaped over potholes filled with ice and puddles. When he finally charged into a thicket of trees, I lost him—fearing what might be on the other side.

"Prozac!" I screamed. "Prozac!"

My hair blew back from my face. I was huffing and puffing, my legs like lead. I plodded straight into the brush, ducking and covering my face as brittle winter branches caught on my jacket and twigs snapped under my heavy, traipsing feet.

When I emerged on the other side of the thicket, my whole body burst forth into an open expanse of white snow dotted with clusters of well-tended green. The lawn was terraced and filled with sculpted shrubs, evergreens, and classically shaped bonsai trees.

I gathered my breath and kept charging, hollering, "Prozac!" His red leash flitted up and down as he tore across that sweeping, almost pastoral landscape. That dog must've had greyhound somewhere in his bloodline.

In the distance, I spied that rising stone turret, that prep school, church-like structure. The building looked even more imposing close up, and Prozac was heading straight for it. As he bolted across the great lawn, a sedan pulled into the long horseshoe drive that led to the front door of the place—along Prozac's apparently intended route. My arms waved and flapped in every direction as a sharp, glaring shriek of "Stop!" scraped from my dry throat.

The silver-haired driver of the car was oblivious to me and the dog. The sedan didn't slow down to accommodate the blurry ball of fur in motion. As the vehicle approached the dark speck that was Prozac, I sent up a bloodcurdling scream that proved enough to shift the dog's course. His velocity dropped off, forcing him to zigzag his way around the looming front tires. I didn't know how he did it, but he reached the front landing of the building miraculously unscathed.

I put a hand over my racing heart. Sweat broke out all over me in the awful cold as I stared at Prozac's muddied paw prints. He'd left dark tracks upon the smooth limestone entrance. On his approach through the archway leading inside the place, the front glass doors parted. As they did, Prozac glanced back at me. With his white teeth gleaming against the swell of his panting, curled pink tongue, he appeared to be smiling, enjoying the fun—laughing, even. Head and snout held high and tail boldly erect, he quickly dashed inside.

The doors slid closed.

# Seven

## PAGING DR. PROZAC

### Meredith

FROZEN AND STUNNED, I STOOD on the vast lawn, staring at a bronze plaque affixed near the entryway of that stately building: *EVERGREEN GARDENS, A Sanctuary for Mature, Independent Living.*

Evergreen Gardens? Was that the place Helen Hendrix's nephew had mentioned in his email—where they wanted me to take Prozac once a week?

I scratched my head, and then it hit me. The unexpected turn of events might actually offer an opportunity. What would happen if I walked away, if I turned on my heels, wandered back through the hedges from whence I came, and simply got in my car and drove off? Prozac would surely be safe in a place like Evergreen Gardens. Someone there, a resident or even a worker, would eventually discover him, swoop him up, and give him a lot more love and affection than I. But abandoning a dog? Bidding goodbye to a living, breathing creature left in my care? Regardless of my disdain for pets and the inconvenience of caring for Prozac, could I really do that? Would I be able to live with myself? I was still carrying around guilt about H&R Block.

Once I stepped inside Evergreen Gardens, how would I explain who I was and why Prozac had just paraded into the place without me, the person responsible for his well-being?

In the end, the temptation to cut and run—to finally ditch the burden of that dog and leave him—was great, but my conscience proved more powerful. I would simply have to walk in there, swallow my pride, and tell the truth. That was all there was to it. I took a deep breath and reluctantly took one stride then another across the great front lawn. I made my way straight toward a row of glass doors topped by tall panels of stained glass, all merging to a curve at the crest to form an arch-shaped pattern.

The word BELIEVETH was etched deep into a narrow strip of stonework set above the row of doors and the stained glass. Once the soles of my shoes touched upon the limestone landing, the doors pneumatically parted as if by magic.

The aged exterior of the building didn't do justice to the ornate beauty inside. Even though it was a cold, wet, and dreary March day, streams of light spewed through the glasswork and spilled onto well-tended interior foliage and a polished white-marble floor. I swiveled my gaze, unable to take in the sheer enormity of the space. In the center of the banquet-hall-sized lobby, a stained glass oculus in the forty-foot-high domed ceiling illuminated an intricately carved marble fountain sporting flamboyant and lively winged angels and cherubs. French Provincial sofas, chairs, and tables filled the space and led toward a wide, red-carpeted staircase brightened by an elegant, sparkly crystal chandelier. On the upper walls was an array of glimmering gold pipes—polished and lined up, graduated in size, as if from an organ—surrounded by finely crafted woodwork and paneling. Gazing around, I could see why Prozac ran to Evergreen Gardens the way he had. The environment certainly gave the appearance of a safe, protective—and plush—place of refuge.

I stood, mesmerized, until a tall, burly high school kid—a teenager whose pouty face underscored his crew cut and who wore a military-looking camouflage jacket—marched by me in a huff.

"Good morning. You look lost," a friendly female voice said. "Can I help you?"

Caught in a breeze created by the kid's wake, I drew my attention toward a stately antique desk, where a woman sat in shadow. A bright-pink baseball cap covered her closely cropped brown hair, and she wore a matching T-shirt with the word *Namaste* screen-printed on the front. Her dangling crystal earrings caught the warm rainbow beams of light spilling forth from an heirloom Tiffany table lamp.

"I, uh…" My voice seemed swallowed up by the immensity of the room. "Um, this might sound peculiar, but did you happen to see a little dog?"

"Oh, are *you* with Prozac? We heard a nice lady would be taking over for Miss Helen while she's recovering."

*Nice?* How *nice* could I really claim to be when, moments earlier, I had been on the brink of ditching that dog and hightailing it back home?

"How is Miss Helen doing?" said the *Namaste* woman, whose name badge read Bobbi Lovett.

"Is Prozac here?" My anxiety over the dog's whereabouts trumped making small talk and speculating on the health of a woman I barely knew.

"You look troubled, honey. Don't worry. I'm the tai chi instructor— filling in momentarily for Betsy. She's in the powder room."

"But have you *seen* Prozac?"

"Yes, he just dashed past—slipped under my reach and zipped up the stairs. Don't worry. He's probably already making his rounds."

"Rounds?"

"Yes, Prozy's always so focused on getting to *his people*."

"So he's here? You're sure?"

When the woman nodded, I splayed a flat hand over the rapid beats of my heart pounding through my chest.

"Thank God." I flung back my head and stared up into the circle of stained glass in that domed ceiling. "Which way did he go?"

The woman glanced at a typed itinerary atop the desk. She ran her well-manicured pointer finger along the grid and stopped at eleven thirty a.m.

"It's no wonder Prozy came charging in here like he did!" The woman's amusement was clear. "It's almost teatime in the solarium, and the ladies from the kitchen always leave special treats for Prozy on the cookie tray."

"Can you point me in that direction so I can wrangle him up?"

"Wrangle him up? But you just got here."

I gathered my scattered thoughts and said, "The thing is... th-th-this was only a dress rehearsal visit for me and Prozac today—a dry run." I pointed to my wristwatch. "We can't stay."

"Oh, that's what you think!" The woman burst out laughing, as if I'd just delivered a punch line to a clever joke. "Prozy's never going to go for that. And neither will his fan club here at Evergreen Gardens."

"Left or right?" I pointed my hands in opposite directions, gesturing toward the two corridors that led away from the lobby.

The woman reached for a small rectangular label and said, "You can't go anywhere without signing in and slipping on a name tag…" The last part of her sentence dangled there, as though she were waiting for me to jump in and give her my name. "It's the policy of the facility."

"Meredith St. John… Meredith Mancuso," I said, fumbling.

The woman looked up at me and appeared puzzled. "Is that it? Or is there more?"

That happened a lot. I had two names—my birth name as bestowed by my parents and the pen name I used for work. I often had to think first before spouting off who I was, depending on where I found myself. And currently I was experiencing one of those times when I replied too hastily and probably appeared in the throes of an identity crisis—or a split personality.

"Meredith is fine," I told her.

"First and last name are required."

I half expected the woman to card me next.

"St. John," I said. "Meredith St. John."

I slapped the rectangular name tag over my heart and dashed away. Bobbi said the solarium was on the second floor, and the easiest way for me to get there was via a tiny, old-fashioned elevator box, the kind where the passenger closes the door and pulls the scissor gate to get things rolling. Once I reached the second floor, I followed the signs and arrows that pointed to the solarium. My aim was to retrieve Prozac, deposit him at Monica's, and be finished with the whole fiasco. I wanted nothing more than to get back to my drab, inert life, which seemed like a dream compared to the nightmare I'd been living for the past two hours.

While hurrying down the hall, I glanced through an open door on my left and thought I spied Prozac sitting alongside the white socks and sneakers of an older woman with gray roots peeking out from her short, dyed-red hair. She was wearing a black zip-up duster with a lace shawl collar. At first, I overshot the room and was forced to backpedal. When I did, I noticed that one panel of a large stained-glass picture window in the room was flung wide open. Chilly air and muted daylight streaked into the mahogany-trimmed space filled with a long conference table, a few chairs, desks, and floor-to-ceiling wraparound bookshelves. A freestanding globe and a dictionary were propped upon a pedestal. The room resembled a library. Prozac rolled onto his back, paws up, and was quick to offer his belly to the fawning red-headed woman who reached down to accommodate him.

"Well, look at who it is—my favorite little four-legged munchkin!" the woman cooed in baby talk to Prozac, who was shamelessly eating up the attention.

I stood, taking it all in from the doorway. When Prozac spotted me, the woman followed his gaze.

"Oh, hello," she said with surprise. She had a youthful voice but old, craggy skin. "Is he with you?"

"He was—is," I said. "But I think he's much more content here with you."

The woman chuckled and gave Prozac an endearing pat on the head. "We all love this little fella. Are you the woman filling in for Helen?"

"W-well, sort of, I guess. But it's… it's not permanent," I stuttered, entering the room.

"You seem frazzled." The woman's mouth curled into a subtle smile. She gestured toward an upholstered armchair adjacent to the sofa. "Please, sit down. Take a breather."

It sounded like the sanest and most rational idea of the day, so I followed her lead and dropped my body into the seat.

"It's something how this guy brought you here today." The woman ruffled her arthritic-looking fingers through Prozac's thick black coat. "It goes to show you, sometimes you simply have to trust where you're being led."

My eyebrows knit. *How does this lady know I didn't willingly bring Prozac here?* I couldn't be sure if it was the old-world aura of the room or the words the woman had spoken, but there was something surreal, even mystical, about the moment. And that indefinable something was making me feel ill at ease.

"Yes, well, I'm filling in for Helen Hendrix. Our visit today was sort of… spontaneous," I explained. "We're just here for a therapy dog dress rehearsal."

The woman looked up from Prozac to me, dead on.

"Oh, I see," she said, bobbing her head. "And how's the *performance* going so far, dear?"

I stared at the woman, noticing her earrings—what looked like dangling wooden hammers.

"You live nearby?" she asked.

"Not far."

"Did you drive here this morning?"

"Yes." My heart pounded inside my chest. The woman's line of questioning made me feel as though she had my number, and the less I said, the better.

"Where'd you park?"

"Outside."

"Outside here—this building?" Amusement filled her hazel eyes that were split by her bifocal lenses.

"Actually, down the block. My sister's accounting office is nearby."

*Who the heck is this lady, and why am I engaging in this conversation?* I hadn't had such a grilling since I'd cut school in ninth grade, eons ago, and my mother caught me at the town pizzeria instead of algebra class.

"So, let me see if I've got this straight. You're filling in with Prozac for Helen?"

"Yes, temporarily—until they can find a more permanent replacement."

"Permanent replacement? I heard Helen only broke her foot." The woman pushed her eyeglasses up her nose. Her hammer earrings swayed. "Is it more serious than they're letting on?"

"She needed surgery, but they say she's doing well. And I'm just Prozac's temporary caretaker. You see, my sister is Helen's accountant, and she was supposed to care for the dog, but the thing is, she's allergic."

"And what's *your* excuse?"

"I beg your pardon?"

"Why, exactly, can't *you* take care of Prozy?"

Prozac swung his head in my direction and locked eyes with me as if wanting to know the answer to that question himself.

"I've never had a dog before or cared for one. I don't have any experience."

"Experience?" She chuckled. "Dogs instinctively know how to love people. That's all the experience *anybody* needs."

"There's a lot more involved—"

"Excuses, excuses!"

"No, but—"

"Oh, you sound like I used to: *I'm not a dog person. I don't want a dog.* The works. And then, one day a couple of years into my marriage, one of my neighbors had a litter of these beautiful little Pomeranians. They couldn't sell the jumbo shrimp of the bunch, so they asked me to take him. My husband fought me, tooth and nail. But that's how I got Charmin. That's what I called him because he was all white and cuddly like the toilet paper in those commercials with Mr. Whipple. You're probably too young to remember. Oh, I could've squeezed that dog all day long…"

The woman's voice cracked. Her eyes grew moist. She sniffled and pulled out a scrunched-up tissue from the sleeve of her black satin shift and blotted her nose and eyes.

"I adored that dog…"

I squirmed in my chair, unsure how or if I should respond to the woman's show of emotion. But Prozac took care of handling that for me and leaped on the sofa. He rested his chin on the woman's thigh as though he sensed she was in need of comfort.

"Charmin saved me when my marriage ended." The woman gazed lovingly at angelic-looking Prozac and stroked him between his ears. "He was the great love of my life. So don't ever underestimate the power of the Almighty or the four-legged messengers he sends into our mundane little lives."

I didn't know what to say, and I feared whatever I did say would certainly be anti-climactic compared to the compassion Prozac instinctively offered.

I went with a safe affirmation. "That's a beautiful story," I said.

"Yes, maybe it's one you needed to hear. Bet you never thought this fella could be such a speed demon." The woman planted a kiss atop the crown of Prozac's head. "The way he flew across that front lawn…"

*Front lawn?* A sick, clammy feeling roiled inside my belly.

"Yeah, had myself a front-row seat to all your dress rehearsal festivities." The woman motioned toward the open window that overlooked the lawn of Evergreen Gardens.

I tried to speak, but when no words tumbled forth, the woman said, "My new hearing aids are practically bionic. And I have to admit, when I first heard someone screaming 'Prozac,' I thought the audiologist fouled something up. But when I realized the hollering was coming from outside, I hurried toward the window. I saw you running and carrying on, and I assumed you were just another nut job off her meds. The world's full of folks like that these days." The woman paused, heightening the drama, and eyed me with suspicion. "But then I saw Prozac. Oh, how harrowing to stand by powerlessly while he was put in harm's way."

"Thankfully, he was smart enough to run for safety."

"But the approach of that car! Prozac could've been killed."

I swallowed hard, not sure what to say next.

"Close call," she added.

"Yes, too close for comfort," I agreed. "All the more reason this dog shouldn't be left in my care—"

"And all the more reason you should try and make things up to him."

I widened my gaze. "Make *what* up to him?"

"The fact that you almost got him killed. Dogs are intuitive creatures, and Prozac here is very special. He's not only exceptionally smart, but he's also very sensitive. He can sense what you're feeling. He knows you don't like him, and I'm getting the sense that he's frightened."

I drew in a deep, exasperated breath. *What is this lady—a pet psychic?*

"You know," she said, "if someone really wanted to, they could report the careless way you've behaved with this poor, defenseless creature. The danger you've put this dog in could be grounds for an abuse charge with the Animal Protection League, I'd bet."

"What?" I was aghast at her sudden shift in tone and her allegation. "That dog jumped out of my car. His getting loose was a complete accident. I had no control of his running away."

"Aha." The lady bobbed her head, enlightened, her hammer earrings swinging. "So you *do* admit you recklessly endangered the well-being of this innocent animal?"

I sat up as ramrod-straight as Prozac's erect, pointed ears. "Not intentionally."

"You're desperate to get out of your responsibility to care for this dog, aren't you?"

I lurched to my feet. "I think we ought to go now—"

"Dear, I know people and their motives very well. And desperate people often take desperate measures, *Meredith St. John.*" The woman flung her nose into the air as she looked at my name tag. She cuddled Prozac closer to her lap. "Helen Hendrix is a dear friend of mine. Once she gets wind of what happened here today, she isn't going to be pleased that her pride and joy has been so ill-treated."

"Ill-treated? This dog has been under my care for" —I lifted the cuff of my coat sleeve and eyed my watch— "for all of two hours and twenty minutes."

"It's long enough for you to scar his fragile psyche, maybe for life."

Prozac, who appeared comforted by the woman's tender touch, stared at me accusingly.

"That's it," I blurted, heat rising as anger spread through my veins. "Please give me the dog. I won't stand here and be falsely accused."

With slow and deliberate care, the woman removed an imaginary piece of lint off the satiny black fabric of her housecoat.

"And what about the scars to *my* psyche?" I said.

The woman shook her head and *tsk-tsked*. "To think that Helen Hendrix had a world of respect for your sister, had so highly recommended her accounting services to the folks in this facility. It would be a real shame for her to lose her credibility—and so many clients, too. I mean, if she'd put a defenseless animal in *your* care, how could anyone possibly trust her judgment in advising folks with their entire life savings, tax returns, and estate plans?"

My mouth went dry. My ears felt molten. "Look, I think you've misunderstood—"

"Oh, there's nothing to misunderstand. I've got it all here—all the proof I need." The woman pulled out a tablet computer from beneath a pillow beside her. She held up the tablet as if it were Exhibit A. "I've captured the whole distressing incident right here on my camera app. It's a good thing I signed up for that iPad video tutorial they had here last week."

I felt like a criminal—a criminal cornered by a conniving, blackmailing old lady with weird-looking hammer earrings. I didn't like her accusations, so I reached across the sofa to gather Prozac. On my abrupt approach, he leaped right onto the woman's lap as if he were taking her side and asking her for protection.

"This is absurd. Ridiculous," I said. "What's your name?"

"You don't need to know my name."

"Yes, I do. I'd like to know just who, exactly, will be responsible for distorting the truth about me and my hardworking sister to the Animal Protection League and/or Helen Hendrix."

"Folks around here call me Judge—Judge Thea. Judge Theadora

Strong—first woman ever appointed to the county bench. Served thirty years. I still have connections…"

*Aha!* The hammers were gavels. Once I considered them along with the black robe duster-shift thing, everything made perfect sense. There I was already mentally conjuring my alibi, thinking I could accuse the shriveled old lady of being mistaken by her dimmed wits, but she was obviously as sharp as the rap of a gavel bringing order to a courtroom. If she was who she claimed to be and was really telling the truth—that she not only witnessed the whole thing but had also recorded Prozac's endangerment—would I really be able to deny my guilt?

"But what we might do," the judge said, her tone softening, "is strike a plea bargain."

"What kind of bargain?"

"If you or your sister don't take Prozac, then he'll probably be pawned off on Helen's no-good, money-hungry nephew. And that man is bound to dump poor Prozy into a kennel."

As if fully understanding the larger ramifications of the conversation, the dog buried his head in the wafting dark folds of the judge's judicial-looking housecoat, right where her arm intersected with her lap.

"And if that happens, then all the good folks at Evergreen Gardens are going to be deprived of their weekly Prozac fix."

With a complete lack of enthusiasm, I asked, "So what are you proposing?"

"If you agree to have Prozac pay us his normal visit for a couple of hours each Wednesday, then I'll zip my lip and keep this video from Helen and the authorities—and from going viral on YouTube."

"YouTube?" I let out a laugh as if I were blowing out a candle.

The judge shot me a stern look. "You know, it would be a real shame if this made its way into the public arena. In this day and age, think of how the whole thing could escalate. I bet the literary community would paint you as the next Michael Vick. Then your books wouldn't have half a chance to nip at the heels of Nora Roberts or Danielle Steel."

The judge paused for dramatic effect and eyed me—and my name tag—square on. When I realized the woman knew who I was and that I was a writer, my fear mingled with indignation. I folded my arms across my chest, feeling totally vulnerable.

"You know, you're actually much prettier, much more youthful-looking, in person than in those airbrushed studio portraits on the back of your books. We have every one you've written, a whole section of them—all hardcover, large-print editions." The woman pointed to the far side of the room. "Your being a local celebrity and all."

I refused to look, choosing instead to stay on point. "Why would you trust me with Prozac in light of what you saw and your so-called video?"

"Because with the right motivation, anyone can be rehabilitated. In and out of the courtroom, I've always been a proponent of second chances. And I think, deep down, there's a dog lover in your soul, Meredith St. John. I get a good vibe from you."

"Good? There's nothing *good* about what you're accusing me of—"

"Do we have a deal or not?" She extended her hand.

I stared at the glimmer of her pearl-sheen nail polish. My hand slowly slipped inside of hers, and I was surprised by the firmness of her grip. She was stronger than she looked.

I tried to pull away, but she gripped tighter. "The folks here at Evergreen Gardens will all be counting on you."

When she released me, she picked up Prozac from her lap and planted a kiss atop his copper-colored head. "After the trauma Prozac has endured today, I think the first order of business should be a treat. How about some ice cream?"

"For him or for me?"

Judge Thea sneered, as though appalled that I would even conceive of rewarding myself.

"Häagen-Dazs Vanilla Bean is his favorite. Why don't you stop at the grocery store on your way home." She said it more as a command than a question as she extended Prozac toward me. Before she let him go, she looked me in the eye and said, "We will expect you on Wednesday, promptly at eleven o'clock. And remember, APL."

I gathered Prozac, his soft hair brushing against me. "APL?"

The judge picked up her iPad and pressed it against her chest as if she were going to breastfeed it. "Animal Protection League. One call," she said, raising a lone, crooked pointer finger as Prozac and I started away from her. "That's all it will take."

# Eight

*ARE WE HAVING FUN YET?*

Prozac

I DIDN'T ASK FOR THE JOB. It wasn't what I signed up for. When they finally called my number and I went before the Canine Dispatch Board and they offered me my next assignment, I thought I'd hit the jackpot. I thought I'd finally been given one of the easiest softball gigs in the history of all mankind—or rather, dog-kind.

I'd been around the block—literally and figuratively—for ages, and I'd had more assignments than I could even recall. I'd scavenged with packs of wild dogs through desert sand and dust and over the knobby roots of olive trees in Galilee and Nazareth. I'd served with shepherds and pharaohs, with emperors and in King Solomon's Court. I'd sniffed more fungi than I cared to admit, clinging to the sandaled feet of Gentiles, Jews, Muslims, Buddhists, heathens, minions, and pagans. I was the canine companion and inspiration for verse 7:6 in the Gospel of Matthew—*the* Matthew. The tax collector-turned-wordsmith and one of the fab-five evangelists whom New Testament Biblical history found much too important and profound for a last name, sort of like Madonna, Cher, and Sting of modern times.

*"Do not give dogs what is sacred; do not cast your pearls before swine. If you do, they may trample them under their feet, and then turn and tear you to pieces."* As can probably be gathered from that well-rendered verse, the Matthew gig didn't end quite so well for me. But I did what I came to the planet to do. That was my job.

Some of my finest moments had been my mongrel roles incarnate—the hours I'd spent with lepers, fearless in licking their wounds; the times I foraged for food scraps to share with the poor, the lame, and the crippled.

There was that time I went AWOL from my post as a noble hound in the royal court of Pompeii. My bark and bite alerted the masses to hightail it away from the path of Vesuvius. And while I navigated countless souls to safety, in the end, I stretched out alongside a little boy crying amid the grip of hot lava. I stayed with him and shared his anguish, ushering him to The Great Beyond.

In happier moments, I served as a quaint Pomeranian who had the privilege of watching Michelangelo paint the ceiling of the Sistine Chapel, and I was a stray mix named Luna who sat patiently alongside Galileo as he kept his eyes pressed to a telescope practically twenty-four, seven.

I was a beloved papillon dog of Edith Wharton, and I'd like to think I was the inspiration behind her "heartbeat at my feet" quote. And I proudly served as the distinguished French poodle sidekick in Steinbeck's *Travels with Charlie*.

So I'd marked my existence in the world—and in the one beyond—working with souls hovering between the material and spiritual planes. My missions always varied, but in my work over the centuries, artistic, creative, and intellectual adult types emerged as my specialty. If I'd had my way in modern times, I would've been assigned to positions like the pseudo-philosopher Snoopy the beagle, who inspired cartoonist Charles Schulz; the role of Eddie, that bright and extremely well-paid Jack Russell terrier on the hit TV program *Frasier*; and also that adorable Brussels griffon who played Verdell in the movie *As Good As It Gets*. What I would've given for that gig, as I'd always admired the films of James L. Brooks and the machismo of Jack Nicholson!

Every time a Spirit Guide Dog such as myself went before the Canine Dispatch Board, we were encouraged to state our preferences and speak up for the positions we desired. In the end, however, the Canine Dispatch Board always had final say.

At one of my CDB evaluations—within the last fifty years or so—one of the board members perused my file and said, "All dogs are not created equal. And *you* are certainly not like other dogs—Spirit Guide Dogs or otherwise. Putting aside your often-atypical canine judgments and your often-conditional love of children, your track record demonstrates incredible instincts and insights into the human psyche. We'd consider you something of a canine Sigmund Freud in your dealings with people. Therefore, the board feels that with your expertise, you have too much to offer for a mere limelight position. There are bigger fish for you to fry, my friend."

A nice compliment, but I hated to be spoken to in parables—and even more so when alliteration about multi-cellular aquatic animals was thrown into the mix. But idioms and parables aside, it showed that some dogs were so much more than simply man's best friend. And Spirit Guide Dogs were in a class by themselves. We were highly evolved and placed in people's lives on purpose. We had explicit jobs and functions to perform during our limited time on earth.

Before we ever arrived, we got an overview of each assignment and saw the big picture. We knew exactly whom we were dealing with, and we fully understood all the reasons we were coming to the planet. Our job was not only to help and love individuals and offer companionship, but we also brushed against human hearts and souls in order to teach something so folks could grow and move on to new levels of living. There were exceptions to the rule, of course, and people didn't always get the gist of our intended partnership. But Spirit Guide Dogs got the best of all worlds: we had the unique capacity to experience a fully human perspective while we also embodied the power of love and the divine. That was what people always really wanted and needed—to feel that special kind of love, loyalty, and emotional support—and that was why so many people, especially in the current day and age, worshipped their dogs.

So there I was—my number was once again called. My incorporeal canine soul was summoned before the Canine Dispatch Board. The human-looking members were constantly updated since, for the sake of fairness, Spirit Guide Dogs were not always evaluated by the same committee. The group appeared to be a wise-looking bunch who sized me up from one side of a long conference table covered with a starched and creased white tablecloth.

"How would you feel about a Border collie position?" asked a senior member of the board. He was a fit, dapper man—bald and with dark, wild eyebrows that gave his eyes a piercing look. A snappy dresser, he was wearing a black suit, white shirt, and a sharp silver tie. "We've recently gotten word of an opening on a sprawling dairy farm in West Virginia. They produce this wonderful artisanal sheep's milk cheese. It's won all kinds of awards. Busloads of people visit every day to see the dog in action, working with the sheep—"

"A farm? Herding livestock? No, I don't think so," I said. "Border collies are brilliant, but they can be too intense and high-strung. Obsessive, even. And some of them can be rather one-note."

"Oh, I beg to differ," said a woman with shoulder-length brown hair. Her bangs were cut severely into a straight line across her forehead. With an ornate gold crown on her head and some more makeup, the woman could've passed for Cleopatra. Oh, the real Cleopatra was a true beauty. She really came to depend on me, her most prized Italian greyhound, especially with all the steamy drama that swirled between her and Julius Caesar and then with Mark Antony. Life with *Cleo* was never dull!

"It takes a profound mental capability to do Border collie work— obedience and discipline," the Cleopatra look-alike said. "Why, with your canine Mensa IQ and extensive vocabulary, you'd be a perfect fit."

"And think of it this way," chimed the second woman of the board, enhancing the pitch. Her long white hair cascaded like a river raging from beneath her black French beret. "You'd have an audience every day."

"No. I don't want *that* kind of audience," I told them. "Besides, I don't take commands well. I'm much too creative."

The last panelist, a quiet man with shaggy steel-gray hair and a beard— and wearing a pilled, old gray cardigan—switched gears. "How about a rescue dog position: K-9 Squad, Detroit. Could be very exciting."

"Smoldering debris? Sniffing out the dead and seriously injured? Searching for drugs and explosives? No. I don't have the stomach or stamina for day-in, day-out trauma. Look," I said, "I'm a good dog. I've got a lot to offer—"

"No one is disputing that," said Mr. Gray.

"And I'm good with people. I understand and connect with them on every level—psychic, spiritual. I haven't been nicknamed 'The Human Whisperer' for nothing."

The members of the board looked at each other, appearing put-off and a bit miffed by my display of braggadocio, but I didn't let the apparent skepticism of their body language daunt me. I pressed on.

"And after thousands of years of going above and beyond, don't you think it's high time I finally have a say in what *I* want?"

"And what is it, exactly, that you want?" Snappy Dresser asked.

"Well, after my last assignment, could we please rule out subzero temperatures and kids—"

"Are you referring to your Siberian husky position in Verkhoyansk, Russia?"

I nodded. "I didn't mind the fur coat. But I don't think I could take another twelve years of hauling broods of little gymnast wannabes by sled, day after day. And all the howling that was required... It was exhausting and gave me a chronic scratchy throat and headaches."

"We can assure you," said Snappy Dresser, "there's nothing of that nature available at this time."

"How about something in the limelight?" I asked, taking a leap. "Isn't it about time I finally stopped working behind the scenes and was noticed by the masses?"

The members of the board again turned to each other and shot suspect glances.

Cleopatra smoothed an eyebrow with her index finger. She said, "Well, we've heard about your prior requests, and as in the past, we've considered them carefully. But at this time, we feel you're not right for an entertainment track."

"Why not?"

"Because you've got an edge, which isn't an altogether bad thing. But you're better when you play to your strengths," said the French beret.

"All I'm requesting is a little less psychoanalysis on my part and a little more tail wagging this time around. Is that too much to ask?"

I stared at the elders seated at the conference table in front of me. They huddled in close, hands cupping their mouths as they whispered and hissed in deliberation—inaudible even to my acute canine hearing—while they flipped open file folders and shuffled around papers and ideas.

Cleopatra held up her manicured pointer finger as if tracking the wind. "Bear with us," she said. "We might be able to offer a compromise."

My hearing perked up. The mere insertion of the word *might* sounded promising, as if they were ready to make a deal.

"How do you feel about the theater?" Mr. Gray asked.

"Theater? As in Broadway?"

"Now, don't get your hopes up," said Mr. Gray, pushing his palms toward the floor. They must've sensed the elation in my tone, as I was already conjuring the bright lights and energizing pandemonium of Times Square. "We're not going to lie to you. There will be a lot of downtime."

"But there will be good PR," added Frenchy. "And you'll be in the spotlight for a majority of your mission."

My eagerness rallied as I asked, "What play is it?"

"*Annie*," offered Cleo.

I gasped in hopeful anticipation. "You mean, the musical? Daddy Warbucks? Miss Hannigan? The-sun-will-come-out-tomorrow *Annie*?"

The foursome nodded.

"You mean, the coveted role of the dog, Sandy?"

Their faces suddenly twisted up with grins, which mirrored the excitement filling my mind and heart as I pictured a full-house theater. The orchestra tuning up. The rise of a red velour curtain. Showers of applause overwhelming the upbeat opening medley. The heat of spotlights centered directly upon me.

Mr. Gray said, "There will be a lot of training—"

"I can do it."

"And keep in mind," added Snappy Dresser, "that every time they launch a revival, they up the ante. The next revival will require your learning some fancy dance moves—"

"I can dance."

"But with your exceptional mental capacities," Cleopatra chimed, "you should know, going in, that after your training, the work won't be mentally stimulating—"

"I don't need stimulating."

"Why don't you take a moment and think about it?" French Beret suggested.

"I don't need a moment."

"But the thing is, the play is currently running on Broadway so there probably won't be another revival for five to ten years," said Mr. Gray. "That's why we thought an interim assignment would serve you best while we get all the variables for *Annie* in place."

"Great. Sign me up. I'm on board—"

"Maybe you ought to hear us out before you answer." Snappy Dresser slipped on a pair of bifocals and stared down at the case file notes in front of him. "The interim assignment is a Classification Eight."

"Eight?" *Uh-oh!* Anything above a seven usually smelled of trouble.

I thought back to my last Class Nine assignment, when I was labeled a "code red" dog on the fast track to euthanasia.

I remembered the acrid scent that filled the house in Taos, New Mexico, where I was adopted from a shelter by a liberal young couple who made it rich in the Internet boom of the nineties. They lived on their investments and, as a hobby, grew and smoked a lot of marijuana. They were the most kind and loving people, always jolly, and they threw the best salty snacks my way. Cheez Doodles were my favorite. But back then, before they rescued me, I was a former underground pitbull-mix fighting dog—with the scars to prove it. I was ultimately one of the very first clients of Cesar Millan when he arrived in America. I hated what I put that poor couple through, but it was all part of a greater plan. They smoked a lot of dope to deal with my anger and temperament issues, but they were as devoted to me as I was to my earthly mission back then. The aggressiveness I displayed in that assignment propelled the young couple to become national advocates for abused dogs, and the problems I presented served as a launch pad for the Dog Whisperer brand. I became Cesar's stepping-stone toward worldwide success. Just my luck, however, that I missed being profiled on his TV show by only a few years.

Thinking back on that mission—and lured by the prospect of *Annie* on Broadway—I oozed confidence as I told the board, "I can handle a Class Eight."

"Wouldn't you like to hear what the case is all about first?"

I gave Snappy Dresser his due as he spouted details from a file in front of him. "Helen Hendrix. Born and raised in Cornwall, England. As a child, Helen and her family moved to the US. Oak Park, New Jersey. Helen's very middle class. Never married. Worked as an elementary school teacher for sixty years—"

"Sixty years? How old is she?"

Snappy Dresser followed the trail of his finger down a page. "Eighty-four."

"Eighty-four? She's not one of those old-timers who has given up on living, is she?"

"No. This one's very well preserved. She has a lot of life left in her—and quality at that," said Snappy Dresser. "Notes indicate that she's very independent, not the type to dwell. She's shared her life with dogs, one pooch at a time. Has a special fondness for toy breeds—especially Yorkshire terriers. Do you have any problem with that?"

"No. My last Yorkie assignment was with Joan Rivers. She was a hoot—I had a blast serving as *her* arm candy."

"The notes for this assignment state that Helen Hendrix is, quote, 'likely to dote on her pet, unmercifully—'"

"But why would a woman in her eighties want to take on a pet now, at this stage of her life? It's a big commitment."

"Companionship, plain and simple," Snappy Dresser said as he plowed ahead with more details. "Helen's always lived on her own. She was forced to retire at age eighty, and ever since, she's become more active in her church…"

*I could always use a prayer—it never hurts.*

"She tunes in regularly to news shows…"

*I'm all for current events.*

"She bakes…"

*I've always had a sweet tooth.*

"Looks forward to her afternoon tea…"

*I'm all for a daily happy hour—whatever shape it takes.*

"She tackles the daily *New York Times* crossword puzzle in ink…"

*Impressive!*

"She makes lunch dates with friends at least twice a week…"

*Could be doggie-bag action involved.*

"And she attends, without fail, her Great Books Club at the local library the third Wednesday of each month. She doesn't seem to love what they read, but she likes the ladies she *kaffeeklatch*es with. It keeps her in the loop as to the happenings in her own hometown."

*I'm a sucker for literature and gossip!*

Helen Hendrix seemed like a good person, a nice lady who led a quiet, unassuming existence—and the life she had to offer me appealed in a mundane sort of way. I mean, how hard could it be for me to live with her?

The only reason I could come up with for the Level Eight classification was that it might present a boredom challenge. After all, being smothered by love and affection wasn't always what it was cracked up to be. Take my mission with Leona Helmsley, for example. The years I spent living as a well-groomed Maltese with that demanding hotel magnate weren't as easy-street as people would imagine. And who ever dreamed that when Leona named me "Trouble," she was prophesying my future. Upon her death, Leona might have made me the richest dog in the world, but dealing with all those strangers who crawled out of the woodwork like cockroaches—all of them wanting a piece of the financial pie Leona had left me—oh, it was more *trouble* than it was worth!

"Helen Hendrix is very healthy for her age," said Cleopatra. "She's very active. Mind as sharp as a tack."

"Then what's the rub?" I asked. "Why is her case a Class Eight?"

Snappy Dresser flipped to the back pages of the file. "That's interesting. In complications, it's listed as TBD."

"*To be determined* by what?" I asked.

"Doesn't say. Maybe not having all the variables in place has heightened the complexity." Snappy Dresser looked to his colleagues, who shrugged and shot each other perplexed glances.

"Can you find out some more before I commit?"

"There's not time," Frenchy said. "You'll have to act on this now, or we'll need to find another dog to fill the position."

"And if I don't take it?"

Mr. Gray countered, "You'll have to forfeit *Annie*."

The optimist in me wanted to believe the Class Eight designation was a clerical error. Maybe it would be fun to serve as Helen Hendrix's fur baby for a couple of years. I could think of the assignment as an intermezzo of sorts—before my big Broadway debut.

Sure, I'd probably have to put on a bow tie and sit for an annual Christmas picture. And I might have to wear a couple of flashy-looking sweaters, be mauled with hugs and kisses, and be charming around a bunch of fawning old biddies. But I could easily turn all that into a cakewalk.

"Okay, I'm in. I'll adopt her," I blurted.

"Are you sure?" asked Cleopatra.

"Yes, very."

"You're absolutely positive?" asked Frenchy.

"Yes. Absolutely."

It was only in retrospect, as I sat on the velour-trimmed front seat of the canine-averse romance novelist's four-cylinder Toyota, that I was suddenly rethinking the *absolutely positive* impulsiveness of my actions.

So much for my cakewalk! So much for a clerical error! I should've known better than to rationalize away that Classification Eight designation. I should have pressed, been more insistent about the details regarding the implications of that *To Be Determined*.

For three years, I had been living a pampered, quiet life. An attentive old lady took better care of me than some folks took care of people. In Helen's modest, middle-class Cape Cod house, I'd enjoyed my own dedicated playroom, complete with a large-screen HDTV tuned to Animal Planet twenty-four, seven. She even invested in an indoor doggie treadmill for me to use when the snow got too deep for outdoor exercise and play. She'd regularly fed me antibiotic-free rotisserie chicken and organic vegetables, outfitted me in merino wool sweaters, and made sure I was bathed, clipped, perfumed, and groomed more meticulously than a metrosexual. I even slept in a plush, baby-safe playpen, cuddled upon the warmth of a hot water bottle on winter nights and a cool orthopedic gel pad in the summer.

And yet, beyond my tunnel vision for the bright lights of Broadway, I never conceived that Helen Hendrix would have designs on certifying me to become a licensed therapy dog—bringing tidings of great comfort and joy to the afflicted, damaged, and lonely. Had I known, I never would've agreed to the gig. It could get pretty exhausting being schlepped from person to person like a peace pipe and having folks *ooh* and *aah* over me every day. It was one thing for a Labrador or a golden retriever, even a schnauzer, to be treated that way. But for a bright-eyed Yorkshire terrier who looked as cute and cuddly as a stuffed animal but with an actual heart beating inside, it could grow blasé pretty quickly.

I thought the Hendrix assignment would allow me to live an uneventful life of news and talk shows all day, *Dancing with the Stars* and reruns of *Murder, She Wrote* all night. But going out, being on my best behavior, and having to make nice with strangers every day?

*Oh, puh-lease!*

Even though my large, active brain was currently confined to the size of a peach pit, I managed to hatch a plan to dissuade Helen from her quest.

Initially, I passed each section of the obedience classes she dragged me to—how could I possibly have allowed myself to fail? I was a perfectionist—but I decided the best way to wrangle out of becoming a therapy dog was to ultimately play the submission card. My strategy was an old one, tried and true. Certainly not creative. Any time I had to meet new people who made eye contact with me, I simply squatted as if trying to squeeze beneath the low bar in a limbo competition and loosened my bladder muscles. And if Helen or anyone else was holding me—too bad, so sad. They'd better hope their clothing was machine washable!

I was convinced my pattern of behavior would be my ace in the hole to become a therapy dog flunky. And when I took the final test and released my bladder as the pièce de résistance in the big finale, I thought that was it. Helen would finally knock off all the therapy dog nonsense.

But Helen didn't give up. She had me retested—sit, stay, come, and lie down—three more times in the Four-Legged Angels therapy dog certification program. That was when it became clear that tenacity was one of Helen's strong suits. She was not going to accept my limitations, my bladder control issues, or the fact that *no* was the final verdict in my therapy dog career. So she moved on to Plan B. She opened her checkbook and proceeded to write down a number with many zeros made payable to Four-Legged Angels, and voilá, I was an officially certified and licensed therapy dog. Helen's dream became a reality for her and a nightmare for me.

For a while, I kept up the bladder control sham, but I got tired of the routine. I ultimately gave it up. Helen and my veterinarian eventually came to think I simply outgrew the issue. Honestly, sometimes humans didn't give their canine counterparts the credit we deserved!

The Helen Hendrix assignment was anything *but* predictable or boring. And who could've scripted that, one morning, Helen would step onto the scale in her bathroom, become peeved that she'd packed on a few pounds, and then take a misstep off the scale, slip, and break her foot? Oh, the poor thing! But what was she thinking, weighing herself in the first place? Did she really expect a weight loss when she'd indulged in two big pieces of Key lime pie—both mounded with whipped cream—at a luncheon she hosted for her book group the day before?

No matter how she sliced it, it was a freak accident that changed both our lives.

At first, after I was wrangled up by that sneezing, high-strung tax lady, I rejoiced, thinking I'd finally get a reprieve from spending every day playing therapy dog—at least for a spell. I tried to look on the bright side—I could think of it as a mini-vacation. But after being dumped on mopey Meredith, who gave off a very strong vibe of being trapped in a whirlpool of grief, it was as though I was about to play therapy dog all day long. My life with Helen—and visiting the sick and infirm and wagging my tail for those who were always so glad to see me—seemed like bliss in comparison.

I didn't know much about Meredith yet, but from the drips and drabs I'd gathered, I got the sense she was rather lost in her life, and she'd been nursing a heart broken by death—the death of a guy named Kyle. Could it be my job to put the pieces of her broken heart back together but rearrange them somehow? Whatever my role, I had a gut feeling it was going to take everything in me—and then some—to figure out a way to untangle Meredith, an emotionally wrapped-up bundle of nerves. Oh, the world could be such a miserable place sometimes, and people, unlike their dog companions, couldn't always see the big picture. Life could sag so low that some people felt as though they would never climb out of the pit.

Meredith Mancuso, aka St. John, was a case in point. But we dogs were relentless optimists, and since I was able to see the wondrous truth of Meredith—a gentle, loving soul at her core—I believed there was hope for her. To the untrained eye, such hope was hard to fathom. But bred with the ability to get inside the spiritual nooks and crannies of the human heart, I sensed that Meredith had been fostering her grief and keeping people at bay. And that was no good. At thirty-three years old, mopey Meredith was still fairly young. She had her whole life in front of her. That was why I was beginning to think that perhaps it was also part of my job, in my new Spirit Guide Dog role, to lead her away from her isolation and back to people.

But the thing was, I was working without a script or a road map. And something in me was starting to think that the wrinkle in the Helen Hendrix assignment, the ineffable *To Be Determined* that appeared to be Meredith Mancuso-St. John, might actually be some sort of test—perhaps my secret initiation en route to Broadway.

When we drove into Oak Park that morning, it suddenly came to me that Evergreen Gardens and the people in it might be the best way to launch Meredith back into the land of the living. Anyone who knew stories and storytelling understood that sometimes, a heroine needed a push to get moving. It made perfect sense, however ironic, that folks in Act Three of their lives could help propel Meredith into Act Two of hers.

It seemed a doable plan. Nonthreatening. It could work. I could make it work. And I gathered from Meredith's body language as we left Evergreen Gardens that morning—the way she firmed her long, bony fingers around my furry carriage and tucked me under her arm as though I were a football she wasn't about to fumble again—that Meredith was an old soul anyway. The lessons of loss she had already experienced in her short life made her spirit vibe register more along the lines of an octogenarian's.

As we made our way back to the Toyota parked at her sister's office, my mud-encrusted red leash hung down and flapped like an unplugged electrical cord. Meredith's hot breath puffed out in misty clouds amid the cold air. I sensed she was seriously contemplating rapping her fist upon her sister's door and giving her a piece of her mind. But feeling chastised and threatened, confused and completely spent—emotionally and physically— was perhaps the reason Meredith got back in her car and drove us away.

The poor thing *was* having one hell of a day. Her shoulders were square, and traces of her antiperspirant were kicking in, overpowering the perfumed body lotion she'd applied to her shoulders and neck after her shower. The energy she was exerting told me, loud and clear, that she was wound up tighter than a harp string. And it confirmed for me that my job was to learn how to play her and tune her up so she'd find a way to live again, out in the world.

Not an easy task. I knew Meredith Mancuso didn't want me in her life any more than I really wanted to be in hers. But life was like that sometimes. It didn't care what we wanted, so we had to go with the flow, as they said. It left me to offer Meredith my temporary obedience. I pressed my head upon the passenger seat and sulked, not wanting to budge, when I looked up and spied the colorful sign for the Stop & Shop sweeping into the vista of the windshield. I was surprised when Meredith parked, cut the engine, and stuffed me inside her ski jacket. She zipped it up so that only my nose was visible. Together, we trudged into the store, past the endcaps promoting super-saver specials. When we hit frozen foods, Meredith made a beeline for the ice cream case, where she rummaged through the cold, rock-hard pints of Häagen-Dazs. When she reached all the way to the bottom and plucked the last container of Vanilla Bean, I rallied, finally lurching my head from her jacket. I sniffed the clouds of sweet, cold air rising from the freezer case and started to reconsider Meredith Mancuso. Maybe I hadn't given her enough credit yet.

# Nine

*LOVE ON A LEASH*

Prozac

Back at Meredith's townhouse, she pulled two spoons from the kitchen utensil drawer then deposited my four paws atop a kitchen chair. Seating herself next to me, she reached for the Häagen-Dazs container, and with one of the spoons, she dug out a heaping clump of cool white cream flecked with tiny brown specks. Waving the spoon in front of me, she said, "Let's call this our peace offering and start again. All right, pal?"

Meredith navigated the spoon toward me, and with wild abandon, I lapped up the soft, melting Vanilla Bean. When I could see my distorted reflection in the clean, concave stainless steel—those triangular pointed ears, those warm, dark-brown pools for eyes—Meredith set me back onto the floor.

I danced around the kitchen, clicking my nails and begging for more, but Meredith paid me no mind. She set down my spoon, and with the other clean one, she heaped a modest dollop of ice cream into her own mouth. No sooner had she swallowed than she rose to her feet and deposited the container amid the frosty cloud that escaped from inside the freezer.

Her actions amazed me. Why would she eat only one spoonful of ice cream, and not even a mounded spoonful, when she had a whole container? Who did that? It was like eating one potato chip or one M&M then walking away from the bag. The controlled modulation of Meredith's ice cream indulgence was surely a contradiction to the gluttonous way she wallowed in her grief.

As I made a trip to the bathroom, I thought about Meredith's two last names and what they signified. On one hand, there was Meredith St. John, the acclaimed romance writer, who probably had several thousand fans on her publicist-maintained Facebook and Twitter pages. On the other hand, I'd bet Meredith Mancuso didn't even have an online presence. Her life seemed more virtual than real—voices on the telephone answering machine, emails, and texts. Where were the living, breathing, three-dimensional people? Outside of her high-strung sister and that voyeur of a postman, who else, besides me, really populated the physicality of Meredith's world? Did she have any social ambition—the desire to reach out and connect with people on any level?

As Meredith lumbered out of the kitchen, I feared the solitude of the Mancuso case might prove even more challenging than that cold, dank French cloister to which I was once assigned in the doldrums of the twelfth century. In that incarnation, my separation anxiety and a barking problem had pushed the limits of patient endurance—and the vows of silence—for those poor sisters to no end!

With rounded shoulders, Meredith made her way to the bathroom. When she flipped on the light, she uttered a loud cry of "Oh, thank heavens at least *one* thing has gone right today!" She dashed into the hallway, waving the amber-marked Wee-Wee pad as if it were a flag of surrender.

---

That night, once Meredith slipped me inside my playpen, I zonked out. By the time the windows were shimmering with daylight, Meredith was already up and restoring order to her disordered life.

I tried not to get in her way as she changed her smelly bed sheets. The overflowing dishes in the sink were washed, dried, and put away. A mysterious stink in the refrigerator was addressed—a squishy, moldy green potato sprouting arms and legs—and the garbage was hauled off, recyclables and all. The floors were dusted. The carpets were vacuumed. The sofa pillows were plumped. And the house became infused with the lemon-fresh scent of furniture polish.

I was proud that my presence had rallied Meredith to tidy up the place. And I took the next few days and tried to get a better read on her. I paid particular attention to her patterns and routines—what made her tick.

Meredith woke every morning and made a pot of coffee so strong, the caffeine-enriched air roused me like smelling salts. She combed her hair, washed her face, slipped on sweatpants and a T-shirt, and wandered into her office. With a cup of coffee steaming on her desk and her computer booting up, she shook her hands and cracked each knuckle. A snapping sigh released from each delicate push, prod, and squeeze until she laced her hands together, and with fingers entwined, she extended her arms, limbering them up to the ceiling and stretching her back muscles from side to side. She looked as though she were about to spring off a high dive, not sit at eye level in front of a computer.

When Meredith finally settled down at her desk, she sat as if catatonically fixated on the blinking icon on the blank screen. Only the low hum of the computer fan interrupted the pin-drop silence as Meredith's fingers remained perched upon the keyboard like a pianist anticipating a conductor's cue. I waited to hear the *clickety-clack,* an adagio of carefully selected letters, but there was nothing. Not a sound.

Hours turned into days of apparent writer's block that went on from nine o'clock each morning until five o'clock in the afternoon—give or take a few coffee breaks and pit stops. At the end of the day, at least Meredith had tried. With her computer finally switched off, she flipped on the TV, which droned on with back-to-back cooking programs all night long.

There was always wine—a budget-priced Merlot—to indulge in along with the day's mail and emails. And with her stocking feet kicked up on the coffee table, she flipped through newspapers and magazines until dinner. She fixed whatever she could find in the cupboard or defrost from the freezer. While she waited for something prepackaged to nuke or simmer, she'd set up my food—Helen's emergency stash of canned dog food labeled "Top Notch." One whiff of the ground, wet mush Meredith dumped inside my dog bowl, and I knew the only thing *top-notch* was the flashy-looking label on the tin.

After dinner, Meredith tidied up then pedaled on her recumbent exercise bicycle. I relentlessly kept bringing toys for her to toss. She was a pretty good sport about playing fetch—had a nice fake and a good snap of the wrist and arm.

By ten o'clock each evening, Meredith dragged my playpen from the living room into her bedroom and set me inside with a dental chew toy. She climbed into bed and, guided by the nightstand lamp, read self-help books—out loud. The latest was titled *Get Out of the Rut Called YOU: Strategies for Getting Your Life Unstuck.*

I mentally rolled my eyes when Meredith read lines like "Get up and get out there again!" or "Find what you love and do it—just go for it!" How was it that grossly under-qualified people got paid to write such drivel while intelligent humans like Meredith shelled out money and spent time reading retread, generic crap? She should've been reading something of intellectual substance more along the lines of *A Grief Observed* by C. S. Lewis. Unfortunately, being a dog had its limitations, and the ability to recommend better books was one of them. But I was well acquainted with Jack's work—that was what those in C. S.'s inner circle used to call him— when I was assigned as his charge. I once consumed half a volume of Plato. Chewed it to bits. That might've put an end to Jack's work on the Greek translation, but I liked to think that my actions served as the inspiration for the talking animals in his Narnia saga.

I decided to look upon Meredith's nightly reading-aloud ritual as an entertaining change of pace. It offered me a chance to curl up on the velour blanket inside my pillow-topped playpen and listen to books far more enjoyable than those I encountered at Read-to-a-Dog programs in schools and public libraries—places that Helen schlepped me to once a week. It was hard work wagging my tail, trying to appear engaged and upbeat while a bunch of slow readers tried to phonetically sound out words from two-dimensional, derivative stories that always seemed to feature vampires, wizards, and/or schoolyard bullies.

Amid pages flipping and Meredith's monotone voice regurgitating all that *get-up-and-go, rah-rah, life-is-grand, stay-in-the-game* cheerleader stuff, I would eventually nod off. After six nights of suffering through the blah-blah-blah of those platitudes, I concluded that Meredith was never going to live the advice those books offered any more than she would ever attempt to whip up the gourmet dishes she saw prepared on TV.

But on the seventh day of our being roommates, the chime of Meredith's smartphone pierced through the quiet morning and woke us both.

Meredith groaned. With her eyes still closed, she fumbled through the dark, reaching over to her nightstand. Once her smartphone was in hand, she switched it on, squinting against the bright glare of the screen. She hit a couple of buttons and read what appeared to be a text message.

"What the... How the heck did Judge Thea get this number?"

Meredith lurched up from bed, clearly annoyed by what she was reading. "Yeah, well, how could I forget? You've blackmailed me!" She launched her words directly at the phone as if lambasting the judge in person.

She kept reading, her pointer finger scrolling the screen. "Meet me about Prozac's itinerary? If you think I'm gonna spend a whole freaking day at Evergreen Gardens, it's not gonna happen, lady. This is a temp job—not my career!"

Meredith lobbed the phone over to the empty side of the bed. Then she drew a pillow over her face and screamed into it.

While she was carrying on, I leaped out of the playpen and onto the bed, thinking I might calm her temper tantrum. But the minute my paws imprinted upon the memory foam mattress, Meredith pulled the pillow away from her face and hollered, "Get down!"

I did as I was told and hightailed it to the bathroom, heeding Mother Nature's call.

When I returned, Meredith, bundled in her robe, trudged past me and slammed the bathroom door closed behind her. It didn't take my canine Mensa IQ to realize Meredith was in a pretty bad mood, and I gathered it all had to do with Judge Thea's text.

I chuffed a sigh, filled with amusement. The tug of war in their battle of wills was sure to make for an interesting day.

When Meredith stepped from the bathroom, I took cover under her bed, poking my head out from underneath the bed skirt to find her hair slick and dripping wet. She slipped out of her robe, and in the mirror, I saw the fabric from the bed skirt covering my head, making me appear illicit in peering at her naked beauty. Meredith spotted me and said, "Yo, mister—some privacy, please." And from the way her chin unhinged, I think I freaked her out when I actually backpedaled and shrank beneath the bed, out of sight.

When I reemerged, I found her dressed in a pair of jeans and a fluffy, angora-soft sweater. She brushed her hair and, looking in the full-length mirror of her closet door, dabbed on moisturizer and sunscreen followed by a coat of base makeup.

A lot of people thought dogs didn't care about what people looked like—the clothes they wore, their grooming habits. And most dogs didn't.

But the nature of a Spirit Guide Dog was to pay attention and explore and perceive everything, in detail.

Through my eyes, Meredith was very pretty, with or without makeup, although I didn't get the sense she saw herself that way. It was as if she were invisible and couldn't see herself at all. And I'd bet the word *attractive* hadn't been a part of her vernacular since that Kyle guy died. Any sense of her appeal to the opposite sex simply didn't register in her psyche. And it was a shame, really, as with the help of Clinique, her brown-green eyes sparkled, and her chestnut-colored hair, when washed, flowed in naturally cascading, silky waves that I was sure any man would've loved to plunge his hands and face into. I'd been around people long enough to know that if I were a human male, Meredith's appearance would've drawn me instantly across a crowded room. She had a dark, alluring look that was brightened by the radiance of her smile—*when* she smiled, which wasn't often. But the thing was, Meredith wasn't allowing herself to enter any rooms, crowded or not, so no man had a chance to notice her.

---

Dogs could read and mirror energy signals, and Meredith's huffing and puffing seemed her means of protest for being forced to go to Evergreen Gardens.

For all of those nights that Meredith spent reading poorly written self-help books encouraging her to rejoin the land of the living, I sensed she was resisting the whole idea of allowing new patterns to unfold. So in keeping with the stress level she'd set for the day, I decided to give her a test to see how flexible she could be.

When Meredith slipped on her coat, ready to take us both to Evergreen Gardens, I waited for her to glance at me, then I turned from her and crouched low, squatting my body beneath the skirt of the sofa in the living room until I was clearly out of sight.

"Prozac. C'mon, buddy." Meredith softened the edge of her voice with joyful enthusiasm. But I could spot the sugarcoat of insincerity a mile away.

"C'mon, Prozy. We're gonna be late." Meredith jangled my leash. "We need to go now."

I didn't budge. *Prozy? Really?*

"Don't you want to go for a walk? Take a ride in the car? C'mon, we'll both get some fresh air. We've been cooped up in here all week."

The gentle tick-tock of the mantel clock sounded between us. When I saw dark shadows from Meredith's loafers suddenly deepen in the direction of the sofa, I had a hunch that Little Miss Honey Tongue was about to turn dragon breath. She got down on her knees and lifted the sofa skirt, her eyes peering through the shadows, fixing straight on me.

"C'mon, good boy. Don't be afraid." Then she muttered, "Listen to me. Look at me. Down on all fours, trying to reason with a five-pound animal."

With my head still pressed to the floor, I shifted my gaze toward Meredith, whose look hovered somewhere between pleading and being completely ticked-off.

Her thinking that I didn't understand took me back to the days when I was a beloved, and quite handsome, shih tzu named Buster who lived with a lovely Korean family who'd migrated to the United States and owned and operated a nail salon. I went to work with them twelve hours a day, and they did a fine job of painting my nails in alternating shades of black and white to match the markings of my hair.

Those Koreans knew how to speak perfect English—grammatically better than some American-born natives, I'd bet—but there were times when pretending not to understand the English language had its advantages, like when a customer balked at a price or didn't like the job of a particular manicurist or pedicurist. It was a similar scenario with dogs and other human pets. We understood English perfectly. Average dogs comprehended roughly one hundred sixty words, and some had better vocabulary retention than others. My comprehension skills were well advanced, but there were times I got in a mood or had a bug up my derriere or I just didn't feel like doing what was asked of me. And sometimes, like in the midst of my under-the-sofa summit with Meredith, we dogs simply chose not to respond to English language commands simply to test humans and bring them down a peg or two.

"Dammit, Prozac!" I could tell she meant business.

She swiped a hand toward me, and I backed away, shy of her reach until her coffee breath blasted into my face. "Get over here. C'mon, we're gonna be late."

And just as I was thinking that maybe I'd exerted my inner alpha dog a wee bit too much, the doorbell chimed.

Meredith dropped the skirt of the sofa like a curtain that made everything go dark.

Her footsteps pounded toward the front door, and I slowly crept out, easing beneath the coffee table, where I had a clear view of the mailman through the front picture window. He was standing on the front steps. He put up his hand and waved, smiling broadly at Meredith. His muffled voice called from outside, "You need to sign for a letter."

Meredith undid the dead bolt and opened the door.

As my paws met with the cool ceramic tile of the foyer, the mailman handed Meredith a stack of letters and a large padded envelope, pointing at where she needed to sign.

"Gee, I almost didn't recognize you with your clothes on," the mailman said playfully.

"Yes, my apologies for the other day." Meredith forced a laugh filled with embarrassment as clear as her blushing red face. "I'm sorry you had to suffer through that—"

"Suffer? Why, that was the most excitement I've had on the job since Agnes Guessbrecht over on Jackson Avenue won the Publishers Clearing House back in the 1990s."

As the postman ripped off the signed card and gave Meredith the package, he said, "Hey, when did you get a dog?"

"He's not mine. I'm pet sitting."

"Pet sitting? A famous author like yourself?" The postman's beer belly jiggled as he sent up a laugh. "Did Hemingway and Fitzgerald also moonlight with a pooper scooper?"

"Wouldn't know," Meredith told him. "But nowadays, anything goes."

The postman flung his bulky bag of mail over his shoulder and squatted down, eyeing me past Meredith's ankles.

I didn't budge or blink. I sat, as regal as a statue, cast in the sunlight beaming in through the front door.

"Here, boy," he said.

Meredith asked, "Aren't postmen supposed to be afraid of dogs—carry Mace, the whole nine yards?"

"No. All dogs love me."

*Oh yeah? We'll see about that!*

I tucked my tail and let out the rumblings of a low, menacing growl. I snarled, baring mean fangs, hoping to intensify my aura.

The postman warily lurched to his feet. "Wow, tough guy, isn't he?"

"Yeah, well, he's got some issues."

"Don't we all." He cast Meredith a suspicious glance. "You have yourselves a good day."

"Yes, you, too." She closed the door and made a quick beeline for me, swooping me up and patting my head. "Good boy, good dog."

We headed for the kitchen, where she dropped the mail onto the table then ripped open the padded envelope. Out spilled my Four-Legged Angels therapy dog badge and blue bandanna, and a whole mess of business cards embossed with a tiny picture of my beautiful self on one side and all of my social networking links on the other—Facebook page, Twitter feed, Pinterest, Google Plus, LinkedIn, and my email account.

In the mix was a small envelope. Meredith slipped her thumb under the seal and stared at a hand-engraved, pearl-white note card embossed with a fleur-de-lis and the name Helen Hendrix. Inside was a message written in flowing, cursive penmanship so perfect—every *i* dotted and every loop fully joined—that whoever wrote that note could've professionally recopied the Declaration of Independence.

Dearest Meredith,

I trust Prozac is being a very good boy, and you are enjoying your time together.

Please give my sweet pea a big hug and a kiss.
Yours,

Helen Hendrix

"Sweet pea!" Meredith gripped me tighter, and while I felt her head slowly leaning toward mine, she stopped herself, unable to plant her lips atop my crown to kiss me. In her hesitation, I took the opportunity to lick her hand. It tasted sweet, like floral-scented soap.

"Yuck," she said, setting the note card free. It fluttered onto the kitchen table as she clipped on my leash and harness. Off we went.

# Ten

Prozac

"I'M SORRY, BUT WITHOUT PROZAC'S credentials, I'm not permitted to let him into the facility."

"Credentials? What credentials?"

Meredith's face went white in the mirror behind the receptionist's desk at Evergreen Gardens. I eyed her reflection—all bundled up in her long, pillow-like down jacket, her large purse flung over her shoulder. She held me close, traces of her perfumed body lotion enveloping me as she clutched me to the warmth of her chest.

"Helen Hendrix is very familiar with the protocols here at Evergreen Gardens," said the gray-haired receptionist, who sat bolt upright. "I cannot believe she wouldn't have provided you with Prozac's identifying paraphernalia, including his business cards."

"What business cards?" Meredith took a deep breath. From the faraway look in her eyes, I could tell she was probably connecting the dots regarding the certified letter whose contents she'd left sprawled upon her kitchen table. "We didn't need any business cards to get in here the other day."

"Was *I* here the other day?"

Meredith gave a short shake of her head.

"Then whoever covered for me did it wrong." The receptionist—a rather nondescript woman with a short bob of gray hair—peeled off her red-framed bifocals. She shot us a suspicious look, revealing a worn face and deep crow's feet. "All therapy dogs are required to have their credentials with them at all times."

"Well, yes, I understand. But since this is technically my very first visit with Prozac, will one of *my* business cards suffice?"

*Snide* was the only word to describe the look on the woman's face. She forced a cosmetically whitened smile—or maybe she was wearing dentures—appearing pleased by the opportunity to exert her power as she uttered, "Are *you* a therapy dog?"

Meredith tilted her head and shot the woman a look filled with displeasure, as if to say, *Drop the sarcasm!*

"It's protocol," the receptionist added, turning the power play of her glance away from Meredith and me and staring down at her computer keyboard. "Every therapy dog that visits is required to wear his bandanna and have his ID badge and business cards listing his social networking pages and an email address so those with whom he connects can stay in touch."

"Stay in touch? But he's a dog."

The woman held up her palms. "Those are the rules of the facility."

Meredith let out an amused sigh. It was clear that the woman behind the desk, her mouth set in a straight line, didn't see the humor or the absurdity.

"Look. I live almost thirty minutes away. By the time I go back and get Prozac's things, it'll take me almost an hour's worth of travel time. Is there any chance, since Prozac is a regular here and we have an appointment with Judge Thea—she's expecting us—that an exception could be made?"

"Rules are rules for a reason." The woman gathered some papers and assembled them into a stack. She tapped them into alignment.

"Could you at least call or page the judge—or whoever's in charge—and see about granting special permission? Just this once?"

The woman shook her head, indicating a firm *no,* and kept staring at her computer monitor.

Meredith countered, "I could try and call Helen Hendrix's nephew and ask him to fax a copy of Prozac's identifying information right here to the nursing home. I'm sure he would do that."

"*Nursing home?*" The woman's head and back lurched visibly straight. "Evergreen Gardens is *not* a nursing home. It's a mature, independent living facility."

From behind Meredith and me, in the wide open and high-ceilinged entry lobby, came a loud voice that beckoned, "For goodness' sake, Betsy.

Based on the way you're acting, maybe we ought to refer to Evergreen Gardens as the Kremlin!"

The receptionist's face twitched. Her eyes gaped wide upon that lady who always talked really loud. In the mirror, I could see the sweep of her salon-tended honey-blond hair. Meredith turned us to face her—a slightly hunched woman who wheeled a rather mod, paisley-painted oxygen cart. She was all made up and wearing an exquisitely coordinated outfit complete with a pastel silk scarf. The loud talker was so well put together that the oxygen tube clipped into her nostrils seemed like a perfectly natural fashion accessory.

"You must be Meredith." The woman's voice grew even louder as she hobbled toward us. The familiar scent of Chanel No. 5 filled my snout. I recognized it because it was Helen's favorite perfume, too. "You'll have to forgive By-the-Book Betsy here. She runs our reception desk as tight as a maximum-security prison. I guess in this day and age, you can never be too careful. I'm Annette," the loud talker said, offering Meredith her French-manicured hand. "You must be the famous romance author-turned-pet sitter."

Meredith shook the woman's hand. "I'm only a temporary pet sitter. And I would hardly call myself *famous*."

"Well, around here you're famous," Annette said. "Our lending library is stocked with all of your Ghost Ranch books. Every time a new one comes out, we Evergreen girls fight over it—all except for Betsy here."

Betsy moved some things around on her desk and said, "I'm a member of Great Books. We only read *quality* literature."

Meredith gave an amused, not surprised, nod of her head.

"Don't mind her," Annette chimed. "Betsy's an unabashed literary snob!"

Betsy shot Annette a wicked glare, but Annette glanced at her watch and said to Meredith, "Hey, we better get a move on."

Meredith's eyebrows crinkled. "Are we going somewhere?"

"Yes, you and Prozac. You're taking me on my errands today."

"But Judge Thea—"

"Oh, don't you worry about the judge," Annette said with a flippant wave of her hands. "It's not like she owns the place."

Betsy cleared her throat, adding, "Well, yes, technically, she does own the place. In a manner of speaking—as a shareholder of Evergreen Gardens, that is."

"Then I'm an owner, too!" hollered Annette, shooting poker-faced Betsy a look that telegraphed, loud and clear, that she didn't appreciate the receptionist adding her two cents.

"But Judge Thea is the president of the board—"

"And I'm a board member, too. So zip it, Betsy." Annette huffed a breath and, looking to Meredith, said, "Your timing is perfect. You'll save me cab fare, and when we get back, I'll square away everything with the judge. Now, let me grab my things." Annette hobbled toward one of the love seats in the lobby, where a purse sat atop what looked like a purple-colored pea coat. Most dogs had red and green color blindness, but I could pick out hues beyond the typical canine spectrum.

"B-but Judge Thea—she's expecting Prozac and me." Meredith's words collided with the back of Annette's head. "She gave specific instructions—"

"Obviously not specific enough, especially if she didn't tell you about bringing Prozac's credentials and warn you about our tight security system named Betsy."

Annette made a valid point, one that left Meredith to bite her lip, temporarily speechless.

"Come on," Annette said, slipping into her coat. "We'll be back in a jiffy."

"Where are we going?"

"I'll tell you on the way." Annette gripped Meredith by the arm and tried walking us toward the front doors.

But Meredith resisted, feet glued to the floor. I stirred and squirmed, trying to encourage her to go with Annette. *Screw Betsy!* After all, Betsy never liked me. She never paid me any attention on my weekly visits to Evergreen Gardens. And she wouldn't even let me in today. *The nerve!* Meredith owed it to me—and to herself—to march straight out of there. So why not take off with that oxygen-toting octogenarian?

"B-but are you sure we can leave?" Meredith said. She turned toward Betsy, pleading for her intercession. But Betsy flung her nose into the air, made a zippering motion across her lips, and tossed away an imaginary key.

"Is she allowed to leave?" Meredith asked again. "I mean, should we check with someone? Is-is this what usually happens when a therapy dog visits?"

"Hel-lo. I'm right here!" Annette waved a hand in front of Meredith's face. Her voice leaped an octave. "I may be hearing impaired, but I have yet to need an interpreter—or permission to leave my own place of residence."

"Do I have any say in this?" Meredith finally blurted, stopping us in our tracks.

Annette moved in closer, and in a harsh, hearing-aid-assisted whisper that released her tomato-juice-infused breath, she said, "Look, I'm trying to make your life easier. Without Prozac's credentials, there's not a chance Betsy is going to let you in. So, do you want to waste an hour's worth of time and gas by driving back home for Prozac's things, only to face Judge Thea's wrath for your tardiness? Or do you want me to serve as your alibi and smooth everything over for you with the judge?" Annette held up her hands as if balancing the options between her empty palm and her other hand, which was fastened to her ornate, purple-patterned oxygen cart.

Meredith inhaled a long, measured breath. She was certainly no dope, but it was clear that she wasn't well practiced in decision-making anymore—least of all spontaneous decisions. I could feel, in the way she clutched me, a surge of clammy, nervous, indecisive sweat seeping through every pore in her body. It told me that she was confused, and her reasoning ability was more tangled up than the wires and cables I'd seen stashed behind her computer desk.

"Come on. Trust me. It's a win-win for both of us," Annette said. "Before I retired, I was an elementary school nurse for forty-seven years. Believe me, if I could deal with the excuses of every snot-nosed kid who tried to get out of class, I can handle the judge."

"All right." Meredith finally caved. "Where, exactly, do you need to go, and how long is this going to take?"

⌒•◦⊂⊃◦•⌒

Annette gestured toward the windshield of Meredith's Toyota and said, "Make a right up at the next traffic signal then hang your next left." She eased her bony fingers along my spine. I sat lulled upon her lap, staring out the passenger-side window.

"You'll have to forgive Betsy," Annette said. "She means well, but sometimes, she gets her girdle in a wad. I guess all those years serving as an executive secretary for the president of IBM made her as rigid as steel."

Meredith said, "She's certainly an excellent gatekeeper—"

"But she could use a few charm school lessons." Annette patted my head. "So, how's Prozac here been treating you?"

"He's a smart dog," Meredith said. "But he's a little weird."

*Weird? Look at who's calling who weird!*

"Weird how?"

"He hides a lot—under the couch, my bed. And the other day, during that rain storm, he even jumped into the toilet."

Annette doubled over, laughing.

"Yeah, I was in the shower, and when I stepped out, I found him crouched inside the bowl."

"Maybe he had to go."

Both Annette and Meredith laughed in unison.

"And I always thought that dogs loved to go for walks and rides, but when he saw me gather his leash this morning," Meredith said, "he went under the sofa and wouldn't come out."

"Oh, I've had my share of dogs in my long life," Annette said, "and I can tell you that even if you get the same breed, each one has his own special quirks and tics. Just like with people."

I craned my neck and looked up at Annette, admiring how my most innocent gaze was reflected in the dark lenses of her sunglasses.

"I've always loved English springer spaniels. They were my breed," Annette said. "Back when I was a girl and even when I was married, we always had one. Some were friendly, others not so much. Some easy to train, others stubborn. The last spaniel we had was my son Brent's dog, Thane. That's what we called him. He was brilliant."

"The dog or your son?"

"Both," Annette said. "Brent and his girls, my granddaughters, taught Thane all these tricks. The girls even used to dress him up in capes like he was a wonder dog. It was the cutest thing."

From the way Annette was telling the story, the lilting pitch of her voice and the grin lighting up her face, it was obvious how much she loved that dog.

"We used to joke and say that Thane was the reincarnation of Liberace. Every time that dog had to go outside to do his business, he'd climb up onto the piano bench, and with his paw, he'd strike Middle C on the old upright. If no one answered his plea, he'd strike the key again and again. Just that one note. We could never understand how he did it, especially with such great big paws. It was amazing."

*Wow! I'd love to pal around with that dog someday. He might even know some show tunes!*

"I gather he's not around anymore?" Meredith asked.

"No, but he lived to be close to seventeen. A really special dog."

"Sounds like it."

Annette looked up at a street sign and pointed. "Okay, make a quick right. We're looking for Picture This. It's a photo shop that's next to the ice cream parlor right on the main drag."

"There it is," Meredith said, gazing through the windshield. "Let me find a parking spot and go in for you."

"Don't be silly. You can drop me and go around the block."

"No, let me help you—"

"There's no dirt on top of me yet. Pull over in that fire zone and let me out."

Annette Mahoney asserted her independence in such a way that Meredith quickly complied, angling the Toyota over the painted yellow street lines.

"Watch for me. I won't be long." Annette dropped her oxygen tank carrier onto the sidewalk and got out of the car. She set me down on the empty passenger seat, right into the warmth left in her wake.

The car eased back into downtown traffic. We stopped for a couple of red lights, and by the time Meredith drove around the block and returned to Picture This, Annette was already outside. She was standing near the curb, holding a manila envelope.

Meredith pulled the car over and swooped me onto her lap. Annette climbed into the car with her oxygen contraption.

"Perfect timing," Annette said, buckling her seatbelt. "Now, if you can drive down the block, I'll need to stop at Andrea's, that restaurant near the corner."

The pulse in Meredith's fingertips quickened as she firmed her grasp around my rib cage and torso and handed me back to Annette.

"Have you ever been to Andrea's?" Annette asked.

Meredith's jaw tightened. She swallowed a gulp and bobbed her head in response.

"What's the matter?" asked Annette. "You don't like it?"

"No. It's fine. It's great," she said, obviously hiding something as she slipped the car into gear and drove down the main street in a queue of slow-moving cars.

"I should only be about ten minutes—tops," Annette said. "I just have to finalize the menu and leave a deposit for my son's party."

I turned to Meredith, expecting her to offer *Do you want me to come in with you?* or something along those lines. But she didn't say a word. Her shoulders were squared, her face stern. Something Annette said or did seemed to have struck a nerve.

"I think there's a municipal parking lot around the next corner. But maybe we ought to recite a little prayer to try to get one closer." Annette laced her fingers together and said, "Hail Mary, full of grace, help us find a parking space."

No sooner had Annette spoken that phrase than a car pulled out of a parallel parking spot on the street.

"Well, look at that!" Annette said, giving Meredith's arm a tap. "Even though I'm a dyed-in-the-wool Episcopalian, that tried-and-true Catholic prayer never fails."

I got a kick out of Annette but was surprised by the seriousness etched on Meredith's face, which was set as rigid as stone. She maneuvered into the parking space located directly in front of a drug store, just one door away from Andrea's. Balancing me on her lap, Annette slipped out the contents of the envelope from the photo store—an eight-by-ten-inch informal portrait of a vibrant, good-looking middle-aged man. His polo shirt was capped by a face with an inviting smile and a full head of hair, accented with touches of gray at the sideburns and temple.

"This here's my Brent," Annette said. "I took this picture the last time the whole family vacationed up at Lake George."

"He's very handsome," Meredith remarked, appearing more engaged. "And you're a very good photographer."

"Oh, everybody's a photographer with camera phones nowadays." Annette was careful to handle the photo by the corners so as not to leave fingerprints on the glossy finish. "I already have a frame. Gonna sit it at the head of the table for Brent's party on Saturday night."

"Is it a surprise—the party?"

Annette stared wistfully into the photograph. "No. Not really. But I guess you could say everybody's *very surprised* that I'm throwing a party at all."

"Is it *this* Saturday night?"

"Once I leave the deposit, it better be." Annette slipped the photograph back inside the envelope and leaned it against the center console. She undid her seat belt, passed me off to Meredith, and hopped out of the car.

With Annette gone, Meredith cut the engine. The two of us sat listening to traffic on the downtown thoroughfare. Meredith held me rigidly, tense. She shifted her gaze to and from Andrea's—a tiny, understated storefront restaurant with a green awning. She fidgeted, unable to sit still. What was making her so uptight and uneasy?

I wormed my way out of her grasp and leaped onto the passenger seat, then jumped up and strained to look out the window. I turned to Meredith and whimpered. When she didn't budge, I cried louder and barked, circling the seat and doing a little dance, hoping she'd translate my body language to read that Mother Nature was calling. I felt we both needed to escape the stifling confines of that car and take a breather.

When she reached into her coat pocket and pulled out my leash, I knew my tactic had worked.

Out on the busy downtown sidewalk, I pulled the slack from the leash, trying to lead Meredith closer to Andrea's, but she pulled me back in earnest. Whatever it was about the place she didn't like, I sensed her anxiousness had nothing to do with food and dining. It went beyond that, as though Andrea's was an old battlefield or perhaps the scene of a crime. An eerie feeling overcame me as Meredith forced me to give up my quest. The two of us trudged down the block the opposite way.

When we rounded the corner and approached the municipal parking lot, Meredith stopped us abruptly as though we'd traced a path toward a seismic undercurrent. Rooted in the middle of the sidewalk, Meredith stood, unblinking. Daylight reflected off parking meters and the shiny roofs and hoods of cars. Pedestrians were forced to step around Meredith, bypassing her like water flowing around a stone in a stream. I gathered that something bad, something very bad, must've happened there—somewhere between Andrea's and the parking lot.

"Meredith! Meredith!" a loud, gritty voice hollered from down the block. I turned and looked past Meredith in her trancelike state, relieved to spy the honey-colored hair of Annette Mahoney and her lively, upbeat face. But it wasn't until I tugged again on the leash, pulling out the slack as I lurched in Annette's direction, that Meredith was finally forced out of her reverie.

The two of us hurried toward Annette, back to the car.

"How'd you make out?" Meredith asked as we all climbed inside the Toyota.

"All set," Annette said. "I've arranged for all of Brent's favorites: oysters, lobster ravioli, Osso Buco, cheesecake…"

Meredith started the car and maneuvered out of the parking space. "Sounds like some feast."

"It better be. I'm going for broke on this party."

"Where to next?"

"The Bottle Brigade, that discount liquor store over on Durie Avenue. I've ordered a few cases of champagne. Giving a bottle to everyone as their party favor."

"Wow! This really *is* going to be some affair." Meredith drove down the street. When we passed that parking lot on the corner, Meredith turned her head and looked. I heard her swallow hard. "How many people are going to be there?"

"Thirty-seven of us. My six children and their children and all their husbands, wives, and significant others, my grandchildren and great-grandchildren—"

Annette's cell phone chimed, spouting Beethoven's Fifth Symphony. It had a much prettier resonance than Meredith's boring, real-life telephone ringtone.

Annette reached down to her purse on the floor of the car and pulled out her phone. She lifted her sunglasses and eyed the number on the small LCD screen.

"Excuse me. I've got to take this." Annette answered the phone in a deafening voice. "Hey, Billy, you get my message? … Right. The Knicks over the Bulls on Sunday… Three-point spread … I'm feeling lucky, that's why, and you know me, I always root for the underdog… I don't care if they're out of contention for the playoffs…" Annette cackled. "Okay, I'll see you on Monday… 'Cause I'm confident they're going to win, that's why!"

When Annette ended the call, Meredith asked, "Everything all right?"

appearing to know the way to the liquor store without having to ask for directions.

"Things will be fine as long as the Knicks win on Sunday."

"You're a basketball fan?"

"This week I am. And in a manner of speaking, I'm counting on the Knicks to pay for Brent's party. He was a die-hard fan, went to every home game."

The wool of Annette's coat bristled against me. She folded her body over mine as she slipped her phone back inside her purse.

"How old's your son?" Meredith asked.

"Would've been his fiftieth birthday this year."

"Oh?" There was an inquisitive, perplexed edge to Meredith's tone, and in the pause that ensued, I suspected she was probably wondering the same thing I was—what was with Annette using the past tense? *He was a die-hard fan. He would've been fifty?*

"Brent passed away nine years ago."

"Oh, gee. I'm sorry," said Meredith.

Through her leather glove, I could feel a quiver in Annette's fingertips.

"I figured it was time for the family to lift the moratorium. None of us have ever really spoken about Brent since he passed. That's why the party. Everyone has agreed to come, except for my daughter-in-law, Brent's widow, and their two girls. They think my idea is morbid."

"Morbid? Really?" Hesitation and care underscored Meredith's words as if she were wary of giving her opinion.

"I don't see it that way," Annette said. "I'm looking forward to finally honoring Brent and his life. Hopefully, we'll talk about him—remembering the good times."

Meredith accelerated onto a busier street. "That sounds like a beautiful tribute."

"Well, my daughter-in-law and my grand-girls wouldn't agree with you. They're still mad. The two girls were only eleven and twelve years old when Brent took his own life. And I was just too shaken and shocked, mired in my own grief, to talk about him or his death back then. I think we all were. And then, the years racked up..."

Annette's words trailed off as she stared blankly through the windshield, her gloved hands still stroking my back. I craned my neck to look up at her.

From behind her sunglasses, I spied her eyes filling with tears. I couldn't tell if Meredith was stunned by Annette's revelation or if she was being astute in saying nothing. She let the quiet hang there for a moment as if hoping Annette would somehow return from her reverie and share more of her thoughts.

"When I last saw the girls and mentioned my idea about having a party to celebrate their father's fiftieth birthday, they became so upset with me. I told them how I needed to do this and how sorry I was that I couldn't be the kind of grandmother they probably needed back then... how I couldn't talk about Brent for a long time. He was my youngest. My baby. And would you believe those two girls, my granddaughters—they're in their twenties now—they shot me these nasty looks, and one of them said, 'Too little, too late, Gram.' And I just looked at them, now these beautiful young ladies, and said, 'You're right. You're absolutely right. And I apologize—for everything. But I'll be ninety on my next birthday. And your father, well, he's been gone for nine years, and all we've done is treat him and his death like some sort of albatross. None of us can deny his end was terrible, but I think he died of his disease like we'll all someday die of our own diseases. And I think it's time we stop this and come together and celebrate how much his life mattered...'"

Annette paused then she gulped, trying to hold back her emotions.

"And that's when the two of them, along with their mother, walked out of the room on me."

"Oh, boy." Meredith sighed, shaking her head.

"They said they won't come, but I've paid for their dinners, hoping they'll reconsider. What more can I do?"

Meredith bobbed her head. I sought out the little patch of bare skin revealed between the space of Annette's glove and the cuffed sleeve of her blouse. As my tongue lapped her skin, I tasted sweet, floral remnants of her perfume. It was my way of telling Annette that she was one hell of a strong lady, and I was on her side.

"I sometimes think they forget that we *all* lost something when Brent died," Annette said. "But the thing is, they all replaced him. My daughter-in-law has a new husband. And the girls have a replacement dad and new brothers. They live in a brand-new house in a brand-new town and have a brand-new life. But I didn't get a replacement son or a replacement daughter-in-law and granddaughters. I lost all of them that day."

Meredith turned up the heat inside the car. She tipped the air vent toward me. The blast of warm air served to stir up all kinds of feelings, until heavy drops of wetness landed atop the fur on my back. When I looked up, Annette Mahoney's cheeks were wet with teardrops.

Meredith pulled the car into the lot of the Bottle Brigade. Once she parked the Toyota, she turned her somber face to Annette, clearly moved by the sight of her emotional outburst.

"Look at me. I never cry, and now I'm waterworks." Annette ran a finger under the dark lenses of her sunglasses and wiped her eyes.

"Why don't you let me go in and get what you need?" Meredith asked.

"Would you mind?" Annette reached into her purse.

"Not at all," Meredith said, cutting the engine. "Tell me what I'm asking for."

"Three and a half cases of Piper-Heidsieck champagne." Annette handed Meredith the credit card and a couple of dollars. "They're under my name, Mahoney. Ask them to carry the boxes to the car for you."

Once Meredith was gone, Annette cleared the sadness from her throat and blotted her eyes with a tissue, fixing her face in the tiny visor mirror.

"Prozac," she sighed. "Sometimes, it's not easy…"

The two of us sat listening to the quiet rustling of intermittent traffic in front of the liquor store. Annette stroked my hair as our breath steamed the windows. I stared past the parked cars and looked over at barren trees that bordered the parking lot.

I knew pets had the ability to take away stress and reduce blood pressure. But in my role as a therapy dog, I always felt more like a truth serum. With every human touch, I became a conduit to memories that people thought they'd sealed off, places in their hearts from which they thought they were safe and protected. How little it took to be gripped by grief all over again, even years after a loved one had died. A moment. A thought. Visiting a place. Being asked a simple question. Petting a dog. It amazed me what triggered human beings to remember things and how those memories often made folks feel vulnerable all over again.

Annette cuddled me closer, taking comfort in my soft fur. She gently pressed her lips to the top of my head and drew herself around me tightly as if wringing out her sadness.

When Meredith returned, she and the store clerk loaded the cases of champagne into the trunk.

"Where to now?" Meredith asked as she pulled out of the parking lot.

"Back home," Annette said. "Evergreen Gardens. I can't be late for my bridge game."

Meredith focused on the road, and I sank low on Annette's lap, snuggling into the warmth of her woolen coat. As we drove toward Evergreen Gardens, none of us uttered a sound. Sometimes, when humans shared things and finally gave voice to their feelings, they cast a light into dark places they'd kept locked inside. In those moments, there were no words.

I yawned, and Meredith lowered the heat. The gentle hum of the warm air that had been blowing from the dashboard vents onto my ears ceased, and I listened to the gears shifting in the automatic transmission. I was comforted by the smooth forward motion of the car, of us all going somewhere. Moving on.

Meredith finally piped up as though anxious to fill the void. "So, do you like Evergreen Gardens? I mean, are you happy living there?"

"Happy? Evergreen Gardens is fine. It doesn't really matter where I live. If I'm not happy, then it's my own damn fault." Annette reached into her coat pocket. She handed Meredith a twenty-dollar bill. "Here. Thanks for taking me on my errands."

"No, that's all right." Meredith shook her head. "But I *would* appreciate your help with the judge."

"Not a problem," Annette said. "She can be a bear, but I know how to handle her."

Meredith flipped on the turn signal. I raised my head from Annette's lap, jumping upon the armrest. As we turned into the long drive for Evergreen Gardens, a bottleneck of cars and flashing red lights swirled near the front entrance.

*Uh-oh, the police?*

"Oh my goodness! What's going on *here*?" Meredith pulled into the closest parking space. "I hope nobody died—"

"If nobody died, then I have a feeling we might have to kill somebody."

Meredith, looking stunned, jerked her head in Annette's direction as she cut the car engine.

"Follow me, and don't say a word." Annette flung the car door open and set me down on the asphalt of the parking lot. She looped my leash around the handle of her oxygen cart and walked us around the car.

Two police officers quickly approached.

"Meredith Mancuso?" one of them asked.

Meredith hopped out of the car and raised her hand. "Y-yes, that's me."

One of the policemen stepped forward and said, "I'm Detective Del Monaco." He studied Meredith's face. "You'll need to come with us."

"Why? What's the matter?" Meredith asked.

"We need to speak with you privately—"

"About what?"

*Gee, Meredith—so much for letting Annette do all the talking!*

"Miss Mancuso, please," the other officer said. "We have a few questions."

As Annette and I approached Meredith, I stared into a crowd of familiar faces, curious residents from Evergreen Gardens standing on the front sidewalk. Some were even gawking through the curtained windows and blinds.

"I don't understand. What's going on?" Meredith's neck and face were turning pink. "Am I under arrest or something?"

"Officers, please," Annette chimed in matter-of-factly. "I think there must be a mistake."

"Are you Annette Mahoney?"

"Yes."

"Ma'am, did this woman here apprehend you against your will?"

At the same time that Meredith's face seared red and she gasped, "What?" Annette burst out in a loud, side-splitting guffaw. She said, "Apprehend me? If anything, I apprehended *her*."

"This woman didn't abduct you from the premises?" the detective asked.

"Abduct me?" Annette said, looking surprised. "No, absolutely not."

The officers and the detective stood there amid fiery, flashing streaks of light from the squad cars. They looked at each other, apparently mystified, as the crowd outside Evergreen Gardens grew larger. There at the front of the pack was Judge Thea. She pinned Meredith with a stern face and a steady, suspicious gaze. She drew her white shawl around herself, stiffly crossing her arms against her black shift that billowed above her white bobby socks and running shoes. Beside her stood gray-haired By-the-Book Betsy, looking rather guilty.

Annette waved a fist in the air. "Betsy, did you do this?" I ducked beneath the shadows Annette created with her accusing outburst. She was livid. "Did you call the police?" As Annette fired off her questions to Betsy, the woman took a step back and hid behind the judge.

"Ma'am, please. Calm down," one of the officers said to Annette.

"This is ridiculous!" Annette cried, her face turning red. "I asked Meredith here to take me on some errands. That's all. There's no crime in that. Since when is Betsy my keeper?"

"There's no reason to be upset, ma'am. You see, when you didn't sign out in the reception register, there was cause for concern," the detective said. "We understand you suffer from congestive heart failure and appeared distressed upon leaving the facility—"

"Distressed? My only distress came from *that* woman, the guilty-looking, troublemaking one. There. That one—the lady who's trying to hide." Annette pointed a crooked finger straight at shrinking Betsy.

# Eleven

*THE FUN STOPS HERE*

### Meredith

THE POLICE INTERROGATED US AT the entrance to Evergreen Gardens. I broke out in a damp sweat, trying to remain calm while telling my side of things, acquiescing to whatever was asked of me. Then I stood back and let Annette Mahoney duke it out with Betsy.

"If you would've just let Meredith and the dog into Evergreen Gardens in the first place, this never would've happened," Annette said.

"This has nothing to do with the dog," Betsy said. "This has to do with *your* leaving the premises without following protocol and signing yourself out."

"But you saw me leave. I said goodbye. Did I really have to pick up a pen?"

Betsy flung her nose into the air. "There are rules to living in this facility, and I wouldn't be doing my job if I didn't strictly enforce them."

"Oh, cut it out, Betsy. You don't like dogs. It was a spiteful move on your part."

Their stubborn back-and-forth went on. Annette was not going to admit she didn't follow protocol. And Betsy was not going to back down in her self-righteousness. As things escalated, the police, having heard enough from both sides, intervened and finally called a truce.

We were ultimately all let off with a warning. The officers stressed that, in the future, all residents and guests of Evergreen Gardens needed to sign in—and out—of the facility.

As she turned on her heels, Betsy stretched her lips across her face, gloating. She wiggled her hips away from us.

"She might've won the battle, but she'll never win the war," Annette said, shaking her head and huffing and puffing as the police and crowd dispersed.

Annette asked the custodian from Evergreen Gardens to remove the cases of champagne from the trunk of my car. Before he carted the boxes inside, she flipped open the top case and reached for one of the gold-trimmed bottles of Piper-Heidsieck.

"Here," she said. "Sorry about the nonsense today."

I waved off her gesture, but she insisted I take the bottle. "After what went on here this afternoon, you deserve two bottles, but then I won't have enough for everyone at the party."

The curved green glass with the gold foil felt cool in my hands as Prozac and I took off.

⁂

The consolation of the champagne was a nice touch, but I'd had it. Enough was enough. I hightailed it straight to my sister's.

Holding Prozac, I rapped my knuckles hard upon the door to her office-apartment, the sound resembling a spray of gunfire.

"Open up!"

The door flung wide, and I was surprised to be greeted by Larry, my sister's long-term beau of bomb squad fame. He was standing there holding a newspaper folded over to the crossword puzzle. A pen was clipped to the page.

"What are you doing here?" I asked.

"Back on a fortnight for training." Larry took a look at Prozac. He slipped the paper under his arm then peeled off his reading glasses. He let them dangle from a leather strap around his neck. "Why? What's up? You in some kind of trouble?"

"Where's Monica?" I looked around him, peering into the office at shelves of important-looking, leather-bound accounting books. "She's gotta take back this dog. He almost got me arrested today."

"Arrested?" Larry's eyebrows knit. "Arrested for *what*?"

"It's a long story."

Larry's hair was crew cut, and he had stubble on his normally clean-shaven cheeks. Wearing jeans and a stretched-out polo shirt, he moved aside. As I entered, I pushed Prozac into his chest, smack against his reading glasses, leaving him no choice but to take the dog.

"I not only got roped into taking care of this stupid animal, but also I'm now expected to keep his therapy dog appointments at that old folks' home down the street."

"You mean Evergreen Gardens?"

I nodded.

"They don't call it a *home*—"

"I know. I know." I held up my palms to stop Larry from saying more. "I've already been called out on the whole politically correct thing: Mature, Independent Living Facility."

"It used to be a church. Evergreen Bible Church."

"Well, I think the place needs an exorcism. The people who live there are all a bunch of manipulators who are far from *mature*."

"I don't know anything about the inhabitants, but I do know the place has a really interesting history," Larry said in his best bomb-squad-calm manner, which overshadowed my outrage. "When the parish started to go belly-up, the congregants pooled their resources and bought it—converted it into a private, independent living space. It was all over the local papers. A great concept."

"Whatever it is or was, I won't be going there anymore."

Larry didn't say a word. He ran a hand over Prozac, smoothing his ruffled fur.

"One resident, a former county judge, is blackmailing me to make me keep this dog's weekly appointment. And today, on my first visit with Fido here, we got roped into taking this other lady on her errands. She's planning a birthday party for her dead son—"

Larry's forehead filled with wavy lines. He looked puzzled, but I didn't leave him a breath of dead air to pursue further questions.

"And to top it all off, after we're done running the errands, we drive back to the place, and the cops are there, waiting for us. They accused me of trying to abduct the lady—"

"Oh, I see. Your so-called arrest. Did they press charges?"

"No, but I had one helluva time trying to convince them that I'm not some sort of senior citizen hostage taker."

A quick smile twitched at the corners of Larry's mouth.

"It's not funny."

"You should hear yourself," he said, patting Prozac's head. "This is the most animated I've seen you in years."

"Believe me, I could live without *this* type of animation."

"Don't worry. It will all look different tomorrow."

"Yeah, probably worse."

"Don't be a pessimist—"

"'Optimist with experience' is what I like to call myself."

"Knowing you, you'll probably find some way to weave this experience into your next novel." Larry pushed away some stacks of important-looking papers and binders from the overwhelmed sofa in Monica's office. He gestured for me to sit down. As I settled, Larry pulled a bottle of water from the refrigerator. He handed it to me then dragged over Monica's high-back leather desk chair and sat across from me. Prozac grew instantly comfortable in Larry's muscular arms, settling inside of them.

"So tell me, where's my sister?" I asked, twisting the cap on the water and letting out a much-needed sigh. "Has she taken the day off or something?"

"A day off? During the height of tax season? Are you kidding?" Prozac, ears erect, sat up majestically on Larry's lap. "She's testifying as a forensic accounting expert at some big divorce trial. She hightailed it out of here all keyed up this morning. You know how she gets with court appearances. And the timing couldn't be worse with April fifteenth approaching."

I rolled my eyes as I swigged a sip of water. It was so cold it hurt my teeth. "Is that girl ever *not* in crisis mode? There's always some pressing accounting deadline or tax loophole tangling her up."

"Well, you two ladies are certainly classic Type-A personalities. Must be in the genes," he said, stroking Prozac gently from head to tail. "Here I make my living trying to figure out how to disarm and defuse bombs all day, and I've yet to figure a way to convince both of you to chill out and lighten up."

Larry bundled Prozac in his big, fleshy hands. He leaned back in the desk chair and held the dog high above him in a grandiose, eye-to-eye *Lion King* pose. It was quite a sight to see the normally macho, muscular military guy fawning over the speck of a pocket dog. But ever since Larry had tragically lost a buddy a few years back—a coworker, on the job—he'd become something of a changed man. The trauma and its aftermath had softened his once hard, steely exterior.

"What a handsome little devil you are," Larry cooed. Prozac's tongue lapped out of his mouth as though he were literally drinking in all of Larry's love.

"You've got the devil part right," I said.

Larry grimaced. He navigated Prozac back to his lap. "Look, Mer. Your taking on this dog... maybe it's not such a bad thing. Maybe you ought to change it up—"

"Don't start with all your bomb-squad psychology." I pointed a finger at him. "I know you're on Monica's side."

Larry held up both hands in surrender.

"It's not right, and it's not fair how I've been roped into this," I said. "Why should I be expected to put my own life on hold to accommodate some stupid dog—and parade him around the county to boot?"

"Meredith, come on. You're not really putting your life on hold. You're simply sharing your home with a temporarily orphaned dog, and you and he are adding to the quality of life for some older people. You're giving back. It's only a few hours a week."

"And what about *my* quality of life?"

"Look," Larry said, gathering his breath along with his thoughts. "Keep it in perspective. This isn't a terminal pathology report or losing a loved one."

The nerves in my scalp prickled. That was all he needed to say to shut me up.

"I know these big, strapping military guys who've been wounded in combat. A lot of them find the companionship of an animal helps them reconnect with themselves and the world in a way they couldn't accomplish on their own. And let's face it, you've been shell-shocked ever since Kyle's murder."

I winced at that word *murder*. Larry knew right where to jab.

"And before you tell me to mind my own business, I just want to say that I know how hard it's been for you. Post-traumatic stress... it isn't easy."

I inhaled a breath, contemplating what he'd just said.

"And you know better than anyone, Meredith, that nothing's forever.

So what's a couple of days or a few weeks? The time you spend doing this might be good for you. Good karma."

"I don't believe in karma—not since Kyle. I never will."

"Well, that's all right, because I'm not a big fan of the words *always* and *never*."

Larry and I sat at an impasse in a shrink-and-patient arrangement—he in Monica's office chair and me slumped in defeat upon the couch.

I took another sip of water, the cold easing back the lump beginning to grow in my throat. Then I barked, "Well, if there are any more surprises like the one I had today, that's it. The last straw. I mean it."

Prozac, who had settled in and fallen asleep on Larry's lap, lurched up, wide-awake.

"Give it a chance," Larry said amid the burgeoning curl of a smile. "I have a good feeling about this."

"Why does everyone but me have good feelings about this?" I asked as I gathered up my purse, took Prozac from him, and left.

# Twelve

*JUST INCHES FROM A CLEAN GETAWAY*

## Meredith

THROUGH THE WINDSHIELD, I STARED up at bare trees and branches that clawed at the last glimmers of light in the afternoon sky. I was tired and spent and lost in thought, and I didn't even realize the dashboard lights had automatically triggered on until we stopped at a traffic signal. I glanced over at Prozac. He was sitting erect on the passenger seat. His eyes looked heavy as he gazed into the sky, which was now softening into purple shades of dusk.

My smartphone buzzed with a text. I reached for my purse, fished out the phone, and read:

> U got lucky 2day! Next week b on time @EG and
> remember P's credentials. APL a mere phone call
> away. Have a nice day! :) Judge T

*Have a nice day? Really?*

Behind me, a car horn tooted. I looked up at the green traffic signal and dropped the phone back inside my pocketbook. As we drove off, I shook my head, massaging my achy neck and shoulders.

*Who does that Judge Thea think she is—my parole officer?*

By the time Prozac and I turned into my townhouse development, the car headlights swept upon the serpentine streets that led to my unit. As I approached my place, I thought I saw a car parked in the driveway. I couldn't be sure at first, as all the units looked the same—brick-built, uniform, and huddled close together—but as we pulled closer, I did indeed see a car in my driveway and the murky shape of a person standing near the front door. As I slowed up in front of my unit, the motion detector on the porch flicked on, obliterating the darkness.

Prozac jumped up on the passenger door to look out the window, tail stub high as if on alert. The person on the doorstep became a growing shadow that moved down the porch steps. The dark shape crossed the ragged grass on the postage-stamp-sized front lawn and headed for the car.

I squinted, trying to decipher the shape silhouetted by the front house spotlights.

"Meredith?" a man's voice thundered.

Prozac let out a low, threatening growl. Somebody big and tall wearing dark clothing—perhaps a trench coat—put up a hand and waved. He called, "Meredith Mancuso?" His voice was muffled by the glass of the closed car window, which I wasn't about to roll down anytime soon.

"Who wants to know?"

"Hammond Cederholm. You're taking care of Aunt Helen's dog. Helen Hendrix—"

The malevolence of Prozac's deep, throaty growl coalesced into fierce barking—a hostile sound I'd never heard from him before. His unexpected show of aggression exacerbated my own nervousness. After all, it was dark outside, and a shadowy stranger had approached us. Prozac would truly be abnormal if he didn't try to protect himself, me, and his turf, right?

I reached over and tried to settle Prozac. But at my touch, he turned to me, drawing his fangs, ready to snap. Startled, I instantly retracted my hand. I got the gist.

"It's okay. It's okay." Hammond Cederholm's well-coiffed hair and dark eyes moved closer, filling the passenger-side window glass. But his literal in-your-face approach only made matters worse. Prozac's bark grew more persistent. He clawed at the window, responding more like a starved, one-hundred-pound Doberman pinscher than a five-pound Yorkshire terrier. His sudden ferociousness forced the Cederholm guy to back off. But his retreat wasn't far enough, as Prozac continued to work himself up into one heck of a tizzy.

Apparently, Cederholm had even less experience with dogs than I did.

He stood there in the shadows, frozen and wide-eyed, looking as pitiful and helpless as I felt.

"Why don't you go and move your car? Put it on the street," I suggested, straining my voice above the incessant alarm of Prozac's Secret Service, to-die-for protection. "Maybe then I can calm him down."

Physically removing the guy from Prozac's sight was all I could think of to enact a cease-fire.

Once Hammond Cederholm moved his black Mercedes from the driveway, I turned in, hit the remote, and activated the automatic garage door. When the door opened, I slipped my Toyota inside. My plan worked, as Prozac instantly quieted. He stopped shaking, and his barking was replaced by heavy panting. His tongue hung out of his mouth like a loose ribbon, as if he'd run a marathon.

I cut the engine then hit the garage remote again. The electric door rumbled closed. I knew it probably seemed rude, but I feared that amid Cederholm's apparent cluelessness, he'd step into the garage to meet us, and whatever progress we'd just made would dissolve.

In the closed quiet, I took a breath and reached out, touching Prozac, who turned to me. I was relieved when innocence oozed from the brown pools of his eyes as if to say, *See, I did a good thing. Never fear, Prozac is here!*

Mean, aggressive Prozac's about-face was chilling. And I never dreamed I'd be so relieved at the return of plain old weird Prozac. I scooped him up and carried him, my purse, and that bottle of champagne into the house. Once I flipped on the light switch, I set the champagne on the library table and, still holding Prozac, opened the front door. Hammond Cederholm was on the front porch. He was carrying a case of what looked like soup cans and wearing a sheepish grin.

He maneuvered the case and extended his hand. "Let's start again," he said. "I'm Hammond Cederholm. You can call me Ham."

"Nice to meet you, Ham." I shook his hand and let him into the foyer.

"I'm sorry if I scared you."

"You didn't scare *me* so much, but I think you did a pretty good job of overwhelming Prozac here."

"Well, his response is probably a good sign. You know what they say—dogs always protect those they love."

I didn't correct him on the love bit. I played along, ruffling the fur atop

Prozac's head. When he licked my hand, I didn't even pull away. I motioned to Ham to set the case down on a living room chair. I was glad that I'd spent the past week tidying up.

"I hope you don't mind my stopping in like this, but Aunt Helen insisted." Ham pronounced the word *aunt* not as the insect, "ant," but more like "ont," as in the last syllable of the word *dilettante.* "While we were visiting today, she suggested I drop off some more dog food and check on Prozac—oh, and check on you, too, of course. We were both curious to know how you made out at Evergreen Gardens."

"Your timing couldn't be better. We're returning from there." I wished I'd stayed and suffered through Larry's pep talk another five minutes. It might've rescued me from the impromptu meeting with Hammond Cederholm.

Ham set down the dog food.

*Why a whole case? Am I in for a long haul?*

"You think it's safe if I try to pet him now?" Ham asked, turning to me and, with a cautious, sideways glance, studying Prozac, who was calm in my arms.

"Has he ever gone after you like that before?"

"No, never. I've never seen him like that," Ham said. "To be honest, he doesn't bother much with me when I visit Aunt Helen."

"I think he's tired, and you might've caught him off guard. Why don't I put him down and see how he responds. Are you game?"

Ham offered a slow nod.

Once Prozac's paws touched the floor, he gave himself a good shaking out. Then he ran around, his nails click-clacking in a frenetic tap dance upon the hardwood floor until he finally settled—ears back, sitting next to me, close at the ankles.

"Gee, look at him," said Ham. "He's sure bonded with you."

I glanced down at Prozac's sweet, angelic-looking face. *Who is this dog?*

"Maybe we ought to try a peace offering." I turned and headed for the kitchen—straight for the refrigerator—where I retrieved a slice of individually wrapped American cheese. When I closed the door, Ham, still in his long coat, rested against the kitchen doorway, while Prozac stood on his hind legs, his paws atop my shin as he kept a laser-like focus on that piece of cheese in my hand.

I ripped open the cellophane and gave Prozac a few tiny pieces. "I think somebody's hungry. Here," I said, thrusting the remainder of the slice Ham's way. "Why don't you give him the rest?"

With hesitation and a quivering hand, Ham took the cheese.

I suppressed a smile. *Ham and cheese. They go together. How bad can this really turn out?*

Ham ripped off a microscopic square of orange and peered down at Prozac circling at his feet. With the speck of cheese between his thumb and forefinger, Ham stretched out his arm as far as possible and dangled the offering as if he were about to feed a sardine to a whale.

When Prozac dashed over and gobbled it up, Ham jerked his hand away, looking stunned by Prozac's eagerness.

"If only the conflicts of the Middle East could be resolved as easily," I joked.

Ham quickly earned Prozac's obedience and complete attention, and his confidence grew as the dog inhaled every bite. When all the cheese was gone, Ham reached over and gave a guarded pat to Prozac's head. The dog took off, his short, stubby tail wagging contentedly.

With great drama, Ham swiped his fingers across his brow and flung off some imaginary sweat. Then he held up his hands my way and wiggled his fingers. "Gee, and I've still got all ten digits," he said.

I chuckled. "So, do you have time for a cup of coffee or tea?" I asked. In my heart of hearts, I was truly hoping he would say no. But I knew it would seem downright impolite *not* to make the offer.

"Well, I don't want to impose..."

I bit my tongue. "No, by all means."

Hammond Cederholm slipped out of his trench coat, revealing what looked like an expensive Armani suit and diamond cuff links. Everything about the guy reeked of affluence.

He carefully folded the coat in half and was about to set it over one of the kitchen chairs when I said, "Here, let me hang that for you."

Traces of musky aftershave wafted toward me as I took the coat from him and headed to the foyer. Prozac happily scampered alongside at my heels.

⁓⊙⟨⟩⊙⁓

I filled the teakettle and flipped the gas on the stove. Then I set down a plate of shortbread cookies—my secret, emergency stash kept on hand solely for unexpected company—in front of Ham, who sat at the kitchen table.

"Hammond. That's an interesting name. Like the organ company?"

"Yes. Hammond organs are famous. But I'm actually named for my great-grandfather," he said, reaching for a cookie. "I like the name now, but the kids in school had a field day, calling me everything from pig and piggy to Hormel and Spam. Nothing worse than being harassed with oinking sounds for twelve grades."

I turned from the kettle and studied Ham, his chiseled profile and his wide, broad shoulders. He chomped on the shortbread. It felt eerie to see a strange man seated in what used to be Kyle's chair. Outside of the gas and electric meter reader and a repairman on the scene every now and then—and my nosy, doorbell-ringing mailman—I simply wasn't used to having a male presence in or around the house anymore.

The teakettle boiled a fierce whistle.

"You sure you don't want me to put on a pot of coffee? I have decaf," I told him, flipping off the gas and silencing the kettle.

"No, tea is fine," Ham said, "and I've really got to get home. I've been trekking out to Jersey to check in on Aunt Helen every other day. I usually stop after work. But today, I drove out from the city earlier than usual—I have a big meeting tomorrow and want to use tonight to prepare."

"How is Helen doing?"

"She's had some complications from the surgery, bursitis in her foot. It set her back a bit."

*Oh, wonderful!*

"But the doctors are optimistic that, for a woman her age, she's probably right where she should be at this point in the healing."

"Well, thank goodness for that!"

Prozac skittered at my feet as I walked over to the table with the kettle. I poured boiling water into two mugs, the handles trussed up with white strings attached to our bags of green tea.

"The little guy looks well. I hope he hasn't been too much trouble." Ham's words were uttered as a statement but carried a touch of inquisitiveness.

As I returned the kettle to the stove, I considered telling Ham about Prozac's toilet bowl escapades and how we almost got arrested today. But I thought better of it.

"It's been a big adjustment, for both of us, but he's been a trouper." As I sat across from Ham, I reached down for Prozac. I set him on my lap and petted him. He stood rather stiffly as I tried to do my best imitation of a dog lover.

"He's a good dog. But today's the first time I've ever seen him in watchdog mode," Ham said, cupping his fingers around the steaming hot mug of tea. "I know how fond Aunt Helen is of him, but personally, I find him a little peculiar."

"Oh?" What a relief to know that I wasn't alone in that assessment.

"Yes, I tease Aunt Helen all the time that Prozac must've lived a past life as a cat—if you believe in that kind of stuff. When he first came to live with her, he used to play incessantly with this little orange mouse on a string. It was a cat toy. And he has this annoying propensity for going into hiding sometimes. He disappears for hours. Has he pulled that with you yet?"

"As a matter of fact, yes, he has."

"I'll let you in on a secret." Ham leaned across the table and whispered, "If you're ever in a bind and want to lure him out, all you need to do is open a can of tuna fish."

"Seriously?"

Ham arched his eyebrows and nodded. "It works. Really. I'd swear it's the past-life cat thing. And don't ever ask him if he wants to go for a—" Ham stopped himself from saying the next word. He raised his left hand, and inverting his pointer and middle finger toward the floor, he moved them back and forth, mimicking the action of walking. "He hates it, so don't even say the word. If you do, you won't see him for hours. Trust me."

I could feel my eyebrows dip. "You mean, W-A-L-K?"

Prozac's ears lifted like active antennae. In an instant, he leaped off my lap and, with tail tucked and nails skittering upon the tiles of the kitchen floor, bolted into the darkened living room.

"Oh my goodness, he can spell, too?" I said.

Ham and I both burst out laughing with great big guffaws. After the day I'd had, it came as a welcome release.

"He's either hypersensitive or extremely brilliant—"

"Or both!" I added.

"He truly *is* a remarkable dog."

Small curls of steam rose from my tea as I took a sip, thinking that *remarkable* was an appropriate word—a safe, neutral adjective—one that I might've chosen myself in describing Prozac.

The tea was strong and warmed me as I studied Ham, listening to him regale me with stories about Aunt Helen and her devoted affection for Prozac. Ham reached for a second piece of shortbread, and after he practically inhaled it, he reached for a third, dunking that one in his tea. He certainly wasn't shy about cleaning the plate.

Ham was likable, and that made me wonder why Judge Thea was so critical of him—making him out to be some sort of money-hungry vulture. His appearance led me to believe he probably had enough money of his own. Why would he want or need Aunt Helen's money?

I tried to size him up as I would a character from one of my books. He was distinctly masculine. But his fingers were callus-free, and his nails were trimmed and neatly manicured. I got the sense he worked with his brain more than his hands. He wore a thin gold band on his right hand—ring finger. It was the wrong hand for a wedding ring. Maybe he was divorced? Widowed? On the prowl? His appearance certainly mattered to him—the mousse in his styled-to-look-carefree hair, the trench coat and charcoal-gray Armani suit, the silk necktie and the diamond glint of cuff links on a crisp white dress shirt with a fine stripe in the weave. Clearly expensive. He could've been a doctor or lawyer. But something about his manner made me lean more toward financial planner. Could also be in high-end real estate. Maybe a stretch, but perhaps even a luxury-car salesman?

"I offered to take Prozac myself, but Aunt Helen doesn't like the idea of his being left alone while I'm at work—and I've been working round-the-clock lately," Ham said. "But my office is moving to a newer, smaller facility—budget cuts and the flagging economy and all. So I won't be traveling for the next several months."

"What line of work are you in?"

"Architect."

I nodded.

*Aha!* Not what I'd guessed, but it sort of made sense.

He opened his wallet and pulled out a business card with a rendering of the Manhattan skyline capping the name of his firm: Baker, Cederholm & Meyers. It looked like a big, high-end operation. No wonder he was driving a top-of-the-line Mercedes-Benz and dressed in a designer suit and diamond cuff links.

Ham went on. "Since I'll be working from home and my building allows for pets, I was thinking that maybe I could take Prozac off your hands. He might be Aunt Helen's pride and joy, but caring for someone else's dog is a big imposition—especially for a stranger."

His offer was tempting. More than tempting.

"Have you talked with Aunt Helen about this?" I asked.

"Not yet. I thought I'd check with you first. But knowing he won't be alone all day, I'd imagine she'd be fine with it. And it might be good for her if I try to smuggle him in to see her at the rehab facility every now and then."

I took a sip of tea, hearing Judge Thea's words from the first day I'd met her at Evergreen Gardens: *If you or your sister don't take Prozac, then he'll probably be pawned off on Helen's no-good, money-hungry nephew. And that man is bound to dump poor Prozy into a kennel.*

If I was making the decision solely on my own, that dog, his Wee-Wee pads, and the stupid playpen would've already been packed up and pulling away in Ham's Mercedes. But out of loyalty to my sister, good old Monica—and my still having the fear of God driven into me by Judge Thea—I felt that a stalling tactic might be more in order.

"It sure sounds like a plan, but I think I should check with my sister first," I told him and then tried to soften my rationale. "After all, Prozac was originally placed in her care. I guess I'm what you'd call the sublet pet sitter."

"Could you maybe phone your sister and bounce it off her?"

I felt my back tense up. "Now? You want me to call her *now*?"

Ham nodded.

Disarmed by his request, I looked at my wristwatch, hoping to buy some time. I didn't like being put on the spot. And the way things were going for me lately—especially after the Annette Mahoney and police ordeal from Evergreen Gardens—something told me that I shouldn't allow myself to be roped into anything about which I had even a slight reservation. What did I really know about Hammond Cederholm outside of his being Helen's nephew? Did I really have the right to keep him from having his aunt's dog?

"Actually, no, I can't reach my sister. Not now," I said, pointing to my watch. "She's in court all day. But I could probably reach her later tonight or tomorrow. Maybe then we can work this all out."

Ham nodded. "All right. That sounds doable."

"How about another cup of tea or more cookies?" I asked.

"No, I better get going." As he stood up, he glanced down at the table and reached for a matchbook propped next to the napkin dispenser and a candle. "Hey, Andrea's Restaurant. Do you know this place?"

"Y-yes. It's a tiny storefront—a BYOB, a bring-your-own-bottle place." I was stunned that, for the second time in one day, I was reminded of the restaurant.

"I ask because when I was visiting Aunt Helen the other day, we read a review in the local paper. She'd never heard of it. But they gave it a really good write-up. Said the grilled octopus is great—melts in your mouth."

"Gee, it's not often I meet another fan of calamari and octopus," I said. "That used to be one of my favorite appetizers."

"*Used* to be?"

I turned my gaze away from him. The scrape of my kitchen chair being pushed under the table resounded like a scream.

"I haven't been there in a really long time."

"That's no fun. And life's too short," he said, placing the matches back on the table. "Maybe one day when I'm in town to see Aunt Helen, I can break away and take you to lunch?"

Cederholm was certainly forward.

"S-sure," I hedged. "That sounds nice, but I'm sort of on a deadline with work."

"What do you do?"

"I'm a writer."

"Yes, I think Monica mentioned that to Aunt Helen. What do you write?"

"Books."

"Wow. That's great," he said, interest flaring. "What kinds of books?"

"Novels."

His eyes flung open wider. He was clearly impressed. "Have I ever heard of you?"

"Probably not. I'm no Danielle Steel or Nora Roberts."

"So you write romance novels?"

"Women's fiction," I told him.

"What book of yours would you recommend for me?"

"I don't think my books would really interest someone like you."

"Oh? And just who am I like?"

I blushed and tried to backpedal. "What I mean is, the stories are mostly geared for women."

"Are men not allowed to buy and read them, too?"

"Oh, of course, anyone can read them," I said, amused by his persistence. "But I don't think they'd really be your taste."

"Let me be the judge of that," he said.

"I'd hate for you to invest in a book that won't appeal to you—"

"I'm sure it'll appeal to me. It's not every day that I can read a book written by someone I know," he said, studying me as though seeing me for the first time.

"Well, you'll have to seek out my books via my pen name, Meredith St. John."

"Aha. A nom de plume—Meredith St. John. I like it. Has a nice ring." Ham nodded approvingly and repeated my name aloud as if to commit it to memory. "Wow. A real author. That's really something!"

He might've been all jazzed about my being an author, but I didn't actually feel like a real author—at least not lately. And I certainly didn't have the heart to tell him that the only thing that was *really something* was that I hadn't written any worthy pages in months, and I was beginning to feel like a fraud, a failure, a flop. Not to mention, my agent and publisher were breathing down my neck, anxiously awaiting a novel that was completely stalled.

"Aunt Helen is going to get such a kick out of this when I tell her," Ham said, charmed by the prospect. "To think that her precious, prized Prozac—say that three times fast—is being cared for by a famous novelist."

"Hardly famous," I corrected.

Ham started out of the kitchen, and on his way to the foyer, he stopped to check out the champagne on the library table. He turned the bottle around to read the label.

"Gee. Nice. Piper-Heidsieck. What are you celebrating?"

"Oh, that was a gift."

Ham bobbed his head. "You ought to share it with someone special."

"Yeah, will do," I said, thinking that I'd probably stash it in my wine rack and wrap it up as a gift for someone at the holidays.

I retrieved Ham's coat and handed it to him. Before he strode out of the foyer and onto the front steps, I asked, "Would you like to say goodbye to Prozac?"

"Oh, right. Right," he said, turning from the front door and following me into the living room.

I scanned the parlor, thinking Prozac might be perched on the back of the sofa. But he wasn't there. He wasn't coiled up in a ball on one of the wingback chairs either. And he wasn't lying on the floor between the sofa and end table.

"Oh boy, I bet he's hunkering down under the couch." As I started in that direction, Ham put a hand on my arm to stop me.

"Don't worry about it. It's probably from the *W* word. Leave him be," he said. "He's had a busy day, and I also gave him quite a fright earlier. He's probably scared to death that I'm going to take him somewhere. It's typical of him, believe me."

I didn't fight Ham on that, and as we walked toward the front door again, he thanked me for the tea and cookies and also for taking care of Prozac.

"So did I pass? Will you give Aunt Helen a good report?" I asked him.

"How could I not?" he said with a grin, the lines around his eyes wrinkling. "Give me a call after you speak to Monica, and if everyone agrees, we'll work out the details for transferring Prozac."

He leaned toward me and gave my cheek a gentle, sweet, yet unexpected kiss.

I tensed, startled at the friction of his face next to mine. His gesture caught me off guard.

"Thanks for helping out with Prozac. Aunt Helen and I really appreciate it," he said, stepping toward the door.

I stood trembling behind the storm glass, watching Ham head for his car.

He gave me a big wave—and an ear-to-ear smile with teeth—as he slipped into his Mercedes. I was too stunned to return the gesture. When the red taillights had shrunk from my sight, I closed the door and leaned against it, putting a hand to where Ham had kissed my cheek.

I didn't know how long I stood there lingering, but when Prozac came crawling out from under the dining room table, shook himself out, and sat down directly in front of me, I looked at him and said, "How would you like to go and live at your Uncle Ham's for a while?"

Prozac turned instantly on his paws. He skulked away, slinking under the sofa as if sending a message to express his reservations and encourage my second thoughts.

# Thirteen

*WAR AND PEACE*

Prozac

THE GIG WAS EXHAUSTING, TOTALLY draining. After piecing together tidbits about Meredith's sad life, I would have thought my mission would be clear, but it wasn't. Without my usual Spirit Guide Dog script to follow—or even a general blueprint outlining the entanglements of the Hendrix case—my mind was reeling. I couldn't make heads or tails of what my next move should be.

All I knew was that the prospect of being uprooted again and hauled off to live with a buttoned-up, white-collar guy like Hammond Cederholm was enough to keep me in seclusion, deep in the dark recesses underneath Meredith's sofa, forever. I was tired of living like a gypsy. Wasn't it bad enough that I was ousted from my cushy life with Helen, deposited at Monica's paper-piled tax office, and then forced into the custody of canine-averse, creatively blocked Meredith Mancuso-St. John?

At least Meredith was fairly pliable, give or take the fluctuating rigidity of her routines. She was meeting my needs and mostly keeping out of my hair. Her house was no palace, but it was comfy and livable.

God only knew what I'd face if I went to live with Ham. He seemed to know more about me than I knew about him. Whenever he visited Helen, which wasn't too often, he paid me little, if any, attention. That was fine by me. And what did I care about where he lived? But since it was fast becoming a possibility that I might be shipped off to room with Ham, I mentally conjured images of a swanky penthouse decorated in austere whites and blacks, clean masculine lines, and sparse decor, as in Scandinavian on steroids. A neatnik germophobe, he'd probably keep me locked like a prisoner in the bathroom or kitchen or laundry room—wherever there was a cold tile floor. But with a name like Ham, for all I knew, he might've lived in a pigsty.

Maybe his offer wasn't genuine?

I traced his presence still lingering in Meredith's townhouse—an antiseptic, hospital odor clung to the path he trod from the front door to the kitchen, along with the protracted scent of his shaving foam and aftershave. I tried to get a better read on him and his agenda. He'd made his intentions sound rather altruistic: "I'll take Prozac to spare you further imposition." The only thing I knew for certain was that Ham knew even less about dogs than Meredith. And that wasn't saying much.

In the end, I'd have no claim to my living arrangements. All I could do was cross my paws and try to decipher my fate via the one-sided telephone conversation Meredith eventually had with her sister.

"Ham seems sincere to me... He didn't have to make the offer about taking Prozac at all. Who would know if he began working from home? ... I don't believe that he's after Helen's money. He appears pretty well-off— driving a Mercedes, wearing an expensive suit and diamond cuff links... Yes, an architect... Oh, *his* firm designed the overhaul for Evergreen Gardens? ... I see... And what? They think he overcharged? ... Could that be why that judge lady referred to him as Helen's 'no-good, money-hungry nephew'? ... I don't know either, but if his firm is as prestigious as his business card indicates, I'd bet he was only the structural engineer and had nothing to do with the budget or finances... So what's the bottom line? ... Well, I could gladly live without this dog, but how many times are we going to move him around? ... Well, I know even less than you do when it comes to animals, but I get the sense this one is very sensitive..."

*OMG! Am I hearing things? Is this really Meredith talking?*

"No, I am *not* softening. But I think it might be in the best interest of Prozac if he stays put..."

*Since when does Meredith care so much about me and my feelings? Does this have to do with Judge Thea's ultimatum?*

"Yes, here, with me... No. I'm not kidding. I'll keep him for now... We'll tell Ham the truth... Then should I call him, or will you? ... No. By all means, go ahead. Make the call."

My heart rose. I bolted from under the sofa and did a little happy dance—complete with tail wagging—at Meredith's feet.

———⊸⊙⊂⌇⊃⊙⊂⊸———

A few days later, the telephone rang after dinner. Meredith, who had been pedaling on her recumbent bicycle and binge-watching Food Network, looked surprised to hear Hammond Cederholm leaving a message on the answering machine.

"I heard from your sister and wanted to say thanks for letting Prozac stay on with you. I think it's probably for the best we don't uproot him again—oh, and I also wanted to tell you that I uploaded an electronic copy of *Under the Moonlight at Ghost Ranch* to my Kindle. I'm hooked. I'm really enjoying it…"

While his flattering message recorded, Meredith hopped off the bike and rushed to the telephone. She hadn't answered the phone for *anyone* since I'd come to stay with her.

What was it about that Cederholm guy that convinced her to take the call? I'd lived with enough writers throughout the ages to know they were a self-involved bunch, and their egos could be extremely fragile. Perhaps Ham—a three-dimensional, blood and bone, living and breathing member of the opposite sex—taking the time to show an interest in Meredith, calling her and making a fuss about her life's work, was what she needed?

With phone in hand, Meredith plopped herself onto the couch—what had become *my* couch. She kicked off her shoes and tucked her legs beneath her as she coiled a stray wisp of hair behind her ear.

With a tilt of her head, she beamed and said, "Really? You liked that part?"

She ate up Ham's compliments as though she were a starved woman savoring each and every delectable bite of a big, juicy filet mignon.

At one point during their conversation, she even reached over to where I'd been resting, sprawled atop the back of the couch, and started to pet me. When I felt her touch, I thought that perhaps I'd been dreaming. But when I raised my head and saw her nail-bitten fingertips gliding through my long hair, I actually leaned into her caress, raised my paws, and offered her my light-colored belly to rub. I was astounded when she followed my lead and even massaged the sweet spots behind my ears. Our physical contact, her offering unsolicited love and affection without an audience, was unthinkable prior to Ham's call. Was she aware of her actions? Or was it some sort of reflex?

Whether Ham's interest in Meredith was sincere or not didn't matter. At least not to me, not right then. I decided to simply bask in the moment—finally, a breakthrough—as God only knew how long it would last.

After the call, Meredith was all smiles. She got up from the couch, and nibbling on her fingernail, she paced the room then walked down the hall to the closed door of her office. Her body language projected fear and trepidation as she reached for the doorknob. In real life, Meredith didn't deviate from her everyday routines and rituals. I had yet to see her enter that room in the evenings, so I was rather surprised when she disappeared inside.

I left my perch on the sofa and quietly investigated. From the doorway, I found Meredith seated in the high-back desk chair, facing me, looking like a hypnotized deer in the headlights. On the wall around her were framed prints of covers from her novels along with a few framed magazine and newspaper articles showing her book covers and her airbrushed face. The sidewall shelves sagged with an overflow of books crammed in alongside a few awards—including several tall gold statues of women in long gowns, each reading a book. Meredith was sitting at her desk, a distant, daunted look on her face as she opened a desk drawer and slapped a stack of rubber-band-fastened pages upon her desk. She fingered the edges and straightened the pile as she read aloud the first sentence on the top page: "Carolina McBride didn't know what she was really made of until the rains came and didn't let up for the next thirty-seven days."

"Not a bad start," Meredith said, bobbing her head, obviously pleased enough with her own words to boot up her computer and settle down to work in the time slot usually designated for fetch and dog chews and playtime. I gave her a pass.

That was the thing that got me about people like Meredith, humans who thought they were islands and believed they were all alone in the world. Life circumstances might have made them feel they were unable to connect with people, that their lives were in a state of perpetual limbo. But they were really not alone. It was other people, sometimes those who passed in and out of life as quickly as a waiter in a restaurant or a seemingly insignificant cashier in a grocery store—or even a well-dressed man who unexpectedly showed up on the doorstep to collect someone else's dog—who had the capacity to restore the life force. It was that simple and that understated. Small acts could become gentle nudges that had the power to plug the holes in the human psyche and fill them with a renewed sense of purpose.

Every day, from that moment forward, I silently cheered for Meredith as she rose from bed, booted up her computer, and worked at her desk for long hours. My heart swelled with joy as I listened to her fingers fly upon the computer keyboard and watched her monitor fill with an overflow of little black marks reflected in the lenses of her reading glasses. Her life once again became all about words, stringing them together to build a story that she tinkered with for hours on end. The monastery-like silence suddenly bloomed as she read sections of work aloud, and I began to hum the "Tomorrow" theme from *Annie* in my head as an accompanying soundtrack to Meredith's voice.

That renewed sense of peace in my world—and Meredith's productivity—went on for a whole week until our next scheduled visit to Evergreen Gardens. That morning, Meredith broke with her new routine and summoned, "Prozac! C'mon, buddy. We're gonna be late, and we can't tick off Judge Thea again!"

*Buddy?* I had already hunkered down, in hiding beneath the sofa, in anticipation of the day that loomed before us. The playful lilt in Meredith's voice piqued my interest, and for a moment, I considered allowing her good mood to lure me out. But I stuck with the tried and true. After all, I considered it my mission, at least for the time being, to find ways to continue to liberate Meredith from old patterns. *Might it be time to offer her another test?*

"Prozac, come out, come out, wherever you are!" she crooned.

And that time, when she lifted the skirt of the sofa and I spied her beaming, made-up face filling my line of vision, I lurched toward her and licked her cheek.

Rather than be disgusted or repulsed, Meredith simply scooped me up, clipped on my leash, double-checked to make sure she had all my credentials, and off we went.

*Wow—this lady is making real progress!*

---

By-the-Book Betsy greeted us at the front desk of Evergreen Gardens. At first sight of Meredith and me, her mouth formed a tight, straight line indicating she was less than charmed by our presence. She closed the thick book she'd been reading, peeled off her glasses, and before she even had to ask for my credentials, Meredith pulled out my business cards from Four-Legged Angels and handed them to Betsy, who aligned them like a deck of cards ready to be cut and shuffled.

"Reading anything good?" Meredith asked.

"By its very nature, all *literature* is good." Betsy put a hand atop the cover of the novel *War and Peace* as if she were swearing on a Holy Bible.

Meredith bobbed her head. "You're surely an ambitious reader."

"Entertainment shouldn't be the goal when you crack the cover of a book. There's no point investing time in something if you don't intend to learn and broaden your horizons."

"I hear you," Meredith told her, astonishingly agreeable. "But don't you think it's possible to be entertained while you learn and broaden your horizons?"

Betsy didn't look up from the desk but instead changed the subject. "Now, before you and this dog go anywhere else today, you are to proceed to the library for a meeting with Judge Thea and the board. Do I need to escort you, or will you do as you're told?"

Meredith offered a mock salute. "You have my word. To the library, we go."

<hr />

Judge Thea and four stern-faced female cohorts were indeed waiting for us, seated on one side of a long conference table in the library.

The minute Meredith and I entered the room, the judge motioned for Meredith to take a seat in the lone wooden chair facing the conference table.

Meredith sat with me on her lap. I felt her fingers pulsing with apprehension as though she were about to be interrogated by a Senate subcommittee—or face a firing squad.

Judge Thea, her nameplate prominently displayed in front of her, was flanked by two women on either side, one of whom was a rather subdued-looking Annette Mahoney.

"This meeting of the board of directors of Evergreen Gardens is now in session," the judge announced, rapping her gavel so hard that Meredith and I flinched.

"After the fiasco of last week, we feel it is imperative for us to set down an appropriate agenda and timetable for future visits. Several members of the Evergreen Gardens Board of Directors have come forward, voicing their objections that another board member was allocated one-on-one time with Prozac last week."

The judge cleared her throat, turning toward Annette Mahoney, who, facing forward and without moving her head, rolled her eyes.

"Therefore, in order to be fair and consistent, starting today," said the judge, "we put forth a new resolution to accommodate all members of this board equally. This resolution will grant each board member a specified amount of time alone with our canine emissary from the Four-Legged Angels program. All those in favor, say aye."

Everyone at the table uttered "Aye" in unison.

"All those who oppose say nay."

The library fell silent. As Judge Thea lifted her gavel, about to strike it, Meredith raised her hand. I cringed at the sight of her fingertips lurching up toward the stucco-painted ceiling.

"Excuse me," she said. "I know I'm only here as Prozac's surrogate handler, but has the board considered the other residents of Evergreen Gardens in this proposal?"

Judge Thea, displeasure scrawled on her face, sat back in her throne-like chair and firmed her arms across her chest—her gavel still in hand.

"It's... it's just that it seems unfair that only board members will get time with Prozac. How do the other residents feel about this arrangement?"

As the members of the board scrambled glances, rosy red filled Meredith's cheeks. Why was she adding her two cents? What had gotten into her?

"Residents can visit with Prozac briefly on his way in and out of the facility. The atrium lobby is our common area," Judge Thea countered. "This one-on-one arrangement will only be in effect for four weeks."

"But—"

Before Meredith could spout off her next thought, Judge Thea lifted her iPad from the table. On the silver back of the tablet, masking tape was fashioned into three big letters that only Meredith and I could read: APL.

"Was there something else you'd like to add?" Judge Thea asked.

Chastened, Meredith stared at the iPad and bit her lower lip. "No. I guess that'll be all."

"Decisions of the board are final and nonnegotiable. All those in favor, say aye."

Those at the table uttered "Aye" in unison, and Judge Thea rapped the gavel hard, putting a final period on the end of the discussion.

"Let the record reflect that all are in agreement." Judge Thea motioned toward Annette Mahoney. Leaning on her oxygen contraption, Annette rose from her chair, holding a small green plastic container in her hand.

Annette gave the container, encrusted with white stains, a good, hard shake. Then she flipped it open to reveal that inside were tiny folded slips of paper.

"Eww. I'm not putting my hand in your germ-laden denture cup," one of the women said. "That's disgusting."

"You couldn't have used a hat or paper cup or something?" another board member said.

"Take it or leave it," said Annette. The shoddiness of her method was a stark contrast to the imposed formality of the meeting.

With great reluctance, all of the board members, except Annette, drew a slip of paper from the denture cup. Each slip had a date scrawled on it—Wednesdays for the next four weeks—indicating when each board member would have her allotted time with *moi*.

Once all the dates on the slips were recorded in a ledger book by the board secretary, Judge Thea announced that Mary Chirichella of Unit 2-A would be first to have uninterrupted visiting time with Meredith and me.

A wide smile filled the wrinkly face of a stout lady, an octogenarian with tightly permed curls of blue-gray hair and pouches, like bulging suitcases, under her eyes. She wore an oversized beige cardigan over her floral-print housedress. She pulled up one of her stretched-out sleeves and looked at her watch. "C'mon. If we hurry," she said to Meredith and me, "I bet we can catch the end of *The Young and the Restless* and *Days of Our Lives*."

# Fourteen

*THE SIREN SONG OF A RAMBLER*

Prozac

"I USED TO HAVE A DOG. A little black Chihuahua mix named Suzy," Mary Chirichella told Meredith and me. She slipped the key that dangled on a string around her neck into the door lock of her unit in Evergreen Gardens. "That dog's coat was like mink. But the poor thing couldn't do stairs, and the building where I lived had this very long wooden flight. It terrified her."

Mary pushed open the door and ushered us inside. A saggy, three-piece sofa sectional was crammed into the corner of the living room. Slip-covered in a wild floral pattern, it appeared bright and colorful and suggested a freewheeling spirit that was the antithesis of the antique-looking end tables, accented with crocheted lace doilies that seemed more in line with Mary Chirichella's modest personality.

"My brothers were unmerciful, always teasing Suzy. They'd stand at the bottom of the stairs and call her. And she'd whimper and cry, wanting so much to come down but never mustering the courage. The poor thing would piddle every time."

*Serves 'em right!*

"Oh, that's terrible," Meredith said.

"Big brothers can be like that sometimes."

"I wouldn't know," Meredith told her. "I only have a big sister."

"They can be even worse."

"You'll get no argument from me there," Meredith said.

"You'll have to forgive the mess. I wasn't expecting company today."

Mary straightened up the coffee table, obscuring a *National Enquirer* and *Soap Opera Digest* beneath a *People* magazine.

As she stepped out of her flats, the arthritic curl of her toes shone through her bulky woolen ankle socks. She rooted her feet inside a pair of overstuffed yellow bunny slippers.

At first sight of them, I squirmed in Meredith's grasp and sent up a grunting yap.

Mary sniggered. "Oh, he does that every time. I don't think he likes these," she said, lifting one of the bunnies into the air. "But I swear by them. They're like walking on a cloud."

"I bet they are," Meredith said.

"How about after I get my stories and shows all set up, you join me in a batch of brownies?"

"Please, don't go to any trouble."

"No. No trouble at all," Mary said. "The mix I have is simple. Just add water. The box even serves as the baking pan. Takes only five minutes in the microwave."

"That sounds like my kind of cooking."

"Yeah, I think my mother and sister, if they were still alive, would've had a ball with all the newfangled stuff they have nowadays. Speaking of which," Mary said, reaching for her reading glasses and three iPads stacked atop the end table, "you can feel free to put Prozac down. The place is pretty doggy-proof. And please, make yourself at home."

Meredith set my paws upon a rather threadbare Oriental rug. I gave myself a thorough shaking out before casing the joint. I shivered when I spied an antique, porcelain-faced doll propped up in a wooden highchair. It freaked me out. At some point in time, the doll must've been pretty. Her yellow-blond hair was billowy, but her porcelain face was chipped and crumbling away like something out of a horror movie.

I hopped onto the sofa where Mary had plopped down and cuddled next to her. She paid me scant attention as she switched on the iPad atop the stack, tuning in to the soap opera *Days of Our Lives*. She positioned the unit atop the coffee table, giving me a pat as she reached for the next iPad and tuned that one to *As the World Turns* and set that little screen alongside the other. The character voices from the two programs overlapped, making it difficult to concentrate on only one show.

The third iPad was tuned to *The Price is Right*, where bells, whistles, cheers, and contestants' shrieks served as a soundtrack to the quiet intensity of the soap operas.

"Look at you, you're amazing with all this technology," Meredith said.

Mary's gaze remained fixed on the *Days of Our Lives* screen. She held her pointer finger to her lips and hissed, "Shhhh! Looks like Philip is going to propose."

Mary pulled me close, stroking my back. I could feel eager anticipation in her touch until the soundtrack for *Days of Our Lives* finally swelled to a dramatic crescendo and the program cut to a commercial.

"Thank heavens for my union pension and Steve Jobs sharing his genius," Mary said in follow-up to Meredith's earlier comment. "My life is so much easier with these gadgets and the app from the cable company. In my old apartment, before I moved here, I used to have three TV sets lined up on my kitchen counter. There wasn't an inch of space left. These iPads are amazing, aren't they?"

Meredith nodded. "If you wanted, I bet you could record all these shows on your DVR."

Mary's face went blank. She looked clueless.

"It's integrated right in your cable box," Meredith explained. "It's like a VCR or a DVD player, but there are no tapes or discs or anything. You just press a button and record any programs you want. Then you can watch them at your convenience."

"Oh, I can't be bothered to learn all that." Mary flapped her hands. "I'm eighty-eight years old. Why don't I just take up twerking!"

Meredith and Mary laughed, and I wagged my tail to join in the amusement. Mary might not have been familiar with DVR technology, but she was pretty hip and cutting edge with her multiple iPads and talk of sexually provocative dance moves. I had to hand it to her.

"All I'm saying is that you could watch these programs whenever you wanted—one at a time, on a real TV, with a big screen," Meredith told her. "Then you wouldn't need three iPads."

"Oh, after all these years, I'm an old pro at watching my stories play out simultaneously. You don't know how it broke my heart when *All My Children* went off the air. It completely fouled up the balance of my multitasking."

I spied the flex of Meredith's eyebrows. Even though Mary's logic didn't make much sense—even to me—at least Meredith was smart enough to let it go.

Once all the programs wrapped up, Mary shut down her iPads, reached for me, and slipped me onto my back. I let her cradle me like a baby. She tickled my belly while she shuffled us into the kitchenette and set me onto the floor so she could put on a pot of coffee. Mary whipped up the brownie mix, placed it in the microwave, and closed the door. As the cardboard baking box spun around beneath the light, Mary sliced a cucumber, cutting tiny pieces for me. She leaned down and fed me each morsel. I crunched away.

When the coffee finished brewing, Mary reached for the pot and poured herself and Meredith a cup. We all headed back to the parlor and sat down.

"That was really something, what happened with you and Annette last week," Mary said.

"It sure was." Meredith inhaled an anxiety-riddled breath as though the memory was as upsetting as the actual incident.

"The police went easy on Annette, but she was reamed out pretty good by Judge Thea in front of the board. It wasn't pretty."

"I had no idea about the protocols at Evergreen Gardens."

"Oh, Annette's a tough cookie. She's been through a lot—including an alcoholic husband who cavorted with her best friend, a woman from our own church, no less. He left Annette to raise five kids on her own. And then poor Brent, her youngest… It's a damn shame about him…"

Mary's words trailed off. She stopped herself as though paying the man homage. In my quest to lighten the mood and serve as a distraction, I lunged for her fuzzy slippers and firmed my teeth around the pink nose of the bunny, giving it a good, hard tug that even shook the bunny's ears.

"They're not real, silly!" Mary said, patting my head.

I let go and gave an affirming lick to a bit of skin on Mary's calf. She giggled like a girl. My tongue must've tickled. She tasted like Ben-Gay.

"Trust me," Mary said, hoisting the bunnies onto the edge of the coffee table, "running errands without signing out from Evergreen Gardens and getting a police warning and a slap on the wrist is small potatoes in Annette Mahoney's world."

I jumped up, trying to paw the bunny's whiskers. They were inches from reach.

Meredith asked, "Do you know how the memorial dinner for her son worked out?"

"Annette said it was wonderful—a fun night. I think it was good for her to finally honor Brent. And the Knicks won. So Annette's been bragging, telling everyone how the ball club paid for her party."

"That sounds just like Annette."

"She's got what we call the Mahoney Midas touch when it comes to gambling. You should see how she cleans up down in Atlantic City."

"Tell me, did her daughter-in-law and granddaughters attend the party?"

"No," Mary said, taking a sip of coffee. "They were no-shows. Personally, I don't know why Annette even bothered. They all said some rotten, unforgiveable things to her after Brent died."

"Yeah, well, in the heat of the moment—"

"But, c'mon. Annette was Brent's mother. It was harder for her than anyone."

"I'm sure it was hard for *all* of them."

"When you've lived as long as I have, you realize that you can't make people like you or change the way they feel. It's like banging your head against the wall."

I'd heard enough. I released an impatient bark as if to say, *Hello! Over here. Did you forget that I'm supposed to be the center of attention?*

"Listen to him," said Mary. "I think he means business."

The timer buzzed on the microwave. As Mary stood up, I flung up my snout, savoring the air bursting with the sinful aroma of hot, melting chocolate. It smelled a lot better than cucumbers!

Mary hobbled to the kitchenette, and I took a few playful pokes at the cotton tails of those slippers.

"Want your brownie à la mode?" Mary asked.

"Are you having yours that way?"

"Of course."

"Then count me in," Meredith said.

Steam rose from the tray of brownies as Mary pulled them from the microwave. "Would you be a dear and drag over those two snack tables? We'll sit by the window."

Meredith set things up in front of two comfy chairs situated by the bright light of a large picture window. Mary shuffled over with a tray that included the brownies in their shallow cardboard baking pan, a pint of ice cream, coffee, and some condiments. After she set everything down, she retrieved a chintz-covered footstool and positioned it in front of her chair. She sat and finally rested the bunnies atop the perch.

"Having you and Prozac here is a real treat for me," Mary said, plating the dessert. "And today, we've been blessed with a sunny front-row seat with Bessie."

I sat down obediently and started my begging routine.

Mary took a dainty bite of her brownie. She looked wistfully out the window toward a snug-fitting gray cover that shrouded an automobile.

"Oh, is that yours?" Meredith asked.

Mary patted her lips with a napkin. She smiled to reveal chocolate on her front teeth. "Sure is. Bessie, she's my pride and joy—a 1968 American Motors Rambler."

"Gee," Meredith said, "that car must be a classic by now."

"Yes. Underneath that cover, she looks as pretty as she did the day I drove her out of the showroom."

"Do you take a lot of drives?"

A dollop of the melting ice cream dotted Mary's lips, but it quickly disappeared as she took a sip of coffee to wash things down. "No. I don't get out much anymore," Mary said. "But Bessie keeps me good company. Always has."

Mary leaned back and reached for a framed photograph in the bookcase. As she handed it to Meredith, she wiped some dust from the glass.

"This was from the day Bessie came into my life. Back then, I worked at a fill-em lab as a splicer."

Meredith looked up from the image in the frame. "Wow, look at you— you look beautiful, like a model standing in front of that car. But tell me, what's *fill-em?*"

"*Fill-em.* Cinema. Motion pictures. I worked for a movie processing and editing company in Manhattan, back in the days of celluloid. It was a very good job, and the pay was good—especially for a single woman."

"Oh, you mean *film?*" Meredith said.

I, too, had never heard the word pronounced Mary's way. But to Mary, it seemed perfectly natural as she went on with her story.

"I first saw an ad for the Rambler in *Look* magazine. And I told myself that if I ever passed my driver's test, I'd save my money and treat myself to that car someday."

I let out a soft whimper to remind Meredith and Mary I was still there, sitting erect at their feet—waiting patiently for a taste of something.

Meredith said, "I gather you didn't ace the test on the first attempt?"

"Gosh, no," said Mary. "Parallel parking always did me in. Took me nine tries until I finally passed. They actually got to know me by name down at the DMV."

Mary's laugh gave Meredith license to show her own amusement. I loved how Meredith's whole demeanor changed, how she lit up, when she gave a broad smile and revealed her teeth. And it was just like the writer in Meredith to be truly engaged and interested in Mary's story. She asked, "After the third or fourth try, or even the seventh or eighth, you never thought about giving up?"

"Oh sure, I did. I mean, we lived and worked in the city. We had public transportation for everything. But I've never been a quitter, wasn't raised that way. When I flunked the test the first time, I knew I'd have to see things through until I finally passed. And the ironic thing was my nieces and nephews were growing older and getting driver's licenses of their own, while I kept flunking. It was the running family joke that with a whole lot of practice and a ton of God's grace, I'd pass the test and get my own license before I died."

"And you made it—good for you!" Meredith studied the photograph. When she finally set the frame down on the snack table, alongside the brownie tray and the ice cream container, I eyed the picture, too. Mary Chirichella looked much thinner and youthful. She was wearing her Sunday best, complete with white gloves, glowing with pride. Mary was probably in her thirties. A hobo-style pocketbook was clenched in her arm, and a sleek black Chihuahua—a real beauty, a hot little number—was tethered to a leash and stood in front of Mary's open-toed shoes on the city sidewalk. Mary's vibrant pastel-pink jacket and matching squared-off hat conjured the colorful spirit of the 1960s, especially as she leaned against that shiny white Rambler with sparkling chrome handles, side mirrors, and bumpers.

"They sure don't make cars like that anymore," said Meredith.

"You can say that again." Mary reached for the picture and eyed it longingly. "Yessirree. My Middle-Class Mercedes, that's what they called it.

A lot of memories attached to that car. It's lasted a lot longer than most of the people I've loved in this life."

The sense of Mary's loss was palpable in her words and expression. But so, too, was the gratitude she exuded. The combination made my heart wince.

"How do you do with parallel parking these days?"

"Oh, I don't drive. Stopped the day I drove Bessie off the dealer's lot." Mary said that as though it were perfectly rational. "Sitting behind the wheel always made me carsick. And Dramamine upsets my tummy."

"That's too bad." Meredith appeared perplexed while continuing to listen attentively.

"Hey, I achieved what I set out to do—I got my license and adopted Bessie. It's nice to be able to sit here and have her nearby."

Meredith nodded. Her lack of response encouraged Mary to continue.

"And the thing is, I feel as though I've gotten the best of all worlds. Bessie was my motivation to accomplish something, and she's always made sure I was never alone. Whenever one of the relatives asked, I let them drive her, and often, they wound up chauffeuring me around. So I became a proud passenger, and I always appreciated the company."

Meredith sat back and grinned in a way that was surprisingly void of judgment. It seemed as though Mary, forthright and uninhibited in sharing her story, set Meredith at ease. And in comparison, Meredith's own quirks, ticks, and insecurities didn't seem so unusual.

"Would you like another brownie?" Mary asked Meredith.

"Sure, why not."

I liked the carefree, easygoing banter between those two—kindred spirits. And I liked being there even better once Mary dabbed the tip of her finger into a bit of ice cream that had melted onto her plate. When she reached down and offered a lick, I lapped it up, anxious for more.

# Fifteen

*WHEN BAD BECOMES WORSE*

Meredith

THE TWO HOURS PROZAC AND I spent with Mary Chirichella went much quicker than I had anticipated. And the coffee and brownies à la mode were delicious.

During our time together, Prozac snuggled on Mary's lap. She stroked him lovingly until he nodded off, his paws twitching as though he were being chased somewhere in his dreams. While he slept, Mary and I chatted more about her beloved Bessie until we ultimately moved on to reading and books. She was an ardent fan of my Ghost Ranch novels and was eager to learn more about the next installment. I told her about the new story, *Shelter from the Rain at Ghost Ranch,* and how it focused on my recurrent protagonist, Carolina McBride, a young, ambitious painter in a serious relationship with Hazzard Braggs, a handsome, flighty cowboy she'd been on a quest to land throughout the series. As we sipped coffee and polished off that cardboard pan of brownies, I hinted at the plot of the next story set in Old West-era New Mexico. I didn't have the courage to tell her that I was overdue on my deadline, only beginning, really, to chip away at the story. When I asked Mary where she, as a reader, would like the story to go, she surprised me by saying, "To want something is a greater challenge than to have it. Case in point, my Bessie. Your heroine seems torn between living the life of an artist and having love in her life. But sometimes a passionate love affair that dies can be more dramatic."

"You mean have Carolina and Hazzard split up? Already?"

"Yeah, it happens all the time—on TV and in real life," Mary said, enthusiasm escalating with her every word. "And maybe the pain of Carolina losing someone she loves is what she needs to become a great artist. Sometimes grief and sorrow need to be borne, not just gotten over. Maybe that's the case for Carolina. Perhaps integrating that loss into her life is more important than a long-term romantic relationship at this point."

<hr />

For days after the visit to Evergreen Gardens, I mulled over Mary's suggestion—intrigued but not sure how, or if, I could make it work. After all, the Ghost Ranch series was a romance, and while complications were the norm, the rules were dictated by Happily-Ever-After.

I rolled up my sleeves and began to hack my way through my novel, honing the storyline and drawing parallels between what Mary said and my own life. *Maybe I should tap into my own grief about Kyle to more fully shape the narrative?*

For the next week—sometimes seventeen hours a day—I plowed through the story, following the thread of lost love and channeling my own emotions into the characters. By confronting my feelings about Kyle and our separation—by remembering the past and the present—and wrestling all that down onto the page, I felt liberated. It was cathartic to resurrect and purge some of the angst I'd tamped down inside myself—to give it form and shape and meaning.

Momentum built. The pages piled up, and on a roll with the novel, I neglected my domestic duties—shopping, showering, doing laundry, washing dishes, sorting through mail, tidying up. I muted my cell phone and shut off the answering machine and even the ringer on my landline. I was aiming for a distraction-free life, with nothing to break my concentration until I was forced to come up for air to feed Prozac and take him for another visit to Evergreen Gardens a week later.

The night before our next therapy dog appointment, I worked late. Bleary-eyed at two in the morning, I crawled beneath my covers and set my alarm for six o'clock, intending to write a few pages before we had to leave. But when I opened my eyes to light edging around the curtains and spied the day-glow green numbers on my clock reading 10:32 a.m., I bolted upright in bed.

Prozac, who'd obviously taken advantage of my exhaustion, leaped off the pillow beside me. He made a fast break off the bed and fled from the room to escape my wrath. But I was too tired to go there.

I must've needed the sleep, but it forced me to leave in record time. I quickly dressed and ripped my coat and scarf from the foyer closet, slipped them on, and slammed the closet door. Then I grabbed Prozac's credentials and therapy dog bandanna and hurried down the hall. I flung open the door leading into the garage, and by the time I slipped the key into the car ignition, I suddenly realized I was leaving without Evergreen Gardens' beloved mascot.

"Prozac!" I hollered, faux cheerfulness filling my voice as I charged back into the house. "Prozac, come on, mister!"

When I stepped into the living room, I noticed how, in my weeklong frenzy of writing, things had piled up. Papers, magazines, books, and junk mail lay scattered on tables. Balled jumbles of clean laundry in need of folding filled the sofa and chairs. I scanned the mess, hoping to find Prozac in his usual hangout—nestled atop the sofa. But alas, he wasn't there. What was it with that dog? He loved people—and they loved him back, especially the folks at Evergreen Gardens. Why, then, did he keep showing agoraphobic tendencies when faced with the prospect of leaving the house?

My futile calls for Prozac went on for several minutes. That dog was trying my patience. Being nice and honey-tongued lasted only so long. I made a sweep of the room and checked to see if he was cuddled in front of the heat vent or beneath the coffee or end tables. I finally got down on all fours in front of the sofa but saw only darkness beneath the skirt. No inkblot of fur or beady little eyes. Harnessing my adrenaline, I instinctively tried to lift the couch. It was so heavy that it toppled backward, taking with it a pile of laundry, an end table overburdened with books and magazines, and two ceramic lamps, which shattered upon impact.

"Dammit, Prozac! Where are you?" My voice projected louder than I'd expected. "C'mon, we don't have time for this!"

Then the doorbell rang.

I froze, breathing heavily, my heart pounding. I was stunned by the eerie sound of silence, as well as the mess I'd made of the living room.

The doorbell rang a second time. I lurched to my feet, heading through the foyer. When I pressed my eye to the peephole, I gasped when I was met with the concave, distorted images of two uniformed police officers.

*OMG! Did someone hear my tirade and call the cops?*

I ripped my face away from the door. I took a deep breath, ran my fingers through my hair, and straightened my coat.

The dead bolt disengaged with a *thunk,* the door sweeping open against the floor mat and releasing a swishy sound.

Two officers stood before me. Their faces were shrouded by the shadows created from the glossy visor brims of their eight-pointed police hats.

"Meredith Mancuso?" The sound of my name was muffled by the glass storm door.

"Yes." I swallowed hard, my heart pumping wildly.

"I'm Corporal Relin, and this is Patrolman Mathis," said a male voice. "We're from the Oak Park Police Department. We've been calling, trying to reach you for days."

*Oh no! My phone. I turned off the ringer and the answering machine, didn't I?*

"May we come in?" the officers asked.

"Why? What happened?" My hot breath fogged the cold glass.

"We're here about an incident involving a car," said the front officer, the corporal with well-tended sideburns. "A 1968 American Motors Rambler."

The second cop, a shorter one standing behind the corporal, said, "There's some speculation it might've gone missing from Evergreen Gardens. Would you know anything about this?"

"No," I hissed, answering quickly. My heart knocked against my sternum. The familiarity of that word, *Rambler,* vibrated through the air.

"Listen," the shorter cop said, stepping forward and offering more compassion. "Why don't you let us in, and we'll talk, okay?" When I heard the voice and spotted red-raspberry lipstick and rouge on the officer's face, I realized Patrolman Mathis was a woman.

"But I'm on my way out," I said. "I'm actually about to leave for Evergreen Gardens."

"It won't take long."

I opened the door and let in the two cops. Their eyes widened upon seeing the mess in the living room—the laundry everywhere, the toppled-over sofa and shattered lamps.

"Is everything all right in here?" Corporal Relin asked.

I laughed, a nervous release. "It's nothing. Just a time management problem."

"It doesn't look like *nothing.* Did someone ransack this place?"

As those words were floating out of the policewoman's mouth, a dull, crying whimper sounded. Our heads swiveled in the direction of the closed foyer closet where I heard a rustling, scratching sound and the rattle of door hinges.

"Oh my goodness," I said, breaking out in a clammy sweat. "When I opened the front door, I must've locked the dog in there."

The two cops exchanged concerned, suspicious glances. I quickly flung open the closet door. Light spilled inside and illuminated Prozac, who was crouched—quivering, ears back—next to the vacuum cleaner.

"What are you doing? Why are you in here?" I asked Prozac, feeling my embarrassment manifest as a flush of warmth in my cheeks.

The minute he saw me, the dog trotted out, making a beeline for the police officers. With his tail wagging, he acted as though he were eternally grateful to them for showing up to his rescue.

*Great! As if my screams and the shambles of the living room aren't bad enough. Now I'm going to look like some kind of dog abuser who locks her pooch in the closet. What else?*

"Oh, your poor little dog," the patrolwoman said, resting her hand atop Prozac's head as if bestowing a blessing.

"No. He's not mine. Well, what I mean is, I'm taking care of him for this lady who broke her foot. He's a therapy dog—visits Evergreen Gardens once a week. That's where we're headed."

Prozac rolled onto his back. He was basking in the moment, as the cops were generous with belly rubs. It was amazing how that dog had shed his whole agoraphobic act since those two had arrived.

"You said you were on your way to Evergreen Gardens. Since we're headed over there, why don't we drive you?" The corporal looked to his sidekick for affirmation.

"No, that's okay," I replied. "The dog and I are going to stay for a few hours."

"Then we'll follow you there," the patrolwoman said. "It might be more helpful if you answer our questions right at the facility anyway."

The way they were pressing, it was clear I didn't have a choice.

<hr />

I turned the car key, and all I heard was a click—nothing else, no purr of the engine.

"Please tell me this isn't happening!" I tried to turn the car over, again and again, but each time produced the same result.

With the squad car idling in the driveway and the officers waiting for my Toyota to slip from the garage, I hopped out to explain my delay.

As the corporal was checking under the hood—diagnosing the problem as the battery, not the alternator—my smartphone chimed.

Judge Thea had texted. *FYI: Your repeated tardiness is not boding well!*

"Oh, great!" I sighed aloud.

"What's wrong?" the policewoman asked.

"Prozac and I are dreadfully late. And the woman who coordinates the therapy dog visits at Evergreen Gardens is not happy about it."

The officers offered to chauffer Prozac and me to Evergreen Gardens, and I took them up on it.

"I guess I can call Triple A later," I said. "The thing is, I don't know how I'll get home."

"Not a problem. One of us can swing back for you," the corporal assured me.

⤍•◦⟠◦•⤏

Prozac sat up front in the police car, cradled on the lap of Officer Mathis, who was deeply under his spell. She had suggested that it would probably be more comfortable for me if the dog rode with her. It soon became clear that was a pretext, as Officer Mathis mauled Prozac with unabashed hugs and kisses. At one point, Prozac broke away from their lovefest. He leaped up and rested his paws atop her shoulder to gaze at me in the backseat. With his teeth parted to accommodate his panting and lax tongue, he seemed to be smiling as if laughing and enjoying every minute of seeing me cooped up and uncomfortable.

The backseat had little room, and I felt as if I were sitting upright in a Lucite and steel coffin. And just my luck, Carlos the mail carrier was approaching the townhouse as the squad car pulled away. Seeing me, he did a double take. I ducked, conjuring all the new rumors he would be spreading about me throughout the neighborhood: *That weird, reclusive author who lives at 22 Rosebush Lane and parades around in the nude... I think she got busted.*

I'd never been inside a police car before, and during the drive to Evergreen Gardens, I prayed I'd never be in one again. The images I'd seen on TV and in the movies gave no indication things were so crowded and close back there. The air supply even felt limited, as the seat was partitioned off with what looked like thick soundproof glass—probably bulletproof—and that made things incredibly quiet and confining, leaving my knees butted up against the front seat. Thank heavens I wasn't claustrophobic or a career criminal!

As the corporal drove, he turned on the intercom system, and through a rather lengthy back and forth Q and A, I told the story about Helen Hendrix and my sister, how Prozac came into my care, and how I was trying to keep his therapy dog appointments at Evergreen Gardens.

They asked me a few more questions, and in my nervousness, I talked too much, my voice stilted, as I said more than necessary. Maybe it was from overwork, exhaustion, and isolation, but I couldn't seem to stop babbling. Eventually, we circled back to the reason the police had tracked me down. It seemed that Mary Chirichella's car, her vintage 1968 American Motors Rambler, wasn't actually missing, but Mary had called the police station in a panic. She claimed her car had been moved—parked in the wrong spot in front of her unit. The officers had questioned the residents. And after learning about my visit with Mary, they wanted me to confirm Mary's accusation.

"I'll help in any way I can," I said.

---

Judge Thea was waiting for us outside, pacing in front of Evergreen Gardens.

"This is a sickness with you," she said, looking at me while pointing at her wristwatch. She didn't seem to notice that Prozac and I were just let out of a police car. She walked straight past me and approached the policewoman, who seemed reluctant to give up the dog.

"He has a very tight schedule to keep," Judge Thea told her. "I need to make sure he gets to his people... his weekly appointment."

A brief tug-of-war ensued until Officer Mathis finally released Prozac into the judge's custody.

"And you," the judge said, looking at me, "do what you have to do, and when you're finished, stop in and see me in the library."

———————◦◦◦———————

With Prozac led away, the officers and I proceeded to Mary Chirichella's apartment. When she opened the door, she was bundled in a sweater. Worry and concern creased her face.

She led us to the big picture window that overlooked the Evergreen Gardens parking lot.

"Now Ms. Mancuso, can you tell us if the covered vehicle has been moved?" the corporal asked.

"I don't know," I said, staring outside. "I don't remember which space the car was parked in. It might've been parked right where it is, or maybe it could've been in one of the spots on either side."

"Were any other cars parked near the vehicle the other day?" the corporal asked.

"I can't recall. It was a whole week ago."

Exasperation filled Mary's tone. "What do you mean you can't recall? The two of us sat together in front of the window staring at Bessie for almost two hours."

I moved closer to the glass, placing my hand upon the windowpane. I so wanted to validate Mary's story, but all I could visualize was the gray tarp-like cover shrouding what looked like a boxy car. I turned and looked from Mary to the officers. "I honestly can't remember, not for sure. I was concentrating more on our chat. I'm sorry, Mary."

The two officers glanced at each other, indicating they didn't put much credence in Mary's accusation—especially since I'd been unable to corroborate her story.

"Keep an eye on things, Miss Chirichella. If you see anything else suspicious, call us again." The corporal handed Mary a business card embossed with a police badge symbol.

Mary took the card then turned to me. Her eyes seemed ready to explode with tears.

"I'm sorry. I really am. I wish I could help," I told Mary as the police escorted me from her apartment.

———⊶o⊙⊂⊙o⊰———

"Well, well, well," Judge Thea said when I stepped into the library. "It must get awfully exhausting for you, stirring up chaos wherever you go."

I held up my hands. "I didn't plan things this way. Believe me."

"The police seem to be regulars around here since Prozac's been assigned to you."

I inhaled a breath that squared my shoulders. What could I say? I swiveled, searching the sofa and chairs and bookcases, looking for Prozac. There was no sign of him, and it appeared as though the judge had the library all to herself.

"He's not here," she said. "Two board members, Lucille Graves and Stella Stanislowski, have agreed to share their visit with Prozac today. They're holding Scrabble Club in Apartment 3-D. It's normally good clean fun. No police involvement. And we're aiming to keep things that way."

# Sixteen

## DISS OR DAT

### Meredith

A PRETTY WREATH WOVEN WITH DRIED purple flowers hung on the door of Apartment 3-D, where music and laughter spilled into the hallway. When was Scrabble ever really *that* much fun?

I raised then dropped the door knocker, waiting for someone to answer. When no one did, I tried again. I finally resorted to pounding my fist upon the door. The laughter quelled. The music switched off. I leaned in closer to the flowers and was met by a hiss of whispers.

"What's the password?" said a muffled male voice from the other side.

I double-checked the unit number: 3-D. I was in the right place. As I stared straight into the peephole set in the door like a bull's-eye in the center of that wreath, I whispered back, "I don't know the password."

Commotion and voices mumbled, and then I heard a woman's voice say, "It's okay. It's that writer lady—she's watching Prozac. Let her in."

*Great. The dog has to vouch for me.*

The door opened. A fragrant wave of Old Spice hit me as I was greeted by a tall, well-groomed gentleman with a shock of white hair. He was probably in his mid-eighties, wearing faded jeans and a gray button-down shirt that made his yellow tie and matching suspenders pop like a blaze of sunshine on a cloudy day. Bright-eyed Prozac filled his arms.

"Are you the author?" he asked.

I nodded. "Yes. That's me."

"Jack," he said, balancing Prozac in his one arm while offering me his free hand. "You're just in time." He turned and led me into the apartment, which smelled like cooked bacon. "You're the perfect person to help us."

"With what?"

Two people were seated at the dining room table: a bald man chewing on an unlit cigar and a rather short, stout woman with a helmet of salt-and-pepper hair. She was wearing large, sturdy-framed, '70s-style tortoiseshell glasses. Four sweaty cocktail tumblers surrounded a Scrabble board.

"Is *diss* a word?" Jack asked me.

"Diss?" I repeated.

"And is it spelled with one *S* or two?" a woman's voice chimed in from the kitchen. I turned toward the galley space and found a spry, petite lady with wrinkly skin—a sun-worshipper from way back when—and a tuft of dyed-brown hair. She was dressed in what appeared to be a tennis skirt outfit. Her sun-spotted legs looked frail and spindly, as though they might snap. With red oven mitts shaped like lobster claws on her hands, she removed a piping hot tray of bacon-wrapped scallops from the toaster oven.

"You're right on time for the last round of appetizers," the woman said, holding the sizzling hot plate toward me. "I'm Lucille Graves. Folks call me Lucy. We met at the board meeting with Judge Thea last week—"

"Yes, I remember," I replied, quickly placing her face. "Nice to see you again."

Jack said, "I understand Judge Thea has been giving you a hard time." Prozac trailed Jack's hand as the man reached past me. He grabbed one of the scallop hors d'oeuvres from the hot plate and fearlessly popped it into his mouth.

Lucy slapped his hand. Prozac jumped. "Jack, honestly! Where are your manners?"

"Forgive me, my lady," said Jack, chomping away on the appetizer while bowing in the woman's direction.

Lucy lifted the hot tray toward me, a bit too close for comfort, so I eased back. I daintily lifted one of the trussed-up scallops by the toothpick skewer. Before I indulged, I blew on it to cool it off. It looked familiar.

"Did you get this recipe from Ina Garten on *The Barefoot Contessa*?" I asked.

"Yes." Lucille burst into a big smile. "You watch her show?"

"All the time," I told her, savoring the bite. "Delicious."

"The soft, tender scallop is a nice contrast to the salty bite of the bacon, isn't it?"

I nodded. "Spoken like a true Ina Garten devotee."

I followed Lucy and Jack as they paraded into the dining room. Lucy announced, "Stella and Stan, this is Meredith, the famous author who's taking care of Prozac."

I nodded at Stan and also at Stella, who slid her thick glasses down her nose to get a better look at me. That was when I realized that I'd also met Stella at the board meeting the week before.

"I'm hardly famous," I told them.

"Like hell you're not. You're the talk of Evergreen Gardens," Stella said, her voice gruff.

"Yeah, and it's like we've got our own live episodes of *Law and Order* playing out around here whenever you and Prozac show up," Stan said.

Everyone got a kick out of his comment, including me. I countered, "I have the right to remain silent."

"What happened with Mary?" Jack said, sitting down at the table. Prozac swiveled his snout in the direction of those hors d'oeuvres. "Has the mystery about her Rambler been solved?"

"I tell you, that broad is losing it," Stan said, removing the cigar from his mouth long enough to pop in a scallop.

"Anyone who's having a love affair from afar with her car probably lost it a long time ago," Jack said. "What's the point of owning a vehicle if you're not going to drive it? It's amazing that thing's not a rust bucket by now."

Lucy reached for a potato chip. As she was about to dip it into a bowl of what looked like whipped chocolate mousse, Stella stopped her.

"Oops, thataway, honey." Stella navigated Lucy's hand toward a bowl of salsa.

"That car only looks as good as it does because Mary keeps it detailed and covered," Jack added.

"What's the point?" Stan said.

"Will you two stop!" Lucy slipped the chip into her mouth and crunched. "It's Mary's thing. Her hobby. Stan, what's the point of your worshipping those Cuban cigars of yours like a dog with a bone?"

Prozac raised his ears at the mention of a bone, his pink tongue peeping anxiously into view, while Stan shrugged, not offering a rebuttal.

Stella elbowed Lucy, shooting her a fiendish grin. "By the way, have you seen the new fella who's been tending to Mary's Rambler lately? He's sure easy on the eyes."

"Not on my eyes—not with this damn macular degeneration!" Lucy said.

"Believe me, Lucy," Stella said, "that hottie would clear up anyone's blurred vision."

Jack leaned my way and whispered, "These two, they're such cougars."

I didn't have the heart to tell him that Lucy and Stella were probably well past that stage.

Stan said, "You know, I asked to borrow Mary's car one day, and she acted like I was propositioning her or something."

"Yikes," Jack said. "Who would proposition *her*? That scowling prune face of hers."

The two guys roared with laughter, and Lucy said, "Leave poor Mary alone."

*Go, Lucy!*

"Don't get in a tizzy, Luce," said Jack. "We're just having some fun."

"Well, Mary's not hurting anyone. So cut her some slack." Lucy reached for her tumbler and sucked up the last drops of her drink. Then she hit Stan in the arm and held out her glass, signaling that she wanted a refill. "And while you're at it, whip one up for Meredith, too."

"No. No. That's okay," I said.

Stan—a rotund little man—rose to his feet. He leaned heavily on the dining room table to support the snap, crackle, and pop of his weary knees. The Scrabble board and tiles shimmied beneath his weight. Hairy legs bloomed from his trouser-like Bermuda shorts as he tottered away.

Stella turned to me. "You're young," she said. "When you get to be our age, it's important to find your joys however and wherever you can. Mary loves her stories and her car. I'm in love with the theater and Broadway show tunes. Lucille loves potato chips, piña coladas, and cooking. Stan is gaga for his cigars and playing bocce. And Jack here, well, he loves to play the ukulele and to bust chops."

"What's your joy, Meredith?" Lucy asked, an eager gleam in her eye.

"Hey, wait a second," Jack cut in. "Did you just *diss* me, Stella?"

From the kitchen, the blender sounded a loud whir.

"Speaking of *diss*," Stella said. "What's the verdict? Is it a word or not?"

Stan returned with Lucy's refill and a drink for me. As he settled into his seat, Stella turned and asked, "Meredith, what's your feeling on *diss?*"

I shrugged and said, "It's probably considered urban slang."

The two guys looked at each other, encouraged by my response.

"But it's not a dictionary word, is it, Meredith?" Stella asked.

"It probably depends on what dictionary you use," I said, trying to skirt further involvement.

From her chair at the table, Stella reached for a well-worn, paperback Merriam-Webster stuffed in the china cabinet. As she thumbed through the pages, her eyes looked magnified behind her eyeglass lenses.

I reached for my drink and sucked a gulp of something thick, cold, and creamy through my straw. My brain practically froze as I was more than a little surprised to find the flavors of coconut and booze—a piña colada spiked generously with rum.

"Nope. No *diss* in here," Stella said, setting down the dictionary.

"Then that's it. Stan and I are out." Jack sounded disappointed. He moved Prozac, mid-yawn, from his lap over to Stella's. After Jack was free of the dog, he said, "But don't rest on your laurels, ladies. Stan and I will squash the two of you next week."

"Keep dreaming," said Lucy. She and Stella began removing letter tiles from the board and packing things up.

"If we're done here, we ought to go and finalize the pool for the Mets-Yankees exhibition game tonight," Jack said to Stan, the two rising to leave.

"Who are you taking?" Lucy asked Stella.

"I've got practically half my Social Security check on the Yankees. How about you?"

"I want the Brooklyn Dodgers," Lucy said.

Stan said, "Lucy, you're dating yourself."

"I would bet on whoever Annette Mahoney picks," added Jack. "She's on a winning streak."

I could hardly keep up with the quick-witted, sharp banter of the foursome.

"On your way out, fellas, would you mind switching on the CD player?" Stella asked.

A musical overture blasted from the boom box, and the two guys burst out singing off-key lyrics to the "Tomorrow" song from the musical *Annie*.

At their crooning, Prozac's ears perked. He stirred in Stella's lap and jumped to the floor. Prancing around with glee, he reared up on his hind legs, paws swaying, as though tap-dancing an old soft-shoe. He let out a few short yaps before flipping his snout to the ceiling and releasing a long, low howl as if trying to join in the chorus.

Jack belly-laughed. "Get a load of him. Sounds like a hound dog."

"No," said Stan, "that's the sound of a man as tortured as we are by Stella's show tune fetish."

"He doesn't sound tortured to me," Lucy said, using her straw in an attempt to spear the maraschino cherry from the bottom of her piña colada glass.

"Don't make fun," said Stella. "The revival is opening on Broadway in a year or two—"

"Again?" said Stan. "How many times are they gonna rehash that one?"

Stella flung her nose in the air and, with forced haughty drama, said, "Truly great theater never goes out of style."

"But we wouldn't know *good* theater. Would we, Stan?" Jack carried the CD remote control over to Stella at the dining room table as he and Stan readied to leave. "After all, we're only a couple of philistines."

Stella said, "Wow! Nice to see how playing Scrabble is increasing your vocabularies."

"Don't forget, Jack, it's your turn to bring the cream of coconut next week," Lucy shouted above the loud musical overture.

"On it," Jack said. "But what happened to Glo's son? Wasn't he supposed to drop us off another half gallon of rum?"

"Yes, David's due to stop over later to pick up Glo's mail," said Stella. "He's been with her all day at the hospital."

"How's she doing, anyway?" asked Stan.

"I don't know. David's not saying much."

"We'll work him over for details later," Lucy said.

Jack marched into Lucy's galley kitchen and paraded back to the dining room, setting an empty half-gallon bottle of Bacardi rum in front of her. "Well, he better not forget us. Our well has run dry."

Jack and Stan left. Prozac's tail wagged like a metronome swinging to the tempo of the *Annie* overture. Stella, Lucy, and I sat at the table, nibbling on the remaining appetizers.

"I suspect there's more to the story than David's letting on. The doctors took out Glo's gallbladder three weeks ago. She shouldn't still be in the hospital," Lucy said, looking at Stella, who nodded in agreement.

"Well, she's fought cancer a couple of times, and she *is* eighty-six," Stella said. "But don't be a fatalist. Sometimes, at our age, it takes a little longer to recover from these things."

"Or maybe David's like my daughter—in denial and not facing reality."

"Don't say that. David is very devoted to Glo. And your Jean, she's a good daughter."

"How *good* is she that I'm gonna have to take a cab to Philly next week to the eye institute?" Lucy turned to me and said, "My daughter doesn't care if I'm going blind—"

"Luce, Jean will come through. Give her time." Stella looked to me and explained, "She's probably trying to adjust her work schedule."

"Wanna bet?" said Lucy.

I kept out of the conversation, listening and taking it all in—Lucy's obvious disappointment and lack of faith in her daughter, and Stella making excuses for Jean.

*Oh, I hope I die before I grow old!*

It came as a relief when the doorbell rang. Prozac hopped around our feet, obviously excited by the prospect of another visitor. Lucy popped a grape into her mouth. "I bet that's David," she said as she rose from the table and hurried to answer the door.

Stella reached for the remote control and lowered the volume of the boom box. In the hush of the apartment, we heard a woman's voice say, "I'm sorry to interrupt, but Judge Thea said I might find Meredith here. I need to speak with her for a moment."

Mary Chirichella stepped in, still wearing that ratty old cardigan. Her face was laced with concern. Prozac, ever the welcoming committee, ran right over to her, threw himself down at her feet, and offered his belly for a rub, but Mary wanted no part of him. Stella and Lucy exchanged glances.

"Is everything all right, Mary?" Lucy asked.

Mary eyed the cocktail glasses, her eyes shifting to the empty bottle of rum. "Is that alcohol?"

"Why don't you sit down? Join us." Lucy scooted out a chair and patted the seat.

"Alcohol isn't allowed on the premises." Mary's back was stiff, her tone accusatory.

Stella said, "Meredith here wasn't aware that Prohibition is still in effect at Evergreen Gardens."

"What?" I cried, my voice leaping above Stella's. I raised my right hand. "I don't have anything to do with alcohol being on-site in this apartment."

"It's okay, Meredith. It's an honest mistake. Anyone could've made it." Lucy put a reassuring hand upon my arm. "Don't worry. Nobody is going to hold you accountable—"

I ripped my arm away from Lucy's touch. "They better not!"

Mary narrowed her gaze on me. I couldn't believe Stella and Lucy were throwing me under the bus like that.

Mary said, "Judge Thea isn't going to like this. Not one bit."

"Oh, c'mon," Lucy said. "You don't need to tell the judge anything, Mary—"

"But you've broken the rules."

"Well, if you want to be *that* way, consider this," said Stella. "It'll be our word against yours—three against one. And ever since you dragged the police all the way over here this morning, your word's not looking all that credible."

Mary opened her mouth and gasped. She turned on her heels and stormed away.

Lucy's words chased after Mary. "What did you want to talk to Meredith about anyway?"

Mary answered by slamming the apartment door closed.

I hauled up Prozac from the floor and said, "Thanks a lot, you guys. You've put me in even deeper hot water with the judge."

"Don't worry. Mary won't say anything," Lucy said. "We'll talk to her."

I rose from the table, carrying Prozac, knowing we ought to get out of that place fast, before all hell broke loose—again.

# Seventeen

## Meredith

THE SMALL, ANTIQUATED ELEVATOR MOVED at a snail's pace. I stared at the numbers on the overhead panel, watching them decrease. When the elevator shimmied to a stop on the second floor, a tall, thin guy—fortyish—opened the elevator door and gate and stepped inside. He rolled a suitcase in one hand while he pressed a bulky grocery bag against his chest. I had to back up against the wall to accommodate him, and feeling all crammed in, I found Prozac growing heavy in my arms.

"I'm sorry," the guy said. "I've got a ton of stuff."

"Yes, I can see." I stared at the guy's wavy, gray-streaked hair and his wild, short-sleeved, Hawaiian-print shirt. Summer and winter seemed to have collided between the bright, flashy colors of turquoise and yellow that were layered over a long-sleeved beige sweatshirt and a pair of well-worn jeans. He looked like a walking schizoid weather report.

With the elevator door and gate once again closed, I stared up at the floor numbers, praying that the light marked "L" for the lobby would soon light up. But instead the elevator lunged and bucked. It stopped abruptly.

"Uh-oh," I said. "Please tell me what I think is happening isn't happening."

"I wish I could," the guy said, pressing buttons on the elevator keypad while eyeing the darkened lights for the three floors above the door.

"We've gotta get this thing moving. I can't stay in here." My voice held an edge much sharper than the one I normally used in front of strangers.

"Are you claustrophobic or something?"

"No. Not that I know of. I just have an intense aversion to Evergreen Gardens."

"I'm sorry to hear that, but stay calm. This elevator is old and temperamental—like a lot of the people in this place. But it's harmless. I've been stuck in here before."

"Oh no. For how long?"

The guy kept pressing elevator buttons. "I don't think you really want to know the answer to that question."

"Please tell me you're kidding."

"Look," he said, "I'm a magician, not a comedian."

"Literally? You're *literally* a magician?"

He nodded.

"Then can't you wave a magic wand and get us out of here?"

The guy offered a bashful grin. "I wish it were that easy. Magic isn't about miracles. It's all about mystery and illusion—toying with the limits of perception. So maybe you ought to change your outlook about being stuck in here."

"I can't. I'm a dyed-in-the-wool realist—and a skeptic."

"A bit of skepticism is always healthy," he said, pushing the red alarm button on the wall panel. When no bells or whistles sounded, the quiet indicated that the alarm, along with the elevator, was broken. When the magician finally whipped out his smartphone and said, "I'm not getting a signal. You mind trying yours?" my suspicion was confirmed.

I set Prozac on the floor. That dog obviously couldn't have cared less about the elevator being stuck or my siege of panic. With a wagging tail, he wove his tidy, compact body around the magician's grocery bag and suitcase as though they were a maze and the prize at the end would be the eager affection of the less-than-miffed stranger.

"Hey there, little fella," the guy said, squatting down and scratching Prozac behind the ears. The dog luxuriated in the human contact so thoroughly that he managed to carve out enough space to roll onto his back and offer his belly for a rub.

Amusement filled the magician's expressive face. "Oh, if only we could all be so uninhibited, right?"

When I wasn't able to get a signal on my smartphone, I interrupted the mutual admiration society and said, "My phone's dead, too."

"All right. Then we'll have to wait it out. They'll find us soon enough."

I let out a long, frustrated sigh. Exhausted and tired—emotionally and physically—I flung back my neck and scanned the ceiling for a hatch or a door, like in books and movies. But the ceiling seemed in one piece. There were no cutouts or trapdoors that appeared to offer a means of escape.

"Do you think the cable will snap?" I asked. "And if we're going to be stuck here a while, will there be enough air for all of us?"

The magician turned from Prozac and grimaced. "You know, for a self-proclaimed dyed-in-the-wool realist, you've got a pretty vivid imagination."

I felt slightly taken aback. "I'm just asking—hypothetically."

"Think of it this way. If the cable snaps, we're only going to fall two floors. At least our bodies won't be beyond recognition for the medics or coroner—"

"That's reassuring!"

"And in terms of suffocating—"

"Forget it." I put up my hands to stop him. "I don't want to know."

"Oh, I see," the magician said, bobbing his head with intrigue. "You don't believe in magic or miracles, but you're all for suspense?"

"Yes. In some instances, ignorance can be bliss."

"Then let's look on the bright side. Evergreen Gardens has about thirty or forty residents. Nobody takes the stairs. Someone will eventually call for the elevator, and when they realize it's not coming, they'll find us. Trust me." The magician stood and scanned the itinerary of daily and hourly events tacked on the elevator wall. "Never fear. Scrabble Club and the Bible Study Group just finished, and it looks like there's a big welcome reception and dinner planned at four o'clock for a new resident and board member."

I lifted the cuff of my jacket and eyed my watch. It was closing in on two o'clock. "Great. That means we could be stuck in here for another two hours?"

"No. Not a chance." The magician pushed his luggage against the wall and piled his grocery bag atop to free up some space. He sat down on the floor and crossed his legs as if twisting them into a pretzel. Once he was settled, Prozac eagerly leaped into his lap.

"You know the elderly," the magician said. "They always arrive places much earlier than need be. I bet we're looking at one, one and a half hours tops."

"Wonderful! What a relief!"

My sarcasm sailed right over the magician's head as he stretched his hand up toward me and said, "I'm David, by the way."

*David? Is this the guy Lucy and Stella mentioned earlier?*

I slipped my fingers inside his warm hand. "Meredith. Your instant friend there is Prozac."

His face lit up. "*The* Prozac?"

"I can't imagine there's more than one," I said. "He's not mine. I'm only filling in for—"

"Helen? How is she?" he asked before I could finish.

"She broke her foot and then had to have surgery."

"I know. How is she doing?"

"Coming along. She's in a rehab now. They say she'll be okay. I hope she'll get better soon, as I'm certainly not interested in becoming a regular here."

David, the magician, let out a laugh. "Gee. Spoken with true affection for the aging population of Oak Park, New Jersey!"

"I'm sorry," I told him. "You'll have to forgive me. I'm having a bad day."

"No apology necessary. I'm an expert at bad days," he said, mussing Prozac's hair. "My mom speaks very highly of this little guy here. She really looks forward to his visits. She'll be very happy to know I finally got to meet him—but she'll be very jealous of me, as well."

"Is your mother the one with the gallbladder?"

"Not anymore," he said, putting Prozac in a trance by massaging his neck. "They took it out."

"I know. I heard—"

"Wait a second. If you're filling in for Helen, then you must be the author lady?"

I nodded.

David studied me a minute. "Gee, you don't really look like the pictures on the back of your books."

Feeling awkward and vulnerable, I looked at my shoes and fidgeted with my right earring. I wondered what he meant. Did I look better or worse?

"My mom, she's a big fan of your novels. Every day since she's been in the hospital, I've been reading aloud to her. We're up to your novel *The*

*Haunted at Ghost Ranch.* She's leading a discussion about it next month in the book group here."

I made a face. "Sorry she's making you suffer through that."

"No. Not suffering at all. It's actually been a very good escape for us. Mom's already read the book. She's read the whole Ghost Ranch series. They're all lined up in her bookcase—*When Shadows Fall at Ghost Ranch, The Miracle at Ghost Ranch, The Stranger at Ghost Ranch.* But I think *The Haunted* is her favorite. It's been a really great way for us to bond—and it's a good story."

"That's nice to hear. It's not often that men like to read women's fiction."

"Oh, don't kid yourself," David said. "My roommate in college always carried a romance novel in the back pocket of his jeans. Claimed reading them taught him everything about the ladies. It's no wonder we nicknamed him Don Juan of the Dorm."

I laughed.

"Personally, I can't wait to see how the book ends. Is Carolina finally gonna give Hazzard a chance or what?"

"Gee, I wrote that book such a long time ago. I don't remember," I said, a lippy grin expanding across my face.

"I don't believe you."

I shrugged as convincingly as I could.

"But what if the cable on this elevator snaps? How will I ever know if those two got together?"

"I suspect there will be someone at the Pearly Gates who can enlighten you."

"Assuming that's where I'm going."

David and I chuckled, and for a moment, I had actually forgotten that we were both trapped in that closet-sized elevator.

"Mom's gonna be tickled when I tell her that I met you."

"If we live that long," I said.

David grinned and puffed a laugh. He ran his fingers through the thick waves of his salt-and-pepper brown hair. "What are the odds of getting trapped in an elevator with the very author of the book we're reading right now?"

"Yeah, truth is always stranger than fiction," I told him. Switching gears, I asked, "So, tell me. Are you the David of bootlegging fame?"

"Bootleg?"

I couldn't be sure, but I thought I spied a twinkle in David's eyes. I brought my voice to a whisper and said, "It's okay. I'm in on the secret."

"What secret?"

David was playing coy.

"Prozac and I spent the afternoon with Lucy and Stella and the Scrabble crew. They were all wondering when and if you were gonna show up with their booze."

A mischievous grin filled David's face. "Gee, is that all I'm good for?" He put his hand inside the grocery bag and pulled out a cumbersome, gallon-sized bottle of Bacardi. "You thirsty?"

"No. No thanks," I said. "I'm actually still feeling the effects of the piña colada they whipped up for me earlier."

David let the bottle drop back inside the bag. "Lucy and Stella—those two sure know how to have fun, don't they?"

"And their boyfriends are pretty funny, too."

"You mean Jack and Stan?"

I nodded.

"Yeah, they're real characters. But they're not *the boyfriends*. They're more like the Casanovas of Evergreen Gardens. The women-to-men ratio here is top-heavy."

"Prozac and I have only been visiting here for a couple of weeks, but I've got to tell you. Sometimes it reminds me of a college dorm. That or an elderly version of Melrose Place."

"Yeah, but it's all good, clean fun," David said. "And you've gotta hand it to some of these folks. They do their damnedest to stay upbeat. They're determined to be only as old as they allow themselves to be."

I nodded. "How'd you get your mom in this place, anyway?"

"She got herself in. She's a very proud, independent lady—didn't want to burden me. I'm an only child. She had me very late in life. And nowadays, I travel a lot with my job. So when our church got in some financial trouble, she and some other folks from the congregation pooled their retirement savings and bought the place. Hired a staff who can help them twenty-four, seven."

"It's really something how Evergreen Gardens came about."

"Yeah, it was some undertaking. But the residents were determined. They set their sights and made it happen."

"It always amazes me how some people have the capacity to simply pick up and keep moving. They press on—no matter what. While others… they cave in and succumb."

I stopped and listened to what I'd just said. My body broke out in cold goose bumps. That last part—I was describing myself, wasn't I?

David's chocolate-colored eyes met my gaze. "Why am I getting the sense that you know somebody who gave up?"

I felt the blood swiftly drain from my face. My heart suddenly felt empty. I ached for Kyle. He was gone. He was really gone, wasn't he?

David turned his face up toward me and asked, "Are you all right?"

My legs felt weak. I put a hand to my woozy head.

"Don't worry. We're not going to suffocate. Elevators aren't airtight. See how these panels don't meet?" David pointed to a seam in the wall. "Right there is our ventilation—plenty of O-two to go around for the three of us. C'mon. Why don't you sit down?"

My mind scuttled back to the moment. "What were we talking about?"

"Giving up—"

"Right. Right," I said, shimmying myself down to the floor. David moved his stuff aside so I could join him and Prozac. "My grandmother— she gave up. After my grandfather died… it's like she didn't see the point in going on without him."

"That's a shame. I'm sorry."

"Don't be. She died only a few months after my grandfather. That was exactly what she wanted."

*Boy! The grief I've been carting around is in my genes, I bet.*

"You know, I've spent a lot of time in this place," David said. "Sometimes, I think we have to do what we need to do and trick ourselves into believing what we need to believe in order to keep living and moving on. For my mother, it's all about escaping with books and movies."

"And you? What do you do? What do you believe?"

"Magic. I believe in magic," he said. "There's nothing like getting people to surrender their disbelief, even if it's fleeting—stepping away from the limits of reality for a minute, maybe two. I guess it's similar for you in writing books?"

"You know, I never thought of it in those terms before, but I guess you're right. It's sort of the same. It's sometimes eerie to create worlds on paper that other people actually want to visit."

"Exactly," David said, bobbing his head.

"Are all magicians this philosophical?"

He shrugged. "I can only speak for myself. But yes, I think a lot. I live mostly inside my head. Always have. You know, the nerdy kid, practicing his tricks in order to be noticed and accepted by people."

"You mean a cape, a top hat, and a magic wand weren't enough to get the job done?"

He nodded. "Oh, believe me, I tried it all."

"What kind of magic do you do?"

"These days, I work mostly concepts. Visual illusions. Engineering work." David stretched his hands over his head and let out a great big yawn. When he brought down his arms, he pulled out a snack-sized bag of potato chips from the sleeve of his sweatshirt and handed it to me.

"Oh my goodness! How did you do that?" I exclaimed, taking the bag and examining it to make sure it was real.

"Tricks of the trade." He laced his fingers together, stretched out his arms in front of him, and produced an identical bag of chips from his other sleeve.

I was astounded.

"Last big project I did was on Broadway," he said. "Special effects for *Spider-Man*."

Prozac lurched up from David's lap as though he'd heard something.

"Really?" I nodded, impressed. "So I guess you're not a run-of-the-mill magician doing kids' birthday parties?"

"Oh, I've done plenty of those, too. They paid my dues. But I haven't been asked to do one in a while. Why, do you have kids?"

"No. No kids," I told him, opening the bag of chips and popping one in my mouth. "But my mother was a teacher. A long time ago, one of her former students performed a magic show at my seventh birthday party."

"Don't tell me your mother was Mrs. Mancuso from Lincolnwood Elementary?"

I nodded, nearly choking.

"Everyone was expecting a rabbit, but the magician pulled a frog out of his top hat, didn't he?"

I swallowed the salty chip and studied him hard. "Do you know him?"

"Intimately."

"Oh my goodness!" I said. "Don't tell me *you're* Razzle-Dazzle Radcliffe?"

"The one and only," he said, his sleepy brown eyes brightening. "I bet your birthday party was one of my very first jobs. Your mom—she was my favorite middle-school teacher."

"Really?"

He nodded. "When I was a kid, I had a terrible stuttering problem, and your mom was able to help break me of that. She got me talking about things that mattered, like my love of magic."

"Gee, what a small world!"

"Sure is," David said.

"How old would you have been when you performed at my party?"

"I guess about thirteen."

"You seemed so much older."

"It was probably my Nehru jacket."

I gasped, a little squeak, bobbing my head as I remembered. "Yes, your Nehru jacket. It was snow white. Not the kind you'd ever imagine a magician would wear."

"That's exactly why my mother bought it. She told me I needed my own look. Oh, I just loved that jacket."

David was getting sentimental waltzing down memory lane.

"That mandarin collar. Oh, I hated to outgrow it."

"So I guess you've moved on and graduated to Hawaiian-print shirts these days?"

David stared into the splash of color covering his chest and torso. He grinned.

"Did you just get back from the islands or something?" I asked.

"Yes, Tahiti."

I looked at him, unsure if he was being facetious.

"In my mind, that is. I've never understood why we northerners are so fixated on the whole don't-wear-white-after-Labor-Day mentality. And it's been such a long and dreary winter that today, I decided to rebel, break the rules of the fashion police, and add some color to life. Do you like it?"

Slowly, I bobbed my head. "Sure. More power to you. Whatever floats your boat."

"My mother thinks I'm deep in the throes of a midlife crisis. *Man-o-pause*, she calls it."

We chuckled, crunching away on chips. We even flipped a couple of small pieces to Prozac, who devoured them, his jaw chomping away.

"I'm parched," David said, rummaging through the grocery bag and pulling out the bottle of rum again. "Maybe we ought to have a nip to wash things down?"

"Better not. And if I were you, I'd keep that bottle under wraps. I have a hunch the bootleg police in this place are going to be on the lookout for it."

David tried to slip the rum back inside the bag, but the contents must've shifted. So he set the bottle down between us, and the moment it touched upon the laminate floor, the elevator jerked. It lurched downward, snapping the elevator—along with me and Prozac, whose ears shot up—back to reality.

"How'd you do that?" I asked.

David blew a puff of air onto his closed fist and polished it over his heart. "Guess it's magic," he said.

The elevator stopped. And before David or I could gather our things and rise to our feet, the door flung open, and the accordion gate smashed across. Standing there and staring down at David, Prozac, and me were Judge Thea and By-the-Book Betsy. Behind them was a towering, burly high school kid with a buzz cut, wearing a military-brown T-shirt and baggy, desert-print camouflage pants.

*Where have I seen him before?*

The judge, with a hand on her hip, stood front and center in the pack of three. She glared down at me and shook her head. "Why, of course. I should've known."

Prozac, tail wagging, tried to dash out of the elevator, but the kid maneuvered his big, cloddy army boots to form a blockade.

Prozac scurried back to us.

"See. See," Betsy said, hitting the judge on the arm and pointing at Prozac, who sniffed all around the full bottle of Bacardi on the floor. "It's like Mary said. There *is* a rumrunner in this place!"

# Eighteen

*WIGGLE ROOM*

Prozac

THAT KID'S OUTFIT MIRRORED HIS military posture as he stood tall outside the elevator like a Great Dane on high alert. His cold, piercing gaze took steady aim on me while I settled into the crook of Meredith's arm.

There was a lot of explaining to do. Meredith, flustered from being sequestered, was all dramatic in wanting assurance that the ancient elevator would be fixed ASAP. But the judge and Betsy were far more concerned about the empty bottle of rum in Stella Stanislowski's apartment and the brand-new bottle of Bacardi discovered in the elevator with Meredith, David, and me.

The more the judge questioned Meredith, the more argumentative Meredith became—clinging to me tighter and tighter as if coiling me up in her lack of defense. She kept skirting the liquor question, lashing out instead about the trauma of being stuck in the elevator.

It was a lame last-ditch effort on Meredith's part, as we'd been stuck for all of twenty minutes, if that. But the desperate rise in Meredith's tone prompted David to put a gentle hand on her arm. His touch calmed her manic energy and proved enough to finally quiet her.

"It's okay," he said, his voice as even as the tile work beneath our feet. "There's no need to be upset."

I couldn't have been more grateful for David's intercession. Finally, someone with a head on his shoulders calmed us all in a peaceful, resolute way.

But before he could continue, the loudspeaker sounded, summoning By-the-Book Betsy to the maintenance room.

"I'll need to go," Betsy said. "The elevator repairman must have arrived."

Betsy motioned to the teenaged G.I. Joe, who marched away with her.

Afterward, David looked at the judge and said, "Have you ever tasted Mrs. Stanislowski's ice cream pie topped with chocolate-rum icing?"

The judge stared at David dead-on. She tightened her lips.

"Trust me. It's delicious," said David. "But Stella uses a very heavy hand with the rum."

"If that's the case, then why did Stella and Lucy try to pin the blame on Meredith?"

"I certainly can't get inside the mind of Mrs. Stanislowski," David replied. "But I'd imagine it might have something to do with the rules and regulations of Evergreen Gardens."

"Stella must make an awful lot of pies if she had you purchase a gallon jug."

"Yeah, well, you know how Stella loves a bargain—retirement pension and all." David looked at the bottle in his hands and, with complete innocence, added, "This size was on sale, and liquor never goes bad. Perhaps it's Stella's hedge against the future."

Gee, I never would've guessed that David used to have a stuttering problem, as he was one heck of a smoothie. In my mind, he was more than just a magician in the traditional sense of the word, pulling rabbits—or frogs—out of top hats. He was clever and convincing, a real quick thinker, sort of like the Foxy sisters who adopted me—then a terrier-poodle mix—in the 1870s. I didn't let their sexy last name fool me. The two widows, Felicia and Fatilda, were portly middle-aged psychics who proclaimed they could also communicate with the dead, and it was the dead who served to make them a pretty decent living. Folks flocked to them like flies on poop even though the two of them were full of, ahem, *doo-doo* themselves. But those sisters sure knew how to twist details and make them prove plausible enough to suit any agenda.

"You'll have to excuse me," David added after he'd spoken his piece. "But I have some things I need to take care of for my mother, and then I've really got to get back to the hospital. Besides, I'm sure everyone is busy getting ready for the big party tonight."

"What party?" the judge asked.

"The welcome dinner," David said, "for the new resident and board member."

"Margo Trilling? Is that today?" The judge seemed surprised by the news.

"The schedule of events posted in the elevator has it listed for tonight," David said.

"Tonight?" The judge strode away and marched into the elevator. She slipped on her bifocals and took a look at the schedule then ripped it from the wall. "This is for *next* Wednesday." The judge stepped from the elevator, waving the paper at Meredith. "On your way out, drop this off at Betsy's desk. Tell her to see me after she finishes with the repairman."

Meredith hesitated, but David tore the paper from the judge's hand. "Yes, by all means, *we'll* make sure Betsy gets the message." He grabbed Meredith by the sleeve and started to drag us away.

"Wait a second. One more thing," the judge called.

We all stopped in our tracks and turned to the judge.

"How about you and Prozac defer your arrival next week until four o'clock and attend the welcome party for Margo Trilling? And you, too, David. You're also invited. Perhaps your mom will even be out of the hospital by then."

Meredith said, "I'll have to check my schedule—"

But David's words crisscrossed Meredith's. "That sounds like fun. Mom will be thrilled for the invitation, and Meredith and I will make a point of being there. Won't we?"

Meredith shot David a look that indicated she disapproved of his answering for her.

"Having Prozac welcome Margo will be a really nice touch." The judge patted my head as Meredith pressed me more firmly against her chest.

When the judge finally walked away, Meredith and David exchanged glances. Meredith said, "Thanks a lot, Harry Houdini."

"Hey, I just did you a favor. Did you want to get the judge's ire up?"

Meredith didn't refute him.

David said, "And nowadays, I'd prefer to be compared to David Copperfield."

Meredith's face contorted. "You mean, the Charles Dickens character?"

"No, the magician, the illusionist—twenty-first century? Big act in

Vegas? Has his own theater at the MGM Grand? A star on the Hollywood Walk of Fame? *Guinness Book of World Records?*"

It didn't matter how many prompts David spouted. Meredith shrugged, oblivious. "All right then. Copperfield it is."

*Gee, with that kitschy shirt of his, I pictured David to be more of a Penn Jillette or Doug Henning disciple.*

Meredith pointed to the rum-filled grocery bag David was holding. "Hey, don't you have to drop off that stuff to Stella?"

He stopped in his tracks. "Yes. It's the other way, isn't it?"

"Give me the schedule. I'll drop it off to Betsy on the way out." Meredith reached to take the paper from David, but he didn't release his grasp right away.

"Wait," David said. "Do you have time for a cup of coffee?"

"Coffee? Right now?"

The rapid beats of Meredith's heart reached me through her throbbing fingers.

"After I drop this stuff off, I mean." David ran a hand through his wavy hair then tugged at his left ear. The poor guy was teetering on a precipice of romantic rejection or acceptance, and he must've feared that by saying another word, he might jeopardize his chances.

"B-but," Meredith stammered, "I-I thought you had too much to do?"

"I do," he said. "But not too much to have a quick cup of coffee with you."

Meredith turned her wrist and eyed her watch. The second hand kept a glacial pace compared to her quickened pulse. It was a dead giveaway that she liked David—the easy, playful banter between them. They'd hit it off. But Meredith was rusty at dealing with people, especially members of the opposite sex. Change was hard for anyone, and for Meredith, it had become almost impossible, like trying to bend a silver spoon with her mind. With each passing second of silence, I suspected that Meredith was probably conjuring a polite brush-off.

"That's very nice of you to ask," Meredith finally told David. "But I really have to get back. Prozac needs to be fed—"

"How about a rain check?"

"Sure." Meredith nodded, swallowing hard. "That would be nice."

*Oh, c'mon now, Meredith! You might be fooling the magician, but you're not fooling me!*

"How about this weekend? Can we make a date?" David pressed.

"A date?"

"Did I just say date? Date is such an antiquated term." David, in Mr. Smooth Talk mode, quickly backpedaled. "What I meant was, do you want to have dinner with me?"

"Dinner?"

Whatever was happening inside of Meredith must've been scaring her senseless. And the way she was repeating everything reminded me of that assignment I'd had in the 1600s, back when I was a Portuguese water dog who sailed the Seven Seas with a band of lewd Spanish pirates and their deranged, potty-mouthed parrot. Give that flashy-colored cockatoo a cracker and a perch at a high-stakes poker game, and that bird's recitations made a sewer look squeaky clean.

"Yes, dinner," David said. "No betrothal or anything. Only a meal. After all, just moments ago, we could've plunged to our deaths together in that elevator. Don't you think, as survivors, we share a bond now?"

"Yes, I guess we do." A smile played on Meredith's lips as she glanced at her shoes. "But the thing is that right now, I'm past a deadline for my next book, and I really need to lock myself in and buckle down. It might be best if we shoot for another time."

"A quick cup of coffee *now* is definitely out?"

That guy was surely on a quest to wear Meredith down.

I sniffed the air. The pheromones Meredith was secreting indicated that she really liked David, but she was torn.

Her being on a deadline wasn't a lie. But if she really wanted to, she could've squeaked out an hour to sit with David and share an innocent cup of coffee. And she could've carved out time in her schedule to go to dinner with him as well. But that was the thing about the human heart and people like Meredith—those whose souls had been badly burned and scarred by tragedy and loss. They feared that once they let someone into their life, even for a measly cup of coffee, they would open themselves up to be hurt. Wounded. That vulnerability became too risky. And some folks were unable to believe that by opening their lives even a crack, they might be enriched, and hope and joy could actually be byproducts that might seep in.

"Thank you for the invitation, but I don't think I can" was Meredith's final answer.

"All right," David said. "Then I'll see you guys at the party next week."

"Yes, that'll be nice," she told him. "I hope your mom rebounds and she's well enough to come home and attend the party, too."

"Thanks. She's going to be so excited when I tell her that I met you." David gave Meredith's coat sleeve a quick pat then turned and started down the corridor in the opposite direction. At one point, he turned back and grinned. "Oh, and next week, it might not be a bad idea if we take the stairs."

Meredith waved, and for a minute, we stood there watching David—Razzle-Dazzle Radcliffe—as the bright, flashy colors of his Hawaiian shirt grew dimmer as he walked farther away. Meredith's shoulders sagged, and she let out a labored sigh as if her body were crying out, *Stop. Don't go. Please, come back. Twist my arm.*

I felt sad for Meredith. She really did want to have that cup of coffee with David. But the pain of the past had rendered her incapable of saying yes.

---

When we arrived at the reception desk, there was no sign of By-the-Book Betsy. Meredith paced around the area, looking for her. She held me in one hand and the incorrect schedule of events in the other. I could tell she was anxious to make the drop and go, but as she scanned the lobby, not a soul was in sight. She finally reached over the desk and plucked out a pen from a cup filled with writing instruments. On the border of the itinerary, she wrote the time and date and *Judge Thea would like to see you ASAP.* She circled the incorrect date at the top of the schedule.

As Meredith deposited the inscribed itinerary onto Betsy's desk, she noticed a hardcover book splayed atop the blotter, face down. She glanced at the entire front and back cover for *War and Peace.* Meredith reached for the book. As she did, she observed that the dust jacket was too large for the binding. Since when was *War and Peace* such a short book? I had always been under the impression that it was a tome, some twelve hundred pages or more. When the book jacket slipped off the binding, the gold embossed lettering on the woven twill spine read *The Haunted at Ghost Ranch,* followed by the last name of the author, *St. John.*

"Well, I'll be."

Meredith thumbed through a couple of pages as if to make sure her discovery was legit.

A prideful smile filled her face. She carefully reaffixed the dust jacket for *War and Peace* and replaced the book exactly as she'd found it.

"That Betsy," Meredith said. "She truly *does* read only great books!"

*Hallelujah! Praise the Lord!* It was about time that lady stopped being ashamed of her own books.

# Nineteen

*THE (DIS)COMFORTS OF HOME*

Prozac

I F I WEREN'T A DOG, I would've been able to remind Meredith that she hadn't taken her car to Evergreen Gardens—that the police had driven us. But instead, Meredith walked us through the lobby, past the cherub fountain, and out through the front doors, where cold air smacked us in the face beneath that word BELIEVETH etched in stone. She scanned the parking lot for her Toyota, and when she didn't find it, she quickly came to that realization on her own.

She could have called the police for a ride. After all, they'd offered. Or she could've walked down the block to Monica's office. But instead, Meredith called a cab. Then, as we paced outside of Evergreen Gardens waiting for our ride, she dialed her town pizzeria and ordered a small extra cheese.

*Yum! Maybe I'll work her over for a little bit of crust.*

Once we got back to the townhouse, we faced the fallout in the living room—the toppled-over couch, the smashed table lamps, laundry strewn everywhere. It seemed like a lifetime since the police had rung the doorbell that day.

With pizza box in hand, Meredith turned from the mess and spied the light flashing on the telephone answering machine. She pressed the button, and Hammond Cederholm's tenor voice boomed through the tiny speaker.

"Meredith, when you have a chance, will you call me? It's about Aunt Helen…"

*Please, let it be good news—news that Helen is finally coming home, and she wants me with her again.*

I expected Meredith to call back Ham immediately. But instead, she made for the kitchen, where she poured herself a glass of wine and dumped a mound of Top Notch into my dog bowl.

I wanted no part of that slop. I wanted pizza, and I set out to get it.

Meredith sat down. She kicked off her shoes and propped her sock-covered feet up on a kitchen chair. Leaning back, she tore off a slice of pie and, straight from the pizza box, started eating.

Tonight there was no TV soundtrack—no jabbering TV anchormen; no gimmicky, jump-cut commercials for products pitched by talking dogs and insects. No, tonight it was just Meredith chomping on cheese, baked dough, and tomatoes, seemingly oblivious to my begging at her feet. As she stared off in a daze, I got the sense she was trying to process all the feelings stirred up by the whirlwind day, mostly those evoked by David.

David Radcliffe.

*Razzle-Dazzle Radcliffe.*

In the past two weeks, two men had shown an interest in Meredith. That certainly didn't fit with her life-without-romance plan, and David's invitation obviously served as smelling salts that had forced Meredith to realize how long she'd been alone and out of commission. I feared that by wallowing in her thoughts, Meredith would stir a tsunami of emotion that could only make her feel mixed up and sad—weird, even. She had been clinging so tightly to the past, there wasn't room for anything new.

But she'd have to make room—and I believed it was my job to help her. Therefore, I took matters into my own paws, determined to shake her out of her funk, even at the expense of my pizza quest.

I started small, pacing around her chair and bumping into her with soft impacts. When that didn't rally her, I stood on my hind legs and pawed her thigh as though wanting to climb up on her lap.

My efforts were annoying enough to make Meredith rip her feet off the chair and send them to the tile floor with a *thud!* She reached down and patted my head, giving a gentle scuff behind my ears. She even flipped me a tiny piece of crust that I gladly crunched on. But the diversion I'd created was short-lived, as she poured herself another glass of wine and returned to her pizza, soon spacing out again.

I moved on to Plan B—plopping my derriere atop her warm wooly socks. But she quickly pulled them out from under me.

That left me no choice but to go big. I squatted and released the contents of my bladder.

"Prozac!" she hollered, jerking away her feet as a yellow puddle formed around the leg of her chair. My bladder was small, but my incontinence-on-demand trick was my ace in the hole.

Meredith slipped off her soggy socks. She lurched from the table and used a wet, soapy paper towel to clean her bare feet before tackling the mess on the floor.

When she was through, she marched down the hall, where she made a stop at the laundry chute on her way to her bedroom.

I waited a minute, expecting her to reemerge wearing a clean pair of socks or her slippers. But when she didn't, I tramped down the hall and found her sitting on the edge of her bed as if alone on an island. Her body was folded over upon itself. She rocked, releasing loud, gut-wrenching sobs. Through the shadows of the room, a dim glow spilled over the open drawer of the nightstand. Wet tears dripped off Meredith's face onto a framed photograph she held on her lap.

I padded into the room and leaped onto the bed, sitting obediently at her side. I expected her to kick me off. But she didn't, so I nuzzled against her. When I put a paw on her thigh and licked her forearm, she gave me a pat then cried even harder. She squeezed her eyes shut, and with both hands, she clutched her head as if in terrible pain. Her body quaked, her grief trembling through the bed as if something inside her was cracking open.

I looked at the photograph on her lap. It was a picture of Meredith and a guy—it must've been Kyle. I hadn't seen a picture of him before. The closest I had ever gotten to his spirit was when I once put my nose to the crack at the bottom of the closet door in Meredith's office and inhaled a shuddering whiff of him. It wasn't until Meredith opened that closet one day, flipping the lid on a case of printer paper situated on the floor, that I'd caught a glimpse—tucked away inside the small space—of a shrine-like grotto dedicated to Kyle. Hanging off the clothes rod was a clear garment bag stuffed with what looked like a perfectly pressed, double-breasted formal dress uniform of a fireman, complete with badges and rank insignia. And attached with clothespins to the other two hangers on the clothes bar were two zipper seal bags. One contained what looked like a set of wrinkly bed sheets, the other a worn Scottish plaid flannel shirt. The objects were preserved like important legal evidence. And displayed on the top shelf were a fireman's formal hat, white with a shiny black brim, and a few autographed baseballs and caps with the New York Yankees logo.

The items in the closet might have been just things, but it was clear they were relics significant to Meredith's life—and Kyle's.

Remembering the contents of that closet and glimpsing the photograph gave me a whole different perspective. It pointed at how grief, when resurrected, could be razor sharp.

I studied the image of Kyle—his bright eyes and receding hairline camouflaged by closely cropped hair. He had a smile that was as warm and inviting as Meredith's, if only she allowed herself to smile. The photo of the two of them—at what looked like a summer picnic or barbeque—showed Meredith wearing a spaghetti-strap dress and seated at a redwood picnic table. Standing behind her was Kyle, who had leaned in and wrapped his big, strong arms around her shoulders, pressing his head alongside the thick waves of her long brown hair. The photo captured the bond they must've shared, and I could imagine Kyle, appearing to be Meredith's protector, inhaling traces of her apple blossom shampoo. There was such familiarity oozing between the two, it was obvious, looking at the photograph, that Kyle and Meredith were a couple who had felt at home in each other's company.

*Home.*

Yes, home.

*That's what real love is, isn't it?* That sense of being able to rest in another's presence knowing there were no pretenses, judgments, or expectations. Trust washed away fear. No wonder Meredith had been steeped in grief all those years. To have had such love and then to have lost it…

One look at that photograph explained volumes. Boy-next-door loved girl-next-door. In bearing witness to that picture and Meredith's grief, I was suddenly struck by the realization that Meredith had been as altered by grief as she'd once been by love.

My heart seized as Meredith flounced back across the bed, her legs dangling over the side of the mattress. She pressed the framed photo against her heart. She closed her eyes and cried herself to sleep until the shrill ring of the telephone woke us both a few hours later. The numbers on the bedside clock read 9:42 p.m.

Meredith lurched up and fumbled for the phone on the nightstand. She cleared her throat and uttered a weary "Hello?"

"Am I calling too late?"

With my super-acute dog hearing, I recognized Ham's voice spilling from the phone.

"No, it's not too late at all." Meredith dropped her forehead into her open palm and pressed her thumb and forefinger into her eye sockets. "I'm sorry I didn't call you back. What's up?"

"I was hoping you and Prozac might be free tomorrow, and we could all pay Aunt Helen a visit at the rehab center."

*Oh, goodie!*

"Do you want to take Prozac on your own?"

*What? Oh no. No-no-no!*

"Actually, Aunt Helen was really hoping you could take time out to meet her."

"Me? Why does Aunt Helen want to meet *me?*"

"Because you've been taking care of her pride and joy. And she'd like to thank you personally."

"Well, I can imagine she must miss this dog like crazy. But the thing is, I'm working on a deadline…" Meredith looked down at me sitting beside her. When her eyes met mine, I shot her my very best *poor-thing, pretty-please* gaze, and she asked, "What time, exactly, were you planning on?"

"How about noon?"

"Later in the day would be better for me. Say around four o'clock."

"Yeah, okay. I can do that."

"If you give me the address, Prozac and I could meet you there—oh, wait, I might not be able to. My car battery died. I have to call Triple A first thing tomorrow—"

"Not a problem. I'll pick you up," Ham said. "And if you're going to be stuck home all day, any chance I might send the groomer over to give Prozac a sprucing up in the morning?"

Meredith sighed. "What's involved with that?"

I feared Ham was going to blow it if he made matters too complicated. So I was glad when he succinctly told her how the groomer drove a van, and all Meredith had to do was answer the doorbell and hand me over. I would be washed and dried, cut and styled right in the truck that sat parked in the driveway.

"That's really all there is to it?" Meredith asked.

"That's it. And the groomer runs a tab for Prozac with Aunt Helen, so you won't have to shell out any money."

After the call, I expected Meredith's pity party to resume. She stared at Kyle's picture, and then, with a few short, playful shakes of her head, she said, half laughing, "Oh, Kyle, how did I ever get roped into all this?" She imparted a kiss on her fingertips, placing them atop Kyle's lips in the photo. Then she slipped the frame into the nightstand drawer and pushed it closed. When she spotted me sitting there beside her, ears erect, she did a double take.

"Sure, *now* you're all obedient," she said, her tone more upbeat.

I remembered the incident from the kitchen, and my ears fell back. With shame and guilt, I slunk down, pressing my elongated body into the mattress.

"Tomorrow there can be no more funny stuff," she said. "We're sprucing you up and going to see your mistress. So you better be on your best behavior."

When she reached a hand toward me, I expected her to boot me off the bed. But I was pleasantly surprised when she ran a gentle hand from my head all the way down to my tail. Then she rose and walked out of the room. I reclined, basking upon the luxurious contours of her memory foam mattress while she set off and took to cleaning up the mess in the living room.

---

Helen Hendrix pulled me into the warm, familiar folds of her belly, and I sank into the sweet scent of a flowery fragrance as though free-falling into a powdery, perfumed cloud. I didn't know who was gladder to see whom, but as Helen greeted me with hugs and kisses and baby talk, I realized how much I had missed her. I wished she didn't have to be relegated to that dreary and drab rehab center. But I burrowed deep into her lap, glad to see her sitting up in a chair with both of her feet, one in a bulky cast, propped upon pillows set atop the edge of her bed.

"Oh, you won't believe the hard time this little guy gave me and the groomer this morning," Meredith said to Helen and Ham. I could tell by the way Meredith was being so talkative that she was nervous and trying to keep the mood upbeat and light. "When the groomer first rang the doorbell, Prozac went into hiding under my sofa like some sort of covert CIA operative. It took us twenty minutes to draw him out."

I turned from Meredith and Ham and peered up at Helen. My cuter-than-cute, groomed, copper-colored face and lapping tongue were reflected in her bifocals as her long nails stroked my back. She was much more charmed by my antics than Meredith had been earlier that morning.

Ham asked, "How did you finally lure him out?"

"I took your advice," Meredith said. "Opened a can of tuna fish, and lo and behold, he came rushing out of seclusion."

Helen beamed, delighted. She went on, with perfect diction and her pretty British accent, "If I would've known Hammond had arranged for the groomer, I could have warned you about *all* of Prozac's pet peeves. Like how he hates having his teeth brushed, taking a bath, and having his nails trimmed."

"The groomer said the bath wasn't so bad. But when she was nearly through blow-drying him, he piddled all over the table," Meredith said. "She had to wash him all over again."

Helen *tsk-tsked*. "He's notorious for piddling. The vet says it's submissive behavior. But I think he sometimes does it for spite—"

*You've got that right!*

"Well, I wouldn't put anything past him. He's a very smart dog," Meredith said.

"And he hates vacuum cleaners," Helen added. "The groomer never has trouble, but I have such a hard time cutting Prozy's nails. The best thing to do is drag out and turn on the Hoover. He's more afraid of the upright than the nail clipper. That always helps get the job done."

"Oh, the lengths you go to!" Ham looked to Meredith and gave a roll of his eyes.

"If you were a dog person, like Meredith and me, you'd understand." Helen winked at Meredith.

During a lull in the conversation, Helen said, "Hammond, why don't you go to the commissary and see if they baked cherry pie today. I'd love a piece. How about you, Meredith?"

Ham's chair let out a loud scraping sound as he lurched to his feet, obviously eager to fulfill Helen's request. He looked at Meredith for her answer.

"Pie sounds delicious," Meredith told him, "but I'd better not."

"Oh, c'mon," Helen said. "Life's too short. Splurge. Let pie make the day sweeter."

"Gee. That sounds like it should be embossed on a plaque or used as a greeting card slogan," Ham said.

"I'll call Hallmark and ask for a job the minute I get out of here," Helen joked.

"If not pie, then how about a cup of coffee?" Ham asked Meredith.

"Sure, that sounds great," Meredith said. "But make mine a decaf."

"I'd like tea," said Helen. "And Hammond, be sure to get yourself something to eat and whatever you'd like to drink, too. Put everything on my tab. And could you also see if they'll give you a kid's cup of vanilla ice cream?"

"For whom?" Ham asked.

Helen pressed down the triangular points of my ears and muffled my hearing. "Guess," she said, her voice muted as she planted a gentle kiss atop my head.

"I should've known," Ham sighed, waltzing out of the room.

I rolled on my side, my body slipping into the crease between Helen's legs, so she could caress my belly.

"Look at him—how he's missed you," Meredith said. "He hasn't been this relaxed in all the weeks he's been staying with me."

"I'm sorry if he's been a handful, but I really appreciate that you've been fostering him. He seems very well adjusted and extremely well cared for."

"You're welcome," Meredith said. "He's certainly kept me on my toes, and I can see why you love him so much."

*Really? Do tell!*

"All my life, even when I was younger, I always prayed that God would allow me to have a dog while I roamed this earth." Helen stared down at me lovingly. "And God has delivered on His promise... until now."

A pregnant beat of silence filled the room and swelled with greater implications until Meredith said, "Well, you still have a dog. Your separation from Prozac is only temporary."

"That's something I'd like to talk to you about—"

"Is everything all right?" Panic seeped into Meredith's voice.

"Yes. My foot is coming along. But let's face it. This is probably going to be a long haul, and I may never run at full speed again," said Helen. "I'm eighty-seven years old. Most of my friends and relatives are underground— or moving in that direction. And I'm not getting any younger. I've been putting my affairs in order, as they say, every couple of years since I turned seventy-five. But now that this has happened, I need to make sure I have solid contingencies in place."

*Uh-oh!*

Meredith sat unmoving. I wondered if she was even breathing. She shot Helen a granite-like stare. It was hard to tell if it was filled with anticipated dread or if her look indicated she was scrambling through a mental card catalog of possibilities.

"Do you have children, Meredith?"

"Children?" Meredith cleared her throat. "No. No kids."

"You might someday. You're still young," Helen said. "I never had kids. Never really missed them. I was one of ten, myself. And when my mother was diagnosed with Alzheimer's, I figured I was probably better off without them."

"Oh, I think you would've made a fine mother," Meredith said. "I understand from my sister that you were a much-loved teacher."

"Yes, my students. They were a blessing. But that's different." Helen eased her fingers through my silky hair. "My mother's illness... well, it created such a rift in the family. It was heartbreaking. Everybody had his own ideas of how best to help Mother. And everyone's true colors came out—who had Mother's best interests at heart and who had designs on preserving her estate to accommodate his or her inheritance. To think that my mother raised and cared for ten kids, and ten kids, all adults, were unable to take care of just one mother..."

"Gee, that's sad. I'm sorry."

"Yeah, me, too. But it happens." Helen gave a flap of her hand as if to wave off Meredith's sympathies. "And it made me realize that even though we sometimes make plans and God laughs, it's still important to prepare for the future."

"Yes. Absolutely. That's always a good idea."

"And I'm thinking that if something should happen to me... Well, since this arrangement with you and Prozac appears to be working out well, would you consider acting as his trustee?"

I flinched, feeling the air get sucked out of the room.

"A trustee?" Meredith's throat shimmied with the question. Her face turned chalk white.

"Yes, if something should happen to me, I'd like to have a plan in place and a trust fund set up for Prozy's continued care. Legally, it's called a Pet Protection Agreement. There'd be money put aside for food, grooming, vet, and whatever else Prozac will face in his life without me. And you'd be compensated for the care you give him."

Meredith said nothing. Her eyebrows knit, indicating that she was utterly perplexed by the whole thing.

So was I. Meredith wasn't a bad person, but to spend the rest of my life with *her*?

"So, would you grant permission for me to arrange things this way?" Helen asked.

Meredith's face shriveled. "I'm flattered that you're considering me. I am. But why wouldn't you put Ham in charge of things? He seems very devoted—"

"Ham? No, he wouldn't be a good fit." Helen shook her head, clear in her assertion. "Don't get me wrong. Ham's very organized. He's competent. And he's a good person. I'm so grateful for the loyalty he's shown in caring for me. But he has way too much on his plate. He works long hours and is constantly traveling with his job. He can't meet Prozy's needs."

"And I can?"

"Yes. And Prozac will thrive with a female companion. I can already see it—the bond you share. Besides, you work from home, and it's important that Prozac not be left alone all day."

I looked from Meredith up to Helen. Her fingers massaged my back with much more vigor.

"I've always had a good sense about people," Helen said.

"Well, to be honest, I… ummm… I've never had a pet before," Meredith said. "Never had to care for one, until now."

I expected Helen's hand to freeze on my back and her pulse to quicken. But she never broke her petting stride. I expected her to change her mind. But with great matter-of-factness, she said, "I know."

Meredith's mouth was ajar before she spoke. "Y-you know?"

"You don't think I'd leave my dog with someone I didn't thoroughly vet, do you?"

"But you left Prozac in my *sister's* care."

"And when I learned that Monica asked you to take him, I did my homework."

"Oh?" Meredith's tone rose an octave. The curl of her lips teetered between insult and amusement. "Well, that doesn't make any sense. If you really checked me out, then why would you deliberately leave your dog with someone who never owned a pet?"

"Look, what happened to your fiancé—it was all over the local papers and the news. And your sister… well, she's been my accountant and confidante for years. And whenever I ask about you, her concern is very obvious. You've been grieving a long time."

*Uh-oh. Monica's gonna be in big trouble!*

"And after everything you've been through, I figured a dog might be what you needed."

Meredith's forehead furrowed. Her face grew pinched and tight. "You don't know what I need."

"And do *you?* Do you honestly know what you need, Meredith?"

Helen's question leveled the playing field of the conversation, which was quickly escalating the emotions in both women.

Helen said, "To think that a person could pick up a rock and take another life simply because of a parking space… It's terrible. Atrocious. No wonder your life's been in limbo."

Meredith tugged nervously at her ear. She bit her lip.

*Yikes! I knew Kyle was murdered. But is that how he really died?*

"When I fell, and Monica offered your help, I figured maybe this was meant to be—what destiny had in mind. You might not have been fond of animals before, but maybe it wasn't the right time. The right season of your life. And there are seasons for everything. I thought Prozac, being as special as he is, might help you. I figured that if you could learn to love him, then maybe that would help you relate to people again, too."

Even though Helen was pushing the envelope with all that talk about love between Meredith and me, her intentions were good and on target— definitely in sync with how I perceived my mission. My tongue lapped at her hand. Then I turned to Meredith and licked my chops—my way of blowing her a kiss. Meredith set her hands on each of her knees. She hauled in a deep breath as if trying to shoulder a great burden.

"Listen," Helen said. "What I've asked about your being Prozac's trustee... I haven't discussed any of this with Ham yet—"

Before Helen could finish, Ham stepped into the room.

"Teatime. Coffee break," he announced.

Ham cheerfully carried in the tray that held two slices of whipped-cream-topped cherry pie, three Styrofoam cups, and one smaller cup that I could smell was filled with a scoop of vanilla ice cream, just for me.

# Twenty

*WHEN YOU LEASH EXPECT IT*

Meredith

THE SUN WAS SETTING BY the time we left Helen's rehab facility. Gentle gusts of heat spewed from the dashboard vents of Ham's Mercedes, wafting the scent of leather from the heated seats and stirring the sound of classical music drifting from the rear speakers. Prozac warmed my lap. He licked his paws while I stared out the passenger-side window, doing a postmortem of the Helen visit and thinking about what she'd asked of me. I regretted there wasn't time for me to tell her, flat out, that I wasn't interested in being Prozac's trustee—that she'd have to find someone else.

A part of me resented Helen. I mean, how could she dare think she knew what was best for me? What had Monica told her? But another part of me couldn't deny that I genuinely liked Helen. Maybe it was the charm of her proper British accent. Or maybe I just felt sorry for her, sitting in that rehab place with that big cast on her ankle—separated from her dog, all alone amongst a menagerie of struggling elderly people propped up in their beds or in wheelchairs docked out in the hallways. Helen seemed with-it and smart and wise. And even separated from her beloved Prozac, she still exuded an aura of peace and confidence—even joy. How was that so?

I examined my feelings. The whole idea of taking on the responsibility of Prozac—permanently—swirled inside my head as I watched the diminishing afternoon light cast houses and small businesses into a passing blur.

"Hey, how about we grab a quick bite to eat before I drop you home?" Ham asked.

I turned away from the darkness descending outside and was met by the dashboard lights and a glimpse of Ham's silhouette—his chiseled profile, his deep-set eyes, his high cheekbones illuminated by the afternoon light.

"Can't. The dog. And aren't you still full from the pie?" I asked.

"No, not really. I know it's a terrible habit, but there's nothing like starting a meal with dessert."

As the car rounded a corner, I chuckled, firming my grasp around Prozac to anchor him more sturdily upon my lap.

"And you didn't have any pie," Ham said. "You must be starving by now."

"I guess I *am* a little hungry."

"You guess?" Ham pointed toward the dashboard clock. "It's almost seven. Don't tell me you're one of those people who forgets to eat?"

"No, not really. Only sometimes in the past couple of years."

"Oh? What changed?"

I hesitated, my mind searching for a starting place in my explanation. But then I thought better of going down that road. I simply responded with, "How much time do you have?"

"For you? All the time in the world," Ham said.

My faced flushed hot. I was flattered. Ham was so kind and sensitive. And he always seemed to know the right things to say. There was something sort of lovable and familiar about him, and the more time we spent together, the more comfortable I felt.

"Ham, you're sweet. You really are. But believe me, I'd probably only bore you—"

"Why do you always do that?"

"Do what?"

"Decide what other people feel?"

"Do I do that?"

Ham nodded. "With me, you do. Yes. '*You wouldn't want to read one of my books. You don't really want to hear my life story.*'"

"Gee, I'm sorry about that. I guess it's the writer in me. You know, always scripting the next scene, staying a page ahead."

"That sounds exhausting! It's a lot easier to let life simply unfold."

"Not always," I said.

An awkward hush hovered inside the car like a cloud waiting to burst. Ham broke the silence. "I think the two of us are just hungry."

"Yeah, maybe."

"Why don't we try that Andrea's place, where they make that calamari and octopus the critics and you were raving about?"

As Ham said that, Prozac stood up on all fours and stared out through the front windshield as if reminding us he was still there.

"It sounds great, but we can't go with the dog," I told him, Prozac settling back onto my lap. "And I really ought to get home. I'm on a deadline."

"Why don't we grab some takeout then? I know a great Chinese place not far from here. The Bamboo House. They make the best homemade pistachio ice cream. It's to die for."

I laughed out loud. "Boy, you sure do like your sweets. You're as bad as Aunt Helen."

"That's exactly what Stephen used to say." Ham nodded his head as he brought his voice down an octave. He added in mimic, " *You and Aunt Helen might not be related by blood, but you're surely related by your sweet tooth.* "

My face shriveled up. "Stephen? Who's Stephen?"

"My significant other. Helen's nephew."

The rusty gears of my mind turned, reconfiguring things. "So, wait… Aunt Helen—she isn't your *real* aunt?"

"Technically, no. But I love her like she's my own flesh and blood." Ham's leather seat squeaked as he sat up straighter behind the wheel. "You see, I met Stephen in middle school, and since I was from a broken home, his family sort of welcomed me into the fold as if I were their own. Helen was always our favorite—we all loved horses and racing, and she used to take us to the track before we were even old enough to place bets. Oh, we had such fun times together. I've always called her Aunt Helen—like she's always referred to us, Stephen and me, as her nephews. But I must admit, that raised a few eyebrows once we got engaged."

"Engaged?" My head swooned trying to take it all in. "You mean, you're married?"

Ham shook his head. He firmed his grasp on the steering wheel. His watery eyes were illuminated by car headlights reflecting in the rearview mirror. "We had the wedding plans all made, but Stephen died before we could tie the knot."

"Oh. I'm so sorry," I said, drawing Prozac closer, squeezing him for comfort. "What happened?"

"Stephen was actually in remission. We thought he was doing really well. But then he had a massive stroke—from the chemo."

"How terrible." My heart twisted. "When was that? How long ago? And if you met in middle school, were you and Stephen together as a couple all that time?"

Ham turned to me, his eyes wide. "Gee, for a person who doesn't like to talk about herself, you don't seem to have a problem asking *other* people questions."

I held up my palms. "I'm sorry. You're right. It's none of my business."

"It's okay. I'm busting you." Ham reached over and placed a reassuring hand on my thigh. He gave it an endearing squeeze. That sense of connection felt good, as no one had laid a hand on me in a long time—not a man and never before a gay one.

"So, c'mon, let's go for a bite," Ham said, rallying his spirits. "You can ask all the questions you want, and I won't make you reciprocate by answering any questions I have about you. Besides, I don't get to talk about Stephen much anymore. I'd love to bring him back to life for a while."

I didn't respond right away. Instead, I studied Ham, the way his meticulously styled gray hair was raked in short, gentle strands away from his face. It all made sense. *He* made sense. As all the pieces of the puzzle were suddenly coming together, I realized Ham and I had something in common. We had both lost someone dear to us, someone we loved. Maybe that was why I felt a kinship, a familiarity, with him.

I asked, "It's not too hard for you to do that—to talk about Stephen, to bring him back to life, as you say?"

"No. Quite the opposite."

"But doesn't it dredge up too much pain, make you too sad to think about what you had and what you've lost?"

Ham shook his head. "Right after Stephen died, people were there, eager to listen and help. But that wasn't always when I wanted and needed to talk. And apparently, some friends of mine think there's a schedule to grief, a timetable—that because it's been almost two years, I should have moved on by now. But sometimes, I don't want to move on. It feels good to bring up Stephen's name—to give voice to him again in conversation. It's like I can still feel him with me. His presence, I mean. Even though he's gone, I don't believe that he's ever really that far away from me."

I nodded. The whole absent-presence thing. I got it. I knew exactly what he meant.

"So, c'mon. Say yes to takeout," Ham pressed. "It's been a really long time since I've shared a meal with someone who wasn't Aunt Helen or a business associate. And it's not every day I get to break bread with a famous author—"

"I told you. I'm *not* famous."

"On Google you are. There's a ton of info about you and your books, reviews and interviews. When I hit the twentieth page, I got tired of reading. Trust me, you're famous," he said. "So, c'mon, make a lonely single man happy for one night."

"You're putting way too much faith in me if you think I can make you happy for a whole night."

"If it'll make you feel less pressured, let's just settle on an hour or so."

"In that case," I told him, "we've got a deal."

---

The Bamboo House was a take-out restaurant located in the middle of an upscale strip mall near my home. Ham offered to place our order, and I gave him carte blanche to surprise me with anything on the menu. When he left, I took Prozac for a stroll along the stone paver walkway of the outdoor mall, toward the Bath and Body Works store at the far end.

With every footstep, my thoughts kept circling back to Ham's revelation about Stephen. What a sad story but also a beautiful lesson of love and devotion. It got me thinking again about Judge Thea's negative view of Ham. I gathered she was under the impression, as most people were, that Ham was Helen's blood nephew. Could Ham's expensive car, fancy suits, and cuff links—and Monica's suggestion that his architectural firm overcharged for the renovation of Evergreen Gardens—have colored the judge's perceptions and comments?

I might've been lost in thought while we walked, but Prozac was in his glory. Several people *oohed* and *aahed* over him—stopping to admire and rumple his freshly groomed puppy cut—along the way. The night held a chill, but Prozac panted and pulled as profusely as a sled dog raring to race. He yanked on the lead and zigzagged around wrought-iron benches and doors that opened to shoppers who burst forth upon our promenade route.

A steady stream of bags from the Apple Store, Williams-Sonoma, and Pier 1 floated by.

Some women liked to shop as a hobby and recreation—even as therapy. Not me. I didn't even like to window shop. The Internet was a godsend. If I went shopping at all, I had a specific destination in mind. As I waited for Ham, I glanced with wonder through store windows and admired the displays, marveling at the bright lights that illuminated merchandise presented with as much thought and care as modern 3-D sculptural art.

When I spotted a pyramid-style display of bath beads and lotions, loofah sponges and scrunchies, I knew Prozac and I had finally reached Bath and Body Works. We turned around and headed back along the walkway. When we neared the center of the mall, we were swallowed up amid a hub of activity at the Apple Store. Consumers congregated there as if held by some sort of magnetic, centrifugal force. Prozac sniffed the sidewalk out front with a patient diligence that rooted me to those pavers. I stared through the large plate-glass windows into the bright, crowded shop. A lighted sign sported the company slogan, *Think Different*. And a gaggle of people—wearing royal blue polo shirts embroidered with the simple white Apple logo—split like atoms and wandered the showroom designed with an understated, Shaker-like simplicity. Beechwood floors and matching long tables were filled with demo computer screens. The place was a bustling hive of consumers, technology, and swelling corporate profits.

I tried to pull Prozac away, the leash in my hand growing taut as he stretched it to the limit. He seemed determined to keep us there. I gave a gentle tug and said, "C'mon, good boy," hoping the soothing quality of my voice would encourage him to follow. But he resisted. He sniffed and snorted at the ground, pulling toward whatever scent had appealed to him on those pavers.

"C'mon," I repeated, giving a sharper tug that finally forced Prozac in my direction. But as he scampered toward me, the doors to the Apple Store swung open, and Prozac danced around, his tail wagging vigorously.

Out stepped a tall man wearing a buffalo-plaid hunting jacket who was as drawn to Prozac as Prozac was to him. Beneath the glare of the strip mall lights and those from the Apple Store, the man reached down to scratch Prozac behind his ears.

"What a good boy," the man said, forming an instant connection with the dog, who flung himself at the man's feet in a frenzy of joy.

Prozac relished the attention. I stared at the back of the man's hunting jacket, thinking how the dark red and black resembled the attire worn by Elmer Fudd of Bugs Bunny cartoon fame. All the guy needed to complete the look was to be shorter and stockier, don a matching hunting hat with ear flaps, and carry a rifle.

Once the man stood up and smoothed the sash of his sable-gray hair, the Elmer Fudd comparison fell by the wayside.

"Well, well, well," the man said. "If it isn't the therapy dog extraordinaire and his busy writer mistress."

My heart fluttered at the twinkle in the man's eye and the familiar beam of his smile.

"David?" I was stunned. It was the magician guy from the elevator at Evergreen Gardens. "Look at you. I-I guess you've left the islands?"

He looked at me and appeared puzzled.

I gestured at his hunting jacket. "I almost didn't recognize you without your Hawaiian shirt."

David grinned. "Well, yesterday it was so mild outside, I thought spring had sprung. But tonight's a completely different story."

"Yes, it *is* pretty nippy out."

Meeting David outside the context of Evergreen Gardens, especially after his proposition two days before, caught me off guard. I felt all quivery inside—and it wasn't from the cold.

*What's happening here? What's going on with me?*

"Gee, are you all right?" David asked. "You look as white as a Vegas tiger."

"Excuse me?"

"It's magician's humor. The white tiger? Part of the Siegfried and Roy show?"

I chuckled. David's kooky sense of humor calmed me. "I think *white as a ghost* is more my speed—and yes, I'm fine." I forced a smile and perked my shoulders to shake off my wave of nervousness. "So, w-what are you doing here?"

"Great minds must think alike, because I was about to ask *you* the same question."

"I live only a few blocks away," I told him. "Waiting for my take-out order from the Bamboo House and getting this little guy out for some fresh air."

*Great! This is just great. How am I going to explain that I'm out with another guy?*

"Aha," David said. "So you're multitasking?"

I nodded. "Sometimes I think it's my new middle name."

"Mine, too," he said. "Especially since Mom's been in the hospital."

"How's she doing?"

"Better. She's responding well to the medications, so hopefully, she'll be back at Evergreen Gardens in a few days."

"That's great news!"

"And she must be feeling better, because she's starting to drive me crazy again. She has no Internet connection from her hospital bed. So I splurged and bought her an iPad—4G." He held up a rectangular white bag.

"Wow, what a good son you are."

"Not for long," he told me. "I'm not always such a patient person when I'm my mother's on-call computer techie. I'm sure she's going to have a gazillion questions in learning this new gadget."

"You never know. You might be surprised."

"I hope you're right," he said. "And speaking of surprises, how is it that the busy authoress-on-deadline is taking time out? Does your slave-driver publisher allow for this?"

I put a finger to my lips and whispered, "Shhh. Don't tell anyone, but sometimes, when it's after five o'clock, I rip out my intravenous feeding tube, finally change my Depends, and make a mad dash for a quick takeout run."

I had no idea where that sudden burst of self-deprecating playfulness came from, but I was grateful for it—and the amusement reflected in David's bent smile.

"Well, if you're going to take the risk, then the Bamboo House is certainly a good choice. They make really great stir-fries. Very fresh. And their pistachio ice cream is the best."

"Yes, I know. I've heard—"

As the thought of Ham breezed into my mind, a masculine voice boomed from behind, "Meredith, there you are!"

David instantly turned toward the voice, and I followed, cringing when I spotted Ham approaching.

A wine bottle, shrouded in a paper bag, was tucked under one of Ham's arms, which also hugged a bulging bag emitting the scent of fried rice and garlic. In his free hand, Ham held a plastic spoon, which was dripping onto the pavers, green splatters that Prozac was only too eager to lap up.

"Here, they gave me a sample of the pistachio. You've got to try this." Ham navigated the spoon with the melting ice cream toward my mouth.

I didn't know which had greater mortification value—being spoon-fed like a baby by tall, towering, meticulous Ham or the fact that tall, towering, rugged David was standing there, witnessing the intimacy of what was actually an innocent act.

I opened my mouth and gulped down the ice cream. A cold shiver of guilt trailed along with it down my parched throat.

I said, "Ham. This is David. His mom is a resident at Evergreen Gardens. Ham is…" My tongue was tied. I didn't know how to characterize Ham and Helen's relationship. I went with "Ham's Aunt Helen… well, Prozac's her dog."

David bobbed his head. "Small world."

After the two men shook hands, the conversation took a nosedive into an even more awkward moment of nobody saying anything.

"What do you think of the pistachio?" Ham turned toward me, awaiting my verdict.

I was too uptight to remember what I'd just tasted, but I said, "Delicious," all the while feeling sick and nauseated. My stomach was in a knot as I gingerly wiped my lips and glanced down at Prozac, who was licking his chops. He stood on his hind legs, paws resting on my shin. He cast me a look of hopeful expectancy, waiting for something else to drop.

Ham said to David, "If you've never had the pistachio ice cream from Bamboo House, I would highly recommend it."

David kept his eyes on me as he said, "Yes, I know. Thanks." Then he firmed his grasp on the iPad bag in his hands and said, "Listen, I better go. I'm late. Nice to meet you, Ham. You two enjoy your dinner."

David seemed as anxious to leave as I was desperate to keep him there. How I wished I could offer an explanation, tell David that Ham was just a friend—that it wasn't what it appeared; it wasn't a dinner date and certainly not a romance—but instead, I blurted, rather desperately, "Will Prozac and I see you at the party on Wednesday?"

"Don't know yet if I can make it." David reached down and busied himself with the dog, his face a mask of hurt feelings. "Hope to be there, but I have a lot going on. See you later, Prozac."

David scratched behind the dog's ear and gave him a last pat on the head before he hurried away.

Prozac stood there—still as a statue, tail erect—watching David depart. It was the first time I'd actually felt that that dog and I were on the same wavelength.

"Seems like a nice guy," Ham said. "But someone should really step in and do a fashion intervention. What's with the Elmer Fudd look?"

# Twenty-One

*THINK DIFFERENT*

### Meredith

HAM INSISTED ON PAYING FOR dinner, so on his way out of my townhouse that night, I gave him the bottle of Piper-Heidsieck champagne I'd received from Annette Mahoney. You would've thought I'd given him a million dollars.

"Thank you. This was such a lovely time," Ham said, the two of us standing with full bellies, mildly tipsy, by the front door. He leaned in and wrapped me in a warm embrace. Instinctively, I firmed my arms around him and hugged back, feeling the rough, woven twill of his gabardine jacket beneath my fingers. Knowing his story, the truth of who he was, had freed me of my former inhibitions. I allowed myself to be enveloped by the friendly comfort of his touch. During dinner, I had opened up and told him about Kyle and what happened. Ham seemed to understand me and how I had been navigating life. Our grief and suffering had connected us, building a bridge between two wounded souls.

"Tonight was the most alive I've felt since Stephen died."

Ham's long, intense hug expressed his sincerity and gratitude. I patted him on the back—inhaling faded traces of his citrus-scented aftershave.

"You and me, we've lost a lot, but we're survivors, Meredith. And love, it outlasts grief. Things'll turn around for us, I just know it," Ham said. "And don't you be afraid to take the leap with this David guy. I felt a very good vibe coming from him—despite his Looney Tunes jacket."

I laughed. "It would never work. I've got way too much baggage."

"Never say never." Ham released his hold on me. He took both my shoulders and stared at me, straight on. "And forget the baggage. If you're not carting around some baggage by the time you get to be our age, then you're probably not living."

"But he'd have every right to misconstrue seeing us out together as a date—"

"Maybe, but I know men. This guy likes you—trust me. Make it a point to show up on Wednesday for that party and *wow* him."

"And how, exactly, am I supposed to do *that*?"

"Hey, I'm an architect. If you want me to design a love nest, draw up plans to accommodate wood and nails, I can make it happen. But creative constructs, conversation?" Ham held up his palms as if in surrender. "That's your terrain, Ms. Writer."

"I can do it on the page, but it's not always so easy for me in real life."

"Be yourself. It'll work out if it's supposed to. Have a little faith."

<hr />

*Faith?*

After Ham left, his parting words resonated, and that one word, *faith*, haunted me. I used to have faith in the world. I used to trust people. I used to believe in the goodness of human nature. But when that kid picked up that rock and hurled it through the air, he didn't kill only Kyle. He also destroyed my faith, didn't he? And after everything I'd been through, maybe I was too far gone to have faith anymore. Maybe I was too afraid to even hope that I'd be able to trust again.

Perhaps my dinner with Ham was a first step. By allowing the pressures of my writing deadline to slip away for one night, I lost myself in our conversation and had a complete disregard for the demands of time. Once I opened myself up just a tiny bit, I began to drop my guard as Ham and I compared notes about what it was like to have someone we loved ripped from our lives. For me, it felt as though a part of my body had been hacked off, amputated, as if I'd lost an arm or a leg. I had learned how to live without it, and I'd adjusted as best I could, but I knew I would never be the same.

"Kyle's toothbrush. Do you still have it?" Ham asked at one point.

I nodded. "Still hanging in the bathroom. His blue brush next to my pink one."

"Me, too. I still have Stephen's. His was yellow. Whenever I have friends over, they tell me it's time to toss it. But I can't. Not yet."

"The day after Kyle died, I came home, stripped the bed, and put our dirty sheets inside a big Ziploc bag. I keep it in the closet. Whenever I have a bad day, I open the bag and take a sniff. I can still smell his scent, the two of us together. I know it probably sounds weird, but something about it still brings me comfort."

"It's not weird at all."

The night went on like that, as though we were playing *can-you-top-this* in the ways of grief. And since Ham had gone home, and I was faced with a sink full of dirty dishes, the events of the day—and my responses to them—started to take on new shape. I wrote off my uncharacteristic openness to having indulged in too much wine. The power of the acidic grapes, all that resveratrol, had loosened me up, including my tongue, and had proven something of a truth serum. I'd probably said way too much— so much that, in retrospect, I was already regretting having told Ham far more than I'd shared with anyone else the past three years. I had conveyed a whole litany of emotions: bitterness, resentment, fear, loneliness, feeling incredibly misunderstood by friends who wandered away from my life, unable to cope with the fact that I wasn't moving on.

I told him about what had happened with David and how he'd asked me out, and I'd choked. And even though Ham identified with many of the experiences and feelings I'd shared, there I was, feeling vulnerable. I stared into the kitchen sink and squirted detergent over the dirty dishes like an arsonist dousing gasoline over a fire, hoping to make everything go away—the past, present, and even the future.

What was wrong with me? Why was I acting in ways that felt so alien and unpredictable, and two times in one day—first with Aunt Helen and then with Ham?

*Think Different.*

That motto from the Apple Store popped into my head as I continued cleaning the kitchen. The more I rehashed the events of the day and tried to understand my feelings, the more encouraged I felt to refill my wineglass.

That was, until the doorbell rang a few minutes later.

Prozac's dog tags jingled as he rushed into the foyer. His nails tapped upon the tiled floor, signaling me to hurry up and see who was at the door.

I followed his lead and pressed my eye to the peephole. My sister Monica's face moved closer. "Meredith, I know you're in there. Open up!"

*Oh, great. Maybe I can go three for three with regrets today.*

The minute I opened the door, Monica pushed her way past me. Oblivious to Prozac at her feet, she stepped on him. He yelped and scurried away as she made a beeline for the phone perched atop the library table. She lifted the receiver. When the blaring sound of a dial tone filled the space between us, she said, "What good is having a working phone if you don't use it? How does anybody *ever* get through to you?"

I spied a bright number six flashing in red on the answering machine. With Ham visiting, I had once again forgotten to check my messages all night.

"And what about your cell?" Monica asked.

"Oh, I shut off the ringer earlier. I guess I forgot to switch it back on." Guilty, I looked away from my sister and bounded into the kitchen. "Why? What's up?"

Monica followed me as I picked up the last of the dirty utensils and dropped them into the sink.

"Did you have company?" she asked, eyeing the white Chinese takeout containers and two empty wineglasses.

"Ham took me over to visit Helen this afternoon."

"I know. That's why I'm here." My sister spun the half-empty bottle of wine around to look at the label. "But I had no idea you and Ham shared a romantic dinner afterward."

"It wasn't romantic."

Monica shot me an incredulous look. She reached for the wine bottle. "Did *you* buy this?"

I shook my head.

"You don't invest in a vintage like this one unless you're trying to woo someone."

"You do if you're a wine connoisseur with high-class taste. And believe me, he's not trying to *woo* me."

"Oh, and why not?"

"Because I'm not his type."

"What *is* his type?"

"Tall, dark, handsome… and oozing testosterone."

"He's—"

"Yup," I said before she could finish her thought.

My sister nodded. She opened the refrigerator and helped herself to a bottle of spring water. "Does Helen know?"

"Yes. She must know. Helen seems to know everything about everybody."

My sister didn't pick up on my insinuation. Instead, she cracked the seal on the water and took a sip. I reached for my wineglass, half full, and motioned for us to sit in the parlor.

Monica plunked herself down into one of the living room chairs and sneezed.

As I handed her a tissue box, I said, "I was wondering when your allergy was going to surface."

"I took an antihistamine about an hour ago. Maybe it's already wearing off."

I sat on the sofa, and Prozac hopped up and settled alongside me. He rolled onto his back, and I stroked his blond belly.

"Ham might not be trying to woo you, but it appears as though this dog sure is. Look at him," Monica said. "He's got you wrapped around his little paws. What on earth convinced you to become his trustee?"

"What?"

"Helen called me. She's practically doing cartwheels in the hallways of that rehab center about your agreeing to take care of him."

"Wait a second." I stopped petting Prozac and sat forward on the sofa. "I didn't agree to *anything.*"

"Then why did she call and ask that I contact the lawyers and start working on her revised estate plan?"

"I don't know."

Monica raised her eyebrows. "Meredith, Helen is under the impression you've agreed to this, and it's a done deal."

"Well, sh-she's mistaken. How well do you know me?"

Monica tossed up her hands. "I don't know anything when it comes to *you* anymore—"

"But you knew enough to tell Helen all about me, and maybe you even colluded with her to finagle this dog into my life."

Monica said nothing. We locked stares. Prozac must've sensed the tension between us. He leaped onto the back of the couch and scurried away from me.

"Yes, Helen and I, conspirators in cahoots," Monica said. "We worked it all out. Helen would intentionally break her foot and succumb to surgery and a rehab center so she could pawn off her dog, the bright star of her life, on me and then you. And that would be the perfect setup to rope you into becoming his trustee... Why don't you stop being a writer for a minute, Meredith, and listen to yourself!"

The way she put it forced me to stick with the facts and press ahead.

"Look, Helen blindsided me with this proposal. She put me on the spot. I wasn't expecting anything like this—"

"Why didn't you come right out and be straight with her?"

"Because we never had a chance to finish our discussion. Ham came back into the room and interrupted. And he doesn't know what Helen is planning."

I ran a rough hand through my hair and gathered my thoughts. As calmly as I could, I started at the beginning, regaling Monica with details about my visit with Helen and our exchange. And just as with Ham, the more I talked, the more things poured out—about Helen and Ham's bond and how Ham wasn't really her nephew.

According to Monica, Helen had mentioned Ham and Stephen's names in conversation, but she had never addressed the nature of the couple's liaison, choosing instead to refer to them as "the boys," presenting them as though they were *both* her nephews—*both* blood relations.

"In retrospect, Helen did make a couple of comments to me about Ham and his being materialistic," Monica said. "That wine you're drinking is proof alone, and it might be another reason she's not totally comfortable leaving Prozac in his care."

"But that's the thing. Why would she ask me? She doesn't even know me."

"She must feel she knows enough. She's read all your novels—she adores them."

"And what does that mean? A lot of people once adored Hitler's *Mein Kampf*, too!"

Monica shot me a limp grin. She sneezed and blew her nose again.

I asked, "So, what am I supposed to do now?"

"You're supposed to pick up the phone and call Helen. Finish your discussion. Tell her straight out, yes or no. I'll be the dog's guardian—or I won't."

I bit my thumbnail, and I turned to Prozac. With his head flush upon the top cushion of the sofa, he shot his tired-looking eyes my way.

Monica studied me, smiling wolfishly. "Oh my goodness," she said, her voice infused with enthusiasm. "You're taking to this dog, aren't you?"

"No. I am not."

"Meredith, it's okay if you—"

"Enough! Stop! I am not going to be the guardian of this dog. End of story."

Prozac stirred, looking annoyed that we were interrupting his nap. He held up his weary head then dropped it again, closed his eyes, and fell back to sleep.

I let out a long breath as blood pooled inside my throbbing skull. My sister didn't say a word. She kept taking swigs from her water bottle, and I kept sipping my wine, considering the implications of Monica's comments. They hung there like a thick, sticky cloud settling over the two of us. I might've been dealing with my own confusion, pain, and fear, but when I looked at my sister seated across from me in the wingback chair—her shoes kicked off and her feet extended atop the hassock—the pale, tired look on her face and the way her gaze held mine told me that she was dealing with her own pain, grief, and worry about me. She knew me too well, as I knew her. Since Kyle's death and my retreat from the world, it couldn't have been easy for her to know how to deal with me. No wonder she often lost patience. Both of us had always been doers. Achievement oriented. We were raised that way—to keep busy and keep pressing ahead despite our feelings. Maybe it was because our father left us when we were in elementary school, and we'd been raised by a mother who never wasted time dwelling on things—especially not when they were upsetting. She simply put her bad feelings on the back burner and plowed on through life. Monica and I followed her example: keep moving and keep the mind occupied. My sister took comfort in the constancy of numbers; I took comfort in words. And while I had often dropped the ball on that life strategy since Kyle died, sitting with my sister—our simply being together and sharing the quiet—evoked a deeper, silent understanding and strengthened our bond.

Prozac broke the spell between us by releasing a string of loud, wet snores. For such a small dog, and one with such a short snout, he could surely crank up the volume. His noisy breath rose to a crescendo like that of a wounded warthog.

Monica and I looked at each other, stifling our laughter so as not to wake him.

My sister ripped her feet from the hassock and leaned forward in her chair. "Listen, you make whatever decision is best for you—but please put your cards on the table with Helen soon. Don't lead her on. She's a nice lady." Monica reached for her pocketbook and pulled out a business card. "Helen's number at the rehab is written on the back of this. Call her and be straight with her. Yes or no. It's that simple—or that difficult."

Prozac's snore was as shrill as a buzzsaw.

"I'm coming back as a dog in my next life," Monica said. "Here I need to drink chamomile tea and pop melatonin to sleep. Hell, I even put in a mouth guard to keep from clenching and grinding my teeth at night. And look at him. Not a care in the world, completely oblivious to everything. Bless his little heart."

# Twenty-Two

*IS THAT YOUR FINAL ANSWER?*

## Meredith

VACILLATION BECAME THE ORDER OF the day. One minute, it was all settled. I'd call Helen and tell her, flat out, that she would have to find someone else to take care of Prozac. And then, in the next minute, as if that dog somehow knew what I was thinking, he'd come sidling up next to me, put on his cute face, and stare at me with those doleful eyes like the kids in ads for Save the Children, of which I was already a sponsor. That was all it took for me to second-guess myself. A few times, I got as far as dialing nine digits of Helen's number at the rehab center, then I'd hesitate before punching in that tenth number and hang up.

Deferring was easier. So I dove back into my novel. By immersing myself in a completely fabricated world from morning until night, I didn't have time to think about calling Helen or giving my final answer to the Prozac question. That was, until three days later when Monica's voice blared through the answering machine I had turned back on.

"Pick up this phone and talk to me…" Monica paused, waiting for me to execute her command. When I didn't, she blasted, "Better yet, pick up the phone and call Helen. The legal papers are being drawn up as we speak. This is it, Meredith! Make that call—or forever hold your peace!"

When she hung up, a surge of cold clamminess washed over me. A niggling voice filled my head, playing devil's advocate.

*"What is the problem here, Meredith? Why are you delaying this? You're not a dog person. You never were."*

*"But does that mean I never could be?"*

*"Oh, please, Meredith, get a hold of yourself. What are you thinking? Stop with this nonsense!"*

I reached for my cell phone. I was in the middle of punching in Helen's number at the rehab center when an idea came to me.

I put down the phone, turned to my computer, and logged on to the Internet. I typed the phrase *Provisions for pets upon death.* Up came a link to the Humane Society. I skimmed the site and read their suggestions regarding state rescue organizations dedicated to specific breeds. It appeared they worked tirelessly to place surrendered pets with people who were carefully screened.

Next, I typed in "Yorkshire Terrier Rescue" and read case histories, testimonials, rules, and regulations. Then I clicked on a video on the main page: "Adopted Precious gets a new set of wheels."

In the blurry footage, a plump woman in a floral print housecoat was holding a Yorkie wearing what looked like a diaper, anchored by a stubby tail. The woman was spouting baby talk to the dog, who couldn't have been more than three or four pounds, and whose hind legs appeared atrophied and completely limp. She fastened the little paraplegic creature into a harness contraption with wheels. Once the dog was strapped in, it took off and joined a pack of six other Yorkies that bolted across the carpet, out the back door, and onto a deck, where the handicapped Yorkie happily scooted down a ramp at rollercoaster-like speed to join them, playing on a dandelion-spotted lawn. The video clip ended with the pack of Yorkies playing tug-of-war with a rope bone and the lady's voiceover saying, "Poor Precious's owner passed away. How could I let them put her down just 'cause she had no one else to care for her? Hell, nobody's perfect, and bad things happen. That's life. Look at Precious hamming it up with Lady Bug, who's blind, and Atlas, who's deaf. Can you imagine killing off these adorable four-legged babies when there's so much life still left in 'em?"

A canned message from the Humane Society warned, "Don't let your beloved, orphaned pet fall prey to the system. In the event of your death, have a plan in place today to ensure your pet's well-being tomorrow."

The video ended, frozen on an image of Precious surrounded by her silver-haired little cohorts swept up in playtime. I felt myself choking up, tears pressing behind my eyes. The devotion and outlook of that woman in the video—the sight of her tribe, those lovable little four-legged misfits—got to me. But before I could burst into a complete emotional cesspool, my cell phone chimed. There was a text from Monica. STOP DELIBERATING. MAKE THE DOGGONE CALL—NOW!

*Doggone? Maybe it's a sign?*

I knew what I needed to do. I picked up the phone and hit all ten digits for Helen. When I heard her line ring, I sucked in a deep breath and prepared to tell the truth.

I was surprised to hear the recorded sound of Ham's low tenor. "Hi, you've reached Helen Hendrix's line. Please leave your name and number, and she will get back to you. Thanks. Have a nice day."

After the piercing beep, I cleared my dry throat and spit out, "Hi, Helen. It-it's Meredith. Meredith Mancuso-St. John. Monica's sister. I've been taking care of Prozac. Well, I'm calling to let you know that I've carefully considered your proposition to become Prozac's guardian and... well... the thing is... well... I'm sorry, but I don't think I can make that type of commitment. However, I've discovered several other viable options you might want to consider. *Plenty* of people out there would be ready and willing to give Prozac all the love, care, and devotion he needs..."

I proceeded to babble on, saying more than necessary about what I'd learned from the Humane Society and Yorkie Rescue. Just as I was leaving my phone number, asking for Helen to call me if she wanted to learn more and discuss things, the machine cut off.

The call ended, and I was besieged by a mix of emotions. At first, I felt a sense of relief, especially that I didn't have to talk to Helen directly. But that was soon overshadowed by the letdown I envisioned Helen would feel. I sat at my desk feeling eerily empty, hollowed out inside. It felt somehow similar to what I experienced the night Kyle died.

I don't know how long I sat, but the next time I looked up, Prozac was seated as still as a statue in the hallway, outside my open office door. He had a forlorn look in his eyes, and his normally erect, triangular ears were flagged down as if they had been blown back by a steady, fierce headwind.

"Please, don't look at me that way." A prickly feeling filled my throat, and a sick sensation roiled inside my belly. "You've got to believe me—you'll be much happier somewhere else."

Prozac, body stiff, locked his deep brown gaze with mine. Drawn in by his stare, I was convinced he understood what had just transpired, and he was shooting me an unforgiving glare.

Maybe I deserved it?

Through my moist eyes, I had a staring contest with Prozac until my phone chimed and pulled me out of my reverie. It was a text message from Judge Thea:

Poor Helen is beside herself.

Call her back and agree 2 take Prozac ASAP or I call APL.

# Twenty-Three

*LIFE OF THE PARTY*

Prozac

MY LIFE WITH MEREDITH HAD been no picnic, but how could she do that to me? How could she let Helen down and cast me off into the surrendered dog system—only to be snatched up someday and cared for by a perfect stranger?

Knowing Meredith as well as I did, I was counting on Judge Thea's text ultimatum to rally her to reconsider. My hopes rose as she sandwiched her phone between her palms, and with her fingers steepled as if in prayer, she bowed her head and closed her eyes. But then, she set the phone atop the desk, dropped her head into her hands, and burst into ragged, wheezing cries that stole her breath until she was practically hyperventilating.

I had the sense that Meredith really wanted to say yes to Helen and to me—wanted to fulfill the judge's order and call Helen back and tell her that she'd changed her mind—but she was mired in confusion. She was conflicted. It mirrored the way she'd vacillated and put off David's proposition to go for coffee. Grief and wallowing had sustained Meredith for years—they had become her comfort zone. But ever since we'd started visiting Evergreen Gardens, Meredith's boundaries had been stretched and blurred, and her sense of security was shaken. She lacked the confidence to make decisions for her life anymore.

Even though I was fuming mad at Meredith, my heart winced at the sight of her completely falling apart. The operatic drama of her recurrent breakdowns brought me back to the 1960s when I was a street dog, a stray who used to rummage through dumpsters behind the Seattle Opera House.

I scammed some pretty good snacks, and the music that spilled out while I dined was an added bonus. But the way Meredith was carrying on today made me as sad as listening to Puccini's *Madame Butterfly*.

When her anguish became too much for me to bear, I climbed under her desk and reached up my paws to her calf.

She rolled back her desk chair and looked down at me. My empathetic face only made her cry harder.

"Oh, Prozac, I'm so sorry," she choked through cries and sobs. "I'm a mess. You've been through enough. You shouldn't have to put up with me on top of everything else."

I clawed at her soft slippers until she picked me up and set me atop her desk. For the first time in the weeks we'd been roommates, she drew her arms around me. She slumped into a bath of tears that trickled onto my back, weighing me down with her trembling grief.

*Oh, the poor thing!*

Meredith pinned me inside her arms as she plumbed the dark depths of her despair. Her hot breath ruffled my hair as she said, "Oh, I can't live like this anymore."

Neither could I. She was smothering me, so I wiggled and pushed through a tiny space between Meredith's elbows. When we both finally came up for air, she pressed her lips to my head. Then she wiped her eyes and blew her nose. She pushed her chair away from the desk, set me down on the floor, and rose to her feet.

Meredith drew her shoulders back and raised her chin. As she tramped out of the room, I was puzzled by the sudden shift in her resolve, so I followed her into the kitchen. She opened the cabinet beneath the sink and reached for a couple of heavyweight paper shopping bags. Then she turned on her heels, marched back to her office, and placed a hand on the knob of the closet door, that hidden shrine to Kyle and their life together. She flung the door open with such force that her hair flew back. Inside, she faced a perfectly captured world: Kyle's fireman's uniform and hat, his flannel shirt, the bundled bed sheets, all that baseball memorabilia. Her face streaked wet, she took great pains to pack everything away with care. When all the mementos were stripped from the closet, she dragged the bags into the hallway. But before she hauled them off, she turned to the bathroom, where she reached for the blue toothbrush in the holder. With puffy, red-rimmed eyes, she stared at it, examining it from all sides.

Her voice cracked with, "I love you, Ky. I do. And I always will. But I just can't live with all this stuff anymore." She returned to the hall and dropped the toothbrush atop one of the bags. Then she lugged the bags away and hoisted everything up onto a shelf in a corner of the garage.

Grief was the price we paid for love. Who would Meredith be beyond her grief?

———————◦◦◦———————

I half expected the Animal Protection League to ring the doorbell at any moment, but all remained quiet on the home front. As far as I knew, Meredith never phoned Helen again. And the judge didn't text a second time.

Meredith went back to work as if her breakdown were merely a passing interlude. I'd learned, over the years, that for humans, grief surged in waves—waves that swept them up and made them tumble. But then the waves passed. They subsided. Humans would then catch their breath and regain their footing, until the waves, over time, ultimately lessened in intensity and became more infrequent.

When Monica phoned a day later, Meredith broke from her writing frenzy and answered the call. She acted as though things were fine—*her* idea of fine—and she seemed peaceful when Monica brought up the Helen decision.

"I know what I'm capable of, and I think I made the only decision I could make—at least for where I am in my life right now," she said.

I begged to differ.

———————◦◦◦———————

It astounded me how the storm of Meredith's life had lifted. She went back to work, fervently polishing prose and tying up literary loose ends. At one point, I heard her on the phone, leaving a message for her agent, saying that she'd finally hit the send button and emailed her the finished novel.

*Does it ever occur to Meredith that my presence in her life has been the force behind that accomplishment?*

I went back into seclusion—disappearing under the bed, the sofa—slinking out just long enough to relieve myself and eat my meals, alone.

A few days later, Ham called and left a message thanking Meredith for "a wonderful time the other night." And when he ended the call with "Be sure to *wow* the magician on Wednesday," I spied the curve of Meredith's lips, a glimmer of her bright, familiar smile.

*I can't believe it!*

It was really starting to peeve me the way Meredith had bounced back—how it appeared as though she had sloughed off all the drama surrounding the Helen Hendrix guardianship dilemma and all the feelings it had unearthed. What was up with that? What about me—my feelings? Maybe I'd let her off the hook too easily.

I studied her more closely, listening to the squeaky mirrored closet doors in her bedroom as they slid open and closed. From my lookout under her bed skirt, I watched as she ripped clothes from the closet. It seemed as though she was in search of the perfect outfit to wear to that welcome party at Evergreen Gardens. But each fashion selection Meredith made—holding blouses, skirts, and dresses in front of her and eyeing her reflection in the mirror—was cause for disappointment. She tossed one outfit after the next onto the floor of her bedroom until the closet was filled with only empty hangers clanging on the bar.

By the time Wednesday afternoon rolled around, I was restless and eager for a day out. The first whiff of Meredith's sweet-smelling perfume served as my motivation to crawl out from under the sofa. I sat, waiting by the foyer closet where Meredith kept my leash and harness. When the bedroom door opened, I tensed with uncertainty. Footsteps clip-clopped down the hall. There was Meredith—showered, hair coiffed, wearing a pretty purple blouse and a tasteful black skirt. Understated. Refined. It appeared that Meredith's manic, emotional turmoil had evolved into a blessing. She seemed ready to move forward with life. I watched her check her face in the foyer mirror, sensing the butterflies fluttering in the pit of her stomach as she applied her lipstick. Was it in anticipation of seeing David again? If so, then purple surely proved to be a "wow" color on her.

---

A bright banner stretched across the atrium of Evergreen Gardens: *Welcome, Margo Trilling*. The room, and the fountain that rose up toward the cathedral ceiling, was decorated with balloons and streamers. Blaring notes and musical arpeggios from the organ resounded through those big golden pipes set high on the wall. When I heard someone remark, "Isn't that Sondheim? 'Send in the Clowns' from *A Little Night Music?*" joy overwhelmed me. I pranced into the room, and with tail up, I wagged it for the gathered guests, swarmed by a whirlwind of love and affection that served to benefit my canapé crusade. The partiers were only too eager to drop me crumbs that sweetened my mission.

At one point, I spied Mary Chirichella sitting alone in one of the chairs by the fireplace. She was daintily sipping a cup of pink sherbet punch, the tight curls of her blue-gray hair blown out into something resembling a storm cloud. My intention in pulling Meredith over in Mary's direction was two-fold. One, I thought Meredith needed to make peace with Mary, and two, I knew if I put on my cute face, Mary might cave and give me a taste of some salmon mousse.

When Mary caught sight of me, she set her glass of punch atop the side table and opened her arms wide in greeting. Then she patted her lap, and I jumped right up—ripping the leash from Meredith's grasp.

"Oh, how I've missed you!" Mary hugged and kissed me as if she'd never let me go. I licked her face.

Meredith said, "Looks like the feeling's mutual."

Mary looked up and nodded at Meredith. "I can never get enough of this little guy."

"Listen, about the other day… your car," Meredith said. "I'd like to clear the air—"

"It's okay." Mary's deeply veined hands drew me closer. "No need to go there."

"Has there been any news?" Meredith asked.

Mary shook her head. "It's probably my old mind playing tricks on me. Nobody likes to admit they're becoming forgetful sometimes."

"Well, I truly did enjoy our visit."

"Me, too," said Mary.

"The brownies à la mode were delicious. And you gave me lots of food for thought about my next book."

"I'm glad," she said. "Most times, all everybody wants to talk about is doctors' appointments or brag about their kids and grandkids. Our chat was a nice change of pace for me, too."

Stan, the guy who always wore Bermuda shorts and chewed on unlit cigars, wandered over, whistling like a teakettle. "Careful you don't smother that dog to death, Mary."

"I would never hurt Prozac," Mary said.

"I think Stan's jealous," Meredith added.

Stan winked at Meredith. "You're darn right I am."

Mary scrunched up her face as though she'd just bitten into a lemon.

"Stan, you are such a flirt!" Lucy Graves chimed in, passing a silver tray of dainty tea sandwiches, crusts removed. When she held the offerings in front of Mary, I inhaled a whiff of egg salad and noticed how the yellow color contrasted so well with the pastel green of Lucille's tennis skirt. She hummed along with "Don't Cry for Me, Argentina," which was piping from the organ. "You're not giving our Meredith here any trouble, are you, Stan?"

Innocence blazed through Stan's eyes. "No, of course not. I'm only trying to take a few lessons from Prozac and figure out why all you ladies fawn over him. What's he got that I don't?"

"Four legs, and he doesn't wear shorts twelve months of the year— among other things," Lucy said, winking at Mary, whose lips unfurled with amusement. "Here, why don't you make yourself useful?" Lucy danced a few steps then handed Stan the platter of sandwiches. She motioned for him to pass the hors d'oeuvres. He crammed two of the triangular sandwiches into his mouth, took the tray, and off he went.

Mary ripped off a tiny corner of her sandwich, and when no one was looking, she slipped it to me. A dab of the creamy egg salad filled my palate. *Oh, how I love that Mary!*

"That Stan. He's something else, isn't he?" Lucy said to Mary and Meredith.

"Sure is," Meredith agreed. "But you really have a way with him."

"Oh, we Evergreen gals, at our age, we all keep praying for nice platonic relationships with rich little old men. But instead, God sends us dirt-poor old geezers the likes of Stan—"

"He sent us Prozac, too," Mary chimed. "And I'd take this dog over most men, any day."

"Amen to that!" chimed in Stella Stanislowski, who joined the group, holding up her crystal glass of punch before taking a swig. "Mary, you didn't spike this punch with any rum, did you?"

"Me? No, that's *your* job," Mary fired back, continuing to pet me. "When are we ever going to taste your so-called ice cream pie with the chocolate-rum icing?"

"I'm working on it," Stella said, winking at Lucy and Meredith.

I was relieved the ladies had apparently resolved their issues.

Stella glanced at her watch and said, "Nice party. But I wonder what's keeping the guest of honor. Did you guys make a wager in Annette Mahoney's pool?"

"I already lost," Lucy said. "I bet that Margo would arrive fashionably late by fifteen minutes."

"Don't feel bad. I foolishly took ten," Stella said.

"I would hate to jinx myself, but I still have a chance." Mary held up crossed fingers on her right hand. "I have her coming in at thirty-five minutes past."

"Knowing Margo," Lucy said, "she probably got sidetracked decorating her place."

"The Regal Suite is all of five rooms," said Stella. "How *sidetracked* could she get?"

"Believe me, the way Margo loves to decorate, she could easily get hung up," Mary added, turning to Meredith to explain. "Margo's the type who needs a twelve-step program to break her shopping addiction."

"All that might change now that Bob's six feet under," said Lucy.

"Don't kid yourself," Stella said. "Bob's probably worth even more to Margo dead than alive. I mean, how many ex-husbands do you know who provide for their ex-wives in their old age?"

"Bob surely didn't make the arrangements for Margo to move in here out of the kindness of his heart," said Mary. "Her divorce attorneys took care of that."

Lucy turned to Meredith and said, "Many years ago, Bob invested the lion's share for the overhaul of Evergreen Gardens. If it wasn't for him, none of us would be living here—"

"And what, we should canonize him for that?" Bitterness seared through Stella's tone. "This place was always just one of his many investments."

Lucy turned to Meredith again. "Bob was a very smart businessman—"

"Oh, he was smart all right—and clever, too," said Stella. "Uprooting Margo and the kids and moving to Oak Park so he could live closer to his tennis instructor-turned-mistress."

*Wow, this story is getting even spicier than Mary's soap operas!*

Meredith asked, "Did Margo know?"

Lucy and Mary shook their heads, while Stella said, "Not until they were all settled, and Margo walked in on Bob and the bimbo all cozy at the club one day—"

"And if that wasn't bad enough," Mary added, "the bimbo was younger than their youngest child."

"Oh, it was humiliating," said Lucy. "Poor Margo having to live in this little town and be subjected to Bob's philandering, right under her nose."

"But it all paid off pretty handsomely for *poor Margo* in the large scheme of things," said Mary, turning to Meredith. "Margo's crackerjack divorce lawyers built in a clause where she would take over Bob's share of Evergreen Gardens after he kicked the bucket—including her having dibs on the Regal Suite."

"Yeah, and it's just like Margo, Mrs. Hoity-Toity—she had to redo everything before she could *officially* move in," said Stella, adding air quotes around the word *officially.*

"I'm sure it hasn't been easy for her," Lucy said, "packing up that big house and downsizing to here."

Mary said, "Yes, I understand her children saw her slowing down and getting a bit forgetful. I heard *they're* the ones who decided she shouldn't live alone in that mansion anymore."

"At least with us," said Lucy, "we made the choice to move here on our own. It must be very traumatic—being uprooted against your will."

Lucy's comments were drowned out by a shower of applause from the fifty or so residents and revelers who had gathered in the atrium-turned-party-room of Evergreen Gardens. At first, I thought all the fanfare might've been for the guest of honor, but when I followed the gazes of everyone in the room, I saw an older woman being wheeled into the room by Razzle-Dazzle Radcliffe—David. He looked sharp in a muted purple shirt and a darker purple tie.

He and Meredith matched.

The woman in the chair was David's mom, Gloria, whose hair looked different—was she wearing a wig?—and she looked thinner than the last time I'd seen her. Regardless, her face beamed from the flurry of hugs and attention.

"Welcome back, *Glo*," some of the partygoers sang out.

I pawed Mary's lap, anxious to see Gloria myself. I had missed her. She was a quiet lady with a bright, warm smile who always baked to-die-for German spice cookies. Whenever I'd visited with her in the past, she'd slipped me a few broken pieces when no one was looking. What I liked best about the cookies was their crunch and the fact that they weren't too sweet—a hint of molasses that I eagerly gobbled up. Those treats made Glo and me friends for life.

When Gloria spotted me, I reacted on impulse, completely disregarding my therapy dog training. I bounded away from Mary and dashed across the room, leaping into Glo's lap. She howled in delight, and when the crowd let out amused cheers, I hoped the collective response would build a case against my disobedience.

"Oh, what a good boy!" Glo giggled while she fluffed my hair and offered me a million kisses. At one point, I spotted a reflection of my wagging tail in the lenses of her eyeglasses. She looked as thrilled to see me as I was to see her.

David was standing behind his mother, gripping her wheelchair. I leaped up and pressed my cold nose to his warm hand to greet him.

As he patted me on the head, Meredith said, "I'm sorry about Prozac's rude welcome."

"No apology necessary." Glo was charmed by my unfettered attention.

Meredith reached down, as though she were planning to snatch me up, but Glo held on even tighter and pulled me from Meredith's reach.

"If you don't mind," Gloria Radcliffe said, "I'd like to make up for some of the therapy dog time I've missed the past couple of weeks."

"Be my guest. I'm Meredith, by the way."

Meredith thrust out her hand to Glo, who hesitated, acting as though she feared that if she let go of me, I might wiggle away, and she'd never get me back.

"I'm Gloria." She released her grasp on me just long enough to shake Meredith's hand. "I love your books. And David's told me all about you."

"Only the good stuff, I hope." Meredith looked to David. His mouth was set in a straight line. He obviously wasn't planning to make it easy for Meredith to win back his favor.

"We've been reading one of your novels together."

Meredith said, "So I've heard."

"David, do you have that shopping bag? I'd like Meredith to sign that book for me."

David unhooked a cloth satchel from the back of the chair and presented it to Meredith.

"Wouldn't you rather visit with Prozac and your friends a while?" Meredith asked.

Glo said with some urgency, "I'm afraid that once I let go of Prozac, you'll be too busy escorting him around the room, and there won't be time for you to sign them."

"Not to worry," Meredith said, shifting her eyes from Gloria up to David. "I promise. I'll sign them later. You have my word."

Glo Radcliffe held me close while well-wishers stopped to greet her. That left Meredith an opening to try to smooth things over with David.

"How'd the iPad go over?"

"Mom loved it," David said.

"She's getting the hang of how to use it?"

David nodded. "I gave her a magazine outlining all the bells and whistles. So I suspect that in no time, I'll be asking her to give *me* a tutorial."

"God bless her. Was she released today?"

"Yes, we left the hospital and made a beeline for the nail salon on our way here."

"Well, she looks good, and she's sure loved. They're welcoming her back as if she's today's guest of honor."

In a moment of silent awkwardness, Meredith and David looked on admiringly at the warm reception the folks were giving Glo.

David asked, "Did you meet your deadline?"

"Yes. Actually, I did. It was a long haul. So I certainly deserve this change of scenery today—"

While Meredith was loosening up, she was interrupted by that towering G.I. Joe of a high school kid from the day we got stuck in the elevator. What was up with him always wearing those army fatigues?

He tapped Meredith on the shoulder and broke into her conversation with David by asking, rather bluntly, "Ma'am, do you know Stephen King?"

*Ma'am?*

Meredith turned. "W-why, sure," she stammered, apparently caught off guard by the intrusion.

"You do?" The kid's brown eyes widened beneath his dark eyebrows and crew cut. "Can you get me his autograph?"

"I don't know about that. I meant that I know Mr. King's work," Meredith said, clarifying. "But I don't know him *personally*."

"But someone said you're a best-selling writer?"

"Yes, but not the caliber of Stephen King."

*Oh, it's just like Meredith to ooze humility!*

"And being a best seller doesn't mean I have the opportunity to literally rub elbows with him, either."

"Oh," the boy said, his hopes obviously deflated. "So you can't get me his autograph?"

Meredith narrowed her eyes, looking suspicious "No. I'm sorry. I don't think I can."

Without another word, G.I. Joe did an about-face.

Meredith looked at David and shrugged. She watched the boy grab a mozzarella stick off a passing tray. As he headed to the other side of the room, she said, "I don't know which is worse—to be rejected so brusquely or to be *ma'am*-ed."

"I beg your pardon?" David said.

"That young man. He referred to me as *ma'am*. I guess I'm past the point of *miss*?"

An amused smile flashed across David's face. "Sooner or later, it happens to the best of us. I've been *sir*-ed and *mister*-ed plenty of times. You'll live."

"But not peacefully," said Meredith. "Who is he, anyway?" She looked at the kid. He was chewing on a mouthful of hors d'oeuvres as he walked past one table that held a communal jigsaw puzzle and another that was laden with assorted canapés, which he took in handfuls. Then he plopped himself down sideways upon one of the nearby French provincial chairs. His back leaned against one of the armrests, while his legs, in camouflage pants, were thrust over the other arm of the chair. He dumped the heaping handfuls of canapés onto his lap and started stuffing his face.

"Oh, that's Randall—Randy—Judge Thea's grandson. His manners and social skills leave a lot to be desired."

"Does he ever smile?"

"Let me put it to you this way—Randy smiling is about as likely as finding a Trappist monk at a Metallica concert," David said. "But don't feel bad. It's not just you. He's abrupt with everyone."

David, Meredith, and I watched as Judge Thea paraded over to Randy. With a firm, staunch look on her face, and the snap and wag of her fingers, she directed her grandson to sit correctly in the chair—two feet on the floor.

He shot the judge a look of displeased annoyance, but he complied.

"What's his deal?" Meredith remarked. "Does he come here a lot?"

David rolled his eyes. "Yeah, almost every day."

"Then he's close to the judge?"

"No, I wouldn't say that. But he's been through a lot. Sad story."

"How so?"

"From what I understand, his mother, Judge Thea's daughter, died. And afterward, his father took off—abandoned him."

"Wow, that's terrible. Is the judge his legal guardian?"

"I gather she is. I don't think he has anybody else."

Glo flipped me a tiny piece of carrot. While I chomped away, I listened woefully to Meredith. The writer in her was at it again, asking a gazillion questions.

"Where does he live?" she asked. "I mean, if he's still in high school, he can't be living on his own."

"All I know is that he sure hangs out here a lot. He's notorious for hogging the computers and keeping the television in the community room tuned to MTV."

"Is he in military school or something?"

"I have no idea," David said. "I assumed the army fatigue fetish was a teenage rebellion thing. What's with all the questions—you writing a book?"

"Yes, currently on the lookout for my next one. Maybe it should be about a teenager who *disses* a woman cured of her writer's block."

When David smiled, a sweet dimple emerging in his right cheek, I perked my ears.

*Diss. Well, listen to her! Little Miss Writer using a word she formerly dismissed as urban slang.*

"If nothing else, at least he gave us something to talk about. An icebreaker," said Meredith. "Listen, I feel really awful about what happened the other night."

David looked at Meredith as if he hadn't a clue what she was talking about, and his nonchalance must've thrown her for a loop. She stammered as she said, "That guy I was with when you ran into me the other night, the nephew of the lady who owns Prozac…"

David let Meredith's words hang undigested in the air. It encouraged her to go on.

"Well, he's actually not her blood relation but close, like a real nephew. Oh, it's complicated, but that afternoon, he had driven Prozac and me to visit Prozac's owner in the rehab center. On the drive home, we stopped to grab some takeout."

"That's nice," David said, looking away from Meredith. His eyes roamed the room.

"No, it's not nice." Meredith was clearly flustered.

"You really don't need to explain things—"

"Yes. I do." Meredith's voice quavered. "I feel terrible for having turned you down for dinner and coffee, and then you saw me out at the Bamboo House. It wasn't what it looked like."

"And what did it look like?" David asked.

"A date. But it wasn't."

"Whatever it was or wasn't," David said flatly, "don't worry about it. You don't owe me an explanation—"

"But I think I ought to set the record straight."

"No need to. It's not a big deal."

But I could tell it *was* a big deal to Meredith, and I felt that as David downplayed things to bolster his bruised ego, he was only deepening Meredith's discomfort. I feared that Meredith might succumb to a full-blown sensitivity attack—have another emotional outburst if she kept explaining herself. Therefore, I took that as my sign to move on from Glo, who had been chatting with friends and daintily pointing her pinkie as she nibbled on a colorful skewer of fresh fruit. I had been sitting on her lap, putting on the cute face, vying for a bite of some watermelon, but I ditched my quest in order to rescue Meredith from digging herself into an even deeper hole with David.

In one flying leap, I lurched off Glo's lap.

The minute Meredith heard my paws hit the floor, she tried to stomp on my leash to stop me, but I took off. I darted out of the room, navigating through the assembled crowd as though I were making my way through a labyrinth cut with sharp corners.

"Prozac!" The sound of my name exploded into the room. A rush of urgency and raw emotion filled Meredith's voice.

I tore past women's bare legs that sported varicose veins and men's legs with their pressed trousers. My paws skidded on the tile floor until I regained traction on the carpeting of a long, empty hallway. I sailed under wall sconces and recessed entryways decorated with small tables and artwork, wreaths, and statuary. Meredith, huffing and puffing, continued hollering for me until the sound of my name grew dimmer.

When I neared the end of the corridor, I followed a brightly lit sign that read EXIT with an arrow pointing toward the Elm Wing. But when I turned the corner, I was stopped in my tracks by something lying across the floor—styled, bleached-blond hair, swept up, as if in a wave. A pocketbook and its contents were scattered about—cylinders of lipstick, a cell phone, a change purse, a rat-tail comb, and a roll of Butter Rum Lifesavers. Meredith's footsteps grew closer as I followed my nose, sniffing the perimeter of a body as if marking a chalk outline around the downed figure in a buff-colored pantsuit. Even a heavy lacquer of hairspray and an intensely overpowering spritz of perfume—Shalimar, perhaps—could not conceal that the woman's beating heart had stopped.

"Prozac!"

The screech of Meredith's crazed, frenetic voice made me freeze. With tail tucked and ears back, I cowered and trembled next to the body, staring at the sight of Meredith's flushed, distraught face. She stood frozen, a hand clamped over her mouth, underscoring her wide, startled eyes, which were glued to the woman on the floor.

Blood, guts, and death didn't normally shake me, but naked shock and fear often did. And I had a feeling that once Meredith's initial upset wore off, I'd be in some pretty big trouble. When Meredith finally took a step toward me, I felt an overwhelming need to make a run for it. So I took off, dashing into the shadows and bounding away from her, down the corridor in the opposite direction.

I didn't look back.

# Twenty-Four

*NIGHTMARE ON ELM*

Meredith

I LET PROZAC GO AND RAN for help.

My mind chided my legs for moving so sluggishly when time was of the essence. When I burst into the atrium, I was so grossly out of breath—partly from physical exertion and partly from emotion—that spitting out even the word *help* became nearly impossible.

With an ache like a knife in my back, I doubled over, heaving ragged breaths amid the loud organ music and the gathered group belting out the glee-filled words to the song, "Put on a Happy Face."

But such communal glee didn't stop By-the-Book Betsy, clipboard in hand, from cornering me and saying, "I understand the board has invited you and Prozac to the dinner for Margo Trilling. However, dogs are not allowed in the dining room. It violates health code statutes."

Lucy Graves, overhearing, quickly approached. "But Prozac *is* a service dog."

"Technically, no. He's not." Betsy eyed her clipboard. "Service dogs are trained to do work or perform tasks for the benefit of an individual with a disability. I'd consider Prozac's role at Evergreen Gardens merely that of a court jester—"

"Enough!" My cringing outburst roared above the singing. The organ music stopped. Heads turned. "Hurry. Call 9-1-1. Someone's passed out in the hallway and needs help—"

I pointed in the direction of the Elm Wing, and several staff members took off running.

I stood there, staring into a crowd of shocked, horror-filled faces.

"It's Margo, I bet," said wide-eyed Stella Stanislowski. "She's the only one who's not here."

"Or Judge Thea," added Lucy.

"No, it isn't the judge," I told them. "This woman has frosted, not red, hair."

Lucy and Stella answered at the exact same time, "Then it *is* Margo."

Moments earlier, there had been singing and laughing. Dancing. Jokes. Sherbet punch. Canapés. Suddenly, the room was silent and still, humming with sobering concern.

I looked at David and was drawn in by the sensitivity of his gaze, which was brimming with disquiet and empathy. His mouth, set in a straight line, certainly didn't correlate with the balloons and streamers, which had lost their vibrancy.

*OMG—Prozac!*

But before I could turn and hurry to retrieve him, uniformed police officers and paramedics, their radios spitting static and dispatching numeric codes, marched through the room, hauling defibrillators, medical bags, and a stretcher.

I started to follow them, but they ordered me to stay put.

"But the dog—"

"I'm sorry, ma'am. You'll need to wait here," one of the officers said, pushing past me into the hallway.

"But I left him down there with the... with the patient."

"Don't worry, ma'am. We'll find him and bring him to you."

"But he ran—" My words strained to reach the backs of the policemen's heads as they hurried away. Could they even hear me?

I felt a firm hand on my arm, trying to hold me back. Loud, hard-of-hearing words blasted, "It's okay, honey. Let the police and the paramedics do their jobs."

In my stunned helplessness, I turned and searched Annette Mahoney's caring brown eyes split by the bifocal lenses of her eyeglasses. I spouted details about what I had seen in the hall, recounting my discovery. Not coming up for air, I gushed over how I must've frightened Prozac and how he'd run away. Not only was Annette listening, but so, too, were other folks gathered around me, straining to hear the particulars.

"What a shame," said Lucy. "I hope Margo's life doesn't end before it even begins here at Evergreen."

Stella said, "Let's not jump to conclusions. Maybe it was just a stroke or something—"

"Sure, just a stroke. Maybe a touch of heart attack," chimed in Stan. "You make it sound as benign as a head cold."

I wandered away, pacing back and forth in the atrium, holding my head and pulling back my hair. The hands on the freestanding grandfather clock seemed unmoving.

A chill of reverence descended as the paramedics wheeled out a stretcher covered in a white sheet that was clearly shrouding a person underneath.

"So much for the *just a stroke* theory," Jack whispered loud enough for all to hear.

"Yeah, but we should all be so lucky to get a Cadillac death," said Stan.

The stretcher was solemnly escorted past us. Some folks covered their mouths, others cried, and some blessed themselves—forehead to chest, shoulder to shoulder. But all I could think about amid the chilling, unexpected loss was Prozac. Where was he?

As the police officers reentered the room, I blurted, "The dog? Did you find the dog?"

"Ma'am, sorry. We didn't see a dog—"

"But he was there. In the hallway. He was frightened…"

The cops shook their heads and said, "Ma'am, why don't you alert everyone in the facility to look for him. We'll notify the station. He couldn't have gotten very far."

My stomach gave a kick. "I've got to find him," I said, pushing past them.

No one stopped me as I ran down the hallway, peeking into doorways and looking under, around, and behind small tables set outside apartment entryways. I hoped and prayed that Prozac was true to form and hiding somewhere.

I reached the end of the corridor and followed the arrow, turning the corner into the Elm Wing. A rush of cold air hit me. At the end of the empty hallway, I spied an open door. A sense of sickening desolation pitched inside my stomach as I spied a slant of afternoon daylight spilling onto the carpeting right below a bright red sign that read EXIT.

# Twenty-Five

*JOYRIDE*

Prozac

FROM THE FIRST MOMENT I laid eyes on him, I didn't like that Randy kid. And since I was wobbling around the bucket seat of his car as he took corners on two wheels and laughed while my body was tossed against the door armrest and the center console, I liked him even less.

It wasn't my choice to take a joyride. I never intended to leave Evergreen Gardens. When I dashed from Meredith, down the hall of the Elm Wing, I wanted only to slip away for a spell—to let Margo's death sink in and let everybody, including Meredith, cool off. After all, death was never pretty, and it was never easy to accept. But I quickly rethought that decision when the door to the men's restroom squeaked open like a house of horrors and filled the eerie quiet of the Elm Wing. I recoiled into an apartment doorway, watching as that Randy kid, the grandson of Judge Thea, emerged from the public lavatory dressed in those military fatigues. He took one look at the body splayed on the hallway floor, and his chin dropped.

"What the—"

With caution, he approached Margo Trilling, keeping a distance as if making an inspection of dangerous roadkill. Then he dropped to his knees and took one of her wrists in his hands. Her frosted nail polish glimmered, and her gold bracelets jangled beneath the fluorescent lights.

"Gee, is that what rigor mortis feels like?" His eyes were wide, and his tone, devoid of sympathy, was impersonal and distant.

When the tremor of fast-approaching footsteps quivered beneath my paws, I suspected help was on the way. I scurried, making a beeline into the Day Room at the end of Elm Wing. I took cover under a desk in the far corner of the room.

While I sat there, panting, a pair of sandy-colored, mid-calf army boots skidded across the tile floor. I knew right away it was that Randy kid who stood unmoving as a noisy commotion filled the hallway.

Cramps gripped my gut as Randy crouched down. His pimply face filled my line of vision. "What's the matter, buddy? Are you bummed 'cause you're not the center of attention anymore?"

*Buddy?* I wasn't that kid's *buddy.* Far from it. I backed away from him, deeper into the shadows, but the wall behind me stopped my derriere. It was time to revert to common dog strategy and ramp up some mean, old-world aggression.

As Randy's eyes bore into my gaze and his fingers reached out for me, I growled and snapped.

He jerked his hand away and said, "Oh no you don't—you little sissy," as he quickly came back at me a second time with a lot more force.

And so did I.

But the kid's big fingers quickly locked around my head and snout like a steel-trap muzzle. I thrashed in his grasp, but he was too strong. He pulled me out into the airy light beneath the vaulted skylight ceiling and sat us down on the sofa. Stunned, I stood chastened and tense on his lap—my front and back legs quivering upon his thick thighs. I fixated on a Monet water lily print and a darkened HDTV screen bolted to the wall while Randy studied me from all sides as if I were a slide beneath a microscope. It didn't take my Mensa IQ to realize that the kid, while fearless, had zero dog smarts. And I would have bet today was a day of two firsts for him: being up close with a still-warm, dead body *and* with a living, breathing dog.

Considering that Randy had two hundred pounds on me, I decided to change my tack. I licked his wrist as if to apologize and plead, "Okay, now. Be nice and go gentle." With a clammy hand, he stroked the entire length of my spine—head to tail. It was true what they said, that dogs could lower blood pressure, and I could feel the pent-up angst inside Randy releasing notch by notch the more we made physical contact.

*If I can keep this kid calm, then maybe I can catch him off guard and make a getaway.*

"Kinda spooky, what's going on out there," he whispered. "Death sucks."

I turned to face him. I had the sense Randy was much older on the inside than he looked on the outside. I stared into his big, troubled, turtle-like eyes—eyes I wasn't sure I could trust. "Maybe you and me ought to walk right out and blow this joint."

*Uh-oh. Walk? The W-word?* I made a sharp about-face, preparing to leap from his lap.

"Not so fast," he said, tightening his no-nonsense grasp. "Nobody would miss me, but I bet they'd sure miss you. Let's see how much."

*Oh no!*

He stood up and stuffed me inside his army fatigue jacket, tiptoeing toward the doorway. When he peered his head past the doorjamb and found the coast clear, he marched us down the hall and flung open the exit door at the end of the Elm Wing corridor.

Out into the fresh afternoon air we went, yet something about the kid smelled of darkness. But then again, Randy really wasn't a kid. He was probably closing in on eighteen. Part of him seemed like an old man trapped inside a teenager's body, and in other ways, he was rash and immature. That became more evident as he flung open the door to his beat-up Honda Civic, in desperate need of a car wash, and tossed me like a rag doll onto the passenger-side bucket seat. The interior could've used one of those pine tree freshener thingies dangling from the rearview mirror, as I smelled a stale mix of raging teenage male hormones, body odor, and dulled, lingering traces of marijuana. Not pretty, and a far cry from my usual fragrance of the inviting perfumed powders and body lotions from the well-tended ladies of Evergreen Gardens.

"So it looks like it's just you and me, buddy. Time to make a man out of you." Randy, in full tough-guy mode, turned over the ignition and peeled out of the parking lot of Evergreen Gardens—as much as a four-cylinder Honda in need of a tune-up could peel. He took the first turn so sharply, my body slammed against the armrest before I finally toppled to the floor. I landed on my back, paws straight up like an upside-down chair.

Randy laughed like a madman as I side-somersaulted amid crumpled-up fast-food bags and empty drinking cups piled in the footwell. When the car stopped at a red light, I maneuvered back on all fours, crouching down low and taking cover under the passenger seat. But inertia didn't last long as Randy gunned the engine, and I slid off some comic books into the rear footwell filled with balled-up, smelly gym socks, shoes, and sweatshirts, along with a couple of CliffsNotes and ancient, tome-like textbooks, which covered a partially obscured girlie magazine.

One look around his car and the reckless way Randy was driving, and it was clear he was not on the fast track to becoming high school valedictorian. I never would have guessed in a million years that he was related to proper, law-abiding Judge Thea.

Our joy ride continued until the car bumped over what felt like a curb and drew to a lurching stop.

Randy reached into the glove box and pulled out a wallet. He thumbed through the billfold and ripped out what looked like a driver's license and a couple of dollars.

"I'll be right back," he said, cutting the engine.

Once he was out of the car, he slammed the door behind him. I leaped onto the backseat and looked out the window. The afternoon was growing gray and dim, which made the sign for Lyle's Liquors and Packaged Goods seem more brightly lit.

In less than five minutes, Randy returned. He flung a bag with Cheez Doodles and a six-pack of Coca-Cola onto the passenger-side floor. The innocence of those purchases, however, was quickly tainted by the sight of a small bottle of Jack Daniels.

Randy tucked what I gathered was a fake ID back inside the wallet that he stuffed inside the glove box.

The car took off. I toppled backward into the crevice of the backseat and stayed put until a sign for a CVS Pharmacy came into view. Randy hung a sharp left. Thank goodness the upholstery was velour, as I dug my nails into the fabric, anchoring myself, until he slowed the car and pulled around the building, following signs for the drive-through lane.

When he finally stopped the car, I heard a girl's friendly voice say, "Hey, Randy. What are you doing here?"

"Hi, Samantha. I need to pick up a prescription for my grandmother."

"Okay, let me check. What's her name?"

"Theadora Strong."

I took that as my cue to leap from the backseat up onto the center console armrest.

"Oh, what a cute dog!" Samantha gushed. She was a pretty blonde with clear skin. She popped her head through the pickup window to get a better look at me.

I jumped onto Randy's lap, my black-brown hair like an inkblot atop his sandy-colored military pants. As I lurched up, tail wagging, I set my paws upon the interior vinyl door to move closer to the girl. I hoped I'd found an ally.

"Is she yours?" Samantha reached out a hand and patted the crown of my head.

"No," said Randy, not trying to pull me back from the girl. If I were in better shape and more acrobatic, I would've leaped through the window. "She's a *he* actually. My grandmother's dog. I'm helping her out for a little while."

"Well, he's adorable," the girl said. "You're lucky."

"Do you have a dog?" Randy asked.

"No. My mom's allergic—even to dogs that don't shed. But if I were to get a dog, he's exactly the kind I'd want. What's his name?"

"Prozac."

Samantha laughed. "That's funny. Like the medication."

Randy appeared mesmerized by Samantha's navy-blue fingernails as they moved through my hair.

"I love his bandanna," she said.

"He's a therapy dog," he told her. "Always cheering people up and making them happy."

"So then his name really suits him."

"Yeah, I guess you're right," Randy said.

The girl retracted her hand from me. As she stepped away to retrieve Judge Thea's prescription, Randy ruffled my hair. It was my hope that his encounter with Samantha, his witnessing her kind response to me, would somehow soften him and turn the tide of our relationship. After all, what could work better at building a bridge to peace than my serving as a chick magnet?

When Samantha returned, she handed Randy a clipboard and asked for his signature.

"It's not *my* rule," she said. "The medication is Xanax. And tranquilizers are controlled drugs, so you have to sign for them. The state checks."

Randy scribbled an illegible signature on the paper and handed back the clipboard.

"Gee, your handwriting is worse than some doctors'," she said.

Randy's bashful face reflected in the mirror. "Never made A-grades in penmanship."

"By the way, did you finish *The Sound and the Fury* for Southern Lit yet?" she asked.

"Almost."

"Don't you love that book? And with Mr. Wilkinson's enthusiasm, he makes it so you don't even have to use the CliffsNotes to understand it."

"Yeah, well, I never use them anyway."

"Then that makes you a lot smarter than me," Samantha said.

Randy handed the girl a credit card. She swiped the card then passed it through the window, back to Randy, along with a stapled prescription bag.

"See you tomorrow in Southern Lit," Randy said.

"Yeah, see you then. Bye, Prozac." Samantha waved at me.

Randy set me down gingerly onto the passenger seat. Then he reached to the floor and stuffed that prescription inside the bag with the Jack Daniel's, the Coke, and the Cheez Doodles. Right there, on the floor beneath the bag, I spied the trademark yellow-and-black CliffsNotes for the novel *The Sound and the Fury* by another old friend of mine, William "Bill" Faulkner.

# Twenty-Six

## MISERY LOVES COMPANY

### Meredith

E VERY RESIDENT AND GUEST FROM Evergreen Gardens pitched in to help find Prozac—and that even included David pushing Glo up and down corridors and from room to room. The more time that went by, however, the less likely it seemed that Prozac was still on-site.

We looked everywhere—behind curtains, under sofas and chairs, on the lower shelves of the kitchen pantry, and behind library books. We checked the public lavatories, looking inside each toilet bowl. The maintenance people even pulled out the washers and dryers in the laundry room. And when we'd combed through every last nook and cranny imaginable, we started our search again. After all, Prozac—notorious for disappearing acts—could've easily outsmarted us.

As we moved into the second hour of our in-house probe, when spirits were growing weary and folks were tired and giving up hope, I gathered the troops, about forty or so people in all. There in the atrium, I stood alongside the puzzle table, which held a half-finished scene of the River Seine—the box lid displaying the full image propped up behind it—and said, "I'm very grateful that all of you have been so helpful in looking for Prozac. And if you're willing and inclined, I hope you'll continue to search. But there's one last thing we might try to lure him out. I know this might sound crazy, but Prozac loves fish—tuna, salmon, sardines. You name it—"

"So if it swims, and it's not a mermaid?" Stan heckled.

Jack added, "What does he think he is, a cat?"

"Maybe," I said. "And with your permission, I'd like to open a few cans and scatter them around the facility in the hope that the scent will draw him out. Any objections?"

By-the-Book Betsy said, "But we should check with Judge Thea. After all, she's the board president. She has final say."

Annette Mahoney chimed in, "Well, the judge isn't here."

"Where is she?" I asked.

I stared into a sea of blank faces.

"Time is of the essence. We can't wait for the judge," I said, marching away with Annette, Mary, Lucy, and Stella.

We headed for the kitchen, where we opened and drained five cans of fish and scattered them in prime locations at Evergreen Gardens. Then we resumed the search.

When someone said that the elevator wasn't responding, a glimmer of hope penetrated my low spirits. Might Prozac have wandered in there?

Thirty-five minutes later, the elevator repairman diagnosed that the lift was stuck on the second floor. Folks huddled around the closed door of the old-fashioned elevator. When it was finally fixed, the door swung open and out stepped a frazzled-looking Judge Thea—her red hair a discombobulated mess. There was no sign of Prozac.

"What in God's name took you people so long?" The judge was peeved. "I rang the emergency buzzer almost two hours ago."

By-the-Book Betsy said, "Judge, the panic button must still be broken. The alert never signaled at the front desk."

"Then don't let that repairman leave today without fixing that as well," she said. Then she turned to me. "And you—I'd like a word with you."

"Have you seen Prozac?" I asked her.

"No. Why?" The judge sniffed the air. She wrinkled her nose. "Why does it stink like a maritime dock in here?"

"It's Prozac. He's gone," I explained.

"Gone where?" the judge asked.

"We don't know," Annette said. "We can't find him."

"It's a long shot, but he loves fish," I explained. "So we've set out a couple of tins of tuna, salmon, and sardines to try to lure him out—if he's hiding somewhere."

"Why would he be hiding?"

"Because of Margo," By-the-Book Betsy interrupted.

The judge asked, "What about her?"

It was clear that Judge Thea must've been stuck in the elevator through all of the excitement. Realizing that, most of the congregants in the room swung their eyes away from the judge and looked at each other or down at the floor.

True to form, Betsy reiterated the facts. Judge Thea looked pale, visibly shaken by the news of Margo's death.

After a few minutes of head-shaking disbelief, the judge said, "Well, it's tragic about Margo. God rest her soul. But there's nothing more we can do for her at this point. Maybe it's best if we focus our energies on Prozac. Somebody ought to start scouring the neighborhood. He might've already left the building, and he's out on the streets somewhere. I'm afraid that if someone finds that dog, they're bound to keep or sell him—"

"That's not what we need to hear right now," I blasted, my voice cold and shrill with exasperation.

"Then get out there and find that dog," the judge said.

I grabbed my purse from a nearby chair. As I was about to traipse out the front doors of Evergreen Gardens, a voice called, "Hey, Meredith. Wait up."

I turned. There stood David. I was tired and spent, and he was truly a sight for sore eyes. If I were less inhibited, I might've rushed over to him and fallen straight into his arms in search of care and comfort.

"Do you want company?" he asked. "It's starting to get dark outside."

"But your mom—"

"Mary's offered to stay with her. Sleep is what she needs right now. Let me come with you."

Care and concern filled David's warm eyes.

I cut right to the chase and asked, "Am I driving or shall you?"

—&sect;—

The quiet inside the car swelled with all kinds of unspoken, dim prospects. It seemed like ages ago since Prozac went missing. Dusk had already fallen, and it made conducting a visual sweep of the largely residential neighborhoods surrounding Evergreen Gardens more difficult. I had a stack of Prozac's therapy dog business cards in my purse, and whenever we spied someone outside—walking a dog or dragging a garbage pail to the curb—David pulled the car over. I'd hop out and show the card with Prozac's picture, asking folks if they'd spotted him. Time and time again, our efforts came up short.

David drove slowly. Porch lights illuminated modest capes, colonials, and split-level houses, and freestanding basketball hoops in driveways looked like giant erector sets beneath the piercing cones of light cast from street lamps. My sight zoomed into shadows accumulating under parked cars, vans, and SUVs that sat in long driveways. At one point, I thought I saw something dark dart around a small concrete lawn jockey holding a lamp. It lit a flagstone path leading to the red front door of a Sugar Maple Split.

But when David slowed and we looked closer, it was only the bushy cotton tail of a rabbit scurrying across the front lawn and taking cover in some sculpted boxwood hedges.

"Oh, this is useless. He could be anywhere." I sighed, my hopes deflating.

A frosty sense of quiet filled the car. The farther we drove and the more time that lapsed, the more anxiety bloomed in my stomach. I feared the judge's words might've already become prophecy, and Prozac might have been stolen. I was tempted to tell David my suspicion, but I refused to voice my fear. And maybe I was naive, but I held out hope that Prozac's blue Therapy Dog bandanna and dog tags around his neck might be enough to niggle a potential abductor's conscience and encourage him or her to do the honest thing and return the dog to his rightful owner.

The negative part of me fired back with, *Who are you kidding, Meredith? Nobody does the right thing in this world anymore. Look at what happened to Kyle.*

My bitter reverie was broken when David asked, "So what are you thinking about?"

"What else? Prozac and where he could be. Whether he's safe. And I can't help thinking about my fiancé."

In my peripheral vision, I saw David's head swivel from the road toward me. "I didn't know you were engaged."

"I'm not. Not anymore."

"What happened?"

"He died."

"Oh." David pursed his lips. "I'm sorry."

"Yeah, well, me, too." I stared at the dark outline of a tall slide in a children's park. It looked as ominous as a great big steel monster.

"How did he die?"

"Instantly. Some young punk hit him in the head, killed him with a rock."

"Wow, what a terrible thing."

"Yeah, pure evil. The world's full of it."

David kept driving. I regretted letting that all slip out, so curt and clipped. But I was tired and spent, and the whole idea of loss—what was already gone from my life and all I still had left to lose—felt as though it were suffocating me like a concrete blanket.

When I realized that my uninhibited response to David made it difficult for him to offer a follow-up remark or ask another question, I said, "Kyle. That was his name, my fiancé. He was a fireman—a forensics expert. Whenever he investigated a possible arson case and was trying to discover a motive, he'd say that if you want to catch an arsonist, then you need to think like an arsonist. And I'm sort of wondering the same thing about Prozac right now. If I want to find this dog, then I've got to think like him. But that might be impossible. I certainly don't have an Einstein brain."

"Is Prozac *that* smart?"

"He's no run-of-the-mill canine, if that's what you mean. I'm certainly not a dog person, but I swear he has a sixth sense about things. Sometimes, I think he can even spell."

David chuckled. "That would be a first."

"I'm not kidding. I've never seen anything like it. You can't say the word *walk* out loud—not even spell W-A-L-K—or he goes into hiding. He becomes agoraphobic—hates to leave the house."

David grinned.

"He has an incredible vocabulary. He truly, honestly understands words—and sometimes, even before I speak them. And his emotional intelligence... Freud wasn't even as perceptive."

"Gee, for someone who claims not to be a dog person, I think this one has captured your heart."

The car slowed. Facing a stop sign, we were forced to make a decision—right or left.

"Let's head downtown and look there." I let out a long breath, relieved that the stop sign allowed us to change the subject.

"I could drop you off near the main drag," David said. "This way, you can check with people on the street and shopkeepers, and I'll scout some of the back streets."

The traffic began to build. David dropped me near a Catholic church, St. Mary's, right where the shopping district began. He told me that he'd meet me in half an hour up the road at a place called Ray's Pizzeria.

Before I hopped out of the car, I handed him a few of Prozac's business cards.

He took them and said, "We're going to find him, Meredith. We are. Believe that we will—and we will."

"Is that the magician, the illusionist, talking?"

"No, the optimist. Sometimes you have to trick yourself, your rational mind, into believing what appears unbelievable. It's what makes the impossible possible."

"Maybe for you, but not for me."

"How could it hurt to hope for a big ta-da?"

"Ta-da?"

"Yeah, the fanfare. The final big reveal. The ta-da!" With a buoyant tone, he took his hands from the steering wheel and spread his arms like wings in mock fanfare. "If you expect it, the universe will deliver it. That's how ta-das work."

I smirked and hopped out of the car with far less enthusiasm than David had.

In my life, ta-das didn't work. They didn't work when my father left and my mother died. They didn't work with Kyle. All I was good at was worry. But I tamped down my worry long enough to stop every person I passed along the way to Ray's Pizzeria, whipping out Prozac's card and asking folks if they'd seen or recognized him.

A lot of folks made comments like "Oh my goodness, he's so cute" or said that their neighbor—or cousin-sister-mother-friend—had a dog that looked exactly like him only his-her hair was shorter-grayer-bluer-blonder-thinner-thicker.

I was met with a lot of swinging heads and downtrodden faces, words like "Sorry," "Best of luck," and "Hope you find him" chasing me as I went on my way.

I got more of the same as I stopped in the pet shop, the camera store, the shoe repair place, the ice cream parlor, coffee shop, the jewelry store, and the florist.

My feet hurt, and I wanted to cry as red neon letters spelling P-I-Z-Z-A shone through the dark, and David's Ford suddenly pulled up in front of the pizzeria.

I climbed into his car.

David's face brightened beneath the interior light. "How'd you make out?"

As I closed the door, the car went as dark as my hopes.

"I think I'm being punished," I said, a slow trail of tears rolling from my eyes.

"Punished? Punished for what?"

"I think someone's put a hex on me."

"Who would do that? What for?"

"It's all my fault."

"You're overtired," said David.

"No. It *is* my fault."

"You're responsible for Margo Trilling's death?"

I said nothing, wiping my tear-streaked face.

"Did you set Prozac free on purpose?" he pressed.

"It's complicated. I should've done things differently."

"What things?"

"We'd better keep driving," I said.

David put the car in gear and drove off. We kept our sights cast out the dark windows, eyes peeled for Prozac. I filled the silence between us by telling him about Helen and her proposition—how she'd asked me to retain guardianship of Prozac and how I suspected I had hurt her feelings.

When I got through telling my story, David said, "I think it would've been *more* wrong of you to agree to take the dog out of a sense of guilt rather than being true to yourself."

"But maybe that's the thing. Maybe I wasn't really being true to myself. Ever since I called and turned her down, I've been second-guessing my decision. I always say I don't like animals, that I'm not a dog person. But maybe I am. Maybe I'm not who I thought I was—or even who I used to be. I mean, I only had Prozac a few weeks, but in some way, it's been kind of nice having him around. Having to feed him and pick up after him, keep his schedule—he's been good company. I haven't felt so alone."

"Well, that's good," David said. "That's great. And people change, Meredith. It's nothing to be ashamed of. It happens all the time."

A shiver ran through me. Had David just encapsulated my true feelings? And if his perception was on target, that I had somehow changed, did I really want to change?

"You know, it sounds to me like this might all be a very easy fix," David said. "Why don't you call the lady back and tell her you've reconsidered?"

"For starters, Prozac is missing. I don't think that'll work in my favor right now. Plus the fact that it's probably too late. It's not just a verbal commitment she's requiring. It's a whole legal thing that has to be drawn up. A Pet Protection Agreement. It's this trust she's creating special for Prozac and his continuing care and support after her death."

David bobbed his head. "I hear what you're saying, but you could be doing all this second-guessing and feeling all regretful and sentimental simply because he's disappeared."

"Maybe," I told him, a catch in my throat. "But this has me thinking that when I finally *do* give him up, I'm going to miss him more than I thought."

I started to tear up again. David took my trembling hand in his. His touch was like a warm, calming wave that filled my heart. My hand felt as though it belonged there.

"Feel what you need to feel, but don't get ahead of yourself. One hurdle at a time, all right?" David's reassurance filled the dark car like a ray of light. When he started to pull his hand away, I held on tighter, and for a moment, I didn't let go.

He didn't either.

We drove for a while longer. Our hands were comfortably clasped together as we wound our way into the outskirts of town. The glow of TVs seeped through closed curtains and the narrow slats of drawn mini-blinds. Dim bulbs lit up front porches, and motion lights over garages flicked on as we drove past. It felt as though David and I were the only two people out and about in the whole world.

In that moment, I vowed that if and when Prozac was finally found, I'd contact Helen Hendrix, first thing, and tell her that I'd changed my mind.

I'd reconsidered. I'd gladly take on the guardianship of Prozac. If need be, I'd even pay to redo all the legal documents to make things official.

Yes, it was decided.

Amid my determination and committed resolve, David yawned, and our hands slowly drifted apart. As he reached up to cover his mouth, a swell of emptiness expanded inside me. It had been such a comfort to feel as though someone had a stake in the situation with me and truly cared about what was happening—that I wasn't all alone.

I was tempted to reach over and take his hand in mine again. But instead, I glanced at the dashboard clock. It was almost nine o'clock. The search for Prozac had been on for nearly four hours.

"You all right?" David asked.

I nodded. "How about you?"

"Tired. But nothing that a good strong cup of coffee couldn't fix to keep me sharp and focused," he said, cruising the car along the dark, windy back streets that ultimately merged onto more brightly lit main roads.

# Twenty-Seven

*HOODIE*

Meredith

A TOWERING PINK-AND-ORANGE ILLUMINATED SIGN WITH the Dunkin' Donuts logo welcomed us like a bright oasis in a dark desert.

"Mind if we stop here?" David asked.

"Be my guest."

David flipped on the turn signal and drove beneath the floodlights that spilled into the parking lot dotted with cars.

"Looks like coffee never sleeps," I said.

"That would make a good title for a book."

We followed the arrows for the drive-through lane and pulled around the building. Three other cars were in line in front of us.

"What can I get for you?" David asked, pulling out his wallet.

I reached into my pocketbook and fumbled for my change purse. "No, this is *my* treat."

"No way," he said.

"But this is an extenuating circumstance. Believe me, I'm so tired right now, you're doing me a big favor by chauffeuring me all over the place."

"It's my pleasure. Besides, maybe we were supposed to have that cup of coffee we postponed the other night."

"You mean, the cup of coffee that *I* postponed?"

David firmed both his hands around the steering wheel. "In the magician's world, if you follow the right steps while performing a trick, then everything usually unfolds just as it should. I believe life works basically the same way."

"Sounds pretty Zen to me."

"No. Magic is about power, supernatural power exhibited over natural forces."

"I thought it had to do with illusions?"

"It's about both," David said. "It's what we choose to believe and cultivate."

I sighed. "Oh, I don't know what I believe about anything anymore."

I thought about that a moment, looking out the side window and eyeing a college-aged couple leaning against a fancy Corvette. They were sipping their respective coffees and sharing, via alternating playful bites, a chocolate-topped Bavarian cream-filled donut. It looked messy but fun.

"At the end of the day," I said, "I don't have power over anything."

"But you write books. You create whole worlds right from your own imagination and fill up blank pages with stories. Isn't that power?"

"No, I'm talking about the things of real life."

"And your writing isn't real life?"

"Well, it deals with real life. But I'm thinking more about three-dimensional things that happen to us. Take Prozac. I don't have the power to find him. And neither do you."

"Of course we have power. We've been cruising around in this car for hours. If we didn't believe there was a chance we'd find him, then why would we be looking for him at all?"

Completely exasperated, I said, "Because it doesn't do any good sitting around doing nothing. Take it from me. I'm an expert at that."

I was diverted from saying more when the car ahead of us rolled forward, queuing up for the pick-up window. David edged his Ford closer to the ordering station.

"So what's your pleasure?" I asked David, staring past him at the flashy fiberglass menu that featured all kinds of choices: sandwiches, croissants, donuts, and more coffee options than seemed humanly necessary.

"An extra-large coffee—plain but with caffeine. How about you?"

"The same."

"And a donut?"

"No. No donut," I told him.

"Come on, you don't go to Dunkin' Donuts and *not* get a donut."

Before he could launch into another diatribe, I said, "All right, I'll take one of those chocolate-glazed donut hole thingies."

"One?" He looked half amused and half aghast.

"Yeah, one." I put a hand to my tummy.

"I don't think they'll sell just one. I'll get us a dozen."

After the day I was having, if he had said, "I'll get us twelve dozen," I don't think I would've balked.

David rolled the car forward to the menu station, slid down the window, and loudly recited our order.

When the attendant's voice spouted the total price and said, "Drive through, please," I noticed something familiar about the car idling in line in front of us.

The car was white and boxy looking. A two-door sedan. Certainly not a new car. The rear taillights were set like two short dashes on either side of the circular gas tank cap, directly below the trunk and above a shiny chrome bumper. The configuration resembled two narrow red eyes, a nose, and a broad glistening smile. On the trunk and to the right of the keyhole was an emblem embossed with the word *Rambler*. Scrolled alongside it, in script, was the word *American*.

"Hey," I said, my voice brightening. "That car looks like Mary Chirichella's."

"You mean you've seen it unveiled?"

"No. But I saw pictures, and it looked just like that. Can you see who's driving?"

David and I leaned toward the windshield. We squinted to get a better look, but between night having fallen and the powerful overhead parking lot lights casting stark shadows, it was tough to see anything beyond the shape of a person seated behind the wheel.

"I can't tell," David said. "I think the driver is wearing a hoodie or something."

"Humph," I said, straining to look closer. "How weird. The police questioned me a few weeks ago because Mary called them, certain that the car had been moved from her usual parking spot at Evergreen Gardens. They thought I might've had information about it."

"And did you?"

"No, and Mary was really disappointed. I got the sense that everyone at Evergreen pooh-poohed her accusation. But this is really strange. I mean, how many vintage Ramblers could still be on the road?"

"You think Mary took the car out for a ride?"

"No! No way." I shook my head, emphatic. "Mary says she hasn't driven since she passed her driver's test in the nineteen sixties."

"What?" David looked aghast. "Are you kidding?"

"Nope."

"Why have a car if you don't drive it?"

I put up my hands. "Not for me to say." I watched as the Dunkin' Donuts takeout window opened and the driver of the Rambler handed over a couple of dollars, along with a smartphone. "What's all that about?"

"They must be scanning the electronic bar code coupon," David said.

That was news to me, a technological illiterate.

The attendant stuck his head out the window. He gave a short shake of his head and frowned as he returned the phone and some change. Next, the order was passed out the window—three large coffee cups anchored inside a corrugated tray and three small bags with the Dunkin' Donuts logo. That was chased by a huge box of donuts and a Box O' Joe, enough to-go coffee and sweets for about six or eight people—maybe more.

"Somebody's having a party," David said.

The bright rear taillights of the Rambler went dim as the car pulled away.

"Hurry up and get our order," I said to David. "Let's follow and see where it goes."

"But what about Prozac?"

"We'll resume the search, but something's telling me that we should see where that car's headed."

"Aye, aye, boss." David slipped the Ford into gear and approached the takeout window.

Before David could hand over his money, I snapped off my seat belt and lunged across the console and David, flinging a twenty-dollar bill out the window toward the attendant.

"Here. We're in a rush," I told the guy. "Keep the change."

David's warm breath brushed against my cheek. I inhaled the scent of his aftershave, and I knew I'd overstepped my bounds.

The attendant took the money, and I settled back in my seat. David soon handed me the tray with our coffee and donuts, and we drove off.

When we turned the corner of the building, the Rambler was pulling onto the main drag.

"Perfect timing," I said.

"Yeah, now that you've accosted me." The glimmer of David's smile telegraphed that he really didn't mind.

We followed the Rambler, keeping a few car lengths back, as whoever was behind the wheel was a slow and cautious driver. We drove on for about three blocks until the Rambler pulled onto a side street and slowed near the drive for an elementary school.

"You want me to pull in there, boss?" David asked.

"No, here's fine. Cut the engine and the lights."

David pulled curbside and did as I asked. The Rambler eased toward a motorcycle parked near a side door of the brick school building, which was illuminated by exterior flood lamps. Stark fluorescent lights from one of the classrooms brightened the windows. We were close enough to see overturned chairs flipped upon rows of desks. A custodian wearing a gunmetal-gray uniform pushed a broom. When the Rambler approached the classroom where the male custodian was working, the short toot of the car horn caught his attention. He looked out the window and waved. Then he walked to the rear of the classroom, opened the back door, and headed outside.

The flood lamps spilled enough light into the Rambler so we could clearly see that the driver was, indeed, wearing a hoodie.

"Let's roll down our windows. We might be able to hear something," I said.

Chilled night air filled the car, along with a rustle of wind and the subtle ding of a pulley ringing against the metal flagpole. The custodian stood at the idling car, where the driver passed one of the Dunkin' Donuts coffees and one of the small bags out the driver's side window. The man's face became illuminated by what looked like the display of a smartphone. He stared down into the light. A dark mustache was revealed on his upper lip as he shook his head and handed the phone back to the driver.

The custodian's words were weak but audible. "I'll keep an eye out and let you know if I see anything. Awfully nice of you to do this for me." He held up the coffee and bag of donuts.

The driver must have said something in return, but we couldn't hear it.

"You take care now." The man stepped into the building and waved toward the Rambler as it drove off.

David started our car, and we resumed tailing the Rambler. It merged onto main roads. A few blocks later, it signaled a turn toward the Garden State Parkway.

"You want me to keep following?" David asked.

"Do you mind?"

The car wound along the circuitous northbound entrance ramp. "If that Rambler is really Mary's, then whoever is driving is going to have to get it back before someone realizes it's gone."

I pulled my smartphone from my purse and pressed the search engine app.

"What are you doing?" David asked.

"Calling Evergreen Gardens," I said, punching in the name and directly dialing the number. "I'll ask Betsy to check and see if the Rambler is gone."

When I heard a busy signal, I said, "That's strange. The phone's busy."

"No, it's not strange." David pointed to the dashboard clock that read 9:22. "Switchboard closes at nine o'clock. Why don't you call my mom?"

"No. If she's sleeping, I'd hate to disturb her. If you wouldn't mind, could we stay on the trail a while longer?"

"Sure. But it might not be the same car."

"Something's telling me it is."

"What something?"

"A niggling inside. Intuition."

"Couldn't be exhibiting supernatural control over natural forces—like the elements of magic—could you?" quipped David.

I shot him an unimpressed frown. Then I stared at the few straggling headlights that beamed upon the three-lane road. The Garden State Parkway was deserted at that time of night—a far cry from morning or evening rush hour, when traffic could be backed up for miles, especially at the tollbooths and ramps. A running question for New Jerseyans was "What's your exit?" The Parkway ran the length of the state, north to south, and the exit where a person lived spoke volumes about his or her neighborhood.

We were nearing the end of the Parkway, which bordered New York State. The roadway median in those parts consisted of grassy knolls filled with weeping willows and pine trees. At points, it literally looked as though we were driving through a park. And the exits on that stretch of highway were close, some less than two miles apart.

As the Rambler began to slow down and veer toward the flashing green light that topped the Cash Only lane, I held up my phone and asked David, "Which button do I push to record a video?"

"The app that looks like a camera," he said. "Tap on it, then hit the icon for the movie camera."

I did as he suggested, staring at the screen and framing the Rambler in the video display as the car steered up to the booth. Our car slowed directly behind it.

I said, "At least we'll have evidence and a license plate number if we need it."

There in the display, I watched the driver hand over a couple of bills and then pass one of the coffees, another Dunkin' Donuts bag, and a smartphone to the attendant in the booth.

"Don't tell me they take coupons on the Parkway now?" I asked David.

The attendant swung his head as he passed the phone back to the driver. The Rambler drove off.

When David eased the car forward and stopped to pay the toll, I focused the camera on the attendant in the booth, a young guy with a New York Jets logo tattooed on his neck. "Your toll's been paid by the car that just left," the attendant said.

David's profile filled the screen as he glanced through the windshield toward the accelerating Rambler. "Do you know the owner of that car?"

"Personally? No. But she's a nice lady. Stops every couple of weeks and brings coffee and donuts to whoever is working the graveyard shift. She always pays an extra fare for the car that comes after her. Today's your lucky day."

"Yeah, guess so. Thanks." David gunned the engine and bolted away from the booth.

"At least we know we're dealing with a woman now," I said.

"Yes, a mysterious Garden State Parkway coffee and donut angel," David added.

"But, what's with the hoodie?" My smartphone recorded the white dotted lines in the road as they moved through the frame of the digital display.

"Somebody's hiding something," said David.

Short red dashes from the Rambler taillights helped me stay the course on the dark screen. Less than a mile after we went through the tollbooth, the Rambler signaled that it was turning off at the next exit for the town of Wild Ridge.

David asked, "Should I keep following?"

"Do you mind—a little longer?"

The Rambler drove up the exit ramp and slowed at a stop sign. It made a right and started up a big hill. We followed, keeping a few lengths behind for about two miles, back to Oak Park.

When the car turned into a CVS and followed the arrows that read "Drive-Thru Pharmacy Open 24 Hours," I said to David, "Park over there and let me out."

"What are you going to do?"

"See those bushes?" I pointed to some hedges that bordered the lane leading to the drive-through window. "I'll hide in them and video what I can."

"You're going to crawl on the ground?"

"No. I'll squat down." I flung open the car door. The interior car light illuminated David's tired eyes.

"Why do I feel like I should be humming the theme from *Mission: Impossible*?" he said.

I hurried out of the car, crouching low as I hugged the perimeter of the hedges bordering the drive-through lane.

When the pick-up window was in sight, I stopped and thrust my hand with the smartphone through a break in the foliage. I pointed the lens at the Rambler, about three yards away. Listening closely, I stared at the digital screen to see what was transpiring on the other side of those bushes.

A muffled-sounding woman's voice asked, "Don't they ever give you a night off?"

"Not lately. I'm saving up to visit Florida over Easter break, so I'm doing some double shifts," a younger, more easily audible voice said.

"Then I'm just in time—here's your mid-shift snack. Share it with your coworkers."

"Oh, Mrs. Strong, you're so thoughtful. I can't tell you how much we appreciate the coffee and donuts you bring us every month."

*Mrs. Strong? Judge Thea? She does this every month?*

I brought my face closer to the video display, eyeing a murky outline of the person in the hoodie. I could make out the silhouette of a face, and when it turned toward the passenger seat, I recognized wisps of red hair emerging from beneath the hoodie like a fiery-colored nimbus enshrouding her head. Then I glimpsed the sway of those tiny gavel earrings. Judge Thea lifted the boxes of to-go coffee and donuts, passing them to the girl at the window.

"While I'm here, I'd also like to pick up my prescription—the one my doctor renews for me every month."

"Oh, I think your grandson picked it up earlier today."

"My grandson?"

"Yes. He had your adorable little dog with him."

I almost uttered a gasp, reeling it back before it could escape.

The judge fiddled with her smartphone and asked, "Is this the dog you mean?" as she passed the phone to the girl.

The girl nodded. "Yeah, and such a cute bandanna, too. Why'd you name him Prozac, anyway?"

When the judge looked down at the display of her smartphone, I spotted the flex of her jawbone. She dropped her forehead upon the steering wheel.

"Mrs. Strong, are you all right?" A look of grave concern filled the girl's face.

The judge quickly regained her composure. "Yes, fine. I'm okay. It's late, and I've had a long day."

"Are you sure? I mean, are you all right to drive?"

"Yes, I'm fine. But I wish my grandson would've told me that he was stopping."

The girl said, "He was probably trying to save you a trip."

"Yes, probably," the judge said, with a nonchalant wave of her hand. "Enjoy the coffee and donuts. I hope you get the funds you need in time for Easter."

The judge engaged the gearshift on the steering column and pulled away.

I stopped filming, hurrying along the hedges to the main parking lot where David was waiting for me. I breathlessly flung open the car door. David was awash in the interior light.

"You're not going to believe *this*." I hopped inside the car, and as we picked up the Rambler's trail, I filled him in on everything I'd seen and heard. He didn't interrupt but kept nodding as though to assure me he was, indeed, listening to each and every word.

When I finally came up for air, he said, his voice steady and even, "Well, there you have it. The *ta-da* moment."

"But we still don't have Prozac."

"Oh ye of little faith. There's one more coffee and another bag of donuts left to deliver—"

"Unless they're for her," I said.

We drove a while longer, saying nothing. Once we turned onto Herbert Avenue, I anticipated the judge's return to Evergreen Gardens. When she made a sharp left, without a turn signal, I quickly reconsidered. The Rambler traveled into the dark heart of an upper-middle-class residential street. She turned into a horseshoe driveway set in front of a sprawling ranch house, where she parked behind a beat-up-looking Honda Civic hatchback.

David pulled over across the street, allowing us a clear view of the house and the judge. She exited the Rambler, holding the coffee and Dunkin' Donuts bag. The hoodie was still draped over her head, under what appeared to be a long raincoat that fell just below the knees. I couldn't quite make it out, but the hoodie seemed to be covering a dress or a skirt—or maybe it was overlapping one of her signature black dusters? Her legs were bare, her ankles sporting white socks rooted inside a pair of running sneakers. When she turned—closing the car door as quietly as she could—the word NAVY, stitched in bright-yellow letters on the front of the hoodie, glimmered through the dark.

Judge Thea walked a flagstone path past the garage and around the house until her face was cast in light shining through a pane of glass in a side entrance. She rapped her fist on the door. When no one answered right away, she knocked again. That time harder.

A dog started to bark. A tiny yet familiar yap-like whimper. A frustrated sound.

# Twenty-Eight

*CREATURE COMFORT*

Prozac

THE KID WAS PASSED OUT cold on the sofa. Had been for more than two and a half hours. While he slept, I pressed my body and head down onto the filthy carpeting—repulsed, but grateful to finally be left alone.

But it wasn't easy to de-stress.

After the liquor and drugstore run, we barreled into Randy's apartment. He unclipped my leash then dropped me on all fours, my weak patellas wincing as I scurried for cover. He flung off his cloddy army boots, launching them like heavy artillery, adding new marks to the already scuffed wall in the foyer. I cowered beneath one of the end tables as he tossed my leash and the bags from the store atop the coffee table. A couple of empty soda cans toppled over, sending an assortment of junk food wrappers airborne. One sniff, and I could tell that kid had a serious penchant for Twinkies.

If Randy had a modus operandi, I couldn't gauge it. Was his kidnapping me—the booze, the prescription meds—some sort of teenaged rebellion, or had the kid snapped? Was he about to do something crazy? After all, liquor and controlled prescription drugs didn't mix.

Randy flipped on the TV. Heavy metal music blared as he cracked open the whiskey. He slugged back a sip, straight from the Jack Daniel's bottle, then ripped open the bag of Cheez Doodles, sending up an airy orange spray. When the puffy noodles landed on the floor, I dove into them, gobbling them up. It was past my dinnertime, and I was starving—and I was rarely fed good junk food. When I finished chomping and licking up every last salty speck, I used the carpet as my napkin and wormed around, wiping my face and beard against the rug, even getting on my back and wiggling against the coarse woolen fibers. In the process of all my gyrations, I loosened the knot on my therapy dog bandanna, wrangling it off my neck. *Hallelujah!* After all those hours of wearing that thing, it was beginning to choke me.

The next time I looked up, I heard Randy wrestling with the safety cap on the vial of Xanax. He dumped a pill out into his palm and swigged it down with another shot of whiskey. I guessed the one Xanax, coupled with the booze, proved enough for Randy to slip into sleep, a semi-coma, in front of the fifty-five-inch HDTV screen that was tuned—much too loudly, I might add—to Comedy Central. It seemed surreal, listening to laugh tracks behind those acerbic, sarcastic pseudo-newscasters and comedians while the state of affairs in the kid's apartment was anything *but* funny.

That was when I decided to take action. With the kid asleep, his mouth open and a trickle of saliva on his chin, I pawed the coffee table until I knocked down the amber vial of Judge Thea's pills. As best I could, I nosed the plastic cylinder, rolling it across the carpeting until it disappeared under the bottom flap of an old, worn La-Z-Boy recliner. That kid sure didn't need to take any more pills.

I tried to get a read on Randy, snuffling my way around his cramped one-bedroom apartment. The stale smell and grimy disarray indicated there was little parental involvement in his living arrangement. How could that be? After all, Randy was still in high school, wasn't he?

The minute I stepped into the galley kitchen, the stickiness on the tile floor made me walk back from the room. I could only imagine the kinds of rare, tropical bacteria and weird virus strains that might have been lurking amid the encrusted stove top and microwave. Crumbs were scattered about the floor and embedded in the grout—certainly nothing worth foraging. The table and sink were piled high with dirty dishes and bowls, and the garbage pail was erupting with cereal and pizza boxes. A couple of dried strands of spaghetti were plastered to the refrigerator. It amazed me that rodents and cockroaches weren't already partying in the place.

But Randy's bedroom was a totally different story. It was like stepping across the threshold into a recreated spick-and-span military barracks. The room had a bunk bed, where both top and bottom were fully made up with sharp seams and crisp corners. A quarter easily would've bounced off the woolen green military blanket with the US Navy logo. Several pairs of boots and sneakers were neatly aligned beneath the bed, where a few US NAVY pennants were pinned to the wall.

But I was most drawn to the corner bookcase. Topping the shelves filled with various military books—both fiction and nonfiction—was a triangular, oak-framed military flag case, where, inside, white stars were set upon the dark-blue background of a folded American flag. Beneath the memorial flag case was a shadow box filled with an array of military medals and commendations, including a Purple Heart. And alongside the flag case was a matching oak picture frame displaying the photo of a pretty young woman with ginger-colored hair and freckles, beaming a prideful smile. She was dressed in full military regalia. Dog tags on a chain were draped off the corner of the frame. Clearly, it was a shrine to Randy's mother, who was a fitter version of her taller son.

A fuller, yet conflicting, portrait of Randy was emerging. He was obviously a sensitive kid—one who loved his mother, was immensely proud of her, and was dramatically affected by her absence from his life. Randy seemed to idolize her to the point of wanting to follow in her footsteps. But if he truly had serious designs on entering the military, what was his game plan? And why did he take me from Evergreen Gardens?

I had a feeling Randy would be forced to put a plan into place quickly when a faint knocking sound was almost lost amid the ear-splitting volume of the TV.

I picked up my head and perked my ears, listening more closely. But I was met with only that annoying laugh track.

When the knocking started again, louder, I looked up at the time displayed on the cable TV box. It was 9:37.

I ran to the door, and when I saw the dark shape of a person through the window glass, I barked in nervous impulse.

*Can it be a savior?*

My hearing was four times more sensitive than a human's. And that the knocking grew sharper implied that whoever was standing on the other side of that door meant business, so I hurried toward Randy, pawing his arm that lay flapped over the side of the sofa. But I couldn't nudge him awake.

Therefore, I leaped up and jumped atop Randy's stomach, scratching his neck and licking the gritty stubble on his chin.

He finally stirred, his eyes flitting open. I yipped a few times and jumped down onto the floor, running circles as I edged toward the door. As Randy gazed at the shape of a person behind the frosted glass, he quickly got the gist. Like a shot, he launched himself up from the sofa. He was obviously dizzy and disoriented, but he quickly capped the bottle of Jack Daniel's, setting it behind a stack of books piled alongside the lamp on the end table. I glimpsed the spine of one book, *A Legal Guide to the Emancipation of Minors*, as Randy whisked me away and dumped me inside the bathroom.

"Now shut up and keep quiet," he hissed, slamming the door.

I cried, offering up a whine of protest. But I quickly simmered down, as barking was never really my style, and I was eager to hear what was happening beyond the door.

I heard Randy shuffling things, and then the TV switched off. The quiet was ominous but short-lived as the door lock disengaged, followed by the sound of creaky hinges.

"Grandma?" Randy said.

*Judge Thea?*

"What are you doing here?" Randy asked, clearing his throat. "Is everything all right?"

"You tell me, Randall."

*Randall? Uh-oh. Use of his full birth name? This kid's in big-big trouble!*

"Yeah, everything's fine. Why? What's up?"

"I was in the neighborhood and thought I'd drop by."

"It's kind of late."

"I think it's time for you and me to have a talk, Randy. You like Dunkin' Donuts?"

"S-sure," Randy stuttered. "But I don't understand. How did you get here?"

"I drove—borrowed a friend's car."

There was a pause. In the time that lapsed, I envisioned Randy stepping aside in order to let Judge Thea enter the apartment. I took that opportunity to let out a few soulful whines and scratch my paws on the door.

"What's that sound?" Judge Thea asked.

The front door clicked closed.

"Oh, I'm dog sitting for a friend," Randy said.

"Why are you keeping the poor thing locked up?"

"Because... because he's not house-trained. Besides, he's a pit bull—and he bites."

"Wow, a pit bull." The judge waited a few beats before adding, "Since when do they allow dogs who bite and aren't house-trained to be therapy dogs?"

"What? He's not a therapy dog."

"That blue thing on the floor over here. It's a therapy dog bandanna. Where did it come from?"

"Gee, I don't know." The vast ignorance Randy was feigning was positively tragic.

"And it looks a little small for a pit bull."

"Oh, he's still a puppy—"

"How long are you going to keep this up, Randall?"

"Keep *what* up?"

"Where's Prozac?"

"Prozac?" From Randy's hesitation, I envisioned a look of clueless innocence scrawled on that kid's face. "You mean that little pipsqueak dog from Evergreen Gardens?"

*Pipsqueak? I'll give you pipsqueak!*

I let out a bark—a shrill, throaty yap. The next thing I knew, the door to the bathroom opened. I was met by Judge Thea's perfume as her face swooped down to mine.

"Oh, you poor, poor thing," she cooed, her cold hands wrapping around my midsection as she pressed me to her rib cage. She marched us both into the living room.

"What is wrong with you?" she scolded, wagging a finger at Randy, who sank into the couch. "Do you have any idea how they're turning things upside down looking for this dog?"

"I wasn't going to keep him."

"How could you do this?"

"That lady dropped dead in the hall. I found him shivering. He was scared. He looked like he needed help—"

"So you stole him?"

"No, I was just gonna get him some air and bring him back after everything settled down. But I fell asleep—"

"How dare you!"

The boy rose to his feet and blasted, "You care more about this stupid dog than you care about me."

"And that's why you stole him—to get my attention?"

Randy's words burst out, shredding through his vocal cords. "I didn't steal him. I-I... I've been trying to talk to you a million times, and you keep blowing me off—"

"We've already had this discussion. You are *not* joining the Navy. I won't lose more flesh and blood to meaningless wars."

"They are *not* meaningless. My mother gave her life in Iraq."

"Then you should wise up and learn from her mistakes—"

"She was a hero." Randy took a step toward Judge Thea. He towered over her and stared her down. "You should know, I've talked to a lawyer. I'm planning to emancipate myself from you."

The judge held Randy's gaze and gave a wide-open laugh. "Just because I pulled some strings and arranged for the nice people who own this house to set you up this apartment, it doesn't mean you can fend for yourself."

"I live here on my own."

"Oh? And who pays the bills?"

"I'm gonna get a job—a full-time job. Then I can make my own decisions."

"If that's the case, and you're making decisions, then maybe you ought to decide to clean this place once in a while." The judge swept her sights around the mess in the living room. "And in the future, it might also be a wise decision if you *not* steal someone else's dog."

"You can't dictate what I do with my life."

"Oh yes, I can. Your mother's gone, and your father is... Oh, God only knows where he is. I'm your legal guardian."

"Not for long."

"I've got news for you," the judge said. "The Navy doesn't accept candidates with criminal backgrounds."

"I don't have a criminal background."

"You will, once you're arrested for dognapping."

Randy was shut down by the force of his grandmother's words.

Still caged in the judge's grasp, I looked to Randy. He dropped himself onto the sofa, crossed his arms, and twisted them as if binding himself in a straitjacket.

"And considering the worth and value of this dog," the judge went on, "what you've done here, by taking Prozac, might even be classified as a felony, grand theft. So you might want to reconsider the emancipation lawyer and get yourself a good defense attorney. You'll need one to keep yourself out of prison."

*Gee, she's sure laying it on thick!*

At an impasse, the judge walked away from Randy. Certainly nothing he could say would refute Judge Thea, who sat us down in the plush La-Z-Boy recliner. She reached for the cup of coffee she'd placed nearby and took a sip, rocking us gently. Through her fingertips, I could feel the vigor of her beating heart. She was upset, and despite her bravado, she was uncertain how to handle things. She surprised me—and Randy, too—when she picked up the bag of donuts and flung it in her grandson's direction. He cringed when it hit him in the chest.

"Go on, eat up. They don't serve Dunkin' Donuts behind bars. Oh, and I almost forgot," the judge said. "Where's my prescription? And don't tell me you don't have it. The girl at the CVS saw you with Prozac. I bet she'll make a good witness for the prosecution."

Randy rummaged around the mess scattered atop the coffee table. Cans clinked together and fell to the floor. When he finally fished out the paper bag that held the prescription, he reached inside. Nothing. Then he pressed his hands around the bag, flattening it. He found no medication vial.

In desperation, Randy got down on all fours and groped through the cellophane Twinkie wrappers and papers strewn on the carpet. He crawled over, reached an arm beneath the La-Z-Boy chair where the judge and I were seated, and pulled out the prescription vial. He handed the cylinder to the judge, who poured the pills out into her palm. She counted them, one by one, slipping each back into the vial.

"There's supposed to be thirty pills here. Why are there only twenty-nine?"

"Because I took one." Randy was bold in his tone as he rose from the floor and returned to the sofa. "If you cared about me one bit as much as you care about this dog, you would know I haven't been sleeping well."

The judge slipped the pill bottle into the pocket of her raincoat. Then she ran her fingers under my rib cage, tickling the blond hair on my chest. She sipped her coffee contemplatively as though preparing to make some sort of pronouncement.

"You know, you and me, Randy, we actually have more in common than you think. We've both lost someone we loved. We're both sad. And we're all the family we've got. I think it's time we call a truce."

Randy didn't budge. He looked straight ahead at the darkened TV screen.

The judge repeated, her voice sharp, "I said a truce—right here, right now. This minute. Tonight."

Randy crinkled open the bag and pulled out one of the donuts. I could smell the cinnamon-sugary sweetness. He split one of the donuts in half, handing a piece to the judge. It was oozing gloppy strawberry jelly from inside. When she took a bite, some powdered sugar and crumbs dropped onto the dark fleece of her hoodie. I lunged to lick them up.

As witnesses to my eagerness, the two of them actually chuckled, and I was glad that my actions served to break the tension. I got the sense it had been a long time since the judge and Randy had shared anything except grief—and animosity.

"Taking Prozac and medication that was prescribed for me... Do you understand the seriousness of what you've done here today?"

"I swear, I *was* gonna bring him back after everything settled down. He was scared. He was shaking—"

"You had no right to take him."

Randy's silence sounded incriminating.

"You won't be let off the hook for this. There'll be consequences to pay. And I'm going to see to it. Do you understand?"

Randy nodded.

"I'm very disturbed by all this, and I'm very disappointed in you, Randy. And your mother, she'd be disappointed, too. But maybe this needed to happen. I'll admit I've been distracted and preoccupied. First your mother, then your father." The judge's tone was softening. She was clearly speaking the thoughts swirling inside her mind. "All your talk about the military... I thought it was just a phase you were going through. I had no idea you've done so much homework and research and checking. You'll be eighteen soon enough. If you really want to join the Navy, I guess I can't stop you."

It took a moment for the judge's change of heart to register with Randy. But when it did, he turned to the judge, his gaze a mix of surprise and suspicion.

"What you did today was not right. But I love you, Randy. I care about you. I *really* do. And it stinks, how unfair life has been to you. I want to see you happy—but you won't be happy if you don't start using your head and getting your morals in check."

The judge wiped her hands of the cinnamon-powdered sugar. The clapping sound encouraged me to stand on her lap. Judge Thea reached for my therapy dog bandanna. She tied it back around my neck then grabbed my leash off the coffee table and re-harnessed it.

"So what do we do now?" Randy asked.

The judge let out a low sigh. "We take this dog back to Evergreen Gardens. You let me handle it. And you give me your word that you will never do anything like this—ever again."

"Yes, ma'am," Randy replied, sitting taller.

They both sat, staring straight ahead. Perhaps the pain of their shared, troubled pasts could finally be put behind them. Perhaps they could face the future with a mutual understanding.

"Okay, then, I think we're finished here." The judge set me down on the floor, and with my leash in hand, she stood up and led us toward the door.

"Wait!" Randy rose from the couch and hurried toward the judge. His big, sad, regret-filled eyes were filling with tears.

"I'm sorry, Grandma." He flung himself at her, firming his grasp, but the judge froze. Her arms went stiff, like two-by-fours, at her sides. I stood there on the leash, looking up at them—two people united by blood but so sadly estranged from each other. Randy's show of emotion and affection was obviously foreign to the judge, as completely unexpected as the judge's show of leniency toward her grandson. But his display of gratitude proved enough to soften the hard edges, the barriers between them. Judge Thea slowly drew herself around Randy, her eyes shining with unexpected joy as Randy sobbed like a baby, his tears pouring down his cheeks and dropping like raindrops to the floor.

# Twenty-Nine

*TA-DA*

Meredith

O**NCE** J**UDGE** T**HEA** **DISAPPEARED** **THROUGH** the side door into that house, I was tempted to hop out of the car and scramble through the bushes to spy.

David must've sensed my eagerness. As if reading my mind, he said, "Unless you want to be spotted, I wouldn't risk it."

"Look at that car in the driveway." I pointed to a beat-up Honda Civic with a rear bumper sticker sporting the word NAVY in the same bold yellow font as the judge's hoodie.

David squinted to get a better look. "Looks like Judge Thea and her grandson are about to have a showdown."

I, too, was connecting the same dots in my own mind.

"I sure hope that kid has the dog," David said.

"He better," I told him.

---

Minutes seemed to stretch on like hours during our stakeout. I leaned toward the windshield and looked up at the stars sharpened by the dark, inky sky. I couldn't relax, and David capitalized on my overtired anxiety. He started asking questions unrelated to Prozac. I allowed myself to be diverted. I told him a little bit about my childhood, and then he asked me how and why I became a writer—and then, we moved on to more about Kyle. I rambled on about the two of us until I spouted some of the details of his death.

At one point, David asked, "Did they ever find who did it?"

I shook my head. "No. He's still at large."

"How terrible." David's voice was grave and calm, filled with empathy. "Not having vindication or closure... that must be really hard for you."

"Even if they found the murderer, it wouldn't bring Kyle back. The police suspect the kid might've been from out of town, just passing through that night. They didn't have much to go on. Not a lot of DNA can be dredged from a murder weapon that's a piece of asphalt."

In talking to David, I realized that I didn't feel so uncomfortable with his questions or afraid of baring the details of my tattered soul. My words and feelings flowed freely, and my heart stayed steady. My hands didn't even shake. That was the second time in two weeks that I'd told the Kyle story. David listened intently. He sensitively affirmed what I shared, underscoring things with an occasional nod or a "hmmm" or "aah," gently letting me know he understood—that he cared about what I had to say.

Pretty soon, I felt talked out, and David and I entered a comfortable, if not contemplative, silence. I reached for the bag of donuts on his lap and popped another chocolate-glazed Munchkin into my mouth, savoring the crunchy, chocolaty sweetness. I imagined that David might've been trying to process things—as I was, too. But I also felt cleaned out in some way, lighter, as if breathing were somehow easier.

David and I were both transfixed on the side door of that house. Parked in the dark on that side street, we sipped our coffees, swapping the bag of donuts back and forth.

"See. Aren't you glad I ordered a dozen?" David asked, to which I realized the impulsiveness of my eating and handed the donuts back to him—for good.

He stared into the bag and said, "Last one. You want it?"

"No. No thanks." Since we'd polished off the Dunkin' Donuts, I realized that I'd done all the talking and learned nothing about David in the conversation.

"How 'bout it's my turn to ask *you* some questions now," I said, gulping the last of my coffee.

"Sure. Fire away, but I must warn you. My life is certainly not as interesting as yours."

"Oh, I don't believe that. A magician's life, boring? Making things disappear and reappear—"

"Nowadays, I work behind the scenes, all alone in a quiet little shop. Hours of tinkering and engineering small details."

"Sounds exactly like what I do—except with words."

"When you get right down to it, I guess you could say magic is my life."

I repeated that line in my head, counting off each word on my fingers. "So that's it? *Magic is my life?* Your whole life story boils down to only four words?"

"I like short stories."

"Aha," I said. "But your life's not over yet. It could still grow into a novel."

David nodded and grinned, open to the possibility.

"Do you travel? Have hobbies? Share your life with anyone?"

David shrugged. "Does a tank of fish count?"

"Fresh or saltwater?" I raised my palms toward the ceiling as if trying to balance a scale.

"Freshwater tropical. The thing is," David explained, "I haven't had time for vacations, hobbies, or relationships the past couple of years. I've been tied up working and trying to keep body and soul together while taking care of my mom."

"I'm so glad she was released from the hospital, and we had a chance to meet. I have to remember to sign those books for her. She seemed in very good spirits today."

"Thanks. She is—she *is* in good spirits, remarkably. The folks at Evergreen, they're good to her. I think she's really going to miss everyone."

I felt my eyebrows cinch. "Is she moving?"

David bobbed his head. His eyes were shining, and he lowered them from me as if he didn't want me to see his sadness.

"I'm sorry," I said. "Leave it to me to ask too many questions. The writer in me—"

"No, it's okay," he said. "No one at Evergreen knows, but Mom's been battling incurable lung cancer."

"Oh." The sound of that simple syllable dragged into a long stillness. "I'm sorry."

"Yeah, me, too. She tried chemo, but it made her too sick. She couldn't handle it. And it was hard for her to admit that. I mean, my mom, she never gives up. She never quits. And now she's calling herself a *chemo dropout*." His eyes grew moist, but he offered a thin, despairing smile. "They gave her three months. But we're going on twenty-six now."

"Wow, two years? That's pretty amazing."

"Sure *is*. And I should be grateful. I mean, I am. Every extra day I get to spend with Mom is a gift." David wiped away some tears that had sprung to his eyes. He took a measured breath and composed himself. "It's really something how she's outlived the odds, how we've gotten to spend more time together—and quality time, at that. But it's hard, too. I mean, on some level, we're all dying. But with my mother being so sick, there's this heightened sense of knowing that every day she lives is one day closer to my losing her."

"It sounds like you've been a real gift to each other."

"It's always been just her and me. My dad died when I was nine…" David's voice trailed off. "The magician in me wants so much to wave a magic wand and take away all her pain and keep her here longer. But sometimes, magic has limits—illusions can't really change reality."

I felt for David. He was a man of few words, but what he'd shared truly seemed to come from the heart. I understood his feelings, and writing seemed so similar to the power of magic. On the page, I could change whatever I wanted, do away with the weight of any burden, wipe out everything with a single stroke of the delete key and reorder the world to make life different—the way I wanted. But writing a book was not the same as living a life.

"See, I knew you had more than a short story inside of you," I told him, forcing myself to sound upbeat. "You already have a novella in the works—"

As I was saying that, David turned and pointed to the side door of the house. "Look, someone's coming out."

Judge Thea emerged. She was carrying Prozac. She pulled the hood of her NAVY sweatshirt over her red hair and headed for the Rambler.

"There it is—another *ta-da* moment," David said, his enthusiasm brimming.

He turned to me. The curl of his smile erased my fear until I was flooded with relief. My eyes filled, and my heart swelled at the sight of Prozac—his blue bandanna contrasted against his black and copper-colored hair, the perk of those triangular ears. The mix of my emotions coalesced into a laugh that sounded like happiness. I reached for my smartphone, clicking on the camera app to activate filming again.

"What should we do?" David asked. "Should we confront her here?"

"No. Not here," I told him. "Let's see where she goes."

After the judge deposited Prozac in the Rambler and pulled out of the driveway, David started our car. We resumed her trail.

Judge Thea stuck to main roads, and it was clear from the direction we were driving that she was winding her way back to Evergreen Gardens. By the time the Rambler pulled into the long drive leading toward the converted church, it felt as though we were coming home again. That immense weight of worry finally started to lift.

"Do you want me to pull right up next to the car?" David asked.

"No, hang back. Let's see what she does."

The judge slowly and carefully maneuvered the Rambler into its parking space. When it was just so, she cut the engine and the lights. Then she exited the car with Prozac, setting the dog on the ground. She threaded his leash around a nearby parking stanchion. When the dog was tethered and secure, she returned to the car. She flung the front seat forward, and from the back seat, she pulled out the gray car cover. It was so large and cumbersome that she had to keep pulling and pulling in order to gather the bulky fabric.

David laughed. "Look. It's like a never-ending hankie a magician pulls out of his hat."

With the cover spilled into the parking lot, the judge pressed down the lock then closed the door as quietly as she could, proceeding to wrap up the car, smoothing out the wrinkles and seams in the cover. She walked around the shrouded vehicle, as if to ensure that it looked exactly as it had before it left the parking lot.

"This certainly appears to be a sneak-the-car-back-in routine," David said.

"I'll say." I continued videotaping the judge while I undid my seat belt. "I'm gonna move in for the kill now."

"Let me go with you—"

"No, I think it might be best if I confront her on my own."

Once I was out of the car, the stride of my footsteps was wide, lengthening with self-assurance as I walked across the parking lot where Judge Thea was untying Prozac. Together, they started toward the emergency exit of Evergreen Gardens. As the judge kicked away a rock that had been wedged into the door to keep it open, I quickened my approach.

"Stop right there," I said, pointing the camera in the judge's direction but holding it unobtrusively down near my hip.

In one swift movement, the judge put a hand over her heart and turned to me.

"Look who I found!" Glee filled the judge's face as she patted the dog with a loving hand. "Prozac, he's back."

"Where was he?"

"I found him loitering about."

"Out here? He never left Evergreen Gardens?"

"Oh, I don't know about that." The judge's eyes twitched as if trying to gauge my response. "All I know is that he's here now—"

"Stop hedging and admit it. You *found* Prozac at your grandson's apartment."

The judge played dumb. "What are you talking about?"

"I've got it all on video. Right here," I said, puffing my chest and holding up the phone as evidence.

Exhaustion colored the judge's pale face.

"Look," she said, taking a step toward me. "Mission accomplished. Prozac's our priority, and we've found him. All's well. I'd think you'd be relieved that he's safe and unharmed."

"I *am* relieved. But I also think you have some explaining to do."

"Please. It's been a long day and night. Let's not escalate this—"

"Oh, I think the fact that Prozac was at your grandson's house, and you seem to be trying to cover up that fact, is escalation enough—"

"I'm not trying to cover up anything."

"No? Well, you just did a pretty good job of covering up Mary's Rambler."

Judge Thea eyed me squarely and said, "We all love Prozac. We were all concerned—"

"Does Mary know you borrowed her car? And does she know you take it out every month and flit around the county delivering coffee and donuts?"

The judge jockeyed Prozac in her arms. The five pounds of him seemed to be growing heavy as she said, "Okay, if you want to know the truth, my father was an ace mechanic. It's a cinch to hot-wire a car manufactured in the 1960s."

My mouth unhinged. I could not believe what I was hearing.

Judge Thea said, "Maybe someday, when you get to be my age, you'll understand."

"Try me now."

"I don't have to explain myself to you—"

"Explain it, or I go to the police."

The judge bit her lower lip then said, "Look, it's hard getting older, giving things up. I still have a lot of love to give and not a lot of people in my life left to give it to anymore. And the world is a mess. It's falling apart. And it makes me angry—all the violence and decadence. I have a need to give back sometimes, to do my part to push against all that evil. You know, get out of myself and do something good for other people. So I do Mary a favor and get her car started and out on the road every month, while I spread some kindness and joy, bringing coffee and donuts to people who work hard and need a lift. It's not much, but it's something. And no harm done. I'm not hurting anyone—"

"But Mary had the police here a couple of weeks ago. She was beside herself about that car."

The judge shrugged. She smoothed her hair, downplaying the situation. "You don't watch daytime stories on three iPads simultaneously if you don't thrive on drama. Believe me, my taking Mary's car out—even the mystery surrounding it—is helping her in a myriad of ways."

"Oh, so that's it? You make whatever rules you want and play God?"

Prozac let out a great big yawn.

"Meredith, please. You're making too big a deal of this—"

"Breaking the law *is* a big deal. You, of all people, should know that. You've repeatedly stolen Mary's car, and it now appears as though your grandson stole Prozac—"

"Oh, c'mon, I only borrow the car. And my grandson didn't steal the dog. He only took him out of Evergreen because of what happened here this afternoon," she said. "The poor dog was petrified—and so was my grandson. He wasn't thinking straight. He was planning to bring the dog back, but Randy, he fell asleep—"

"But he didn't just take the dog for a walk. He carted him across town. He kept him for hours. That seems an awful lot like stealing to me."

"Look, I'm not saying that what he did was right, but he's a troubled and confused kid. A teenager. And he's lost a lot." The judge's tone was pleading. "I think he got spooked and very frightened after seeing Margo—and then all the commotion. It must've brought back the trauma of his mother—she died in Iraq. She was a nurse. Please, as a favor, I'm asking you *not* to pursue this."

I looked at the judge, trying to gauge her sincerity, and at Prozac, who licked the judge's hand.

"Why should I do *you* a favor when you've spent all these weeks making me feel guilty about this dog—all that APL nonsense?"

"Look, are you forgetting that a woman died today? It's been a traumatic day for all of us. And the car—it's back. And the dog—he's safe. That's what matters…"

Prozac wriggled amid the judge's grasp, clearly wanting to get down.

"… But go on. If it will make you feel better, then out me to Mary. Go on. Tell her everything," Judge Thea said. "But my grandson can't get in trouble right now. It could foul up his whole future."

The judge shot me a beseeching look. But I wasn't about to let her off the hook.

"I can't believe you," I told her, shaking my head and almost laughing at the absurdity of what I'd just heard. "The *Honorable* Judge Thea, hot-wiring cars—and now you're asking me to give a delinquent kid a pass? What's *that* going to teach him?"

"It's going to teach him that his grandmother loves him—and believes in him. I've already spoken to him about what went on here today. And don't worry, I'll personally hold him accountable for this—"

"How?"

"I don't know, but I'll see to it that he pays a price—even if he mops the floors and cleans the toilets of Evergreen Gardens for the next several months."

Prozac settled his furry head, burying his eyes in the bend of the judge's elbow, as if trying to shield himself from hearing any more of the conversation.

"Look, Randy's all the family I have left in the whole world," the judge begged. "He's all I've got."

I stared at Judge Thea—the tired colorlessness of her face, the impatient sway of her gavel earrings.

"So that's it?" I said. "We're gonna tell everyone that we searched all night and then we just happened to find Prozac wandering around out here?"

As I posed the question, a beam of light passed over the building then swept over the judge, Prozac, and me. Prozac perked. I turned, squinting into headlights that grew brighter on us. A car, a police squad car, was cruising up the drive leading toward Evergreen Gardens. On its approach, a startled Prozac shifted his eyes back and forth. He squirmed furiously. He refused to be contained any longer, finally freeing himself from her grasp and flying to the ground in a soaring arc. He landed on all fours and took off, charging directly toward the approaching squad car until it swerved, slamming on the brakes and shrieking in a bloodcurdling skid that sounded like a terrifying cry.

*Thud!*

I screamed, a deep, primal keening that I'd never heard from myself before, as the dark shape of Prozac's tiny body was tossed across the parking lot.

# Thirty

*EN ROUTE TO CLOUD NINE*

Prozac

I NEVER WOULD'VE SCRIPTED THINGS THAT way. But that was how it was with animals. No matter how obedient and integrated we were in human lives, we were never completely predictable, were we?

There I was, caged in the crux of the judge's arms. I let out a yawn, wondering how much longer that banter, that power struggle, would go on between those two in the darkened parking lot of Evergreen Gardens. It was late, and we'd all had one helluva day. By then, I was worn out from the melodrama, and I had a throbbing headache on top of everything, swinging my sights between the verbal tug-of-war engaging the judge and Meredith.

At one point, I longed to shout, *Okay, enough, ladies! Let's take this debate inside. It's time for me to get some shut-eye.* But the moment those headlight beams swept through the parking lot, I welcomed the distraction. With my eyes squinting against the intruding glare, my heart raced, and my senses were suddenly sharpened by the sight of a fluffy white cotton tail—a garden-variety rabbit. I guessed the little gray rodent-in-hiding took the flash of light as his cue to dart away from the hedges where we stood. He hopped out in a zigzag pattern across the grass, over a couple of gnarled roots twisting out of the earth from a tall pine tree and onto the blacktop. Envious of his escape, I wanted a piece of that critter, and something inside told me to snap to it and go after him wholeheartedly.

In the end, a dog was a dog, and our inherent primal, predatory instincts would ultimately win out over any kind of human logic. In my ratter-bred, terrier mind, all I was focused on was that white cotton tail glinting away into the shadows. I took off, and the next thing I knew, the wailing screech of that police car consumed me along with the smell of burning rubber and *boom!* I was out like a light.

The consequences of my impulsive action proved fatal—not for the rabbit, but I didn't feel a thing.

Dying wasn't all it was cracked up to be—literally and figuratively. Folks got all riddled with anxiety at the mere thought of it, but in the end, the last whispers of life were usually quick and painless. Anticlimactic, even. The final breath was always quite a relief. It was the getting there, that fear of the unknown—losing oneself piece by piece, breath by breath—that scared most people. But I knew better as I'd had multiple death experiences, having faced the slow, labored death of old age and progressive terminal illness. In my demise at Evergreen Gardens, I got lucky. I was still young and in my prime. My death was instant, my life snuffed out like a candle. And it was the best kind in that I never saw it coming.

Neither did the judge or Meredith, who stood there, horror-struck, as if their feet were nailed to the blacktop.

The great scenes of my short life passed before my eyes: my snuggling with my over-zealous puppy brothers and sisters. My years with doting Helen. My pseudo bladder-control issues. All those tests and retests at Four-Legged Angels. Helen always slipping me too many treats. Those stupid sweaters she used to parade me around in. All those kids who bored me—but tried so hard—with their phonics at libraries, and the great gossip I'd gobbled up at the weekly Stitch 'n Bitch meetings. The good folks at Evergreen Gardens. I even saw Meredith, the toilet bowl incident… *Priceless!*

Once that car made impact with me, the trajectory of my short life, as dictated by a series of small choices I'd made along the way, suddenly took shape. My spirit left my body, and as I hovered weightlessly above the blacktop where my paws gave a last twitch and the beats of my heart slowly petered out, I admired my once beautiful self splayed upon the pavement. *I sure was a good-looking dog this time around. A real cutie,* I thought, while doused in those squad car headlights as if a spotlight were shining directly on me. The poor cop driving the car hurried out of his vehicle and reached down to check for a heartbeat and my respiration.

When he found none, he swayed his head somberly at the judge, who stoically let out a track of silent tears, and Meredith, who had lost control and started to shiver and shake. She sobbed lung-choking noises. Gulps of deep, wild despair.

David bolted out of his Ford and tore across the parking lot, quickly enfolding Meredith in his embrace. The two collapsed into one another.

The policeman radioed for backup. He took off his jacket and draped it over me.

As David calmed Meredith, the judge blurted, "It's all my fault. If I hadn't—"

"Stop it!" Meredith pushed away from David. The pain of her sadness was evident across her face. "It's nobody's fault."

Meredith's words were jarring. Her wet, pale cheeks brightened with resolve as she explained to the cop how she and David had spent hours combing the area for Prozac and how they had just returned to Evergreen Gardens, pulling into the parking lot, when they spotted the judge wrangling up Prozac, who must've been loitering in the shrubs.

"What were you doing outside, Judge?" the policeman asked.

Before Judge Thea could respond, Meredith answered, "She was looking for Prozac. We all were. All night."

"So he was here, all along?" the policeman asked.

Meredith shrugged. "The judge and I… we… we were so happy and relieved to have finally found him. We were just about to bring him inside the building when you pulled up. And then, he took off…"

David and the judge looked to Meredith, as though expecting her to fill in more details. But she offered nothing more, outside of a few sniffles. There was no talk of the Rambler that was still warm under the car cover or the Dunkin' Donuts or even the mention of Judge Thea's grandson.

And that was when I knew I'd achieved my goal, fulfilled my mission. That was it—Meredith's moment. Her finest hour. Her reckoning. The past few weeks we'd spent together at Evergreen Gardens had finally melted her heart.

There was no blame game, only a sad, faraway look that filled Meredith's bloodshot eyes as she wiped them dry. "I thought we were home free. It all happened so fast."

"I know, and I'm so sorry," the officer said. "I honestly didn't see him. And by the time I did, I couldn't stop."

Meredith shot the judge a knowing glance, and the two of them stood face-to-face, finally wordless. No more animosity. No more back-and-forth bickering. No more pretense. Just the two of them sharing—despite the sadness and pain—a perfect, almost rapturous moment.

My heart enlarged with what felt like all the love of mankind, and it seemed to lift me higher and higher, taking my spirit farther away from the scene until Meredith and David, the judge, the policeman, and the earthly shell of my body became mere specks on earth.

Clearly, my job was done. Dogs could never replace human love, but they could guide people to it. And it was obvious that the next chapter in Meredith's life was about to begin.

# Thirty-One

*ALL'S WELL THAT ENDS WELL*

Prozac

SURE, MY JOB WAS DONE, but what about the trail of broken hearts I'd left behind? And what about Helen—poor Aunt Helen?

After the accident, the police brought me over to the animal hospital where the veterinarians pronounced me gone from the world. Meredith cried on David's shoulder as she walked out of the hospital, grasping my harness and leash and blotting her eyes with my therapy dog bandanna. It was well after midnight when she phoned Monica and woke her up. Monica was as devastated as everyone else to learn of my passing, but she offered to make the trip over to the rehab center at dawn to break the news to Helen. Meredith instantly cut her off and said, "No. It's *my* responsibility—"

"But she's my client—"

"I need to do this on my own."

"Let me at least meet you there," Monica said. "We'll tell her together."

"No. This has to come from me," Meredith said. "I'll call you later."

---

The long day and night became even longer. Meredith and David sat together on a couch in the quiet, empty atrium of Evergreen Gardens. They drank coffee and chatted, finally deciding to view the smartphone footage Meredith had captured that night from start to finish. When the video clips ended, Meredith hit the delete button, and David put his arm around her. She moved closer to him, resting her head on his shoulder. David reached for her hand. He carried it to his lips then pressed it against his heart. The two sat quietly, studying the whimsical-looking cherubs buried in the foliage surrounding that ornate fountain until they fell asleep in each other's arms.

When the first traces of daybreak streamed down in a shaft through the oculus in the dome ceiling and cast a puddle of sunlight on Meredith's feet, she stirred. She woke David and said, "C'mon, I think it's time."

———◦◦⟨⟩◦◦———

At seven thirty that morning, David and Meredith pulled up to the rehab center where Helen Hendrix was convalescing.

"You can drop me off at the front door," she said.

"Why don't I come in with you?"

"No, I need to do this on my own."

"Meredith, why do you do that?"

"What?"

"Try to act so stoic all the time. There are people who really want to help you… love you, even. You should let them."

Meredith reached over the console. She put her hand atop David's and squeezed it. She leaned over and looked up at him, staring deep into his compassionate brown eyes. Then she raised her face to him. Her lips sought his, and he found her. The two shared a kiss warm with promise.

"Thank you," she whispered, as she exited the car.

———◦◦⟨⟩◦◦———

Moments later, Meredith, her body stiff and her shoulders square, tidied her bedraggled hair, moving wisps of bangs on her forehead. She took a deep breath, clenching tightly to my leash, harness, and therapy dog bandanna. Then she rapped her knuckles upon the open door of Helen's room at the rehab center.

Helen looked over from where she was seated in a chair alongside her bed. "To what do I owe this honor?" she asked. A cup of coffee and a half-eaten slice of pecan pie rested on her tray table. She motioned for Meredith to enter and sit down.

Helen's response surprised Meredith, especially after Meredith had declined my guardianship via voicemail. She half expected Helen to order her out, demand that Meredith do an about-face and go away. But Helen seemed genuinely pleased to see her.

"Shhh. Don't tell anyone about my breakfast," Helen said to Meredith, wiping her mouth daintily with a napkin. "My caretaker girl baked this herself. She brought me a nice big piece from home this morning. She wanted me to save it for later, but when you get to be my age, you don't wait for *laters*. You become a dessert-first kind of person. You want the last forkful?"

Meredith shook her head. The words she'd come to deliver somehow wouldn't budge. She stood there, face flushed and mouth open—silent.

Helen must've sensed Meredith's awkwardness. She set down her fork, twisted her wrist to look at her watch, and asked, "Wait a second. What's going on? Why are you here, and why do you look so troubled?" When Helen's bloodless gaze landed on Meredith wringing her hands around my leash, harness, and bandanna, she cried, "Oh no. What's happened to my Prozac?"

Meredith cleared her throat and said, "I have some very bad news."

Helen firmed her fingers onto the edge of her tray table. She held on and squeezed her eyes closed, listening as Meredith spewed an edited version of how Margo Trilling died the day before and how, in the commotion, Prozac ran out of Evergreen Gardens and was found on the grounds later in the night, only to be run over by a police car.

When Meredith finished, a burble of grief, a tiny moan, escaped Helen. A single tear tumbled out of Helen's right eye, casting a moist track across the wrinkles of her cheek until it sank into the dollop of whipped cream topping that last forkful of pie. Meredith sat down on the edge of Helen's bed. She reached across the tray table and put her hand atop the bulge of blue-green veins on Helen's hands.

Helen clasped her other hand atop Meredith's. And for a moment, the two women sat that way, staring at the deflating whipped cream crater that deepened atop the creamy cloud.

"I've had a lot of dogs in my life, and every one of them has softened my heart and made it grow larger, probably to hold all the love I have in here." Helen's voice was low and warm as she pointed to the left side of her chest. "That Prozac, he sure was one special dog. He made my life so much sweeter."

"He made a lot of lives sweeter," said Meredith, her voice reedy. "Mine included."

Meredith's eyes welled up. She listened as Helen regaled her with stories and confessions about me—the day she first fell in love with me; my crazy name and how it was always a topic of conversation; a litany of my quirks and the mischief I'd made; how I was a therapy dog flunky and how she'd greased the palms of the powers-that-be at Four-Legged Angels; and the joy and privilege Helen felt in sharing her life with me those three years.

It was good for Helen to talk and remember. I knew it was the start of her healing.

"You'd think I'd know by now, at my age, that this life, everything in it, is all so fleeting," Helen said, wiping her face. "I'll never understand why dogs never get to live for very long. But it's something how they always manage to live just long enough for me to want to share my love with another one someday."

The corners of Helen's lips lifted. She reached for her fork and submerged it into the sticky, syrupy pecans and the flaky crust. Then she deposited the last bite into her mouth, savoring the richness of flavor.

# Epilogue

*EVERY DOG HAS HIS DAY*

Prozac
Two Years Later

I T WAS ALL WORTH IT—EVERYTHING.
After my stint with Helen Hendrix, my Spirit Guide Dog turnaround time was brief. In what felt like a matter of seconds as I was transferred from one life to the next, I was birthed as a plain old mixed breed onto the streets of St. Louis on a crisp April morning—the last day of the month. While my brothers, sisters, and I foraged as strays for eighteen months—braving the wind and wet, the sweltering heat of summer, the crispness of fall leaves beneath our paws, and the frigid chill of winter—I had all but thought the powers-that-be at the Canine Dispatch Board might've forsaken me and the deal we'd made. And especially when I wound up separated from my mother and my siblings, wrangled up one night by Animal Control. All hope was lost. I found myself alone in a kill shelter, a sandy-colored mutt living a hard-knock life with no takers. The writing was on the wall—my time on earth was dwindling. I had less than forty-eight hours to live.

And then I heard them coming for me, a dead dog walking. The gate of the poorly lit, mildew-infused shelter creaked open, and footsteps approached. A tall man and a shorter one stood before my chain-link cage turned prison cell. In my despair, I didn't even pick up my head. I lay there, eyeing those guys, two suited city slickers, who scrutinized me, comparing me to a picture the tall guy had displayed on his smartphone.

"He's got the right look," the short guy said.

"But do you think he'll be able to dance?" said the tall guy.

My ears perked. *Did he say dance?* I picked up my head.

When they opened the gated pen, I sprang out. And with a treat dangling from the short guy's hand, they lured me to stand on my hind legs, where I walked back and forth for them. I even twirled around.

"Well, I'll be damned," the tall guy said. "Look at 'im—he's a natural. A star is born!"

*And the rest, as they say, is history!*

Of all the shelter dogs in the world at that point in time, I was the one the producers of *Annie* found and chose. They were looking for the perfect mutt to fill the coveted role of Sandy. At the last minute, the canine star of the show and his understudy came down with a gastrointestinal virus. It was later diagnosed as colitis, a nasty condition brought about by stress, which barred both pooches from the bright lights of the big city.

Once I was discovered in that St. Louis shelter, I was flown on a private jet to New York City. My training was last-minute and vigorous—much more challenging than I ever dreamed and certainly more physically demanding than anticipated. But when I finally reached opening night, the whole trajectory of my rags-to-riches story made my worldly moment of glory all the more profound—and newsworthy. Just what I'd always wanted!

Several times a week, I wagged my tail in the wings and watched as the stage lights started to dim. A hush settled like a warm blanket over the crowd. The conductor marked a single beat of his baton on the corner of the music stand, and the orchestra—eyes riveted behind clarinets and flutes, the piano and timpani drums—launched into the bright notes and triumphant chords of the overture.

Every time I burst out on the stage, the rousing applause at my entrance made my heart sing with notes more beautiful than those that accompanied the hopeful, heartfelt "Tomorrow" theme. I basked in the hot spotlights, following Little Orphan Annie's curly red locks and the steady trail of treats that lured me to stand on my hind legs as I danced with her across the stage.

During my most recent performance, when commanded to lie at Annie's feet, I peered into the audience. And seated in the front row was the old crew from Evergreen Gardens. I should've known that Stella Stanislowski could never resist organizing a New York City bus trip to one of her all-time favorite Broadway shows.

My heart did leaps and flips at the sight of Lucy and Stella—and the usually poker-faced Mary Chirichella—smiling. There sat By-the-Book Betsy and Annette Mahoney, who kept fiddling with her hearing aids throughout the performance. Also present were Jack and Stan, yawning and nodding off between the big numbers. Judge Thea sat next to Helen Hendrix. The pocketbook Helen clung to on her lap revealed, through the opened zipper, the short snow-white snout of a tiny Maltese pup—I always knew she'd get another dog! Next to Helen sat Hammond Cederholm and a good-looking guy I'd never seen before. Beside him was Randy, crew-cut and outfitted in full military regalia, and the pretty blonde from the CVS, followed by Meredith's sister, Monica, who rested her head upon the shoulder of Larry of bomb squad fame. I didn't know how Meredith ever dragged them there, but they both finally looked relaxed—and amused.

Meredith sat at the end of the row. Her fingers were laced with those of Razzle-Dazzle Radcliffe. Good old David, the magician. He must've been very gifted at his craft, earning Meredith's trust so she could finally translate romance from the page into real life. And then I looked closer—there was a sparkly diamond engagement ring on her left hand!

The only missing face in the crowd was that of Gloria "Glo" Radcliffe. But I knew she was there with the lot of them—and me—in spirit.

No life was insignificant. We all played a part. And dogs often led people to other people. At least that was always my job description. Sitting before me, staring up at the stage, was the cast of disparate characters from the previous chapter of my life—souls I had helped connect. I looked out at the mesmerized, joy-filled faces filling that front row. While I could identify the individual pain and hardships, disappointments and sadness that had marked each one of those lives, I could also identify what each person did to keep going past the point of heartbreak—be it the love of a good book or cigar, a fine wine, a piece of pie, or a Broadway show. Maybe it was board games, gambling, magic; soap operas, cooking, shopping; or writing, numbers, the law. Admiring a car that was rarely driven or sharing life with a dog. Or maybe it was about cultivating a passion for doing good in the world.

Annette Mahoney captured it best when she said, "If I'm not happy, then it's my own damn fault." How right she was, because happiness was a choice, as was living despite the pain of losing and having to put two feet

on the floor each morning and face the unknown, the future—again...
and again... and again. No life was perfect. Everyone carried some kind
of burden, some heavier than others. But we pressed on. And just like the
drama of the theater, there were good days and bad. Each night, a different
performance emerged for a different crowd. And the thing was, the curtain
rose no matter what. The lights bumped up. And the show... it went on.

Dear Reader Friend,

I hope you enjoyed your journey through *The Thing Is*. When my last novel was published—*In Transit*, a woman-in-jeopardy story—some of my closest friends were disappointed there wasn't a dog, or even the mention of a dog, in that book. They knew how much I love my Yorkies, as I've been fortunate to share my life with three Yorkshire terriers, one at a time, and each has served a unique purpose that has enriched different phases of my life. There was Daisy, the clever, energetic companion of my youth. Jonathan, a gentle and regal long-haired Yorkie devoted to me while I experienced many years of illness and disability. And there's Sicily (aka Sissy), a petite little charmer (with many quirks, including agoraphobic tendencies) who creates a fanfare wherever she goes.

I've found Yorkies to be smart, happy, and extremely lovable—although there have been times when I've referred to my own as *Yorkshire terrorists*! Armed with that knowledge, I took the comments of my friends to heart and decided to channel my inner Yorkie. And *voilà*! Prozac emerged on the page. While my imagination conceived of him as a Spirit Guide Dog, his "doggieness" is a composite created from all the Yorkies I've known, lived with, cared for, and loved.

Thank you for reading! Please note that since this book was written, my home state of New Jersey has enacted a law requiring that all pets, for their safety and protection, be restrained when traveling in vehicles.

If you enjoyed *The Thing Is*, I'd appreciate your recommending this book to others. Hearing from readers is always a special treat for me. Therefore, I encourage you to like me on Facebook, follow me on Twitter, sign up for my newsletter, and contact me via my blog, "Reading Between the Lines," at www.kathleengerard.blogspot.com.

Until the next book... Happy Reading!

Kathleen Gerard

# About the Author

Kathleen Gerard writes across genres. Her work has been awarded many literary prizes and has been published in magazines, journals, widely anthologized and broadcast on National Public Radio (NPR). Kathleen writes and reviews books for *Shelf Awareness*. Kathleen's woman-in-jeopardy novel, *In Transit*, won "Best Romantic Fiction" at the New York Book Festival.

# Acknowledgements

Special thanks to Ellen Bass for her poem, "The Thing Is." Her words deeply touched my life and planted a seed that grew into this story. Sincerest gratitude to the team of professionals at Red Adept Publishing who supported and shepherded this novel—with care and respect—every step of the way: Michelle Rever, Angela Webster McRae, Jessica Anderegg, and Streetlight Graphics. Most of all, thanks to God... for everything!

# Other books by Kathleen Gerard

*In Transit*

*Cold Comfort*

40149922R00171

Made in the USA
San Bernardino, CA
24 June 2019